A CHRISTMAS KISS

Bundled up, Ben and Samantha headed homeward, through a magical wonderland. Clusters of large, wet snowflakes floated down from a darkened sky, lamplight sparkled underfoot like a path of diamonds, and the slight breeze that caressed Samantha's cheeks had lost its chill. Not a sound but their own footsteps broke the silence; any conversation would only have spoiled the enchantment.

When they came to an icy stretch, Ben took her arm, only to span her waist with his hand, drawing her to his side, pointing skyward. Her cheek resting lightly against his shoulder, she saw a smattering of stars in a distinctive shape.

"Looks like the Big Dipper," she said, forcing levity while her heart thumped faster and faster at his closeness.

"Everything looks like the Big Dipper to you, Sam," he teased. Pulling her closer still, he placed his chilled cheek against her temple. They had stopped walking and stood still, their gaze on the stars. He smelled faintly of bay rum. Beneath the scents of aftershave and soap and out-of-doors, she discovered another distinctly his own, undeniably male. He shifted slightly until he faced her, his lips brushing her temple where her pulse fluttered wildly, giving encouragement. He feathered her face with kisses, and then touched one corner of her lips with his . . .

BOOK YOUR PLACE ON OUR WEBSITE AND MAKE THE READING CONNECTION!

We've created a customized website just for our very special readers, where you can get the inside scoop on everything that's going on with Zebra, Pinnacle and Kensington books.

When you come online, you'll have the exciting opportunity to:

- View covers of upcoming books
- Read sample chapters
- Learn about our future publishing schedule (listed by publication month *and author*)
- Find out when your favorite authors will be visiting a city near you
- Search for and order backlist books from our online catalog
- Check out author bios and background information
- Send e-mail to your favorite authors
- Meet the Kensington staff online
- Join us in weekly chats with authors, readers and other guests
- Get writing guidelines
- AND MUCH MORE!

**Visit our website at
http://www.zebrabooks.com**

SAMANTHA'S HEART

PAMELA QUINT CHAMBERS

Zebra Books
Kensington Publishing Corp.

http://zebrabooks.com

ZEBRA BOOKS are published by

Kensington Publishing Corp.
850 Third Avenue
New York, NY 10022

Copyright © 1998 by Pamela Quint Chambers

Zebra and the Z logo Reg. U.S. Pat. & TM Off.

First Printing: December, 1998
10 9 8 7 6 5 4 3 2 1

Printed in the United States of America

FOR
TRADITIONS AND CELEBRATIONS

THIS BOOK IS DEDICATED TO
MY COUSINS
GINNY, PEGGY, HELEN, AND ESTHER,
WHO BEAR LITTLE RESEMBLANCE, IF ANY, TO
SAMANTHA'S.

AND TO
MY SISTER, SANDRA,
AND
MY BROTHER, LEE—

THANKS FOR THE MEMORIES
ALL MY LOVE, Pam

ONE

At your quilting, maids, don't dally.
Quilt quick if you would marry.
A maid who is quiltless at twenty-one
Never shall greet her bridal sun.
                    —Devon folk saying

Wednesday, November 27, 1889

At 9:40 A.M. on Thursday, November 14, aboard the Hamburg-American Company White Star steamer, *Augusta Victoria*, out of Hoboken, New Jersey, Nellie Bly embarked on her journey "Around the World in Eighty Days," for Joseph Pulitzer's newspaper, the *New York World*. According to Samantha Spencer's lapel watch, at the same moment the woman whose accomplishments she most admired set off on her greatest adventure yet, she herself had been waiting outside the city editor's office at the *Chicago Evening Star* exactly forty-two minutes. That she was being called upon the carpet by her employer, Robert Whittier Reed, she had expected, and richly deserved. That R. W. intended to make her sit in full view of her fellow reporters, like a naughty scholar outside the principal's office, until he was good and ready to speak with her, she had not the slightest doubt. By 10:45, when she had all but given up hope of gaining admittance before noon, R. W.'s glass-paned door abruptly opened. Samantha rose expectantly. The silver-haired veteran of countless successful journalistic campaigns of his own pushed wire-rimmed spectacles up onto his forehead to pierce her with his eagle-eyed stare.

"Miss Spencer, *do* join me."

He waved her in with a wide sweep of his arm.

"Yes, sir."

Congratulating herself on keeping the quiver out of her voice, she followed him inside, standing at attention in front of his mahogany desk until he had positioned himself on the other side. He gestured to a straight-backed chair beside her, and did not sit until she perched on the hard seat's edge.

"Miss Spencer . . ."

"Sir?"

"Tell me, Miss Spencer, *exactly* what reporter worth his . . . or *her* salt lets himself . . . or, ah, herself . . . be *scooped* by a *competitor's* newspaper? And just how *did* Nell Nelson get wind of the exclusive *you* promised *me?* I *do not* enjoy reading *our* story in someone *else's* paper."

With each characteristically emphasized word, he stabbed his finger at the bold banner headline on the front page of the rival *Chicago News* on his desk.

As he expected an excusable explanation, she should attempt one. She could share some of the blame with the other *Star* reporter in whom she had confided the story idea she stumbled upon, the cause she was certain would set her upon the road to success equal to that of Nellie Bly's. Having spoken of it to no one else except, of course, R. W., to obtain his reluctant go-ahead, she had few doubts that Harold Clarke somehow betrayed her, if only inadvertently, being the friendly, loquacious fellow that he was.

"Well, Miss Spencer?"

R. W.'s bark brought her back from her wool-gathering. She made no attempt to defend herself. A good reporter made no excuses. A good reporter got the story despite all odds, unlike herself, who had not.

"I blame no one but myself for my failure with this assignment, sir."

R. W. harrumphed. "Assignment, *hah!* As *I* remember, you badgered me *relentlessly* until I gave in to your request to attempt this exposé. Though, if you'll recall, Miss Spencer, I had *grave* doubts about permitting an *unseasoned* cub reporter, and female at that, with but a few months' experience—"

Samantha stiffened her spine, tipped her chin upward, and dared to interrupt.

"I am twenty-two, the same age as Nellie Bly, and have been employed by you for nearly a year."

One corner of R. W.'s generous mouth lifted in a fleeting grin.

"I stand corrected, but nevertheless this *lengthy* term of employment has apparently proceeded *without* your having acquired the necessary skills to attempt what most *older, toughened* newsmen would not. After yesterday's *fiasco,"* he poked the paper before him for emphasis, "I cannot *help* but conclude that this town isn't big enough for *two* female stunt reporters. Nell Nelson, who has already made her name in what is rightfully a *man's* field, more than fills the bill. The sweatshop in question has been shut down. The family you befriended . . . the Klines?"

"Klem. Wilhelm . . . Willie Klem, his mother, and two older sisters."

"That's the same lad who sells newspapers down on

our corner, isn't it? An *excellent* salesman despite his youth. How old . . . ?"

"Seven."

"As I said, *in spite* of his youth, one of our *best.* Always full of good cheer, rain or shine, broiling heat or bitter cold . . . Harrumph . . . What's become of little Willie? Not *ill,* I hope?"

"I . . . I heard that his mother and sisters have already relocated to another sweatshop . . . across town . . . and that Willie obtained work . . . delivering a different paper . . . closer to his new home."

She found it increasingly more difficult to speak. Nothing had been changed for them by her interference, nothing at all except that she might never again see the plucky lad she'd exchanged many a cheery good morning with, shared a bag or two of hard candy, and from whom she'd learned of the cause she championed with such disastrous results.

"Yes, well, it would seem that all's well that ends well. *You,* Miss Spencer, on the other hand are *obviously* neither hard-headed nor hard-hearted enough for stunt reporting, and *far* better suited to the social events column, as before."

Samantha's chin rose a notch higher, her eyes burning with withheld tears.

"And if . . . if I choose not to return to the Society Desk. . . . ?"

R. W. rocked back in his leather swivel chair, lacing his fingers over his vest.

"Is that your choice, Miss Spencer?"

She refused to glance away, or blink so gathering tears might spill.

"I-I-I cannot allow myself to be demoted in lieu of continuing to pursue my most cherished dream."

Leaning forward to support elbows on his cluttered desk, drywashing his ruddy cheeks with both broad hands, R. W. sighed heavily, spoke with finality.

"Then you may consider yourself unemployed, Miss Spencer, *as of now.* Clear out your desk, and be on your way by noon. It would seem you shall have the lengthy holiday you requested, *and then some."*

On the twentieth of November, a week after Samantha's dismissal, Nellie Bly reached England, and the next day France, where she conversed with Jules Verne, whose book had inspired her journey. Packing books into a trunk for her move back home, Samantha held Nellie's volume, *Ten Days in a Mad-House,* in her hands. Two years ago, upon reading this compilation of Miss Bly's newspaper accounts of her adventure masquerading as mentally ill behind insane asylum bars, she realized she had finally found her calling. A way to do something as meaningful with her writing talents, and her life, as had the dauntless Nellie Bly. It took an entire year to overcome her parents' many objections to her living and working in nearby Chicago, a wild and wicked big city, where muggers were commonplace even in broad daylight, and a murder rate that had quadrupled in less than two decades. A year to wear them down, another in R. W.'s employ to convince him to give her this chance to prove her writing abilities sufficient to attempt stunt reporting. Only to be vanquished in the end, not because of lack of talent, but because she placed her trust unwisely.

Searching her conscience as she packed up the last of her belongings, Samantha had to believe with all her heart that she had wanted to help Willie Klem, his mother, and his sisters, more than to write up an exposé to rival Nellie Bly's. If she did not, she wasn't sure she could ever bring herself to write again. In all honesty, if R. W. hadn't fired her, in every likelihood, she would have resigned anyway. She had failed abysmally, and now she was running home in defeat. And not even a flurry of last-minute Christmas shopping for family and friends, the anticipation of the celebrations ahead, or seeing her loved ones again after so long, lifted the heaviness from her heart.

Wednesday, Thanksgiving eve, while Nellie Bly headed for the Suez Canal by steamer, Samantha stared morosely out the window of the passenger car, ignoring, for the most part, the ceaseless chatter between her Aunt Jane and cousin Olivia sharing the bench seat across from her. She would have much preferred to make this train trip alone. Thanks to her mother's sense of propriety, her relatives' return from their annual Christmas shopping venture into the Windy City had been arranged to coincide with her own leave-taking. They mostly ignored her, as well, their chitchat meandering from the latest fashions, to the latest scandals, to the latest social amenities, and back again.

Left to her own devices, Samantha brooded, knowing that once she confessed to having lost her job, her parents would insist she remain at home like a proper, single young woman, awaiting some proposal of marriage. Without doubt, Mama and Grannie, and every last one of her aunts, had made at least one selection for her consideration from the bachelors and widowers in town, probably in the entire county. No one took seriously her vow to remain single and pursue her chosen career. Except now she had foolishly thrown away that opportunity by refusing to resume her former position on the Society Desk. Pride once more got in the way of good common sense, leaving few choices of future action. She could stay at home. Heaven forbid! Or look for work on other Chicago-based newspapers, likely with no better success than before. Or she could swallow her pride, if necessary, beg R. W. to take her back, in any capacity, as long as she was allowed to write. If he would have her. If he did not . . . well, Samantha fought down choking panic, afraid to put words to the possibilities spinning in her thoughts.

The clatter of iron wheels on iron rails sang a constant refrain in her ears. *You can't go back. You can't go back. You can't go back.* The leaden, polluted skies of Chicago, all shades of gray no matter what the season, reminded her of other unpleasantnesses she so hated about big-city living. The never-ending wail of the noisome wind through the tunnels made by tall buildings, carrying with it the smell of garbage, the scent of blood from the slaughterhouses. Fine sand blowing in off distant dunes, turning clean clothes dusty, teeth gritty. People with closed expressions, hurrying, always scurrying someplace else. No one knew her, no one cared. Constant homesickness hovered just below the surface.

As gray skies finally gave way to blue, revealing snow-dappled brown fields, and the last scraps of scarlet, gold, and russet clinging to stark autumn branches, self-pity gave way to the renewed tenacity her mother affectionately labeled a stubbornness "just like your Grannie Spencer's." To the wheels' refrain of *You can't go back!* she silently countered, fists and jaw clenched, *I will go back! I will go back! Somehow, by Providence, I will go back.* If it meant telling no one that she had lost her source of income and given up her room in the boardinghouse, so be it. If she must grovel before R. W. on bended knees to get her old job back, that she would do. She could not be deterred from her purpose in life so easily, not by one single setback. Relief, like the gray skies turned azure, lifted her spirits, fortified her sense of purpose.

With that settled in her mind and in her heart, Samantha leaned back against the upholstered bench, closed her eyes, and listened to the new refrain thrumming through her head. *I'm going home. I'm going home. I'm almost home.*

"—stay, Samantha?"

Samantha awoke abruptly at a sharp kick to her shin from her cousin's high-buttoned walking boot. Leaning forward to rub the throbbing spot, she glared up into Olivia's serene face, wondering anew how the loveliest of all her female cousins ended up having the worst disposition.

"I didn't much like your attention-getting tactics when we shared classes together in school, and I appreciate them even less now that we are grown."

Cousin Olivia's tight little smile on perfect Cupid's bow lips in an angelically beautiful face was as malicious as the glint in her heavily lashed violet eyes. Ivory-complected, with a touch of ruby in the cheeks, and ebony hair having just enough wave in it to remain forever tidy, Olivia Frances Tyler presented a picture of perfection that also included a slender, hourglass figure, voluptuous in all the right places. Always fashionably attired, overindulged by well-to-do parents, she was the envy of nearly every other female in town. Yet Samantha had never known her cousin to be anything other than mean-spirited, especially when bored, which was frequently. Samantha noted that Aunt Jane dozed, her round little chin bobbing up and down upon her generous bosom, matching the rhythm of the train, likely occasioning Olivia's attack.

"I merely meant to get your attention, cousin dear. I enquired how long you planned on staying in River Valley before returning to your journalistic endeavors."

"I asked for a six-week leave of absence after Papa

wired me about Mama breaking her arm," she said, feeling not at all guilty in implying that she had been granted the requested time. "They both seemed to feel Eliza couldn't manage without my help, under the circumstances. I promised to do what I can. I'll leave for Chicago right after Eliza's wedding. January second, or third at the latest." *Praying all the way I'll have something to go back to,* Samantha silently added.

Olivia's full lips drew back over equally perfect teeth. "Ah, yes, the wedding. Who would have guessed that poor, plain, orphaned Eliza would be the first cousin to wed? And to one of the most desirable of the Morgan brothers, at that. What Charlie sees in her, I can't imagine."

Samantha bristled at the slight to the cousin who'd been raised in the Spencer home like her younger sister since her parents' untimely demise when she was still in diapers.

" 'Pretty is as pretty does,' Grannie Spencer always says, and as sweet and kind as Eliza is, she ought to be downright gorgeous by now.

"Oh, I don't deny she's kindhearted, poor dear, but so painfully shy, why, what with Charlie's outgoing high spirits, I simply meant—"

"I know what you meant," Samantha snapped. "Your little jibes are better left unsaid, Olivia, especially in Eliza's hearing. If I catch you making her in the least unhappy before the wedding I'll . . . I'll—"

"You'll *what,* cousin?" Her violet eyes glittered at the challenge in the implied threat.

"I'll tell Aunt Jane about a certain incident—"

The old, familiar threat never failed to work.

"Oh, all right. You know I wouldn't do anything to ruin dear cousin Eliza's wedding," Olivia pouted, while obviously seeking some other line of attack, and finding it. "I always thought *you* would end up with Charlie . . . or maybe Duncan, if he hadn't run off. Duncan was *always* sweet on you, wasn't he? You didn't chase him away, did you, with all your talk of a writing career?"

Refusing to honor the barrage with answers, Samantha countered question for question.

"Why this sudden interest in the Morgan brothers' love lives? Do you have your cap set for one of them?"

Olivia blushed furiously and looked away, over Samantha's shoulder, not meeting her scrutinizing stare.

"You have! You're taken with one of them. Which one? It better not be Charlie, he's spoken for."

She took the barely perceptible shake of Olivia's head to mean no. Eyes narrowed, Samantha speculated.

"Not Duncan, gone for, what is it? Two years? Three? Andrew, then? Or Ben? The others are still children." Watching closely, she saw Olivia's flush go darker. " 'Fess up, who is it?"

Olivia pointedly ignored her. Samantha prodded.

"Can't be *Ben.* He's never taken his nose out of a book long enough to notice the opposite gender."

Except to tell me in no uncertain terms I'd never succeed in Chicago, she thought bitterly. He'd told her she hadn't the heart for hard reporting, for the big-city life, that she'd always be a small-town girl no matter how far away she roamed. She disagreed vehemently, vocally, and they had not resolved their differences before she left town. Wouldn't her nosy next-door neighbor be happy to know how perilously close she was to making his prediction come true. Well, he *wouldn't* find out; she'd make certain of it!

"Not Ben."

"What?" Samanatha almost missed the quiet confession.

"Not Ben . . . It . . . It is Andrew. But don't tell Mama."
Olivia's voice was barely above a whisper.

Samantha leaned forward to catch her words over the
rumble of the train, then fell back against the upholstery
at her cousin's surprising confession, asking, "Does he
know? Does he feel . . . ?"

Olivia's frantic "shhhh" left the question unanswered,
but the misery in her eyes told the story, and the faint
shake of her head confirmed it. Samantha watched as
Olivia drew an invisible cloak of indifference around herself like a garment. Her perfect little nose tipped upward.

"Mama feels the Morgans are not of our social standing. She has been searching farther afield than River Valley . . . New York or abroad . . . for a suitable match."

Samantha interrupted with a very unladylike sound.

"Aunt Jane'd have to go a lot farther than that to find
a more upstanding, responsible gentleman than Andrew
Morgan. He works in a bank, for goodness sake."

"But only as a clerk. It is Uncle Preston's bank."

Samantha came close to telling her cousin that her father had spoken of making Andrew a partner sometime
in the not too distant future. Olivia was beyond arguments.
She might have feelings for the eldest Morgan brother,
but she was as much of a snob as Aunt Jane. More. She'd
end up doing what was socially correct, and smother the
natural longings of her heart.

"I like your outfit, Samantha, it's really quite stylish.
Did you pick it out yourself?" asked Olivia in a saccharine
tone, her switch of subjects occasioned by Aunt Jane's
rousing herself from slumber.

Her aunt stifled a wide yawn with the back of one
gloved hand, her sleepy blue eyes studying Samantha's
garments, missing nothing.

"That shade of navy is flattering to your unfortunate

coloration," Aunt Jane stated. "I imagine it's difficult to find hues to complement that odd brown of your hair and eyes. And those freckles! You should at least have listened to your mother about shading your face from the sun, my dear, to preserve your complexion."

Not at all certain how to respond to their barbed remarks, Samantha thanked aunt and cousin anyway, confessing, "I purchased a few new items for the holidays and the wedding."

Self-consciously, she smoothed the rich lamb's-wool fabric of her new coat over her lap, and straightened the high black chinchilla collar that matched her cuffs, cloche, and muff. Secretly pleased that her purchases had elicited the notice she hoped for, she had not yet overcome her initial guilt over her exorbitance. On the coat and its accessories, as well as dresses and shoes and lacy unmentionables, she had squandered all but her last few dollars, hoping to appear sophisticated and successful in the eyes of her family. And had pulled off the charade, if the barely concealed envy in Olivia's tone was any indication. No one would guess that she was an unemployed pauper. Especially her know-it-all neighbor, Ben Morgan.

Near midnight, the train pulled into the River Valley Station. Samantha immediately recognized the lone figure on the dimly lit platform. The sight of her father's familiar face brought on an unexpected prickle of happy tears. As distinguished and proper as ever in his long tweed overcoat and black felt bowler, still he graciously suffered her exuberant hugs and kisses when she hurriedly disembarked to throw herself into his arms, and even became a bit misty-eyed himself.

"You missed me, too," she accused, then to avoid his further embarrassment, added, "How is Mama? Is her arm bothering her? How's everyone else? Have Grandpa and

Grannie Spencer arrived from Colorado yet? Oh, there's so much to get caught up on."

He smiled indulgently, with that bit of humor that cropped up now and again no matter how proper he seemed otherwise.

"There, there, I would have thought your aunt and cousin would've answered all your questions between here and Chicago."

"Oh, pooh! They talked fashion and gossip, and little else, for the entire trip."

"Preston." Down the way, Aunt Jane signaled her cousin with a beckoning wave. "Our luggage is unloaded. Bring the buggy around."

The father and daughter camaraderie of which they were both so fond, would have to wait until later. So would catching up with the rest of the family, Aunt Jane having much more newsworthy subjects to discourse on during the homeward trip.

After taking Aunt Jane and Olivia home, Papa let her off in front of the house and headed around the block with horse and buggy to the alley and the barn behind the house. No welcoming lights greeted her from inside the two-storey frame house with wraparound porch. Her father had already warned her that the female members of the household, Grannie Spencer included, retired hours earlier in anticipation of arising long before dawn to begin feast preparations. Disappointment tempered with thoughts of the happy reunion in the morning brought on a sense of contentment Samantha found nowhere else. She fell to soaking up the sights and sounds of home like a starving soul. Papa's old mare, Dolly, nickered, grateful for her warm stall and a bucket of oats for a job well done. The Morgans' hound bayed at the moon, bright and full in a starry sky. A block away, a wagon rumbled over the cobbles of Main Street, muted with distance, so different than the never-ending racket on the streets of Chicago.

Shivering with happiness more than the cold, Samantha wrapped her arms around in a self-hug, letting her gaze dwell upon the smallest details that for a year had been only memories to fall asleep with. Papa had again forgotten to take the porch swing down after Labor Day, she noticed. He'd talk one of the Morgan brothers into helping him with it after Thanksgiving dinner, as always. Mama had written that the old oak off to the left had been lost to a spring ice storm; how bare that corner of the yard looked without it. Future generations of Spencers would miss out on the sheer joy of swinging from its boughs and climbing into its concealing heights to read or write or just get away.

Next door in a similar frame house as familiar as her own, a single light glowed upstairs in the back bedroom window. Scholarly Ben Morgan likely burned the midnight oil. She'd expected no welcoming greeting from him anyway. Tomorrow, Thanksgiving, the traditional blending of Spencer and Morgan families for the midday feast was soon enough for confronting the irritating third son of the Morgan clan.

Samantha smothered a yawn, gave the beloved house a last, long once-over to assure herself she was really home, and made her way quietly up to her room. Undressing post haste in the unheated chamber, she crawled beneath a pile of Grannie Spencer's warm patchwork quilts, and instantly fell into the first deep sleep in a year.

TWO

" 'Can she bake a cherry pieee, Billy boy, Billy boy? Can she bake a cherry pieee, charmin' Billy? She can bake a cherry pie, quick as a cat can wink her eye, but she's a young thing an' cannot leave her motherrr.' "

Samantha groaned and buried her head beneath two down pillows, but couldn't drown out the off-key caterwaulling that passed for Grannie Spencer's singing.

" 'Can she make a puddin' welllll, Billy boy, Billy boy? Can she make a puddin' welllll, charmin' Billy? She can make a puddin' well, I can tell it by the smelllll, but she's a young thing an' cannot leave her motherrr.' "

Lifting her head enough to peer out from under her pillows, Samantha snagged her lapel watch from the nightstand beside her. The hands on its face stood at twelve and four. Four o'clock—in the morning.

The mingled scents of the feast in preparation, wafting up through the heat register set in her floor, tantalized her senses. Grannie's mincemeat pie, her favorite, predominated, making further sleep out of the question.

Throwing back her quilts, sitting on the edge of the bed, Samantha anticipated a foot-freezing rush across cold floorboards to her clothing. But the cookstove below, stoked early and red hot with Thanksgiving preparations, offered up a welcome, toasty warmth. She slipped into her flannel wrapper and settled herself amid a pile of pillows stacked against her headboard, decorously covering her bare feet with a log cabin quilt. Grabbing up the pencil and pad of paper always at the ready nearby, Samantha ignored her stomach rumbling with sustenance temporarily denied. Tapping pencil against chin, she meditated for a moment, then began to scribble as fast as her fingers could fly.

Home for the holidays! I was awakened this morning to what our family fondly calls Grannie's singing and to the clatter of pots and pans of Thanksgiving dinner under way, sights and sounds and smells universal to the holiday, yet as unique to our family as Grannie Spencer herself . . .

Pencil poised over pad, Samantha lifted her head, smiling, sniffing the heady aromas from below. Grannie finished with "Billy Boy" and went on to "Clementine"—" 'and her shoes were number nineee' "—in a tone midway between a screech owl's cry and the screak of a rusty barn door hinge. Samantha privately suspected her grandmother purposely exaggerated her lack of singing ability for Grandpa Spencer's benefit, he complained so about it. Glancing out her rear window, she saw that he had escaped the house for the woodshed out back. Still vigorous and strong at seventy-two, he was splitting kindling in a growing heap that suggested he'd been there for quite some time. No one slept in once her grandmother was up and about.

Samantha deliberately avoided looking out through the side window of her corner bedroom, the one directly across from Ben Morgan's. As youngsters, Ben had shared the room with his brother, Duncan, three years his junior and a year older than herself. Two of a kind, she and Duncan—always into some mischief one or the other of them thought up—had strung a rope on a crude pulley system between that window and hers—at great peril to life and limb, as she recalled—so that they could send secret messages back and forth clamped on with clothespins. Now Duncan was long gone to parts unknown, and as far as she knew, Ben roomed with no one. Mama had written that Adam and Charlie, both employed by Papa's bank, shared accommodations near work. Leaving only Ben and his three youngest brothers, Edward, Frankie, and Georgie, to rattle around inside the big, old Morgan house. Once it had been full to overflowing with the seven boys— her best friends, playmates, the brothers she never had—a mother and father she considered her own second parents, and all the lighthearted happiness one would expect of a family where offspring were named alphabetically. Then the boys' parents perished in a tragic boating accident. Adam was twenty, Ben eighteen, the littlest, Georgie, just three. Adam became the wage-earner and Ben held the family together. After that lamentable day, childhood ended for all of the boys, even the youngest, with the exception of Duncan, who stubbornly refused to face reality, and finally ran away from it altogether.

" 'In my dreams she still doth haunt me, Robed in garments soaked in brine, Though in life I used to hug her, Now she's dead, I'll draw the line.' "

Samantha giggled, but quietly, into her hand, for she knew that as soon as Grannie sensed she had awakened, her peaceful interlude would quickly come to an end. As Grannie swung into "She'll Be Comin' 'Round the Mountain," Samantha returned to her reminiscences, and wrote.

In this melting pot society of ours, Thanksgiving is one of the few wholly American holidays, and the one I most associate with my paternal grandmother, the product of more than one culture all by herself. Daughter of a New York gentleman banker and a Southern plantation belle who had followed her heart onto the performing stage, Grannie's adventuring spirit, so like her mother's, sent her journeying West long before such travel was popular or easy. In the vast wilderness, she found her own happiness in the love of a rugged mountain man. She made friends with the Natives, as well, and to this day, her contribution to the bountiful Thanksgiving feast reflects the best, and the tastiest, of these diversities.

Samantha's thoughts strayed to little Willie Klem, the newsboy, wondering what kind of Thanksgiving he and the rest of his German immigrant family would experience this, their first year in the land of opportunity. If only she could have done more . . . Before she had time to dwell upon their fate, Grannie's song rose an octave.

" ' . . . when she comes,' " screeched Grannie in response to the slam of the back door and Grandpa Spencer's admonition to "Keep down that hellacious racket, old woman. You tryin' to raise the dead?"

Quiet laughter broke into loud chuckles Samantha couldn't control.

"Samantha? Samantha Sarahannah Spencer, I hear you up there," Grannie called through the grate from below. "Get out of that bed right now and come on down here. Make yourself useful. There's more'n enough work for every willing pair of hands . . . what with your mama's having only one that's working."

Responding as expected to the guilt heaped upon her, Samantha scurried out of bed, shouting a quick promise down the vent. Tossing her pencil and pad on the bureau, she suspected, with regret, it'd be quite some time before she resumed her attempts to capture her grannie's unique qualities in mere words. Through the grate, she heard her mother say something to Eliza, and her cousin's soft reply. As the last female in the household to respond to the duties of the day, she knew it would be hours, maybe days, before she'd hear the end of it from Grannie Spencer.

An hour before guests were to arrive, feeling like she'd melt if she remained in the sweltering kitchen a moment longer, Samantha caught up a shawl hanging on the hall tree beside the front door, and slipped out onto the deep front porch. Scanty blue skies peeked out between thick, cottony clouds with dark underbellies promising snow to coat the patches left behind by yesterday's sun. Samantha shivered, relishing the cold. Pulling the woolen shawl taut around her shoulders, she leaned against the glass-paned door at her back, inhaling deeply, filling her lungs with crisp, clean air—an impossibility in Chicago, where every breath felt tainted.

How quickly life slipped into an old familiar pattern, she thought. Laboring side-by-side over the feast to come with Grannie and Eliza, and Mama doing what she could one-handed, Samantha felt as if she had never left. The cheerful chatter of family, the gossip, and the out-and-out matchmaking on her behalf, left her longing for a few moments' solitude after a year of little else. For just five minutes, ten or fifteen if she could steal them, she needed to be alone.

As soon as she turned toward the porch swing, anticipating a gentle ride, she saw that someone had beaten her to it. With legs stretched out and a red plaid mackinaw jacket collar pulled up around his ears, he could have been any one of the older Morgan boys.

"Andrew? Andrew Morgan, is that you sitting out here in the cold? Or is it Charlie?"

Her query held light humor that she was unable to distinguish one brother from another. He turned at the sound of her voice, expression guarded; lifting his lanky frame out of his seat, he ambled toward her over the worn, painted planks of the porch.

"It's only Ben, Sam. Welcome home."

Face to face with the brother she least desired to encounter, Samantha wasn't surprised she had not immediately recognized Ben. Struck with how his appearance had altered in a single year's time, it occurred to her that the process had likely begun long before she left, and she simply hadn't noticed.

"Where are your glasses?" she blurted.

"W-what?" he asked, bemused.

"You're not wearing your glasses," she amended, feeling foolish and frustrated.

His face, rugged and angular, bore long, deep creases in each cheek that passed for dimples when he smiled, as he did now.

"I only need them for reading. Mama made me keep them on all the time because I regularly misplaced them. Now that I pay for my own, I have the luxury of wearing them only when needed. How was Chicago?"

Mesmerized by the changes in him, Samantha forgot to answer. Once he'd been the epitome of the skinny, loose-jointed scholar, awkward and somewhat clumsy, with wire-rimmed eye glasses and ragged, cropped hair that looked like he'd chopped it off himself. Always the loner on the sidelines, book in hand, judgment or disapproval—or both—on his face at their harmless antics, he was teased mercilessly, she recalled with some shame. The brunt of many a childish prank, excluded, by his own wishes, he acted as if it mattered not at all. Now, with regret she wondered, *had it?,* remembering how carelessly cruel she and his brothers had sometimes been.

Before her now stood a handsome, well-proportioned man who had finally attained self-assured maturity. Whip-lean he would always be, but muscular, broad-shouldered, and slim-hipped. Ash blond hair tidily hugged the back of his sturdy neck and fell away from his forehead in a graceful wave. Midnight blue eyes, identical in shade in all the brothers, clear and candid without glasses, held wry amusement at her obvious discomfort in a way that struck her as all too familiar and all-knowing. As certain as she was that he had no idea she'd proven his parting words right, that unless she told him, he'd never be able to issue an "I told you so," on principle alone, she bristled, demanding, "What are you doing here so early?"

Oblivious to her rebuff, he continued to study her from toe to crown in the most disconcerting manner. At length, having completed his slow perusal without comment, he replied.

"Delivering extra chairs for the dinner table."

"Oh! I see."

That said, what more could she add?

Ben's voice held a rumble of humor. "You aren't still mad, are you, about my prediction?"

"Prediction?" She pretended to search her mind for a long-forgotten memory. "Ah, yes! The prediction. That I would fail to find employment on a newspaper in Chicago . . . wasn't that it? . . . and come running home within a week? I hadn't given it another thought 'til now," she responded icily, lying blatantly, as he deserved.

"You proved me wrong on all counts," he admitted. "You're a better writer than I realized back then."

Her eyes narrowed, suspecting a trick.

"How did you happen to come to that conclusion?"

He shrugged with studied nonchalance.

"Your father subscribes to the *Chicago Evening Star* and passes the paper on to me when he's done with it." His cheeks went ruddier than the weather occasioned. "For educational purposes, of course. I teach school now, you know—"

"I didn't." She was surprised her nose didn't grow with all her lies.

"The new Townline School, servicing both River Valley and Isadore. One room, twelve grades. A real challenge."

"As reporting the news is not?"

"I didn't say that. I'm sure there are many subscribers in Chicago needing to know who went where with whom, what they wore, what was eaten. Someone has to . . . aw, Sam, don't go off mad just when we—" The front door slammed behind her indignant, retreating figure. "Just when we were starting to—"

To what? Get along? Not bloody likely! Leave it to Sam to turn tail and storm off, as usual when someone expressed an opinion that wasn't her own!

"Some things never change," Ben muttered at the resounding slam of the front door.

Stuffing cold hands deep into his pants pockets, he flung himself down on the porch swing. As the erratic rocking resulting slowed, so did his ire, dwindling to self-recriminations. Bearing his fair share of the blame for triggering her temper, as only he—of all the Morgan brothers—seemed capable of doing, he cursed himself for bringing up exactly what he'd promised himself he wouldn't. His parting words to her then had ended the same way, and not at all as he'd intended.

Hell's bells, Sam, when're you going to learn to hang around to give a fellow a chance to explain?

And when, in bloody blue blazes, was he going to learn that a little tact went a good long way? Dammit, if seeing her again after a long year's absence hadn't knocked every last bit of common sense and good intentions clear out of his head!

He'd been sitting out here in the cold trying to work up the nerve to invade the kitchen overflowing with Spencer womenfolk, when she came outside to him. Well, not to him, he amended, a bitter taste on his tongue; she obviously hoped for any other Morgan *but* him. He saw disappointment replace happy anticipation on her face, a face at the same time as familiar as his own, and newly, beautifully all grown up.

At first he took her for the same old Sam, then with a few seconds before she noticed him, managed a long, hungry once-over. He almost gave his presence away with a chuckle at her appearance. Her whiskey-colored curls she'd caught up haphazardly on top of her head, tendrils escaping and clinging to her moist skin, where dabs of flour dotted her forehead and shapely nose. She wore a pin-striped shirt, blue and white and open at the throat, matched with a brown corduroy split skirt from her tomboy days by the patched look of it—probably something she dug out of her wardrobe—and over all a big once-white apron speckled with stains of an unknown origin.

Same old Sam! Except not the same. Not in the way she stood, not by her expression, her far-off gaze. Before he could figure out exactly what the differences were, she sensed his watching presence.

He knew the instant when she realized she was not alone, and he turned away just in time, burying his chin in his collar. When he couldn't avoid it any longer, he admitted to his identity; heart thudding hard and heavy somewhere in the region of his knotted stomach, he watched her expression turn to one of surprise and curiosity at the changes he knew she saw in him, changes for the better if he said so himself. She didn't miss a thing; he held to silence and tried to keep from squirming. *Maybe all's not lost!* he remembered thinking, just before he opened his mouth and put his foot squarely into it.

Nothing had changed; he was no more skilled with the opposite sex now than as a skinny, scholarly, twelve-year-old discovering, and falling hard for, the annoying little girl next door. Once he'd had hopes . . . and hung around waiting for Sam to grow up, notice that he was the best match for her of all his brothers, better than ever-practical Andrew, wise-cracking Charlie, or her temperamental confederate in crime, Duncan. But he waited too long. About the time she matured into irresistible womanhood, she took off for Chicago. Not even his best attempts to keep her in River Valley, which sounded like criticism to her, kept her Highness from going her own stubborn way. Quite successfully. Without his help. Without him in her life at all.

So how had he welcomed her back, but with exactly the same topic that sent her away mad as a hornet before they'd been alone together for more'n five minutes!

Smart move, Morgan, smart move! What're you going to do for an encore? See if you can talk her into slugging you next time you feel compelled to run off at the mouth?

Someone, in rare good humor, had set Samantha right across the table from him. If they hadn't been so danged annoying, her efforts to pretend he wasn't there would have amused Ben. As it was, he choked on every bite of his dinner from appetizer straight through to dessert. Ignoring him, she spoke at length with each of his brothers, from Andrew down to little Georgie. Sixteen-year-old Edward hung on her every word, for all the world like a hopelessly infatuated fool, poor kid, and who could blame the boy. Her year's absence left Ben himself just as greedy for the sight of her, unsatiated with their brief run-in earlier, he feasted—hopefully less obviously than his smitten sibling.

He saw now what it was he couldn't quite pin down before. Living and working in the big city had given Sam an air of confident poise that only enhanced her natural beauty. She'd gone from coltish to contained. Wrapped in a tailored blue suit that looked like it'd cost a pretty penny—a testament to her success—her tomboyish angles had gone soft and round. The fine, flyaway whiskey-colored mane of tiny curls Sam so hated as a child, she had somehow tamed since noontime into a twisted and coiled concoction she wore like a crown, with small wisps escaping to caress each temple and the back of her pale, slender neck. The peaches and cream of her complexion looked downright delicious, leaving a hollow emptiness no meal could satisfy—Thanksgiving included.

Hungry and hurting, figuring everyone'd notice him noticing her, Ben applied himself to his pie, but couldn't keep from glancing her way. Sam gave him an amber-eyed glare guaranteed to freeze the hottest ardor, that put certain things back in perspective mighty quick, dreams and fantasies in particular.

After their little chat on the front porch earlier, so much for second chances. Was he willing to try for a third? How much rejection could one man's pride withstand before he finally got the message that she just plain wasn't interested? Ben would've taken the hint, he wasn't stupid, except for that look, that flash of intrigued curiosity he'd seen on her face as he was coming toward her. Just maybe there was a chance for the two of them after all, *if* he could figure out a way to catch more than her interest. Her heart, for instance. Odd how a little hope went such a good long way when a body wanted something as badly as he wanted Samantha Sarahannah Spencer.

Samantha concentrated on a generous bite of Grannie's mincemeat pie, trying to distinguish each distinct element of the delicious whole, in a futile attempt to ignore the enigmatic stare Ben leveled on her throughout most of the meal. Having reacquainted herself with the brothers and with her numerous cousins and aunts and uncles, she'd applied herself to the feast with relish. She'd skipped breakfast altogether in anticipation of overeating now. After a year of mediocre restaurant food and what she could whip up on a gas hot plate in her room, every morsel tasted like ambrosia, and Grannie's pie the best of all, despite Ben's blatant efforts to give her indigestion. Ignoring him, she told her grandmother, "It's better even than last year, Grannie, if that's possible."

"Too much cinnamon and not enough wine," grumbled Grandpa, and everyone laughed at the annual, and much awaited, criticism. If it wasn't too much of one thing—the spices, nutmeg, cinnamon, cloves, or allspice—it was too little of another—be it the apples, raisins, or citron. She had boiled the beef too long or the suet tasted off, or she'd stored the preserved mincemeat too long in the crocks covered over with butter. Teasing—never malicious—defined the marriage between her grandparents. An oft-related story of Grannie's, one of hundreds it seemed, told of her not knowing a thing about cooking when they met, and of her first success, a perfect mincemeat pie Grandpa swore she'd yet to create again.

The thought occurred to Samantha that it wouldn't be a bad idea to write down Grannie's recipe, and the tale behind it, for future generations to come, and might even make an ideal wedding gift from her to Eliza, who cherished family traditions as much as she herself.

Ben's annoying behavior forgotten for the moment, Samantha looked down the long, heavily laden table to where Eliza and Charlie sat side by side, oblivious to everyone but each other, including herself. Samantha experienced a twinge of jealousy at being ignored by her best friend, more like sister than cousin, though she couldn't begrudge Eliza at last finding all the happiness she so richly deserved. The sweet but plain young woman with mouse brown hair and soft gray eyes looked almost ethereal with love; and Charlie of the sunny nature, golden hair, and blue eyes twinkling like sunlight on a pond, grinned until his cheeks looked about to split. The deep affection in their locked gazes, far too intimate for candid perusal, left Samantha feeling like an interloper. To her immediate right, Olivia and Aunt Jane chattered ceaselessly on topics of real interest to no one save themselves. Curiously, Olivia's end of the conversation consisted primarily of "yes, Mama" and "no, Mama," her beautiful cousin's attention having wandered to where Andrew sat beside her father at the table's head, engrossed in discussing business even today.

Samantha admired Andrew tremendously, she always had. Never as opposed to fun as Ben, upon the demise of his parents, he had shouldered the burden of supporting the remaining family without complaint, earning a position as Papa's right-hand man in a few short years. In the process, though, he had lost the ability to have fun and, in fact, had grown rather stuffy. What had attracted Olivia's interest, she couldn't imagine, unless she was inspired by his very promising financial prospects, or the fact that he was without a doubt the handsomest of the Morgan brothers—honey blond hair, bold blue eyes, and chiseled features to rival the gods—and very possibly the best-looking man in town. To dear cousin Olivia these attributes were always, first and foremost, of greatest importance.

With growing amusement, Samantha watched Olivia plying her many charms to attract Andrew's attention. Incredulous, she observed Andrew, on several occasions, with fleeting glances Olivia's way, lose the direction of what he was saying or force her father to repeat himself.

She found their surreptitious exchanges more unbearable than Eliza and Charlie's open mooning, and looked away, right into Edward's love-struck gaze, directed at her. She had tried to ignore the sixteen-year-old's unwavering, admiring stare all through dinner, hoping his attention would prove to be a passing fancy of which he would quickly tire. Unfortunately, his interest only intensified as the meal progressed. The boy, so near to attaining manhood, looked to be skinnier than Ben ever was, lucklessly the plainest of the brood, with somewhat protruding ears and a pug nose liberally spattered with freckles. Sitting diagonally from her, elbow propped on the linen tablecloth, a forkful of pie poised near his mouth uneaten, the puckish lad unblinkingly focused only on her. Unable to bear his undivided attention a moment longer, she turned away, catching Ben watching her, too. At least *he* did not look demented. Simply annoying in the way only Ben could, as if he read her very thoughts, and found them amusing.

The Morgan boys, in her estimation, had lost their collective minds. With the possible exception of the two youngest, Frankie and Georgie, towheaded charmers of twelve and ten, whose only peculiarity this day seemed to be their capacity for consuming one dessert after another on top of the feast that went before.

Unbidden, the one Morgan missing from their midst came to mind. Duncan. Who'd loved her so much more than she had him. Whose heart she'd broken with the rejection of his ardent declaration and impassioned proposal. Who ran from the truth that she did not care for him in *that* way, rather than accept the sisterly devotion she offered. Whose dear, teasing, often brooding face she might never see again.

Love. What foolishness. What folly. As far as Samantha could see, love was nothing but a nuisance that spoiled perfectly good camaraderie. Thank fortune she herself was immune to that troublesome emotion. Writing was her only true love, her passion. Always was and always would be. Love, romance, marriage. Silly sentimentalities. Pah, who needed them? She faced matters in her life of far greater importance at the moment. Such as convincing R. W. Reed to take her back at the *Star.* In any capacity. And keeping anyone here at home from finding out she'd been fired. Especially the infuriatingly observant Ben Morgan.

THREE

"Did you bring your famous fruitcake with you this trip, Maddie?" asked plump Aunt Jane, running the tip of her tongue around her lips in anticipation. "After that marvelous mincemeat pie yesterday, I have such a craving for some."

Grannie chuckled. "Knowing there'd be more of us here than usual because of the wedding, I brought three. And, yes, Jane, I brought a tin of Christmas cookies for each family as always."

"Did you make lebkuchen and pfeffernusse this year, Aunt Maddie?" Aunt Rose's daughter, twenty-year-old Lucille, wanted to know.

The German recipes garnered from Samantha's mother's side of the family were the most popular. Cordelia Spencer, nee Gilbert, boasted of the Schumann on the family tree with his own bakery in the Old Country. Recipes passed down from him through Cordelia to her mother-in-law had soon become legend in Spencer heritage with Grannie's baking expertise.

"Lebkuchen, pfeffernusse, and springerles. And sand tarts, almond crescents, macaroons, walnut rocks, fruit and nut cookies and . . ." Grannie Spencer paused, pretending to try to remember.

"Gingerbread men?" cried the youngest cousins, Prudence and Sally, together.

"Gingerbread men, and women, children and babies, and even a few animals thrown in for good measure," agreed Grannie with great glee. "And kisses. And true-lover's knots. I didn't forget anyone's favorite this year, did I?"

Every woman, young and old and ages in between, gathered around the quilting frame set up in the back parlor, shook their head no. Fingers flew, needles passing from the hand under the layers of fabric to the hand poised over the tumbling blocks pattern on top and back again, up and down without ceasing. Pleasant female chatter accompanied the happy task of completing this traditional thirteenth quilt for Eliza's hope chest, already crammed to the top with twelve other family-made quilts and hand-work-embellished linens. Holidays when relatives traveled great distances and stayed for a number of days occasioned these sewing bees several times a year. All the unmarried female cousins, from Willa (whispered to have become the family spinster at age twenty-seven) down to thirteen-year-old Sally, were fully outfitted by the time they left their parents' home for their husband's. A matter of family pride. Anything less would be unthinkable.

Samantha, sitting in a rocker in the bay window beside her temporarily handicapped mother, personally thought her hope chest a waste of time and effort. She'd been unable to dissuade the women from working on it on these occasions, though she herself was not allowed to help. Sewing any kind of a fine seam proved to be beyond her early on, and she had been gently asked not to participate after her first few disastrous attempts. She retaliated by writing down nearly everything that was talked about, from recipes to cures for whatever ailed a body, to the latest in fashion, the most current of gossip, and the family stories old and new. She filled reams of paper with her small, tidy script over time, no thought in her head what to do with them, except that it seemed of great importance to keep the records as accurately as possible, though she suspected many of Grannie's tales to be as embroidered as the linens.

"Are you planning a church wedding, Eliza?" asked Aunt Dorothy, Cordelia's older sister.

Though only forty-five, she tended to be forgetful. Mama said she just didn't listen, never had, or she wouldn't've married Clifford Burgess, the town mortician, who was, the ladies all agreed, a hard man to get in a good humor, ever. Aunt Dorothy herself said little on the subject, except that her husband took his job, and his position in the community, very seriously.

Eliza briefly lifted her head from her small, tidy stitches. Passing the back of her hand over her forehead to push away a straight wisp of mouse-brown hair, she threw her aunt a shy gray-eyed glance, her pale cheeks staining pink.

"Charles and . . . and I would like to be married here, in the parlor," she admitted in a quiet voice, but could not hide the joy in simply saying "Charles and I."

Unable to let Eliza experience a few moments of undivided attention unchallenged, Olivia announced, *"I* shall have a *church* wedding. A very *large* church wedding." Her perfect nose tilted upward in disdain for anything less.

Thoroughly annoyed, Grannie Spencer spoke up, tone tart.

"And just when will this grand event occur, Olivia dear?"

The young woman flushed red, but would not back down even to the family matriarch.

"As soon as Mama and I have the opportunity to travel to New York where so many rich and titled men reside," she responded crisply.

"I see," said Grannie, and chuckled.

Young Sally, at thirteen included in her first quilting bee, spoke up with the candid innocence of youth. "I thought you were sweet on Andrew Morgan, Olivia. You stared at him all through dinner yesterday."

Olivia's ire rose, and accordingly so did her hauteur. "I did not, Sally Parkin. What would a child like you know of such things?"

Sally pouted. "I am not a child, and I know what I saw."

"Girls, girls, let's not quarrel," Sally's mother Kate, ever the peacemaker, intervened. Then, with a sly smile, she asked Grannie Spencer, "What kind of wedding did you have, Maddie?"

Everyone tittered; all gazes turned expectantly toward Grannie Spencer. Maybe this time she'd finally break down and confess just what oddity of a wedding she had had, so bizarre that she would not speak of it even among the women of her family. Who knew for certain how such matters had been attended to in the wilds of the Colorado Territory so long ago? Or—and none dared think it let alone say it aloud—what if Maddie and Sam Spencer were not really married at all? Wouldn't that make most of them present today—horror of horrors—bastards, and many of the rest, too?

Without hesitation, Grannie replied, as always, "Beautifully wed and happily married for all these forty-two years. You were married at home, weren't you, Kate? And Dorothy, and Eliza's poor departed mother, Ophelia. All the Gilbert sisters but Cordelia here, as a matter of fact." Turning to her daughter-in-law, she suggested, "Tell them about your wedding, Cordelia. Even better, tell us how you and Preston fell in love. Now that's a story worth the telling."

It was Mama's turn to look flustered, and more than a little embarrassed. "It is also one that's been told so many times, there's not a soul in this room who hasn't heard it."

"I haven't, Aunt Cordelia," said young Sally.

Everyone raised a voice encouraging Cordelia to tell her story once again, for Sally. Samantha knew each one who'd heard it before, some many, many times, found the story wildly romantic, even she herself. In their late teens, both Mama and Papa had been telegraphers, Cordelia employed by her father's bank here at home, and Preston by the town of Luckless, Colorado, where her father had an investor with extensive holdings. Through the process of communicating between the investor and Grandpa Gilbert, Cordelia and Preston fell in love. Over the wire, he proposed. She accepted sight unseen, then traveled across country to meet him for the first time, and marry him. Though happily wed, the couple remained without family for years. Cordelia miscarried with every pregnancy—six in all—and they'd about resigned themselves to childlessness when Grandpa Gilbert passed away. Having no sons, he left Preston his bank and investment holdings. As soon as Preston and Cordelia settled down in River Valley, Mama became with child once more. Samantha's birth proved testament to this fertile valley in the midwest, where the climate and terrain were far less harsh than in the Rockies.

As Mama began her tale, Samantha dropped her pencil into her lap, flexing cramped fingers. Massaging one hand with the other, she let herself be distracted from the familiar retelling by the gurgling and cooing coming from the basket nestled in the bay between her chair and her

mother's. Cathleen's baby, Betsy, born six months before
in June, represented the first of the next generation, product of the daughter of Mama's sister Dorothy and her husband Clifford—the mortician—and Cathleen's husband
Martin Murray—mortician's assistant. Beautiful in the
way all babies are, infant Betsy Murray had yet to develop
features Samantha could define as those of the new
mother or father, though everyone else claimed she had
Cathleen's tiny nose and Marty's round chin. Until this
moment, Samantha had not really given the child much
thought; now, some latent maternal instinct caused her to
bend down to gather the happy baby into her arms, blankets and all. Freshly diapered, recently fed, and relieved
of gas, little Betsy snuggled contentedly against Samantha's bosom; succumbing to the gentle rocking, she settled
in for a nap in Samantha's arms.

Entirely unprepared, Samantha felt a totally unexpected
sense of peace and well-being settle over her and the baby
like a warm, comforting cloak. Pressing her lips, then her
cheek to the infant's downy crown, she breathed in the
mingled scents of freshly bathed baby and talc, her heart
swelling with undefined longings she didn't dare examine
too closely.

"Is she asleep?" asked Cathleen, standing over her,
arms open to receive her child.

Nodding, Samantha reluctantly relinquished the baby
to her mother. Glancing through the window overlooking
the adjoining back lawns at the slam of a door, she saw
the youngest Morgan boys, Frankie and Georgie, tear out
into the snow-covered yard, with Ben in close pursuit.
Several inches of heavy, wet snow had fallen overnight,
and the Morgan boys took full advantage of this first thick
layer to engage in a free-for-all snowball fight, with much
shouting and laughter. Then they industriously set to work

building a snowman. Red-cheeked but warmly dressed and oblivious to the cold, the trio worked together with good-humored industry to roll an enormous ball for the snowman's base.

Watching them brought back memories of some of the happiest times in her life. Winter, that magical season of childhood. Christmas aside, she recalled endless, aimless hours spent skating and sledding, snowmen making, and snow forts—one in her yard and one in theirs. Choosing up sides for snowball fights without end, until spring thaws turned snow to slush.

When Samantha could stand it no longer, she offered some mumbled excuse and made a dash into the front hall for her outer wear. Bundled warmly, she stepped outside, standing behind a porch post so as not to be observed, knowing full well those Morgan fellows would not spare her. Any more than she'd spare them. Stepping down, she scooped up two generous handfuls of snow, patting them into a perfect sphere with easily recaptured skill. She suppressed chuckles of anticipation. Sound carried across snow the way it did over water, and she had no intention of giving any warning.

Taking careful aim, Samantha threw her snowball, striking her target—Ben's head—as intended. Ducking behind the closest tree, she watched him glance around sharply this way and that. Seeing no one, he even looked up, as if expecting an overhanging tree limb to have dropped its load of snow, though there was none nearby. He shrugged, then went back to helping roll a ball for the snowman's middle. Samantha quickly formed more ammunition, and launched with the same accurate results. Ben repeated his search with the same lack of success. He whipped off his stocking cap, scrubbing his cowlick at the base of his skull, deep in thought. With a second shrug, he pulled on his cap and helped Frankie and Georgie lift the middle-sized ball in place.

Smug at her success, exerting great caution, Samantha moved from cover of one concealing tree trunk to another. Her third snowball caught Ben in the rear as he bent to tie his bootlace. Except that actually he'd been forming his own ammunition. With a quick swivel of his upper torso and swing of his pitching arm, he caught her on the shoulder with a huge, soft ball. Snow exploded in a cloud, covering her coat front, splashing into her face, leaving her to sputter and step out from behind the tree, accusing, "You knew I was there all the time, Ben Morgan."

Grinning, he admitted, "Not till the second hit. Good throwing, Sam. You haven't lost your accuracy with a ball, for all that city living. Come join us."

His brothers, who had fallen to the ground laughing, now stretched out flat, waving arms and legs to make snow angels.

She hung back. "I will if you promise not to try to get even for the one you owe me."

"Two. But who's counting? We promise, don't we, lads?" Ben turned to his brothers with an exaggerated wink visible to Samantha even at a distance. The boys sat up to nod innocently in unison. Ben said, "See, Sam, you have our word. Come on over and play."

How many, many times those words had been shouted between the Morgan and Spencer houses! Sensing treachery, still Samantha was unable to resist the prospect of an afternoon of harmless fun in the bracing snow and cold. She and Ben rolled the final, smaller ball for the head, while the boys ran inside for a carrot, some coal, a hat, and a scarf. Samantha contributed the worn broom from her back porch. They all stood back to enjoy their handiwork. The snowman grinned happily back with coal-black teeth, stocking cap at a cocky angle over one coal eye. Samantha tipped her head sideways.

"He looks like his head is sliding off."

Ben scooped up snow, patting it in place to brace up the snow sculpture's head. Taking advantage of the distraction, Samantha hastily formed a snowball, holding it behind her back as he turned, face stern, eyes merry.

"Samantha Spencer, if your intentions are what I think they are, you might want to reconsider. We're three against one here, in case you hadn't noticed."

"Three against one. Three against one. Three against one," chanted his brothers.

At that moment, some children passed by out front, calling to the boys to join them for sledding, crying out a greeting, too, to their teacher, "Hi, Mr. Morgan." Frankie and Georgie, sleds in tow, disappeared in an instant, leaving their elders standing alone together, suddenly awkward. Samantha cleared her throat.

"There went your troops, *Mr. Morgan*," she teased.

Ben fisted his hands against his chest. "Deserted in the face of the enemy," he declared with great drama. "I surrender. You can drop that snowball you're holding behind your back now, Sam."

"What snowball?" She brought it out in front of her as if surprised to see it there. "Now how do you suppose that got there?"

Ben gave an exaggerated shrug. "I can't imagine." A pause. "You going to drop it, or throw it? I should warn you that if you throw it, I'll be forced to wash your face with snow."

She studied the snowball and studied the mock serious look on his once-plain face grown handsome, not knowing quite how to deal with this Ben, so familiar and yet so changed. The subtle differences in him made her feel most peculiar inside. She didn't mind change, not in herself or her circumstances, but she liked old familiar things . . . and people to stay comfortingly the same. She experienced a strange, not unpleasant, premonition that changes beyond her wildest imagination were soon to occur.

"Well?" demanded Ben with a chuckle. "Are you planning on dropping that thing or throwing it, or to just hold it till it melts come spring?"

"I . . . mmm. How about some nice hot cocoa?"

He gave her a quizzical glance.

"Sure, I could use something hot to thaw me out. You inviting yourself over?"

Samantha rose to his baiting with indignation. "I *can* boil milk."

"Your kitchen, then."

He waved her toward the back steps of her house with a sweep of his arm, all proper and gentlemanly.

"After you," Samantha suggested, sugar sweet.

Caught up in the moment, Ben made the mistake of turning his back at her. A loud, wet *splat* alerted him too late, as her well-aimed snowball struck him squarely on the bare skin at the back of his neck. Snow slithered down under his collar. He tore off his right glove, frantically trying to extract the stuff, turning a murderous gaze her way.

Bent over, arms wrapped around her waist, Samantha laughed loud and long.

"Very funny! I'll get you for that, Sam, sure as snowmen melt in sunshine."

He started toward her, looming large. For one brief moment she was afraid she'd gone too far, before coming to her senses. This was Ben. Ben Morgan, the least threatening of all the brothers. Who always accepted a prank against himself without retaliation. She stuck out her tongue at him.

"Catch me if you can, Ben Morgan," she challenged.

Always the quickest of the neighborhood children, Samantha had forgotten the heavy wool coat she wore, and underestimated Ben's lengthened stride, increased coordination. He caught her in two steps, hauled her tight against his hard body, and fisted a handful of snow within inches of her nose. She frantically twisted this way and that, to no avail.

"Don't wash my face, Ben. Please, Ben. It'll make my skin all red and raw. Please, Ben, don't."

He tossed the snow away, but bent closer.

"A different punishment, then."

His face came dangerously near, then nearer. His cold lips covered hers, and he kissed her long and deep. Until she grew uncomfortably hot, certain the snow must be melting under her feet. He let her go so abruptly, he had to brace her with a hand on her elbow to keep her from falling down. His face wore the strangest look, his eyes a bit unfocused. As if suddenly realizing she stared at him equally mesmerized, he offered up a poor imitation of his habitual know-it-all grin.

"Remember the price you were forced to pay today next time you challenge me to a snowball fight." His voice sounded husky, labored. With a deep breath, he added, "How about that hot cocoa?"

Without a by-your-leave, he turned his back on her and strode up her back steps into the house. In the Spencers' cozy kitchen, smelling faintly of yesterday's Thanksgiving dinner, Grannie Spencer, Olivia, and Eliza set out refreshments, Mama directing the proceedings in her domaine with her usual efficiency. Panic instantly fluttered in Samantha's stomach. What if one of her cousins or Mama, or worst of all, Grannie—ever the matchmaker on her behalf—had seen Ben's impetuous, retaliatory kiss and misinterpreted it? Thankfully, no one seemed the least aware of her and Ben until he closed the door behind her.

"Greetings, ladies. I hope there's something good and hot ready to drink for a pair of frozen laborers," Ben spoke up cheerily.

"Harrumph! Laborers, my Aunt Fanny. I know larking about when I see it," said Grannie Spencer with mock severity.

"An hour frittered away I'd call it," Cordelia agreed.

Eliza spoke up, but softly, "It looked like great fun," adding with regret, "Sometimes I wish I could spend an afternoon at play instead of with my painting or reading or embroidery, though it isn't half so ladylike."

Olivia spoke up, voice bitter, jealous. "Don't let your grandmother hear you say disparaging remarks about needlework, 'Liza." Although Grannie had, as everyone well knew. "It's *tradition* for a female family member to fill her hope chest before reaching twenty-one, whether she'll ever have need of or not. With the exception of Samantha, of course."

Samantha, too giddy with relief that the kiss had apparently gone unnoticed, refused to let her cousin bait her. Shaking the snow out of her coat, she hung it on a hook behind the cookstove to drip dry.

"If I were capable of learning to sew a straight seam, I would gladly join you all. Instead, my contribution seems to be writing down every gem of wisdom, every tale told, for future generations," adding, tongue-in-cheek, "Careful what you say, Olivia, your words could stand for hundreds of years to come."

"Pish posh!" responded Olivia, pert nose in the air. "As if anyone *would* read those silly stories you write down, Samantha. You give too much importance to your scribblings. Mother says your articles haven't even been appearing in that newspaper of yours for weeks and weeks. Most disappointing, for her at least. She followed your reporting of the Chicago society quite closely. Myself, I find only the East Coast social scene to be of significance." She leveled a piercing stare on her cousin. "Why haven't your articles been appearing, Samantha? You haven't been dismi—"

Before Olivia finished asking the question she most dreaded hearing, Samantha spoke up. "I've been researching an exposé."

"Oh, Samantha, you promised your father and me to pursue no dangerous assignments like that reckless Miss Bly you so admire." Alarm evident in her voice, her mother paused at her task of placing cookies in a precise spiral on a plate.

"Mama, I was in absolutely no danger."

"What were you reporting on?" asked Eliza, wide-eyed, awestruck, clearly envious.

"When will your story appear?" Grannie wanted to know. "I'll have your grandpa subscribe to the *Star* for the occasion."

Samantha evaded Eliza's query to answer Grannie's, hot color rising in her cheeks. "It won't. A reporter from another paper printed her article on the same subject before I could. I was scooped."

All feminine faces except Olivia's expressed sympathy; everyone—except Olivia—murmured condolences. Ben's candid blue eyes studied her with an intensity Samantha found most disconcerting, containing, what was it? Censure? Curiosity? Kindness?

Ignoring him, and the jumble of emotions his scrutiny aroused, Samantha said, "I'm enjoying this time at home simply writing up family memories. Rest assured, ladies . . . and gentleman . . . after the holidays I'll be re-

porting the social news of Chicago and beyond, as before."
Not a lie, she rationalized, but a promise to them and
herself that she'd get her job back in the new year, no
matter what.

"You ought to see about getting your stuff printed lo-
cally, Sam," Ben suggested mildly, helping himself to another cookie on Mama's carefully arranged plate, already
half-empty thanks to him.

"I do not report on *stuff,* I write the news." Samantha
bristled, slapping his hand away as he reached for more.

Smiling amiably, Ben took a sip of cocoa, oblivious to
the ridiculous chocolate mustache resulting.

"You are also making a record of recipes and remedies
and anecdotes involving the town's history. I'll bet a lot
of the local folks, the older ones especially, would enjoy
seeing them in print."

"And have everyone in town know our personal business? Heaven forbid!" chided Olivia.

Ben barked a laugh. "As if they didn't already. I'm sure
Sam would know what to write about and what to leave
out for propriety's sake, wouldn't you, Sam?"

"One of the first rules of reporting," Samantha agreed
tongue-in-cheek. "Assuming the editor of the *River Valley
Weekly Review* would be interested."

"Jasper Cooper is a friend of mine. I'll see what he
thinks. Can't hurt." He stood, backhanding his cocoa mustache into oblivion. "I hear the boys, back from sledding
and probably starving. I'd better go feed them before they
tear the pantry apart foraging for something to eat."

"Nonsense," Grannie interrupted. "Dry them off and
bring them and yourself back over here for dinner. We've
enough leftovers to see us through till Christmas if they
wouldn't spoil. Which they will. You'd be doing us a favor

by adding three more hungry appetites to the supper table."

Ben gave Grannie Spencer a bear hug and a smacking big kiss—nothing at all like the enervating one he'd pinned on Samantha earlier.

"Thanks, Grannie. We'll be back in a while, then. Afternoon, ladies." He tipped his cap and was gone.

Samantha followed his long-legged lope across the snow, already patterned with hundreds of footprints, happily recalling the frolicking earlier. With the exception of the kiss at the end, of course.

The others watched his progress, too, observing Ben's affectionate, playful behavior with his brothers as he hoisted Georgie onto his shoulder, then stole Frankie's cap to ruffle his hair.

"That's one of the finest young men I've ever known," said Grannie. "As is Charlie," she added for Eliza's benefit. "Ben Morgan'll make a wonderful husband for some lucky woman one day soon, wouldn't you say, Samantha?"

"I—I hadn't given it a thought, Grannie," she lied, her thoughts having strayed precariously near that same conclusion not so long ago. Not as a prospect for herself, naturally, since she intended to remain single and self-sufficient, thanks to her writing. With added thanks to Ben, should speaking with his editor friend result in additional income for her, a nestegg for the future. Her encounter with the Klem family, if worth nothing else, had made her most painfully aware how close abject poverty hovers over anyone with a run of bad luck and—

"Andrew would make a good catch, too," Olivia interjected, tone brittle, tinged with tears, "if he didn't keep himself so poor helping Ben keep that big old house and support those children."

With a knowing smile, Grannie asked, "Just what concern of yours would that be, Olivia, dear?"

Olivia became her haughtiest. "None whatsoever except as a disinterested observer. Soon Mama and I shall be leaving for New York. Spring is when personages of royalty begin arriving for the season—"

"Personages of royalty, is it? And what's the likelihood of any princes and dukes and such being left over after the Astors and the Vanderbilts and so on get through choosing husbands for *their* daughters?"

Olivia's chin trembled at the truth in Grannie's gentle assault.

"Perhaps I shan't marry at all. Maybe I shall choose to remain single like Willa, and . . . and Samantha. Maybe I shall become the old maiden auntie who moves from relative to relative until she overstays her welcome because . . . because she has nowhere else to gooo." The last was said in a great sob, and Olivia fled the house, having grabbed up Samantha's new coat on the run.

"Well, I never . . ." began Mama.

"Oh, yes, Cordelia, you have," said Grannie. "You've seen and felt that very agony before, as have we all who've been in love, but too afraid to pursue it."

"*That* I remember all too well," agreed Mama.

"Me, too," added Eliza timidly, as was her way.

Not having had a similar experience to share, Samantha sipped her cooling cocoa and contemplatively chewed on a frosted sugar cookie, mulling over what a painful, chancy thing love was, thankful to be free herself of that annoying emotion. It had not escaped her notice that Grannie had been attempting a bit of less than subtle matchmaking between herself and Ben Morgan. This time, however, her grandmother's notorious skills in that area were destined to fail. Marry Ben Morgan? Not if she were down to her last cent with fingers too arthritic to hold a pen. Andrew maybe, if Olivia found her prince; or Duncan, if he ever came back. She might even consider the smitten Edward, though he was six years younger than herself. He'd soon grow up. But Ben? Ben Morgan? That was about as likely as the hot springs in Johnson's Pond freezing over. And *that* had *never* happened, never would.

FOUR

Ben pretended to adjust the lens on the telescope aimed at the stars through his bedroom window. His fingers fumbled at the familiar task because his gaze continually strayed to Samantha's window across the way. Disappointingly, no light illuminated her room. Ben was no voyeur. All he wanted, needed, was a glimpse of her to see if *she* glanced *his* way. Anything to give him hope.

Never in all his born days had he done anything as impetuous, or as purely stupid, as kissing Sam this afternoon, but, good Lord, he needed it. She needed it. She needed to accept him as a force to be reckoned with, no longer the gangling, gawking teen she and his brothers liked to taunt.

Kissing her was the only way he could think of to learn if there was any hope at all for them. And he still wasn't sure of a blessed thing more than before their wind-chilled lips locked. Oh, she kissed him back. He had no doubt on that score. But hell if he could figure out what it meant to her, deep down, where it counted. If it meant anything to her at all. As likely as not, nothing he could say or do was as important to Samantha Sarahannah Spencer as her writing. She could easily cast him aside the way she had poor, hapless, heart-on-his-sleeve Duncan. And look what happened to him. Ben nursed the sore spot buried somewhere in the region of his heart, missing the one brother who'd not remained in the fold. He wondered anew if there was anything he could've said or done to keep him home after Sam's rejection. Knowing there wasn't, wishing there had been.

Losing Duncan had hurt Sam as much as Ben and the remaining brothers, though she never let on. Writing in those days meant everything to her, as now, to the exclusion of those things most folks longed for—courtship, marriage, family—things he wanted for himself before he grew too old to enjoy them. Twenty-five and still a bachelor! How much longer could he hang around waiting for Sam to come to her senses?

Forever. He'd live his entire life unloved, unwed, before he'd give up on Samantha. She was as much a part of him as every breath he took, always had been, always would be. And if that wasn't stupid, Ben Morgan didn't know what was! Especially since she hadn't a clue how he felt. Particularly since she'd probably head back for Chicago in a few weeks not knowing. And, if it killed him, he'd have to let her. As close as she was to fulfilling her dreams of being a stunt reporter like Nellie Bly, why would she ever want to settle for small town life again? If she knew how he felt, and assuming she reciprocated his feelings— a mighty big assumption—would she reconsider going back, would she stay, always secretly wishing she hadn't, or—and this was the most likely—would she run like a scared rabbit back to Chicago to escape him? How the blue blazes would he know which, unless he did something about it? Said something, like "Hey, Sam, I love you, always have, always will, and I want you to marry me. Stay home, settle down, and we'll raise a family. I don't mind if you write when and if you can find the time."

"Oh, damn!"

Ben bolted across the room, blew out the lamp on his desk, and stormed down the stairs calling for Zeus, his aging hound, already settled in for the night beside the banked heat of the cookstove. Well, tonight the damned worthless old mutt was going for a walk, Ben had no intention of going alone. He had to talk to someone, anyone, or explode, and Zeus was the only living, breathing soul available. Top on his endless list of topics, why in the world had he volunteered to talk to Jasper Cooper, editor of the *River Valley Weekly Reporter,* to get Sam *more* writing assignments. To remind her of the bigger and better things awaiting her in Chicago.

Shoot, she deserved them. Sam was one damn good writer. Her talent, her gift from God, whatever, was her life's blood, and come hell or high water, even if it sucked out every last drop of his, he'd do whatever was in his power to see that she got where she wanted to go with it.

It was just too damn bad he wasn't a saint, or a eunuch!

"Zeus, get your worthless old bones out of bed. We're going for a walk. One *hell* of a long walk."

Ben's light went out. At last. Samantha crossed her darkened bedroom from the doorway, where she'd stood watching him make adjustments on that telescope of his for an interminable length of time, feeling like a spy, a snoop. She reached her window unerringly, looking across, then down as Ben's back door slammed. She followed the progress of the familiar figures over the white lawn, through the back alley, behind his barn, then hers, then out of sight.

She discovered she'd stood all this time with fingertips pressed against her lips, remembering the sensation of Ben's impetuous kiss. Of course he'd meant it only to tease, to pay her back for lobbing snow down his neck. Or had he? Would a punishing kiss linger so long, feel so impassioned, induce that hot melting sensation in her most private parts? *Blast you, Ben Morgan! What could you possibly have been thinking?* What impulse possessed him to embrace her, kiss her every bit as though he were her beau, her lover? Was she reading more into the simple gesture than he intended?

Wishful thinking?

Most decidedly not on her part. And not in regards to Ben Morgan, of all people. The boy next door, ever-practical bane of her childhood. Definitely not Ben. What silly nonsense. Preposterous even to consider the possibility.

So what if she'd come home expecting a lanky scholar with his nose in a book and interest in nothing else, to discover a lean, handsome, funny, thoughtful, caring man? There were many, many men with at least some of those same qualities, probably right here in River Valley. None of them was Benjamin Franklin Morgan, though, blast his hide. What'd he have to go and change for? Why'd everything have to change?

If only it were six weeks from now, Eliza's wedding over and done with, and herself safely on a train back to Chicago. No one—least of all Ben Morgan—was going to keep her from her writing, or steal her hard-won independence.

"There's to be a Christmas party at Sissy Chester's on the fourteenth," announced Olivia to her cousins.

The three sat before the hearth in the back parlor, Olivia stringing cranberries, Eliza making paper chains, and Samantha supposedly threading popcorn into a long rope, but mostly stuffing it into her mouth instead. When her audience failed to respond, Olivia continued anyway, addressing Eliza.

"I'm sure you and Charlie will be expected to attend, what with Charlie's position at the bank; and Samantha and I must naturally join you for propriety's sake. Eliza," the young woman lifted her head from her cutting and pasting, "please do pay attention. It will have to be left up to you to arrange for Ben and . . . Andrew to escort Samantha . . . and myself to Sissy's party."

Olivia's ploy proved so transparent even sweet Eliza saw it for what it was, and indulged her. Samantha held her tongue to see where the conversation would lead, Olivia being a mistress of manipulation. Eliza's hesitation fueled her crafty cousin's impatience.

"You and Charlie *are* planning to attend, aren't you?"

"I-I-I suppose so." Eliza sighed. "Charles does so enjoy parties."

"Well?" Olivia persisted.

"It would make going less trying if we all attended together." Eliza brightened at the thought. "I'm sure Charles won't mind speaking to his brothers. I'll ask him about it this evening."

As his fiancée, thought Samantha, the shy young woman would have to learn to at least tolerate them for his sake. What better way to begin than with her family beside her? Easing Eliza's obvious distress almost—but not quite—made up for being paired with Ben, for without a doubt that was Olivia's plan, leaving Andrew for herself.

Samantha was silent up till now, observing Olivia's guiding Eliza in the direction she would have her go. Seeing, too, that Eliza used Olivia's manipulation to her own advantage, whether or not she realized what she was doing. But enough was enough.

"I don't plan on going to Sissy's party," she said.

Olivia paled.

"You have to go," she insisted imperiously.

"Why?" demanded Samantha. "Why should I go? Sissy's your friend. I don't like parties. And I haven't a single party dress to my name." She dumped her string of popped corn into the bowl to count her objections on buttery fingers, all but upending the popcorn bowl. "The only reason you want me to tag along is so people won't assume you and Andrew are a couple."

Her cousin's cheeks turned an unflattering scarlet.

"That's not so. Everyone knows of my intention to go to New York in the spring—"

"And catch yourself a prince or duke. In the meantime, you think you're infatuated with Andrew and plan to let him haul you around from one gathering to another during the holidays, as if he were your beau. What about after you leave? Is everyone in town supposed to assume he jilted you, or you him? How beneficial will that be for his squeaky clean banker's image?"

"What nonsense! You're making far too much of things, as usual, Samantha. It must be that writer's imagination of yours." Olivia resorted to snobbery to cover her visible discomfort. "It's only one party. No one will think Andrew and I are together, anymore than they would pair you and Ben as a couple."

"That *would* be the logical conclusion. Ben and me as a couple, I mean."

"You and Ben? Why that . . . that's just silly."

Olivia's brittle laugh rankled. Samantha wasn't sure why it mattered, but she had to know.

"Why is it silly?"

"Because, for one thing, it's common knowledge you don't even *like* each other."

"I like Ben. I mean, I don't *not* like him. We all played

together as children. He's our neighbor, for goodness sakes." Before she blundered any further, Samantha clamped her lips tight and watched Olivia's smile go smug.

"So is Andrew, don't you see? Merely a neighbor to whom we are being . . . neighborly. So you *must* come, it's the neighborly thing to do, and I shall loan you one of my dresses to wear. Fortunately there's time enough to let the seams out in the waist."

Eliza spoke before sparks could fly. "Samantha, please do come with Olivia and the others. I'd feel so much better knowing I wouldn't be facing my first social outing as a bride-to-be without the support of my family," she offered each cousin a small smile, "and my two best friends."

Samantha threw up her hands, then barely caught the popcorn bowl before it slid off her lap.

"All right. I'll go. But only if we can all go in a . . . in a bunch, and *not* as couples. And if Andrew and Ben are willing."

"I can't speak for my brother, but I'm willing to do just about anything three lovely young ladies ask of me. What am I volunteering for?"

The three conspirators jumped guiltily at the sound of Ben's voice in the doorway. This time, Samantha's bowl did hit the rug, scattering popcorn over the floor like a winter snowfall.

"Samantha!" her cousins chided in unison.

Ben laughed heartily. "No longer suitable for eating, but still fine for stringing. Let me help." He picked his way through the mess, then cleared himself a spot to sit cross-legged in their midst. He picked up Samantha's half-finished chain and set to work.

"You're doing a better job of that than I was," Samantha admitted begrudgingly. Looking into his eyes, like bits of midnight sky, Samantha felt an odd compulsion to explain herself. "I'm more comfortable with a pen than a needle."

Gazes locked, Ben assured her. "I can sew on a button, mend a drooping hem, and even stitch up a finger or a forehead if need be."

"That's all very practical, but can you dance?" Olivia's blunt query broke in.

Like dreamers awakening, Samantha and Ben acknowledging Olivia.

"I can dance as good as I can fly," Ben admitted.

"You can't fly?"

"Exactly."

"Pooh!" Olivia pouted. An instant later she brightened. "Neither can Samantha. You'll be perfect together."

Uncertain, Ben remonstrated. "Practically perfect at best, ma'am, and at your service. What are we talking about, anyway?"

"Sissy Chester's Christmas party, of course."

"Of course. Mayor Chester's annual attempt to find a husband for his wayward daughter among the eligible bachelors of River Valley. Too bad Sissy's reputation preceded her. I'd much rather be the one and only in some fair lady's future, instead of one of many." He winked at Samantha.

Olivia flashed her charm. "You're not to be companion to Sissy, silly. Samantha and I promised to help Eliza get over her shyness at social gatherings by accompanying her and Charlie to Sissy's party. Naturally, we'll need escorts."

"Naturally."

"Don't interrupt. Eliza suggested that she ask Charlie to invite you and Andrew to join us."

"Great idea, Eliza." Ben's voice boomed with enthusiasm, noticeably false.

Eliza started, thoroughly flustered. "I didn't . . . that is . . . well, thank you."

Now Olivia looked frustrated, and Ben mighty pleased with himself. This nonsense had gone on long enough!

"What *did* you come over for?" Samantha demanded of him.

His self-satisfied grin never faltered. "For the pleasure of you ladies' company. And to tell you, Sam, that I spoke with my editor friend, Jasper Cooper. He'd like to discuss with you the possibility of contributing to his paper." He leaned back against the leg of the sofa to study her face, better to judge her reaction, and was rewarded with the eager pleasure that turned her brown eyes amber.

"When?"

"I said we'd stop by his house around seven tonight."

"We?" she challenged. At once genuinely contrite, she amended, "I suppose it's only right you make introductions." But her face looked as though she'd just swallowed a bitter tonic.

"A 'thank you, Ben' wouldn't be out of order here, Sam. Or if you like, you could fling yourself into my arms and plant a thank you kiss on my——"

"Thank you, Ben, will do."

Unwilling to press his luck, Ben thrust into Samantha's hands the popcorn bowl, empty except for unpopped kernels and a neat string of popcorn for the tree. He dusted crumbs off his pant legs.

"I'll come by for you at quarter to seven."

She threw him an if-you-must glance.

" 'Bye, then, ladies."

As soon as the front door closed behind him, Olivia chided, "That was rude, Samantha. A young lady sees a young gentleman to the door, especially one who has gone out of his way to help her."

"Ben's been finding his way in and out of this house alone for a number of years," Samantha countered.

"Ah, but that was before he started courting you."

Samantha glared at her smugly smiling cousin. "Ben *is not* courting me, and don't you dare let that rumor begin circulating, Olivia Tyler, or I shall tell the whole town of your infatuation with Andrew Morgan. In print!"

Olivia blanched and fell silent, though she pursed her lips in a disapproving, definitely unflattering moue of displeasure.

"I was only trying to help by pointing out what has become painfully obvious to everyone but you, and this is the thanks I get."

"And all you're bound to get from me for some dreamt-up fantasy you only *imagine* to be the truth. For your information, cousin dear, I have every intention of remaining that old maid you predicted I'd become the other day. *If* I ever took it into my head to marry, rest assured it wouldn't be Ben Morgan. Friends and adversaries we've always been. A loving couple? Never! Impossible! Is that perfectly clear?"

Undaunted, Olivia offered her tiny, confident smile. "Perfectly clear, Samantha dear."

Bowl in hand, Samantha picking her way through the remaining spilled popcorn to the door into the kitchen. Shouldering the swinging door open, letting it fall shut behind her, she set the bowl on the central worktable with hands that trembled slightly. From what, she wasn't certain, rationalizing the tremor came from an afternoon spent in Olivia's company. No one frustrated her more than her beautiful cousin. Except . . . except for Ben Morgan. How could he be so incredibly thoughtful on one hand—speaking to his editor friend on her behalf—and so incredibly cocky . . . and dense on the other? She'd never in her lifetime be able to understand that infuriating man.

"Olivia wound you around her little finger this afternoon," Samantha chided.

She and Ben made their own path down the sidewalk headed toward Main Street through a couple more inches of new snowfall.

"Correction. I let Olivia think she had," Ben amended cheerfully. "I enjoy seeing how your lovely cousin's mind works. I was going to the party anyway. Command performance by the school board of the newest teacher in town."

"You were going anyway!" Samantha echoed, wondering if he'd planned on asking anyone to go with him. Maybe he was expected to be the flaunting and flirtatious Sissy Chester's escort. The very idea riled Samantha's sensibilities, though she had no right to feel as she did.

"Can you keep a secret?"

"What?" She recovered with difficulty. "Of course. No society reporter worth her salt tells all she sees and hears, or she'd soon be out of a job."

Ben leaned close, too close, whispering though they were the only souls out walking at the dinner hour.

"Andrew stopped by today, asking me to make the same arrangements for the party that Olivia wheedled out of me."

Samantha pulled back, clutching her notebook of family anecdotes more tightly to her chest with wrapped arms, stopping in her tracks, almost as disconcerted by his news as his nearness.

"Well, I'll be . . ."

"Told him I'd see what I could do." He chuckled.

"Didn't want to make it too easy on either of them, though they're as smitten as a pair of lovebirds."

"Don't say that."

"Why not? It's the truth."

Samantha started walking fast enough that Ben had to lengthen his strides and hustle to catch up.

"What's the matter, Sam? Aren't you pleased that true love conquers all?" he teased.

"Love, pah! All this mooning around is . . . is crazy. It's just plain insanity."

He studied her profile long and hard. "Or the sanest thing in the world," he amended quietly, then aloud, "We're here, Sam. This is Jasper's house. And there's Jasper at the door to greet us. Hello, Jasper. How are you?"

Samantha saw a portly, balding, bespectacled fellow backlit in the open doorway who, on closer inspection, proved to be only in his early forties.

"Fine, just fine. Come in, come in! Never mind the snow," he said genially as Ben and Samantha stamped their feet on the stoop. Once they were inside, Jasper Cooper held out his hand. "Miss Spencer, I'm so pleased to meet you at last. I've heard so much about you."

She took his hand, throwing a questioning glance Ben's way, and found him red-faced, avoiding her stare.

"What have you heard?" she asked, suddenly suspicious.

Mr. Cooper chortled, missing nothing. "Only the best. Only the best. Come on into my study. My housekeeper has made tea and biscuits."

They walked into a crowded but immaculate room, with books, newspapers, and periodicals stacked everywhere. He gestured to the laden tea tray set out on the corner of his mahogany desk, adding, "Mary's British, don't you know."

Samantha and Ben took the two large, leather wing chairs he offered; he himself perched on the edge of the desk, precariously close to the tray of refreshments.

Samantha patted the notebook on her lap. "I've brought some samples of my recent work," she told the editor without preamble.

"No need. No need. I've been reading your articles in the *Chicago Evening Star*. Ben clips and saves them for me. Very good style, Miss Spencer, very good."

Samantha darted a look at Ben. He reclined in the leather chair as if it were a comfortable old friend, with his legs stretched out and crossed at the ankles, elbows on the chair arms, hands linked loosely over his flat stomach, completely at ease. His face wore a relaxed, confident expression shamelessly without guilt, smile wide, dimpled creases deep, eyes crinkled with good will—or was it wicked humor? He'd set her up for this interview with all the skill of a puppet master and she his marionette, and she had half a mind to—

"We'd be most pleased for you to write for our little weekly . . . that's the editorial we, by the way. There's only me and Old Gus, who sets the type and runs the press. What kind of column did you have in mind?"

"Column? A weekly column?"

Jasper Cooper looked faintly troubled. "I'd offer you more frequent publication, but we're only a weekly newspaper, don't you know."

"No, no. Once a week is fine." She tossed a glance between Jasper and Ben. "Ben did tell you I'd be going back to Chicago after the first of the year, didn't he?"

She saw real regret on the editor's face. "Yes, he did. He did. And I was hoping we could work something out for your columns to continue after you leave River Valley.

If not, maybe an occasional article, subjects of your choosing, of course."

Samantha opened her mouth and closed it again. This offer was nothing less than an answer to her prayers. Before this moment, she hadn't a clue how she could survive in Chicago, without funds as she was, until she found work. Now here lay the solution, with absolutely no effort on her part. Thanks to Ben. How irritating to be peeved at him for interfering, and at the same time feel she owed him a debt of gratitude. Especially with him sitting there looking so self-satisfied over his charitability.

"Miss Spencer?" Jasper's query held a note of concern.

"Excuse me? Sorry! I'm a bit overwhelmed by your offer. I had not expected it to be so generous."

"Generous in everything but pay, I'm afraid, Miss Spencer. A few dollars per column is all I can manage, much less than you get at the *Star*, I'm sure."

A blatant lie sprang surprisingly easily to her lips, too easily, she thought guiltily.

"Pleasure at sharing hometown tales with friends and family is added compensation, Mr. Cooper."

"Jasper."

"Jasper. I'll be pleased to join your staff."

"You are my staff," he reminded her with a grin. "I'll need an article from you by Wednesday of each week for publication on the following Saturday."

"And you shall have it."

Samantha stood, extending her hand. He enveloped it in both of his large paws, shaking vigorously. Ben rose up beside her, fortunately silent as they made their way to the front door. It crossed Samantha's mind that they'd never sampled the housekeeper's repast; leave it to a man to forget the amenities. She was too excited to care for food or drink in any case, her mind already brimming with ideas for her first and future articles for the *River Valley Weekly Review*. She did, however, have one additional question for Jasper Cooper.

"What do you hear of Nellie Bly's progress? The papers have not been arriving from Chicago because of the holiday."

"Nellie Bly. Nellie Bly. Oh, yes, that young woman attempting to circle the world in record time! Why, I hear very little. Tempest in a teapot, don't you know. As near as I can figure, only her own paper, that *New York World* Pulitzer puts out, has been reporting on it. You're the first to ask, Miss Spencer—"

"Samantha."

"Samantha, you're the first to show an interest, don't you know. But I'll see what I can find out, if you'd like."

"Please do. I'd like to be kept apprised of her progress. Thank you."

"Will do. Will do. Good night then, to both of you. Good night. And watch your step. Temperature's dropped. Bound to be icy under foot. Icy." Muttering his parting warning, the wool-gathering editor gently closed the door behind them.

FIVE

Snow fell lightly, sparkling crystals in lamplight. Flakes, unique and individual, settled on the dark blue of Samantha's fur-trimmed coat, caught in the whiskey-colored curls framing her face, melted on her cold-reddened cheeks like diamond tears. Lord, she was beautiful. Ben stored away that image of her to sustain him after she returned to Chicago. In fact, he'd already lost her. Though at his side, she'd traveled as far away in thought as the farthest star, probably planning her first newspaper column for the *Weekly*. Of all the stupid things to do, by mediating between her and Jasper, he set in motion events to take her out of his reach for good, and all in pursuit of her goals.

The walk home, the long way through the heart of town, proceeded as silent as the night, with only the crunch of their matched footsteps to break the stillness. Ben stuffed his hands into his jacket pockets, nestled deeper into his upturned collar. This wasn't the way he'd planned on the evening going. Not by a long shot.

The clop-clop of horses' hooves on icy cobbles, the hum of buggy wheels passing by, alerted Samantha to her surroundings. Through one window cracked open at the First Methodist Church, came the harmonized voices of the church choir practicing "Silent Night." How fitting on this magnificent wintry evening!

Beside her, Ben plodded along, saying nothing, his rugged profile craggy in shadow and lamplight, so striking she momentarily lost her train of thought. And hated that simply looking at him did that to her. Hated the confusion his contrary behavior wrought on her concentration, and in her heart. Remote and reflective, of what was he thinking? Or whom? Was there a special someone he fancied, someone who reciprocated? This handsome, personable man at her side most assuredly turned the heads of every eligible young woman in town. Had he singled out his choice, or was he biding his time in his usual methodical manner? And what, pray tell, did it matter to her one way or the other?

More important than such nonsense, she should be asking herself when and why Ben had become such a supporter of her writing efforts. By his own admission, he routinely read her articles in the *Chicago Evening Star*. He also shared them with Jasper Cooper and put it into the man's head to consider hiring her. During all their growing-up years, he had teased her for her fantasies, challenged her lofty ideals, as much as told her she would perish away from River Valley. In the end he went out of his way to further her goals. Whatever his unfathomable reasoning, belatedly, Samantha realized the debt she owed him, and the thanks stubborn pride made her loath to express.

Instead, she teased, "You're awfully quiet. At the very least, I'd expect a lecture on the stars."

Rusty-voiced, Ben pointed out, "No stars tonight. Overcast skies."

Conversation died before it began.

"Thank you for speaking to Jasper on my behalf," she

finally conceded. "I have more ideas for the column than I can use in a lifetime. I was thinking of calling it "Seasons and Seasonings" . . . because of the recipes I hope to include . . . and after Grannie's favorite Bible passage, 'To everything there is a season, and a time to every purpose under heaven.' "

"Everything hoped for comes in its own good time," Ben agreed with sarcasm.

Ignoring his tone, she asked, "What are your hopes?" She needed to know the answer, not at all certain why.

Briefly he glanced at her, expression shuttered, response terse. "I have everything I need. A home. A job. Family. Friends."

She persisted. "No special loved one? No great ambition?"

Ben's jaw jumped, muscles tight, but he swallowed his ire. He answered evenly, evading her prodding about someone special; she wouldn't thank him for admitting it was her.

"My only ambition is to pass on the love of learning I've enjoyed all my life. Not like your own lofty aspirations to shape the world through your writing."

Furious that he made her feel embarrassed and superficial, she defended herself. "I aspire to follow in Nellie Bly's footsteps. She's helped bring about great reforms, exposed great wrongs. There are women on many major newspapers, including myself, who've been inspired to follow her example because of what she has accomplished."

"And you'd rather be one of her imitators than true to your own talent?" he pressed.

Her lovely features taut with displeasure, hands wrapped around her notebook white-knuckled in lamplight, she refused to look at him.

"I don't know what you're talking about."

"Don't you, Sam?" he prodded gently.

"I'm doing exactly what I want to do."

"And?"

"And *what?*" she demanded, thoroughly exasperated.

"You want nothing more?"

"No, nothing," she lied, no longer knowing herself where truth lay.

"Fine!"

"Fine!"

They stomped along side-by-side, not speaking, scarcely noticing the direction of their meanderings until they reached the square at the heart of town. A towering northern pine marked its center, more magnificent than any decorated tree, adorned only with snowflakes and icicles and a pair of cardinals—scarlet and rust against evergreen—perched on a couple of the highest branches. An arm's-length apart, like two strangers, they shared the captivating scene until the almost palpable silence shattered at the sound of happy, childish voices.

"Hi, Mr. Morgan," a number of his students chorused.

Ben raised his hand in a wave at the group of children headed for the slopes on the far side of the park, sleds scribing slashes in the snow. Among them, Frankie and Georgie attempted to hide from their brother behind the taller children. Feigning sternness, Ben warned, "You two'd better be home by nine. Sharp!"

Shouting compliance, the two lads ran to catch up. Ben turned to Samantha, wearing his first smile since their walk began.

"Kids."

She marveled at the affection in his light tone. It could have turned out otherwise, Ben having to take on the responsibility of his younger siblings before he himself had left youth behind. As substitute parents, Ben, at seventeen, cooked and cleaned and raised his brothers, while twenty-year-old Andrew shouldered the financial responsibilities. There'd been no complaints—well, few—from any of the Morgan brothers, from oldest to youngest, as if each understood that staying together depended on presenting a united front. The parents of the seven Morgan boys would have been so proud of how well their young men turned out, thought Samantha, eyes suddenly misty.

"Let's watch for a while," Ben suggested, unaware of the pedestal upon which she'd inadvertently put him.

Feeling foolish and fanciful, she agreed.

He took her arm as they walked down the steep sledding slope to the river. At the crest of the swiftest hill, they stood watching, reminiscing over similar good times in their shared past.

"Remember when Duncan made it all the way downhill to the river?" asked Ben.

"All the way there, and on into it, as I recall," Samantha amended. "You and Andrew had to rescue him and wrap him in your own coats to thaw him out. With him hopping mad at both of you for not fishing out his sled."

Ben chuckled. "Oh, we went back for it. Never did find that darned sled, though. Either it buried itself in the mud or washed away down river."

Samantha shivered, but not with the cold. "I almost washed away down river myself. Remember? On that log raft Duncan and Charlie built and convinced me was safe. That time you rushed to the rescue all alone. Did I ever thank you properly for saving my life?" she asked, with a sidelong glance.

"Oh, you thanked me, all right. You kicked me in the shins with those hiking boots you always wore. I believe your exact words of gratitude were 'I can take care of myself.' We used to hear those words a lot from you in those days." His voice went thoughtful. "Apparently nothing has changed. Time to head on home. I can't feel my toes, and I'll bet you're as frozen as I am, though you probably wouldn't admit it."

Out of habit, she started to contradict him. A resounding thud, followed by a long, drawn-out wail, interrupted.

Some small child had run her sled into a tree and lay where she fell crying loudly, surrounded by the other children. No one rushed to her aid except Ben and Samantha. They found the little girl not nearly as hurt as frightened. Ben calmed her with soothing assurances and a gentle touch, washing her scraped cheek with his big white handkerchief and a dab of snow. Samantha, her own apprehensions eased by his words and the kind concern in his voice, recounted an encounter of her own with that very same tree—or one very similar, since she'd run into most of them during her sledding years. The child quickly forgot her fright. With a whispered "T'ank you, Mr. Morgan," she ran off to play, little the worse for her experience.

Samantha rose, brushing snow off her coat where she'd knelt on it. Ben rose, slapping snow off his pant legs with his gloves.

"You're very good with children," Samantha told him with grudging admiration.

"I get plenty of practice. So are you."

He appeared genuinely surprised. To forestall starting another argument, Samantha changed the subject.

"Shall we go? I'm more than ready for hot cocoa and a piece of Grannie's mince pie."

If he had more to say, he changed his mind. He offered his arm. She took her hand out of her warm muff to wrap around Ben's elbow on the uphill trip, her fingers cozily tucked up against his mackinaw-clad side, enjoying his body heat. At the top, suddenly self-conscious, she quickly withdrew her hand, returning it to the muff.

Ben missed the light pressure of her small hand the instant she snatched it away. For one brief moment, he had gloried in her closeness at his side, where every instinct told him she belonged, whether or not Sam ever saw it that way. To ease the tension—his anyway—he asked, "That story you told Ruby, about running into the tree? How much of it do you figure was the truth?"

Her smile shattered the distance she'd wedged between them.

"Probably about half . . . maybe all of it, in theory."

"You were as adventuresome a child as you are an adult."

Samantha suspected Ben of teasing, taunting her. He wasn't; no dimples creased his cheeks, no wicked twinkle lit the midnight blue of his eyes.

"Mama and Papa would have said I am foolhardy," she countered, trying for a rebuttal the old familiar Ben would have been quick to offer.

His response was a thoughtful half-smile.

"You've always marched to a different drummer, not at all like Olivia and Eliza, or any of the other girls in town. You're uniquely yourself, Sam. I guess that's why I was surprised how well you got along with Ruby."

Hurt, not certain why, she insisted, "I like children."

She recalled the quilting bee, holding her cousin Cathleen's baby girl. How from the moment Betsy settled into her arms, she understood completely what all the *ooohing* and *aaahing* over infants was about. The euphoric sensation of unbelievable intensity, the inexplicable longing so overwhelming her, she gladly thrust the sleeping babe back into her mother's arms.

"I like children," she repeated.

"But not the idea of love, marriage, and family," Ben stated rather than asked.

Suspicious, Samantha retorted, "I love my family. And marriage's all right for others, just not for me. As to love, if you mean the romantic kind, it seems like so much foolishness to me." To make her point perfectly clear, she elaborated, "Look at Eliza and Olivia. Eliza's besotted with Charlie, not at all like her normal self. Olivia longs for both Andrew's affection *and* a rich man's security, unwilling to be satisfied with one or the other. And it's become painfully clear young Edward is as infatuated with me as Duncan was, and we know how *that* turned out. Why can't everyone just be friends?" she implored. "Why must everyone suddenly feel a compelling need to be paired with an individual of the opposite sex? And why," she asked ruefully, "must every married woman in my family feel honor-bound to find me a proper mate, when I have always made it perfectly clear I don't need or want one?"

Her speech, which should have had Ben sick with discouragement, instead inspired an idea of sheer genius.

"I know just what you mean, Sam. There isn't a mother in town with an unattached daughter who hasn't invited me to dinner to show off her domestic skills and, on occasion, her other attributes. Nothing I say or do discourages any of them." He paused for effect, pretended deep thought, his heart thumping so loud he figured she might hear it. "At least not until I give evidence of having settled down to a young lady of my choice." He shrugged, apparently defeated. "Too bad we're both faced with the same problem. If *you* come up with a solution . . ."

"Oh, but I have. At least I think I have. That is, if you'll agree to it." Sam bit her full lower lip, a sure sign she was plotting. Ben's hopes rose. "What if you and I started going around together?"

Ben fought to hang on to composure, when he'd much rather have danced a jig right there in the snowy path. She'd taken his bait—hook, line, and sinker.

"We already do," he reminded her without betraying his anticipation.

"Socially. Beginning with Sissy's party. And make it seem like something more. . . ."

"You and me, Sam? No one would believe it."

"I can be very convincing if I have to; you know I've always had a flare for make-believe. Remember all those little plays I used to come up with and badger you all to perform in? We can do it, Ben. We can convince the relentless matchmakers in town we have found our choice, lead them to believe we are a couple so they'll leave us alone."

He made a big pretense of mulling over the solution she thought of as hers for possible complications, knowing—hoping, praying—that the most likely one might be that their play-acting would become reality. He doubted it would even occur to her. It was up to him to make darn sure, come hell or high water, that's exactly what happened. Ben Morgan was going to somehow convince Samantha Spencer to fall in love. With him. Before she headed back to Chicago. *If* she went back.

Samantha continued, "As long as you remember this arrangement is for appearance's sake alone. If you go and fall in love with me like your amorous brothers, I . . . I'll never speak to you again, Benjamin Franklin Morgan."

Somber-faced, Ben thrust out one leather-gloved hand to seal their bargain. She advanced a step nearer, hit an icy patch, and they went down hard together, Samantha on top. For a startled moment, though unhurt, neither moved, chest to chest, face to face, limbs entwined.

An irresistible urge overcame Samantha's better judgment. Intending only a quick, punishing kiss to pay Ben back for his of yesterday, she found warmth in his lips that left hers lingering there. Lingering longer still as she explored texture and shape, the slight prickle of whiskers around the edges. Exploring for experimentation purposes only. Amazingly, Ben offered no resistance. His breath hitched, his lips parted. The tip of his tongue pressed lightly, inviting her lips to open. Lost in discovery, inundated with that same inexplicable heat as last time, Samantha indulged her senses. Expecting to discover some solution, she experienced only deeper and deeper levels of confusion. His tongue danced quickly into her mouth and out. She shuddered, not with cold, and imitated the movement. His hand came up to the back of her head, pressing her closer, kissing her harder. Harder, too, became the pressure of his thigh against her. She squirmed, trying to find a more comfortable position.

With a gasp, Ben's lips broke contact with hers. He flipped her off him, dumping her unceremoniously on her rear in snow the exact color of his face except for bright red spots high on his cheeks. He lifted himself into a sitting position, simultaneously raising both knees to brace crossed arms on them.

"Good . . . Lord . . woman . . . have mercy."

Disappointment greater than she dared examine, Samantha retorted.

"I believe that makes us even—"

"E-E-E-even?"

"And demonstrates perfectly how far we have yet to go to perpetrate our farce. We are sorely in need of practice, you and I, with this . . . this kissing business . . . and all the other folderol that goes with a courtship, most especially a fabricated one. When should we attempt it again?"

Ben held up a restraining hand, palm out. "Not just yet, okay, Sam? I've had enough practicing for one night."

"You find kissing me wearying? Maybe even repugnant?"

The hurt in her voice seared his heart.

"No! No, it was . . . fine. Men react differently to kissing than women . . . that is, I mean . . . Sam, I can't explain. Ask your mother . . . or Grannie."

"I can't tell either one we're pretending to be a couple to ward off matchmakers. They're the worst of the lot."

"I meant kissing in general. And those other things between men and women . . ."

Clearly, she didn't understand. Sam might have lived a year in a large, cosmopolitan city, but she was as virginal in thought and experience as her unmarried cousins here at home. Damned if he was going to give her a lecture; he had no desire to be her teacher . . . at least not without becoming her husband first. The images that thought conjured up kept his knees bent protectively for several long minutes more.

"Trust me, Sam. Your mother and grandmother will understand exactly what it is you need to know, and have the appropriate answers. They were young ladies once themselves, and had the same talk with their mother or some other experienced female." He attempted humor to cover his discomfort. "In the meantime, if anyone passes by, how do we explain why we're sitting here in a snowbank?"

Samantha grinned generously. Some considered her mouth to be too wide. Ben didn't, it fit his to perfection. It also foretold her mood, and he'd early learned to read each small variation. One corner quirked higher than the other, like now, indicated trouble. He scrambled backwards, leapt up, turned to run, not quickly enough. A hard ice ball struck him squarely in the center of the back. He spun.

"No fair, Sam, that hurt!"

She lifted a hand, pretending to need assistance in rising. "I have no idea what you're talking about, Ben Morgan. And if you expect to share hot cocoa with me in Mama's warm kitchen, I suggest you behave like a gentleman the rest of the way home."

SIX

Hours later, Samantha climbed the stairs, hand trailing the banister, mulling over the evening. She'd come up with fewer answers than questions she wasn't sure she'd dare ask Mama or Grannie, or anyone else. Ever. Like, why had Ben abruptly pulled away from her just as their tentative explorations became the most intense; why did she feel bereft with the ending of what she intended to be only a playful, retaliatory kiss; and concerning yet another puzzling matter, why did her arms feel so empty after Cathleen took baby Betsy out of them, and why did merely remembering the feel of that child in her arms make her breasts and belly ache so sweetly.

She lit the lamp at her bedside, intending to clear away the cobwebs of confusion by reading for an hour or so. Her lapel watch beside the lamp showed the time to be well past midnight. No wonder she could scarcely keep her eyes open, though her mind raced from one thing to another, not only the warm, fragrant fit of an infant in her arms, or that pretended courting nonsense. Fortunately, after the kiss in the snowbank and Ben's odd behavior afterwards, talk over cocoa settled down to saner topics— good literature, current events, her column for Jasper Cooper. Ben had so many good ideas for what she might include and leave out, she'd scurried for pencil and paper to jot them down while they lingered in Mama's kitchen. She couldn't remember a more pleasant or productive time in Ben's company. Or with anyone else, for that matter. Thank fortune, Ben required nothing more than friendship of her, unlike those foolish brothers of his.

Stifling a yawn, she undressed and slipped into her flannel nightgown. Snuggling deep into Grannie's quilts, she lay with eyes closed, suspended on the verge of delicious sleep.

"Samantha? Are you awake?"

Samantha's eyes flew open at the tearfulness of Eliza's query and darted to her door, cracked open. Her cousin stood backlit by the dim light of the gas wall sconce, waiflike and forlorn. Propping herself up against her pillows, Samantha patted the quilts at her side.

"Come get in bed with me, it's cold out there."

Barefooted, Eliza scurried across the hardwood floor to slide in beside her, looking slightly less desperate than when framed in the doorway.

"Remember how we used to crawl in together either in your bed or mine and talk half the night?" asked Eliza, slightly less timorous.

"Remember how Mama used to call up the register from below 'The two of you settle down now'?" Samantha imitated her mother's exasperation exactly.

They giggled together like those little girls.

"What's troubling our bride-to-be?"

Eliza's lower lip began to tremble, her eyes to fill.

"Has Charlie done something?" Samantha prompted.

Eliza found her voice.

"No! Oh, no! . . . That is . . . not exactly." She burst into tears. "He-he-he wants us to-to . . . move to-to . . . Coloradooo." The last word came out in a heartbroken wail.

Arm around her cousin's shoulder, Samantha let her weep until the flood dwindled to a trickle.

"Why Colorado?"

She barely kept the envy out of her voice, recalling how Mama and Papa had adamantly refused to allow her, as a child, to visit Grannie and Grandpa in Colorado. It had been Mama more than Papa, actually; and in affairs of home and family, Mama reigned supreme.

"Grandpa Spencer mentioned that the bank in Luckless had recently closed after losing its manager. A golden opportunity, Charles says, that we cannot let pass us by. He insists we pack up everything, leave family and friends behind, to move there. Oh, Samantha, how can I move so far away from all of you? I love Charles, but . . . I . . . I don't think I can dooo w-w-what he w-w-wants."

Samantha patted her arm. "If Charlie loved you as much as you claim, he wouldn't ask it of you, knowing how you feel."

Her cousin looked up with stricken eyes.

"He doesn't know. I didn't tell him. Because he loves me, I fear he would agree to give up his heart's desire, stay here simply to placate me. And he *does* love me, of that I am certain, though everyone else seems to doubt it."

Samantha caught up Eliza's hand in both of hers. "I have never doubted that someone would discover your finer qualities under all the shyness. But how can you be so sure of Charlie? He's always been the biggest flirt in town, loving every girl who'd have him equally and often. How can you not doubt he is ready to settle down with one. With you?" Blunt words, candidly spoken, but better from her than never broached.

The shine in her eyes no longer from tears, Eliza offered her plain, gentle smile.

"I know Charles loves me because . . . because I love him for the man that he is, and can be. He has confided in me that, being the middle child, he always felt passed over, first by his parents, then his brothers—"

Samantha interrupted with a protesting sound.

"It's true," Eliza defended. "He never got the attention he deserved, that he needs, that I alone can give him. He knows he will always be the center of my world—"

"Until your first child is born. I hope he is willing to share you with a little one, and all the others to follow," Samantha cautioned, well knowing Charlie's propensity for requiring undivided attention for himself to the exclusion of all others.

Eliza studied their interlocked fingers, cheeks flushed.

"I . . . cannot . . . I cannot have children."

Startled by such frankness from her painfully modest cousin, Samantha did not press for elaboration. "Does Charlie know?"

"I would not let him marry me without telling him," Eliza declared. "He . . . seemed a bit shaken at first, but he was so kind. He insisted it didn't matter. He would be husband and child and brother and father to me all rolled into one. He's so sweet, so understanding—"

"Then tell him you don't want to go to Colorado."

"I cannot. He has his heart set on finally emerging from Andrew's shadow at the bank, to be in charge of his very own. I cannot deny him this opportunity to prove his worth, especially to himself. I will go," she drew a shuddering breath, "but, oh, Samantha, how will I bear leaving you all behind?"

"Grannie and Grandpa will be there."

"And I love them as if they were truly my grandparents. But they live up in that mountain cabin of theirs . . . snowed in half the year."

"There are aunts and uncles and cousins by the cartload in and around Luckless—"

"Your relatives. All strangers—"

"Who will love you as much as we do once they get to know you. Soon Colorado will seem as much like home as here with us."

For the first time, Eliza looked hopeful.

"Do you really think so?"

"I know so."

Soon thereafter Eliza tiptoed off to her own bed. Samantha slid down under her covers, offering up a hasty prayer that her words prove true. Adding concerns for Eliza's future to the thoughts crowding her mind, Samantha lay awake until nearly dawn.

She slept in through the hour for church, awoke to an empty house, glorying in the solitude. She took a thick turkey sandwich and an apple to her room and decadently indulged in writing all day, virtually undisturbed by the family who'd long ago become accustomed to her prodigious sessions when in the throes of creativity.

The scents of Sunday supper cooking, and the cramps in her fingers, finally forced her to put down her pencil when daylight waned and shadows grew long across the braided oval rug on her floor. Reluctantly she left her labors to join her family for rich beef stew, crusty bread, and the last of the pumpkin pies. Afterward Eliza persuaded her to help make ornaments from last year's Christmas cards and bits of tinsel, lace, and yarn. Samantha went from that to forming cornucopias from paper doilies and ribbon to fill with candy and small gifts, while Eliza began construction of a mistletoe kissing ball.

"Whoever dreamed up a Christmas decoration that forces men and women into an unwanted display of affection must have been a desperate spinster," Samantha commented dryly.

"Or a hopeless romantic," Eliza countered dreamily, in far better a mood than at midnight, probably because after church Charlie had promised to call this evening.

The doorbell rang three quick bursts, then two more.

"That must be Charlie," Samantha commented, twisting a paper doily into a deep cone, securing it with a daub of paste. "Only an amorous fiancé would crank that bell so impatiently."

Eliza hurriedly removed the Mother Hubbard pinafore she wore over her dress, smoothing her mouse brown hair with both hands. Her cheeks bloomed rosy, her eyes sparkled.

"Do I look presentable?"

"Radiant."

She scurried to the front hall. Samantha heard the door open, heard disappointment in Eliza's soft voice as she greeted their visitor, obviously not her intended. A moment later she reappeared, perplexity clouding her earlier anticipation.

"It's Ben. For you. He brought . . . flowers."

Ben peered over Eliza's shoulder, wearing an incorrigible, wide grin Samantha found herself responding to with a welcoming smile of her own. He entered the room behind Eliza, a small, blooming violet plant held outstretched in one large hand.

"For you, m'lady."

Samantha cupped both hands around the pot and breathed deeply of the sweet, faintly woodsy scent of spring. She glanced up warily, not trusting his motivations, intrigued nevertheless.

"Where in the world did you find violets in December?"

Ben slipped out of his mackinaw and tossed it onto the nearest chair, followed by the scarf loosely draped around his neck.

"Jasper has a huge greenhouse attached to the rear of his house. He's passionate about his plants summer and winter. You'd've thought I was asking for his firstborn son instead of one small plant."

"I had no idea Mr. Cooper was a floriculturist. How fortunate he is to have the space to pursue his interest." Envy laced Eliza's gentle words.

She picked up the plant Samantha had carelessly set on the tablecloth to smell the flowers' heady aroma. Absently, she brushed soil off the tablecloth.

"Do you mind if I take this to the kitchen for a drink of water, and to find a saucer to catch the drippings?"

Agreeing it was a fine idea, Samantha waited until Eliza was gone before she challenged Ben.

"Flowers? You brought flowers? Isn't that carrying things a little too far?"

Ben pulled up a slipper chair and sat at the draped table overflowing with ornaments and the makings. He picked up the kissing ball, tossing it from hand to hand, his smile having gone from pleased to bemused.

"Considering that I'm over here most every day anyway, I thought flowers would state that my intentions had changed, without having to come right out and say it."

Immediately contrite, Samantha agreed. "You're right, of course. No one will notice that things have changed between us if we ourselves don't make a point of it."

Ben held the kissing ball over his head. "In that case, how about a little more practice?"

Panicked, Samantha glanced around the room, vacant except for the two of them.

"S-s-someone might come in and see us."

Ben dropped the ball to throw his hands up in exasperation.

"That's the point."

"Oh. Oh, yes. I—I—forgot."

Samantha caught the ball as it rolled to the edge of the table. Remembering the heat of past kisses, she faced away from his scrutiny.

Ben leaned back in his chair, stretching his feet out before him.

"If you'd rather, we can just talk."

"Perhaps . . . for now . . . that would be best."

"For now. But I'll expect a good-night kiss when I leave," he insisted, teasing now like the Ben of old.

Samantha tucked the kissing ball into her smock pocket, smiling smugly.

"We'll see."

Ben clutched locked fists to his chest, his expression an exaggeration of the lovesick swain.

"I shall count the moments until we part. 'Parting is such sweet sorrow—' "

"If you are going to make a mockery of our bargain, Ben Morgan, we can just forget the whole thing."

"Not up to a little play-acting, Sam? Aren't you the one who claimed to be so good at it?"

Samantha turned up her nose. "I am, but not if the other participant won't take the matter seriously for more than two consecutive seconds. Can't we simply sit and talk the way we would have in past times, before all this silliness began?" she implored.

"As you wish, m'lady." He settled more comfortably in his chair, crossing left ankle over right knee. "Good news. Jasper told me when I stopped by for the flowers that he should be hearing about Nellie Bly's progress sometime tomorrow. Thanks to you, he's become intrigued with her story and this whole concept of female stunt reporters. He'd like to interview you for an article he intends to write along those lines."

"He would write it?" asked Samantha, making no attempt to hide her disappointment. "Wouldn't it be more reasonable for me to write the article, having long admired Nellie Bly, and having been a stunt reporter myself?"

"Jasper thought an article written by him might be more objective. He'd really prefer you use your short-term employment at the *Weekly* to compose as many columns for him as you can before you return to your job on the *Chicago Star*."

"Of course. That's wisest, I'm sure."

Samantha hated continuing to deceive Ben and Jasper. Silence regarding her position on the *Star*—rather, the lack of one—remained of utmost importance if she dared plan on being allowed to return to Chicago unopposed.

Watching her closely beneath half-closed lids, Ben added, as casually as he could manage, "Jasper is hoping you'll decide to stay home and write for him permanently."

"Mama and Papa wish I would, too," she evaded. "No one understands, or accepts, my dedication to pursue my dream of writing for a major newspaper, and not just articles for the society column. I may have had unforeseen difficulties with my initial attempt at stunt reporting, but I've learned my lesson. Next time, I shall succeed in being the first to uncover an intolerable wrong, help bring about needed change. I shall . . . I shall . . ." She paused for breath.

"If you don't fall off your soapbox first. What was the cause you championed that another reporter beat you to? You never said."

It was on the tip of her tongue to tell him, to lambaste

the loathsome sweatshops Nell Nelson's exposé had done little to reform. Knowing Ben would listen intelligently, maybe even agree with the need to end such deplorable conditions, she dared not speak of it to him, for fear it might get back to her parents. They would never let her return to Chicago if they suspected the full extent of danger to their darling daughter, past and future.

"It's something I'd rather put behind me, especially during the holidays. Particularly since I now have this reporting job for Jasper on a lighter vein. Let me get the list of column ideas we came up with last evening. I'd like your opinion which to write up first."

"You sure you want *my* opinion, Sam?"

She never hesitated.

"Who else would tell me the absolute truth about suitability for the *River Valley Weekly Review* but Jasper Cooper's best friend . . . and mine?"

Before Ben could wipe the openmouthed incredulity off his face, she left the room. He heard her run lightly upstairs, stunned by the words he'd never expected to come from Sam's pretty, generous mouth. A friend! Whose opinion she valued! How about that! And how much closer was he from friend and confidant to lover, husband? His hopes soared, and for once he threw caution to the wind to indulge in the sensation.

Samantha returned with a sheaf of paper completely covered with ideas in her small, neat script. For an hour they argued, sometimes heatedly, the merit of each and every one, as only companionable friends could. When the grandfather clock in the hall chimed eight times, Ben rose reluctantly.

"Wish I could help you with those last few pages, Sam, but I have essays to correct for school tomorrow."

Samantha stood beside him, looking so darn pretty, he

impulsively pulled her to him for a quick kiss full on the lips.

"W-w-what was that for?"

"Practice."

Not five minutes after Ben left, before the heat of Ben's fleeting kiss had cooled, the doorbell impatiently rang again. A smile on her well-kissed lips, she threw open the door.

"Forget something? Oh, it's you, Andrew."

Ben's oldest brother, gloriously blond and blue-eyed and the handsomest of the clan, cleared his throat. Always proper in every degree, this impromptu visit, occasioned by whatever reason, was clearly out of character for the man Samantha recalled him being.

"Were you expecting someone?"

"Ben went home not five minutes ago. I thought he might have left something behind. Come in, come in."

He stood hesitantly just inside the door, stomping snow off his boots onto the Oriental runner rather than the hard-wood floor.

"I saw him go. I was waiting for him to leave," he admitted with equally uncharacteristic hesitancy. "I'd like to speak with you about something. Privately."

He glanced about, rather furtively, Samantha thought, and seemed relieved no one else in the family appeared.

"Eliza's baking cookies in the kitchen with Charlie. Mama and Papa have taken Grannie and Grandpa to visit Aunt Jane and Olivia. Uncle Noble and Noble, Jr., are back from a buying trip to New York."

Her uncle and cousin, father and son traveling salesmen, were away more than at home. Samantha personally thought her strong-willed Aunt Jane preferred it that way; probably cousin Olivia did, too, for her mother was far

looser with the purse strings when it came to frippery and
finery than her hardworking father.

"Let's go into the back parlor, it's the coziest room in
the house besides the kitchen. Can I offer you some cocoa
and oatmeal cookies fresh from the oven?"

"No, nothing, thanks."

She led him past the closed pocket doors of the formal
front parlor to the room behind, where a cheery fire
burned in the small parlor stove and Christmas decorations in the making lay spread out over every available
surface. She waved him toward the slipper chair Ben had
so recently vacated and took the one across from it. He
perched uneasily on the edge of the seat, uneasily twirling
his black bowler hat between his hands. Belatedly, Samantha realized he still wore his long overcoat, and chided
herself for being a less considerate hostess than either of
her cousins would have been. He refused her belated offer.

"I, ummm, won't be here that long. I was merely wondering what the status might be regarding Sissy Chester's
Christmas party."

His blatant discomfort left Samantha wondering
whether to chuckle or commiserate.

"Didn't Ben tell you? It was decided we would all go
together. You and Ben and Olivia and me, and Eliza and
Charlie, of course."

"Of course," he echoed absently. "Ben did say something about you and he, umm, leaving Olivia and myself,
well, does Olivia understand that she and I. . . . ?"

It was pure misery watching him struggle, and a pure
shame that infatuation had brought him to this pitiful pass.
Another strike against love, by Samantha's estimation.

"Olivia's looking forward to accompanying you, Andrew. She was the one who suggested the arrangement."

The puppylike happiness on his face was almost as painful to observe as the uncertainty of a moment before.

"She did? Well, then, I, that is, we mustn't disappoint her, ah, or the rest of you." He stood, still absently twirling his hat. "Please tell your cousin, I'll be most pleased to accompany her, that is, all of you to Sissy's party." He made no move to go. "One other matter, Sam . . . Samantha. Would you happen to know, umm, is Olivia, I mean to say, does she seem to be, well, pleasantly disposed to, ah—"

Sick to death of all his hemming and hawing, Samantha interrupted. "For mercy's sake, Andrew, if you're trying to ask if she wants to go with you in particular, the answer is yes. Why do you think she manipulated all the rest of us so you and she would be left paired together?"

"Did she, now? Well, well."

The sappy, happy look on his face made her want to shove him out the front door. She rose, hoping he'd take the hint. Unfortunately, he had more to say, in a burst of words long held back.

"I find Olivia's apparent interest in being in my company most confusing, Sam, as she seems so set on looking for a husband in New York. I-I-I'd like to try to change her mind on that score and would appreciate, umm, any help you—"

Appalled, Samantha held up both hands, shaking her head.

"I will not get in the middle of this, even for you. You'll have to get someone else to—"

His face lit up, he interrupted eagerly.

"Someone else, of course, to make her jealous—er, come to her senses. That would clear up the confusion fast enough. Great idea, Sam, damned good idea."

"No, no. I didn't mean—"

He caught up her right hand, pumping vigorously. "Thanks, Sam. Thanks."

Then he was gone in a burst of cold. Samantha shut the door behind him, leaned against it, shaking her head in disbelief.

Everyone but her was going mad! She was sure of it. What else would make Andrew, staid, self-contained, and—she'd always thought—the Morgan with the most common sense, turn into a blithering idiot before her very eyes, but mind-numbing infatuation, pure and simple! What if it were somehow contagious? The thought all but sent Samantha scurrying upstairs to pack her bags. She could not afford to fall in love, not now. Not ever. She had her life all planned out to the last detail. And nothing, especially not the love of a man, or for a man, was going to stand in her way.

SEVEN

Monday morning dawned gray and dismal and fit Ben's mood exactly. Damn, he was sick and tired of being good old patient Ben, when all he really wanted to do was sweep Sam off her feet and into his marriage bed! That her kisses were more passionate than friendly offered his only encouragement, and might simply be due to her inexperience and/or her eagerness for new experiences. Hell's bells, he was no better off than before they made their pact; he still didn't know where he stood.

Deep in morose thought, Ben scarcely noticed when Frankie and Georgie left his side on the daily walk to school. As usual, he walked and they cavorted all over the place until Ben swore they covered five miles rather than the two it took to get there. This time, though, they didn't come racing back with some found treasure or profound ten-and-twelve-year-old idea to share with him. He caught a glimpse of the young scamps disappearing into the woods out behind the school.

"Frankie. Georgie. Get back here."

One shouted, "We will!" and the other added, "Won't be late!" Then they joined a couple of smaller children Ben didn't recognize at a distance, and the four of them were gone.

His youngest brothers hadn't arrived by the time Ben

rang the bell, or for the Pledge of Allegiance. Not until morning recess was nearly over did the pair of them put in an appearance, dirty and disheveled with muck-caked boots smelling more of manure than good clean earth. To top it all off, Frankie arrived in the schoolyard coatless, blue-lipped, and shivering. Ben caught each by the scruff of the neck and hauled them inside, no farther than the cloakroom, considering their condition.

"Where the bloody blue blazes have you been? And what the he—heck have you been wallowing in?" He all but gagged on the smell.

The boys exchanged guilty glances. Neither spoke up.

Singling out the older of the two, he demanded, "Frankie, why aren't you wearing your new winter coat?"

The lanky towheaded lad, on the verge of his teens, wore a closed, uncommunicative expression Ben had seen on the boy's face far too often lately. Young Georgie, ever the imitator of the brother closest to his age, glowered, lower lip outthrust, managing only to look more like a petulant infant than defiantly independent. These two, mere toddlers when their parents died, were more like sons than brothers, the age difference being what it was. The older brothers all had a hand in raising Georgie and Frankie—who would have been Howard, or Harold, or maybe Hank except for his mother's miscarriages after Edward—but nine times out of ten, discipline fell to Ben. As now.

"Your coat?"

Head down, Frankie mumbled something unintelligible.

"What?"

The boy lifted his chin, all anger and belligerence. "Musta lost it."

"Lost—? How—?" Ben ceased his sputtering to take

a steadying breath. He saved weeks for that coat. "Why did you take it off?"

Frankie shrugged and glanced away, over his shoulder, in the direction of a small sound.

"Mister?"

Ben spun, ready to pounce on one of his scholars for interrupting. The kid, a boy, had to be the scrawniest, shabbiest, filthiest bit of humanity ever, but out of gray eyes the shade of tempered steel, shone strength of will Ben had never seen in one so young. He couldn't've been more than Georgie's age, but this was not the face of innocence. Spine stiff, he gave Ben stare for stare, every bit as if they were equals.

"Mister, you got no call to light into my friend Frankie. He give his coat to me."

"He what?"

At second glance, the coat he wore was indeed Frankie's, and about two sizes too large. He pulled it more tightly around his skinny body, as if fearing its loss. Chin up, he declared, "Tol' him I wanted to go to school like everybody else, but couldn't 'cause my duds wasn't good enough. He give me his coat to cover 'em. I wanna get me some learnin' an' I'm in a mighty big hurry. Ya gotta teach me all ya know 'fore I get caught up with an' sent back."

Dumbfounded, Ben couldn't figure out which issue to address first.

"What grade are you in?"

"What's grade?"

"T-T-The level at which you read and write."

"That's easy. Zero."

"Zero?"

"Cain't read. Cain't write. That's why I'm here. Only, like I said, we gotta hurry."

Impatient to begin, the boy pushed past Ben on into the classroom, taking a seat in the front. Ben looked from Frankie to Georgie and back again, until Georgie, who couldn't keep a secret to save himself, piped up.

"That's our friend, Henry Baxter."

"With whom you spent the morning playing?"

"Naw, we were helping him clean out old man Miller's barn so he could come to school with us. We were going to bring Molly, too, but she had to wash clothes 'cause it's Monday."

"Molly?"

"Henry's sister. She's only five. She'd couldn't't've kept up with us anyway. Henry's twelve, same's Frankie."

So many tangled issues and no time to resolve them, Ben saw by the clock over his desk.

"Recess is over. Frankie, ring the bell. You two are off the hook for right now. Just don't make any after-school plans. You're going straight home and take a bath, then off to bed without supper."

"Aw, Ben. We didn't do nothing wrong. And it ain't even Saturday," Georgie protested in a whine.

"What am I supposed to wear, going home?" sullen Frankie wanted to know. "I ain't got no coat."

"First of all, you two might be friends with a boy who can't speak correct English, but I know *you* know better. As for your coat, Frankie, I'd say that's gone for good. Henry appears to need it more than you do, anyway. There are blankets in the shed for emergency use. You can wrap up in one of those, then dig your old coat out of the mission box when you get home."

"It's too small."

Ben hung on to the shreds of his temper by sheer will.

"You should've thought of that before you gave your new one away. The old one's more Henry's size. Maybe he'll trade with you. We're not going to argue about it now. Go ring the bell before recess runs into lunch. Go."

His students had no more than settled onto their benches, and he was preparing to introduce the new boy, when the schoolhouse door slammed against the wall hard enough to shake the roof rafters. On a wave of frigid air, a burly brute of a man stomped in, threw a quick narrow-eyed glance around the room, honed in on his prey, and thundered down the aisle straight to Henry. He caught the boy by the coat collar and hauled him out of his seat and up into the air to face him.

"Git home. Now." He set the kid on his feet, pulling the coat off his back in the same movement, exposing tattered coveralls and long johns. "This ain't yern. Where'd'ya steal it?"

Clearly terrified of the man, Henry still held his own.

" 'Tis too mine. Was give to me." He made a grab for it.

The man Ben figured was old man Miller caught the boy by both arms, and shook him hard enough to rattle the boy's brains.

"Enough of that. Release the lad. I gave him the coat."

Ben stepped up to the gigantic farmer and caught an overpowering whiff of rank body odor. Miller turned on him, gave Ben a once-over, and complied as if Henry were no more than a bothersome mutt. Spitting a stream of tobacco juice on the floor through the vacancy of two front teeth upper and lower, he sneered.

"Don't need no charity, an' the boy don't need no coat. How's he goin' toughen up all wrapped up like a sissy? Ya leave what's mine alone, an' I won't have ta bust open yer head. Git home, boy."

"Your son—"

"Ain't no son of mine, nor no business of yers. Hired

'im fair an' square outta one of them orphanages. Ya see
fit ta interfere again," the burly fellow raised a fist inches
from Ben's nose, "I'll smash yer face 'til yer own maw
won't know ya. Git home, I said, boy, an' don't come back
here again, 'less ya want one hell of a tannin'. Ya can
thank yer sister fer tellin' me where ta find ya."

Ghost-white, scared and furious, Henry raised doubled
fists.

"Ya better not've hurt her."

Miller chuckled without humor.

"No more'n she deserves. An' if I have to tell ya ta git
one more time, ye'll get double."

The fellow's leave-taking proved no less violent than
his entrance, as he pushed and shoved the boy out the
door over Ben's unheeded protests. The class, as one,
turned accusing eyes his way as soon as the door slammed
shut; and to save himself, he couldn't come up with any
defense for his lack of gumption. The fact that Miller
probably had the law on his side was no excuse. The best
he could manage now was to try to right the wrongs, his
and Miller's. Something had to he done to save the boy
and his sister from the monster who virtually owned them.
More skilled at reasoning than fisticuffs, he ought to be
able to come up with a solution.

Late in the day, when a headache threatened to take off
the top of his head, and the classroom had emptied after
a day wasted to learning, it came to him. Who better to
help him help liberate Henry and Molly than trial lawyer-
turned-journalist, his friend Jasper Cooper.

"Samantha, shame on you. I was so embarrassed. It
was all over church yesterday," scolded Olivia the moment
she came in out of the cold, dressed more for fashion in
an elbow-length cloak and high-heeled buttoned shoes

than for the shopping excursion downtown. She appeared chilled to the bone in spite of her hot indignation.

"What am I supposed to have done?" Samantha suspected she knew, though, and Olivia's scandalized words confirmed it.

"You were seen Saturday evening rolling around in the snow in Ben Morgan's embrace."

An explanation, the partial truth, came far too easily for Samantha's conscience, "What a tempest in a teapot! We were walking home from Mr. Cooper's and I slipped on an icy patch, knocking us both down into a snowbank. It proved quite a struggle to extract ourselves."

Olivia's scandalized pleasure dissipated into a disappointed "Oh!"

"Mrs. Taylor was certain she saw you kissing."

"Isn't Mrs. Taylor that nearsighted woman who mistook the Wilson's large dog for a bear a few years back?"

Olivia pouted. "Pooh! I hoped you'd caught yourself a beau at last."

"I suppose you also hoped I'd reel Ben in, a keeper? Sorry to disillusion your romantic expectations, cousin dear, but they are extremely premature concerning Ben and me."

"I wouldn't say that," declared Eliza, coming down the stairs behind them. She had an uncharacteristic teasing little smile on her lips that made her look quite pretty. "Ben brought Samantha flowers last evening."

A questing glint sparked anew in Olivia's eyes. "Flowers? In winter? What kind?"

"A small pot of violets."

"What color?"

"Blue."

"Ah ha!" Olivia gloried in conquest. "Blue violets represent faithfulness, steadfastness. Ben Morgan has declared himself at last. A pity they weren't roses, particularly red, as he would then also be proclaiming his great passion for you, Samantha. However, a steadfast lover is better than none at all, I suppose."

"Stuff and nonsense. Where do you come up with such fanciful notions?"

"Not fanciful, Samantha, but scientific fact. Every flower, indeed every green growing thing, implies a specific emotional significance between giver and receiver. I'm surprised you are not more informed, having lived in a cosmopolitan city like Chicago. The subject has been greatly reviewed in all the best women's magazines and etiquette books of late."

"And I am surprised you give credence to such absurd—"

"Young ladies," intervened Eliza. "Hadn't we best be on our way? Samantha, didn't you have a stop to make before we begin our shopping?"

Olivia tapped her foot impatiently, her face petulant. "Where must we go now?"

"To Jasper Cooper's house, only long enough to drop off some material for him to look over." Ben had said the editor planned on working at home this afternoon. "It's on our way, Olivia, and won't take more than five minutes."

Samantha checked her appearance one last time in the nearby hall tree mirror. Beneath her new coat, she wore her most businesslike costume of starched white shirtwaist, trim gray gabardine skirt which barely brushed the vamp of her shoes, and matching gray tailored jacket with a touch of navy braid at collar and cuffs, serviceable and appropriate to her brief meeting with Jasper. Her fur cloche covered all but the fringe of curls around her face, but there was nothing she could do about it. She envied her cousins their sleek, smooth hair, Eliza's brown, Olivia's black, always in control. Accepting that she had done the best she could with what she'd been given, she caught up her portfolio from the seat of the hall tree.

"Shall we be off then, cousins?" Brimming with energy and expectations, she preceded them out the front door.

The overcast day promised more snow on top of the several inches already accumulated. Edward Morgan had spontaneously volunteered to keep the Spencer sidewalk cleared. Yesterday, Samantha caught him more than once leaning on the shovel and staring moodily at her house instead of shoveling; and the day before, Olivia, on arrival, had teased her mercilessly about her new admirer, so she was certain it wasn't only her imagination. As much as she pitied the lad his infatuation, she fervently wished he'd find someone else upon whom to focus it.

"My, my," commented Olivia, "look what a good job Edward did on your walk, Samantha. With so few to appreciate your many charms, Samantha, how fortunate you are to finally have someone who does."

"Good grief, Olivia, he's sixteen."

Eliza, once more the peacemaker, intervened. "And he has an admirer of his own, if he'd only but notice. I have seen Lydia Snow eyeing Edward from her front porch whenever he shovels our walk or his. And she follows him to school most every day, too."

Samantha glanced toward the Snow house diagonally across the street from the Morgans' and two down. "They're about the same age, as I recall."

Eliza concurred. An idea bloomed, a way to shift Edward's attention from herself to someone far more suited and, apparently, appreciative.

Five minutes later, Samantha cheerfully stated, "Here we are."

By daylight Jasper's house appeared larger, grander, if a bit scruffy around the edges like Jasper himself. Samantha could see where there'd easily be room for a conservatory of whatever size the man chose. She gave the doorbell a confident twist. Mary, the British housekeeper, answered almost immediately, a round rosy woman in her fifties, whose voice held a bit of cockney.

"Do come in, young ladies. 'Imself is working in 'is office. I'll fetch 'im for you directly."

"Samantha, hello. Hello. I thought I heard the bell." Jasper spoke from the far end of the hall. He bobbed his head twice, acknowledging the others, returning to her. "Have you brought me your first column for the *Weekly* already?"

"Only some ideas to go over with you so that I'm certain they're what you want. By the way," she responded to Olivia's nudging, "these are my cousins, Miss Olivia Tyler and Miss Eliza Upton. We're on our way to town for some Christmas shopping. Eliza would like to see your conservatory, if you don't mind." Now Eliza nudged her, though it was more of a sharp jab to the ribs.

Jasper's shaggy eyebrows rose, his faded eyes alight at the mere mention of what was obviously his greatest passion. "And so she shall then. So she shall. In fact, Miss . . . Miss Upton, is it? If you and Miss . . ."

"Tyler," contributed Olivia, piqued.

"If you and Miss Tyler would like to wander about a bit, go on ahead. I'm quite proud of my plants, don't you know." He waved them down the hall.

"I'll show 'em the way, sir."

"Just so, just so. Thank you, Mary. Samantha, let's have a look at your ideas."

The meeting proved brief and profitable, with enough approved ideas for several weeks beyond the allotted few. Samantha promised to continue writing for Jasper even after her return to Chicago, for which he was exuberantly, and repetitively, grateful.

Departure took somewhat longer, for once Mary retrieved Eliza and Olivia from the conservatory, Eliza could not contain her enthusiasm. The usually quiet young woman effused over Jasper's handiwork.

"You are so fortunate to have the space to grow plants so lavishly. I have only a small Wardian case in the east-facing bay window of the dining room. No matter what I try, my poor plants do not flourish."

Jasper's face lit like a lad's at Christmas, making him appear younger, almost handsome.

"What specimens have you chosen? What soil mixture do you favor?"

As quickly as that, the two had their heads together, deep in conversation and completely oblivious to Olivia and herself. Samantha fell to watching Eliza's animated features, noting how the subject under discussion completely transformed a drab little mouse into a vision of delicate loveliness. Olivia found no such distraction to hold her interest, and after a few minutes of failing to be the center of attention, insisted that they must go before the shops closed for the day.

At the door, Jasper invited the three of them to come to visit his conservatory any time they wished, he enjoyed having it appreciated, but his gaze never left Eliza's happy face. Surprisingly, Eliza answered for all of them that they would gladly take him up on his offer, as frequently as possible. At the door, Jasper remembered something more.

"By the by, Samantha. The word on Nellie Bly is that

she is expected to arrive in Aden sometime today and journey on to Colombo by Sunday. I'd like to discuss Miss Bly's trip and other noteworthy exploits with you, don't you know, when you have the time. More time. You might bring Eliza, that is Miss Upton, with you to browse among my vegetation while we work. That is, if you'd like, Miss Upton?"

"Indeed I would, Mr. Cooper. T-T-Thank you."

Samantha thanked him, too, for keeping her abreast of Nellie's progress and his generous acceptance of her column ideas, but she doubted he even heard her, he and Eliza having taken up their horticulture conversation once again until Olivia insisted, quite rudely Samantha thought, that they leave.

Olivia grumbled all the way to Main Street, though Samantha paid her little heed, trying to come up with an appropriate Christmas gift for Ben. Eliza, who was usually Olivia's captive audience of one, proved inattentive as well, which did little to improve Olivia's disposition. Given the season, Samantha gave in, vowing to be charitable.

"Can you suggest a gift I might buy for Ben, Olivia? To thank him for making working with Jasper possible. I was thinking a book would be appropriate."

"You know I haven't time for reading, Samantha. I have much better things to do with my—Oh! Oh, nooo!" Her voice fell off in a anguished moan.

Across the way, Andrew Morgan stood outside the mercantile, intimately close to Sissy Chester, his head dipped near to hers as if to catch her every word. He cocked his head, and Samantha thought he observed the three of them across the street. If he did, he gave no indication. He rested his hand on Sissy's shoulder, threw back his head in a robust laugh over something she said. She tittered, her expression both pleased and smug, with a sidelong glance at her audience. Finally, Andrew tipped his hat and walked away. Sissy watched his departure. With a self-satisfied grin, she turned and sauntered off in the other direction, without so much as a word of acknowledgment to those who watched.

Olivia's lovely face crumpled, her violet eyes swam with tears, mirroring genuine distress for the first time in Samantha's memory, though she felt little sympathy for her usually shallow cousin. Olivia had brought this on herself. Recalling her conversation of the evening before with Andrew, Samantha thought she knew what it was he was trying to do with his blatant show of interest in Sissy, and promptly decided to help him along.

"It would appear Andrew has come to appreciate Sissy Chester's many charms."

"Don't say that," Olivia snapped. "He would never . . . He couldn't possibly . . . It is certainly no concern of mine who he . . . I-I-I have suddenly lost interest in shopping. I've developed a horrid headache." She fled toward home.

"Now look what you've done," Eliza scolded.

When Eliza would have gone after her distraught cousin, Samantha gave her pause. "I did exactly what Andrew would have wanted me to in his attempt to make Olivia jealous by flirting with someone else. Maybe now the silly girl will finally decide what it is she really wants. Personally, I don't know what Andrew sees in her but—"

"I think the latest Dickens novel would be a good choice for Ben, or perhaps a volume on the stars, wouldn't you agree?"

Samantha gave her remaining cousin a quick hug. "I think you are completely unable to abide an unkind word, even of those who deserve it. Astronomy sounds like a perfect choice."

Ribboned wreaths hung on every lamppost on Main
Street, festive storefronts inspired the desire to shop.
Samantha found no astronomy book she felt confident
Ben wouldn't have, but instead chose a rip-roaring adventure tale she knew he'd like, fresh off the printer's presses.
Though she was sorely tempted, with her temporarily de-
pleted funds, she dared spend nothing on herself. The rest
of her Christmas shopping she had completed in Chicago,
so she trailed Eliza from store to store in her quest for
the perfect gift for Charlie, noticing that Eliza didn't seem
to lack the Christmas spirit, and yet she couldn't make a
choice. In the bookshop, Samantha suggested several different possibilities. Eliza shook her head absently and
wandered over to browse in the horticulture section, handling each volume with an almost ardent attention. In the
mercantile, Samantha suggested a warm woolen muffler,
a stocking cap, gloves, to no avail. She mentioned stationery, printed calling cards, pen and ink—one of her own
personal favorites. Not, apparently, what Eliza would
choose for Charlie. Gift ideas exhausted, Samantha suggested refreshments at the nearby tea parlor, and finally
found Eliza agreeable.

"I want my gift to Charles to be precisely what he would
most enjoy receiving, but I haven't the least idea of his
tastes," Eliza confessed over cups of steaming hot brew,
her fine, high brow furrowed with distress, eyes clouded
with concern.

Samantha curled her hand over Eliza's.

"You will learn his likes and dislikes over time. After
you're married. Once you move to Colorado, every new
adventure will be a shared one. In the meantime, don't
try so hard. Anything you give him for Christmas will be
just what he always wanted, because it's a gift of love from
you to him."

Reassured, Eliza's smile trembled back to life. "You're right, of course. I'll get him the scarf you suggested. And the cap, *and* the gloves. He'll have need of them all in Colorado."

EIGHT

Samantha ran next door as soon as she thought Ben would be home from school, unable to wait longer to share with him the good news that Jasper liked all the ideas they worked on together, knowing his pleasure at their success would enhance her own.

The Morgans and the Spencers never knocked. Samantha found the kitchen deserted, the cast-iron stove banked. No lamplight illuminated the midafternoon gloom except in the family parlor. He sprawled in the comfortable easy chair close to a cheery blaze in the stove, his stockinged feet warming on the fender. His fair head rested against the plush back, and Samantha heard a gentle snore. As she tried to back out of the room unnoticed, a floorboard creaked. He shot out of the chair at the sound, spinning to face her. It wasn't Ben. Samantha's heart leapt.

"Duncan! Duncan, is that really you? Oh, Duncan, welcome home."

She flung herself into his arms and clung, afraid he might disappear again if she let go, and released him only when it occurred to her he might interpret her enthusiasm as something more. She stepped back quickly, locking her hands behind her.

"Welcome home."

Duncan fisted his hands on his hips, tossed back his head, and laughed loudly and long.

"Scared I've returned to throw you over my shoulder and carry you away with me, are you, Sam?"

His puckish features had grown lean and angular over time, and his body muscular under the leather jacket he wore. He was inches taller than she remembered, and his hair several shades lighter. Whatever he'd been up to in his absence, it set well with him. He was handsomer now than Andrew, his face so full of life and joy he far outshone his older brother's rather stuffy, always sober demeanor. Her overlong perusal only made his grin wider.

"Ah, sweet Samantha. Second thoughts about turning me down?"

Surprisingly, she was no more tempted than when he first asked. She shook her head.

"Not in the least. Why have you really come back after all this time?"

"I'd like an answer to that question, too. What brings my wayward brother home after vowing—at the top of his lungs as I recall—never to set foot in River Valley again. Ever."

Ben's taut voice held no welcome, and his jaw jumped with anger scarcely contained.

Duncan spread his arms wide.

"Is that any way to greet the prodigal brother's return?"

"Knowing you like I do, it's the best I can come up with. What'd you want? And how long are you planning on staying before you take it into your head to run off again?"

Duncan's smile faltered and fell, his arms dropped to his side, dauntless cheerfulness drowned under hurt he made no attempt to hide.

"Sounds like no matter how brief the stay, it would be too lengthy for you, brother Ben."

Ben held to silence, making no denial. A glance from one brother to the other told Samantha it would take more than a long-awaited homecoming to mend the wide rift between these two. A great deal more. And not without her personal intervention.

"You might at least give your very own brother the benefit of a doubt, Ben Morgan," she stormed. "You wanted to know where he's been and what he's been doing. Well, I for one would like to hear his answer before you toss him out on his ear."

Ben's throbbing head hammered with each beat of his pounding heart. Faced first with the need to deal with Frankie and Georgie—and they sure as heck'd better be bathed and in bed like he ordered—now here was Duncan after nearly three years. Big as life and bright as a new penny, looking all the world like he'd only been off on one of those overnight and weekend jaunts that used to drive Ben crazy. Never an explanation of where he'd gone and what he'd been doing then, either, or any attempt to make amends. No promises not to run off again. The only one of his younger brothers over whom he had absolutely no control, who never listened, defied his authority day by day, hour by hour, until it was almost a relief when he was gone for good.

"He won't answer. Never did before—"

"Colorado."

"—before . . . Where?"

"Luckless, Colorado. Heard Grannie and Grandpa Spencer tell such stories about the place all my life, I just had to see it for myself. Mined gold and silver. Saw a lot, learned more."

Ben squinted, rubbing the bridge of his nose with two fingertips to ease the ache.

"Not that I don't believe you," which he didn't, "but how come Sam's grandparents never mentioned that you lived in their neighborhood?"

Duncan looked shamefaced, probably, Ben reasoned, because he'd caught him in another of his notorious lies. To Duncan, truth and tale were usually one and the same.

"I kept to myself, away from most folks. Until recently. I paid them a visit at their cabin before they left for home, made them promise to let me come back on my own terms."

"Nothing new there. You've always lived life on your own terms." And now he'd come back for Samantha; the thought struck Ben like a staggering blow. The big question was, if Duncan asked, would she go away with him? He had to know. "Staying through Christmas?"

"Maybe, maybe longer. If I'm welcome, that is, and if my old bed's still available."

"If you don't mind sharing with Edward," Ben reluctantly agreed, deciding it was better to have him underfoot than living somewhere, like a hotel, where he could come and go unobserved, and with whomever he pleased, maybe Sam.

"Never did. Ed and I have always been able to get along."

"Unlike you and me."

Duncan's expression had gone closed and tight, the very look he frequently wore as a rebellious teen.

"Right." He picked up a carpetbag setting next to the overstuffed chair. "Eddie's in the same old room?"

"Same one. Most of your stuff's in mine, just where you left it last time you ran off."

Ben had finally baited his brother enough to get a rise.

Duncan's eyes burned blue-black, his stance became combative with widespread legs and free hand fisted midwaist. Forcing self-control, he let his hand drop to his side open-fingered.

"I won't come to blows with you, Ben, no matter how much you want it."

Samantha stepped between them, chin jutting.

"If either one of you lays a hand on the other, I—I'll leave for Chicago that very minute." She knew her bluff was weak and she hoped neither would call it. She tried another approach. "You're men now, not boys, and it's Christmas. Don't you dare spoil the season for your brothers and . . . and everyone else by acting like a pair of foolish . . . asses."

Duncan grinned, good humor restored. "Now that's the Samantha Spencer I remember," to Ben, "and I guess she means business, brother. Can't have Sam missing Christmas with her family on our account, now can we?"

Ben made no comment, which the other two took as assent. Duncan glanced from one to the other.

"Looks like you two have more fighting to do, and I'm all fought out for the day. Been on the train for two. Didn't get much shut-eye."

He left Ben and Samantha behind to face off. They spoke at the same time.

"Shame on you, Ben Morgan, treating your brother that way."

"Bet you're glad Duncan's back, now you don't need me pretending to be your beau."

And again.

"His fault."

"*What* did you say?"

Once more.

"You and he can pretend—"

"Oh, no you don't, Mr. Morgan. You're not getting out of our agreement that easily." Sudden panic fluttered high in her chest.

They started to speak at the same time again. Samantha clamped her lips together, gesturing for him to go first.

"Duncan's back," he stated with grim finality.

"What's *that* got to do with anything?"

"Everyone's going to think he's come back for you."

"Do *you?* You do, don't you?" she accused. "And you're trying to get out of our bargain. Well, I won't let you, Benjamin Franklin Morgan. We've begun courting, you and I, and we're going to carry on with the plan to the bitter end. It was for our mutual benefit. Remember? We agreed. You are stuck with me whether you like it or not."

Her reason for coming over long forgotten, Samantha turned on her heel and stormed out of the house. Too furious to face her family and their questions, she headed back toward town, no purpose in mind except to outrun her outrage.

Before she got more than a block away, Ben caught up with her, still buttoning his coat, head and hands bare.

"What do you want?" Samantha refused to give him more than a glance.

"Just performing my courtly duties, Sam, as you requested. Where are we going?"

"Going?" She glanced around, and stopped stock-still. "I have no idea," she admitted grudgingly. Where did one go once the shops were closed, when everyone she knew was in the process of preparing or eating supper?

"We're almost to Jasper's, and I need to speak to him about a matter." He pulled on one glove, then the other, his face somber.

"Must be something unpleasant." He neither agreed nor

denied. Samantha tried another approach. "Eliza and Olivia and I visited Jasper this afternoon. He and I talked about the ideas we went over last night, and he approved them all." She told him everything that had transpired, including Eliza's having found a kindred spirit with the same gardening interests. "Olivia practically had to shove her out the door to get her to leave." She mentioned Andrew's blatant ploy to make Olivia jealous by flirting with her cousin's arch-rival Sissy Chester. "From the way she ran off in tears, I think his plan worked."

Ben made comments and laughed in all the right places. Their earlier quarrel forgotten, or at least delegated to the background, they climbed Jasper Cooper's haphazardly shoveled steps. Ben's hand on her elbow kept her from slipping, then rested there possessively long after the need had passed.

Mary responded to his impatient tugs on the doorbell after a lengthy pause, flinging open the door still wiping her hands on her copious apron. "My word, Miss Spencer again? And if it isn't Mr. Morgan, too? Come in, come in, the both of you. Was I to be expectin' you for supper? Mr. Cooper is that forgetful—"

Ben patted her arm. "Mary, we're not expected. Sorry to invade the dinner hour, but if you don't mind, I have a matter of some urgency about which I need Jasper's advice."

"Well then, supper can wait. 'Tis only stew, it'll keep. Maybe he'll talk the pair of you into joinin' him, save himself from havin' to eat alone. He's in his office, as usual. Go on in. I've me biscuits to check before they burn to a crisp."

Ben knocked on Jasper's door, then pushed it open to a muffled "come in, come in." Papers piled everywhere on his scarred mahogany desk fluttered in all directions.

Jasper stretched out spread-eagle over them, muttering expletives, then begging Samantha's forgiveness when he realized Ben wasn't alone.

Ben stated the problem without preamble, leaving out no detail of the incident in the schoolroom between Henry and old man Miller. His friend listened attentively; Samantha listened, too, appalled, and curious why Ben would bring his problem to an editor. Ben concluded with Miller's claim that he got the brother and sister from an orphanage, fair and square.

"The man doesn't deserve those kids. He's treating them in a way no children should have to suffer. How can I get Henry and little Molly out of the brute's clutches? There must be some law—?"

Jasper was shaking his head. "Been a long time since I practiced law, don't you know, and I've forgotten more'n I ever knew," he grunted a laugh, "but it seems to me possession is still nine-tenths of the law. Nine-tenths. Now, now," he waved away Ben's attempted interruption, "let me see, let me see, now, what I can find."

He swiveled his chair to face the barrister bookcase behind him. Each glass-fronted section gaped open, too overstuffed for the doors to close, but Jasper headed unerringly for what he wanted, and turned back to them, thick volume from a large set in hand. He blew on the top edge of the leather-bound book and a cloud of dust arose. Samantha sneezed.

"My apologies. Been a few years since I've consulted one of these. Figured they'd come in handy someday." He opened the book on his desk, flipped to the index, and started down the column with a pointed forefinger.

"I had no idea you were a lawyer. Why—"

Jasper glanced up. "Why'd I quit? Simple as pie. Simple as pie. Was my father's idea I study law. I didn't take to it, nor it to me, don't you know. Too much speaking. Too much. I'd rather write my thoughts than say them. Rather write."

He attacked the index columns again, thumbed to a page, read and frowned, his high brow creased with lines. He slammed the volume shut and reached for another, and another, repeating the process three more times. Ben and Samantha remained respectfully silent until he regarded them, expression solemn.

"You say the man—Miller, was it?—mentioned an orphanage? Any idea whereabouts it might be?"

"None!"

Jasper pondered.

"It's my guess a man like that would not travel far afield or put himself out much to obtain his help. The nearest orphanage is a couple of days away at the least. My guess is he got the children off one of those Orphan Trains passing through headed West. We see one or two of them every month or so, don't you know. Easy to pick and choose what you want, no questions asked, and no legal papers to sign as a rule."

"That's horrid, inhuman," Samantha interjected.

"Some feel it's more important to find a home for the homeless than to question too deeply those willing to take them, don't you know. First thing we have to find out is, does the man have papers to substantiate his claim of possession."

Jasper threw Ben a questioning look.

"I don't know anything about Henry and Molly other than what I told you, but Miller didn't appear to be the kind to let a few legalities get in his way in any case. If he has no papers, does that mean the kids aren't his?"

"That it does. That it does. On the other hand, without papers, they don't belong to anyone else either. Tell me,

Ben, if you manage to get these children away from that brutish farmer, what'd you plan on doing with them? Like I said, those Orphan Trains come through regularly. I suspect anyone hereabouts needing or wanting a child or two has made a selection by now."

By the look on his face, it was clear to Samantha that Ben hadn't thought that far ahead, but the solution came to her readily.

"Their plight should be dealt with in the *River Valley Weekly Review*. Someone might step forth to take them in." Her suggestion met with no enthusiasm. "Why not?"

"Because we're just guessing. We need more information. What if my conjectures are totally wrong, and right is on the man's side?"

Neither Ben nor Samantha had an answer.

"Let me wire to my friend, Judge Harper, see what he thinks. We were law students together, don't you know, and I helped him pass the bar. I'd say it's time he returned the favor. Should hear back from him in a matter of days."

Ben and Samantha declined sharing his supper. Bundled up, they headed homeward through a magical wonderland. Clusters of large, wet snowflakes floated down from a darkened sky, lamplight sparkled underfoot like a path of diamonds, and the slight breeze that caressed Samantha's cheeks had lost its chill. Not a sound but their own crunching footsteps broke the silence; any conversation would only have spoiled the enchantment; neither spoke.

When they came to an icy stretch, Ben took her arm, and did not relinquish it.

"There's Cassiopeia, or at least most of it."

He released her arm only to span her waist with his hand, drawing her to his side, pointing skyward. Her cheek resting lightly against his shoulder, through a break in the clouds she saw a smattering of stars in a distinctive shape

that appeared vaguely familiar. And it should have, after
all the evenings Ben put in trying to educate her and his
brothers in their youth, behind the lens of his telescope.

"Looks like the Big Dipper to me," she challenged,
forcing levity while her heart thumped faster and faster
at his closeness.

"Everything looks like the Big Dipper to you, Sam,"
he teased. Pulling her closer still, he placed his chilled
cheek against her temple. "See the widespread W that
cluster makes? That's Cassiopeia, no mistaking it."

They had stopped walking and stood statue-still, their
gaze on the stars, attention on their physical proximity.

He smelled faintly of bay rum. Beneath the scents of
after-shave and soap and out-of-doors, she discovered another distinctly his own, undeniably male. His jaw jumped
against her cheek, his breath warmed her skin, his unfamiliar nearness heated her, heart and soul. Suddenly afraid
to remain so close, she could not force herself to be sepa-
rated from the security and the sensuality of his embrace.
Standing perfectly still, she waited, scarcely breathing.

Whiskey-colored curls escaping Sam's fur hat brushed
his cheek, light as down. Her skin pressed against his chin
felt like velvet. She wore a tantalizing floral scent, barely
discernible, violets, he thought. More subtle, another
scent, uniquely her own, all feminine. She fit into the
curve of his body from shoulder to thigh like she belonged
there, forever. And she did. He'd always known it, and
someday she would, too. He counted on it, held on to the
belief, even when it seemed impossible. For now, just for
a little while, he forgot to worry that he could be dead
wrong, and gloried in her nearness.

He shifted slightly until he faced her, his lips brushing
her temple where her pulse fluttered wildly, giving encouragement. He pressed another kiss between her brows

and felt them lift in surprise. She wrinkled her nose when he feathered kisses, first there, then all the way down to her chin, missing her mouth, though it pursed in invitation. He touched one corner of those inviting lips with the tip of his tongue, then the other. Her mouth opened ever so slightly on a shuddered inhalation, allowing him entrance. He delved more deeply than he'd ever before dared, and glories of glories, she allowed him to explore, finally initiating an investigation of her own. His body responded with excruciating pleasure he fought to ignore. He could feel her pulse beating beneath his lips, as erratic as his own; she clung to him as if unable to stand alone. Love him or not, she wanted him as much as he wanted her. Ben's heart soared far and away, beyond reason, beyond control, straight on to the blissful heaven of anticipation. He swore he heard a choir of welcoming angels.

Samantha heard them, too, and froze, recognizing the sweet music for what it was. The children's choir from the First Methodist Church, out caroling, heralding the advent of the season. Pressing flattened palms against Ben's chest, she pushed against his resistance until he conceded, with the reluctance of an awakening dreamer. He lifted his head, cocked to listen, craggy features collapsing into a chagrined grimace as he recognized the singers. He dared one small peck, missing her mouth altogether, before setting her away from him to brush gathering snow off the shoulders of her coat.

"You're starting to look like our snowman," he told her with a loving chuckle.

She brushed snow off his lapels, trying to ignore the almost shattering bereavement at being free of Ben's embrace, refusing to examine why that might be. Willing her breathing to steady, her pulse to settle back to normal, she forced a playful tone.

"You shall look like a snowman, *I* shall be a snow *woman*. Probably with a pencil and a pad of paper firmly gripped in my stick fingers."

Instead of the usual bitter disappointment with the mention of her chosen vocation, Ben experienced a flash of brilliance, a way to bring Samantha closer—closer to him and closer to home—helping him with the cause it seemed he'd been chosen to champion whether he wanted it or not.

"Stick fingers or flesh and bone, it'll be great having an experienced journalist like you helping Jasper and me right the wrong perpetrated against the Baxter children, Sam."

A heavy silence followed, lingering too long. Samantha started walking toward home, leaving him to follow or not, as he chose. He caught up in two strides.

"Sam?"

"I can't do it."

She spoke against the fur of her collar, and he almost missed it. She stopped walking abruptly and faced him.

"I can't write an article about those orphans."

A battle raged across her lovely, troubled face. A decision was reached, but not without a price, for she looked even more distressed, and sad.

"Ben, because of that story I initiated and was attempting to write before being scooped, the Klem family—mother, two daughters, and a son, Willie—very nearly lost everything they came to America for. Only relocation to another sweatshop, equally as vile as the one they'd left, kept them from starving on the street; and I lost a young friend whose friendly face and cheery 'good morning' I'd come to count on in a cold and faceless city." She told him everything, except, of course, her greatest shame— that she'd been fired.

"It's regrettable all sweatshops weren't closed down as a result of the investigation you initiated, Sam. And it's too bad the Klems were unable to better themselves, but that's the way of big cities and the poor. It was out of your control, Sam, but helping to get Henry and Molly away from old man Miller isn't."

"No, Ben, no matter what you say, I won't go mucking around in other people's lives. What if what you're planning to do only makes things worse for those children? Can you live with that? I couldn't."

"How could it be worse than being overworked and underfed, forced out-of-doors in the winter without a coat . . . probably abused in a hundred other ways we don't even know about, including physically? *Anything* we could do for them would be better than what their lives are now, don't you see?"

"All I see is trouble and sorrow ahead for them, one way or the other. Prove to me that we can be of real help, Ben, and I'll write an impassioned plea on their behalf that will shake this town to the core. Until then, count me out."

Shaking her head, Samantha started walking, eyes straight ahead, chin jutting. Ben stood his ground, feet planted.

"You're afraid of failing again, Sam, that's the real issue," he called after her, his voice ringing down the quiet street.

Her steps staggered, but she never paused.

"Damn it, Sam, I never took you for a coward."

Her pace increased until she was running. He let her go. If she was ever to come around to his way of thinking, he'd have to give her time to mull things over on her own. If Henry and Molly Baxter had that kind of time. He hoped to Hades Sam didn't take too long.

NINE

"*Where* have you been? We held dinner nearly an hour," Samantha's mother accused, holding open the kitchen door with a shoulder, cradling her injured arm with the good one.

Cordelia Spencer's usually even temperament became daily shorter as her incapacity progressed, especially given the holidays—which she loved—and Eliza's wedding to prepare for—which she clearly gloried in. Guiltily, Samantha realized that one of the reasons she had planned an extended holiday home had been to help her mother.

"Sorry, Mama. Ben and I were visiting Jasper Cooper . . . the editor of the *River Valley Weekly Review* . . . and I forgot the time."

"I recognized the name readily enough," Cordelia all but snapped, "Eliza has spoken of little else since this afternoon. I believe I could quote from her a list of every bit of flower and foliage in that conservatory of his. One would think that with a wedding only weeks away, both of you would have more important matters to attend to. Have you eaten? I thought not. Grannie saved you a plate."

She shoved the door wider, leaving her daughter little doubt what was expected.

Tossing hat and coat on the seat of the hall tree, Samantha trailed her mother into the kitchen, when she would much rather have slipped off to her room to mull over Duncan's return, the plight of the Baxter children, and the kiss. Most especially the kiss. Which had left her so shaken, all else paled by comparison.

"Hello again." A relentlessly cheerful voice broke through her reverie.

"Duncan."

He sat at the worktable in the center of the room, a wedge of dried apple pie on the plate before him equal to one third of the whole, and that half-consumed.

"I might have known you'd make this kitchen your second stop with Grannie here for the holidays, to resume your ongoing battle over who has the sweetest tooth."

Grannie spoke up from the kitchen sink, where, elbow deep in suds, she washed dishes and Eliza dried.

"Considering that's his second piece since he got here less than a half hour ago, I'd say the boy's well on his way to catching up, though I have a head start on him in years alone."

Grannie chuckled, a deep and throaty sound. In her youth, Madeline Preston Spencer's beauty had rivaled Olivia's. Ivory skin, raven hair, violet eyes. Colorado had weathered her skin into aged leather and creased permanent laugh lines around her eyes; her hair, now heavily laced with silver, she wore in a thick, braided coronet, without concern for the latest fashion; her pretty eyes sparkled still, but from a rounder face to match her comfortably plump body, testament to her excellent cooking and her notorious love of sweets.

"You might have mentioned that Duncan was back, Samantha," chided her mother.

She sat in an old wooden rocking chair beside the cookstove, rocking as vigorously as if she expected the chair to transport her somewhere. Cordelia did not take well to inactivity, as she continued to make everyone well aware. A pretty woman, though not the beauty her mother-in-law had been and was still, she was tiny and trim, fashionably dress and fashionably coiffed as befitted the wife of the local bank president. Propriety her goal, a stickler for correct deportment, Cordelia found Samantha forever and always at odds with her sense of right and wrong. A second apology for her oversight in this instance fell automatically from Samantha's lips.

Grannie slid a heaped plate from dinner out of the warming oven and set it on the table, gesturing for Samantha to sit.

"Tempest in a teapot, Corrie. Duncan's home and came running over here before his bags were unpacked, I'll wager. That's good enough for me, and should be for you. Our boys are all together again, at least through the holidays."

She winked knowingly at Duncan, who returned the gesture with a grin and offered up his clean-scraped plate for more pie. Grannie traded the empty plate for what remained in the pie tin.

"Could've saved myself a plate to wash," she grumbled, but clearly pleased. As much as she loved her sweets, she loved seeing others appreciate them more.

Mildly offended at her mother-in-law's candor, Cordelia left the rocker to announce to no one in particular that she was going upstairs, and if Preston was through shuffling bank papers on his desk in their room, to bed. Grannie and Eliza finished the dishes and, with transparent excuses, left the room as well. Samantha rose to pour herself and Duncan brimming cold glasses of milk, then sat to watch him finish his pie, her dinner scarcely touched.

"Grannie implied you won't be staying," she said

bluntly when he was no longer left with anything to eat or drink.

He raised one eyebrow. "Missing me while I'm still here?"

"How long before you disappear on us again?"

"Now, Sam—"

"How long?"

"I'll be going back to Colorado with Grandpa and Grannie Spencer right after the wedding," Duncan admitted quietly.

"Oh! I see!" Her words came out tight with disappointment.

His puckish grin spread wide.

"You've missed me," he declared, tone smug.

"I did not. Well, some. But then, I was not at home either this last year."

"I know. Working for the *Chicago Evening Star*. And doing a great job, from what I've read." He laughed outright at her surprise. "Newspapers are mailed out west, too. A few days late, or sometimes not 'til spring thaw, but arriving eventually. We've come a long way since stagecoach days, Sam."

"Then why must you leave so soon?"

"Will *you* be staying on?" he countered.

She evaded. "Ben and you have more things to resolve between you than a few short weeks allow. Please, promise me you won't take off while you two are still at odds."

She reached for his forearm, resting nearby on the worn worktable, and clung as if she could keep him by force of will.

"Sorry, Sam. I can't make that promise. I have responsibilities back home—"

"Back home?" she echoed, a sinking feeling in the pit of her stomach.

"Colorado's my home, same's Chicago's become yours."

"That's different."

"How?"

She refused to elaborate. Quick tears smarted behind her eyelids. Duncan patted her hand on his arm.

"I can't stay on more than a couple of days after the wedding, whether Ben comes around by then or not. I can't have Alice worrying and wondering about me."

"Alice? A sweetheart?"

"Sweetheart . . . and wife."

"Wife?" Samantha squeaked.

"And pregnant. That's why I can't have her wor—"

His words choked off at Samantha's bear hug, as she threw herself into his arms. She kissed his cheek resoundingly. Married and settled down, glory be, and soon to be a father. The life she'd hoped for him since the day he left her behind, feeling guilty and responsible because she couldn't love him and marry him.

"Sam, I can't breathe," Duncan gasped, then when she released her choke-hold on him, added, "I take it you're happy for me. No lingering jealousy?"

Samantha fell back into her chair. "Of course not, I haven't a jealous bone in my body." But the fleeting thought crossed her mind: what if it had been Ben announcing he loved another woman enough to marry her? She felt a sharp, physical twinge. Or maybe it was Duncan poking her in the ribs to get her attention.

"I thought you'd be busting with questions about the girl who stole my heart from you."

"I am, I am. Tell me everything, and don't leave out any details from the moment you stormed out of town until this very second." She pretended rapt attention while picking up her fork. "I'm as famished for your news as

I am for Grannie's buttery mashed potatoes." She forked up a pile and stuffed her mouth full.

Duncan laughed. "Sarcasm aside, I bow to your request, ma'am."

He proceeded to talk her ear off through her meal and over a shared pot of coffee—made by Duncan after Samantha admitted she didn't know how. He confessed he had always longed to head west and that he'd used her last rejection as an excuse to go—that and the fact that he and Ben could never see eye to eye. Slipping away without awkward goodbyes made sense to him at the time, angry as he was. Only after he arrived alone and low on funds in Luckless did it occur to him he'd taken a coward's—and a fool's—way out. Winter was coming on, though it was barely September, and he had no place to stay and not a soul to care. Too ashamed to look up Grandpa and Grannie Spencer—if he could've made it through the mountain passes to their cabin high in the Rockies—he couldn't bring himself to face them. He panned some and mined some and generally lived from hand-to-mouth that first winter. He admitted to doing more than a few things of which he was not proud, gambling—losing more than he had to lose—hard drinking, soft women.

"I wasn't a man you'd've been proud of then, Sam. Didn't feel very good about myself, either, 'til I chanced to meet up with Alice, and her father Matthew Fletcher . . . a Methodist circuit preacher—"

"Her pure love saved your wicked soul and captured your wayward heart," Samantha's creative mind supplied.

Duncan roared with laughter, head flung back, mouth wide, until he had to wipe tears from his eyes, speaking when he could.

"Nothing all that dramatic. You know me, Sam, always

needing to explore, check things out, learn something new. Alice is a beautiful young woman; I listened to Matthew's sermons hoping to get on her good side, and found myself listening. Really listening. Lo and behold, I discovered what I'd been looking for all my life. I'm a preacher, too, now, Sam . . . well, studying to be one. And when Grannie said Eliza was getting married, I just had to come back to offer to assist at the wedding. It was time to come home, mend fences and . . . Close your mouth, Sam. You'll catch flies, as Grannie would say."

"Y-Y-You? A preacher? I-I-I can't believe it." She looked into his eyes, suddenly suspicious. She punched his arm with her doubled fist. "You're making it all up, Duncan Morton."

Duncan placed a hand over his heart and raised the other one to pledge, "If I'm not telling the gospel truth, may God strike me dead on this spot."

Samantha glanced quickly upward, fully expecting a lightning bolt to split the smoke-weathered, fly-speckled ceiling down the middle. She let out her breath in a *whooosh* when nothing happened.

Still suspicious, she leveled him with a challenging stare. "If this whopper is really all true, and not just something you and Grannie've cooked up for a practical joke, why's it such a big secret? Why didn't you tell Ben and me in the parlor the moment we discovered you were home?"

"Planned on it." At a rude, disbelieving sound from her, "Ask Grannie. I was going to tell Ben, all of you, right off. But Ben was being such an—excuse the expression— ass, I figured he needed more time to welcome me back into the fold first, before I sprung the rest on him. And I sure as heck wasn't going to keep it from him and tell the others." He gave her a pleading grin. "You won't tell on me, will you Sam, before I'm ready?"

"To help keep the peace, you can count on it," she vowed.

He gripped her hand. "Thanks, Sam. Knew I could count on you."

Samantha took a deep breath, shaking her head.

"Well, I never."

"Me neither. But I'm happy, Sam. Happier than I ever figured to be in my lifetime. I've found my calling, and I found my Alice. All that's left to make things perfect is for everyone here to accept me as I am, and be happy for me, too."

Duncan laid an upturned hand on the table and Samantha slipped hers inside, quick, unexpected tears splashing down on their linked fingers. She impatiently brushed them away, offering a shaky laugh.

"I am happy for you, Duncan. I couldn't be happier. When will we get to meet your bride?"

"After the baby's born, we'll come for a visit. Right now, she's sick every morning and sometimes all day. Your grannie assures me that's not unusual in the early stages of pregnancy." He squeezed her hand. "Now, Sam, tell me what's been going on in your life since I left."

Afraid this new minister might catch her in her tangle of lies, she confessed.

"I got fired from my job in Chicago. Only, please, *please,* don't tell anyone. If Mama and Papa find out they'll never let me return after the holidays. I'm determined to get my job back, even if I'm forced to remain on the society desk forever."

Promising nothing, with a few probing questions, Duncan got the entire story out of her. He had a natural flair for it, she noticed. The story of the failed exposé poured out, and when she had finished with her trials and tribulations in Chicago, including how she missed young Willie, she told him of Ben's request of her, and her refusal to help.

"I'm afraid to do more harm to those poor, orphaned children than good, as I did with Willie Klem," she revealed.

"Are you so sure Willie's no better off where he is now? Or is it just that you missed seeing the boy around every day to cheer you?" Not waiting for an answer, he suggested, "Why don't you write to this editor of yours on the *Star?* Tell him your concerns for the boy, see what he can find out for you. It's an opportunity to keep the man from forgetting you while you're gone," he teased.

"I doubt he'd forget the cocky young reporter who barged her way into his office to badger him for a job, then threw that job back in his face the first time it didn't suit," she admitted ruefully. "He probably never wants to see or hear from me again."

Duncan shrugged. "The only way to be certain of that is to correspond with him. Maybe he'll give you your job back before you even leave River Valley. Maybe he's only waiting for you to come to your senses and ask. Swallow your considerable pride, Sam. Write."

"I will. I'll do it tonight."

"And write that article for the local paper, too, as soon as all the facts are available. Public awareness has its value. Even if you can't change circumstances for Henry and Molly Baxter, you might just salvage some other unfortunate orphan's life."

"You're right."

"What about you and Ben?" Duncan asked in an abrupt change of subject.

"What about Ben and me?"

"Rumor has it he brought you flowers, that you spend every waking hour together. That you and he are courting."

"Oh, that." She chortled, explaining. "Ben and I made a pact. Both of us were so weary of well-meaning matchmakers, we decided to pretend we had chosen each other on our own."

"I see." He drew the words out suggestively.

"You don't see a thing, Duncan Morgan. Disbelief is written all over your face, plain as day."

He raised both hands palm up, shaking his head.

"Whatever you and Ben have cooked up between you is no concern as mine. A word of advice, though, Sam. Be sure you and Ben know for certain it's only everyone else you're fooling, and not yourselves. Think about it, Sam. You might be pleasantly surprised."

Promising nothing, she said her good nights at the back door, then sat alone in the kitchen over a cup of cold coffee, her head so full of so many things she couldn't sort them out. Her solitude was woefully short-lived. The swinging door to the hall swooshed open.

"Duncan? Duncan? Oh, pooh! He's not here. Samantha Spencer, were you keeping Duncan's return all to yourself? We wanted to welcome him home and tell him the good news." The pouty petulance in Olivia's voice couldn't hide the excitement just beneath.

Samantha rose to the bait. "We?"

"Andrew and me, of course, silly."

Olivia pulled the oldest Morgan brother into the room with both hands wrapped possessively around his arm. He seemed to mind not at all, in fact, wore a decidedly pleased expression on his somber, handsome face.

"Duncan's had a long day. He's gone home. You can probably catch him before he retires if you hurry."

"That'll wait 'til morning. We want you to be the first to know, don't we, Andrew dear?" Flush-faced he only nodded, looking bewildered but pleased. *Probably because I'm the only one available, Samantha thought uncharitably.* "Andrew and I are engaged. To be married. There shall be a double wedding come the new year. Isn't it wonderful?"

"M-M-Married? That's . . . that's . . . sheer madness! That's what it is!" Samantha exclaimed, too loudly. "You aren't . . . you haven't even . . . gone together. How can you possibly be engaged?"

"Oh, pooh! You could at least *pretend* to be pleased. Honestly, I told you days ago how I felt about Andrew. And when I went to confront him after I left you, he confided that he has worshiped me from afar for just ages. It's not as though we're strangers, Samantha. We've known each other all our lives, and we know what we want, don't we, Andrew?" She gave him no chance to respond. "We'd like you to be happy for us. It's the very least you can do. That, and be my bridesmaid as well as Eliza's."

"What if Eliza objects—?"

"Of course she won't. Why should she? There, it's all settled."

More beautiful than ever in her happiness, Olivia had everything worked out, except one looming problem Samantha couldn't resist mentioning.

"What does Aunt Jane think of all of this? I thought she had her heart set on your marrying nobility, or at least someone very, very wealthy."

Olivia paled noticeably, but rallied quickly. With a toss of her lovely head, she announced, "If Mama is not pleased—though I am sure she shall be as soon as she realizes it's what I want—we shall simply elope, won't we, Andrew?"

The once-sensible Andrew appeared so besotted he couldn't think straight.

"Whatever you say, my dear."

"For mercy's sake! Enough is enough. Why don't the two of you go see who else you can pester with your announcement. This chirping about like a pair of lovebirds is giving me a headache."

"You're just jealous," Olivia snapped, but her eyes held triumph.

"Not where this love and marriage nonsense is concerned. It's nothing to me who's married and who's going to be. I have more important matters to think and write about. No time like the present to start. Go find someone else to share your good news with, I'm busy. Good night."

She unceremoniously ushered them out through the swinging door, then sat, alone and brooding. Sometime later, Grannie Spencer found her there. Samantha turned her head, propped in palms with elbows on tabletop, and sighed heavily.

"Why the long face?"

"Grannie, please explain love to me."

A bemused smile on her age-thinned lips, Grannie Spencer set on the table a tray of cups containing the last dregs of hot cocoa and a plate of cookie crumbs.

"What aspects of love confuse you, my dear?"

On a second hearty sigh, Samantha admitted, "Everything."

"Mother love? Platonic love? Puppy love?"

"You're getting closer." Samantha rubbed her temples with two fingertips on each hand. "I went off to Chicago, leaving behind sensible family members and friends going their separate ways, as always. I haven't been home a week, only to discover that sweet bucolic life has vanished, and everyone I know has leapt willy-nilly into the throes of . . . of mindless infatuations and . . . and—"

"Love? Devotion? Intimacy?"

"Well, yes . . ."

Grannie sat beside her, her liver-spotted, callused hand pressing against Samantha's cheek to force eye contact.

"That's courting, plain and simple, as old and as natural as time."

"I know that, Grannie. I just can't accept that it's happening to everyone at once. It's not catching, is it?" Samantha gave a brief, rueful smile.

Grannie joined her. "Not like measles, my dear. But it's been my experience that once a wedding is in the planning, all the single young men and women among family and friends take to the idea and start looking around. I'll bet we'll see at least a couple more weddings come out of Eliza's and Olivia's."

Samantha's eyebrows rose.

"That's been settled already? Without even consulting Aunt Jane and Uncle Noble? What did Andrew have to say for himself at this turn of events?" How much else had she missed by lingering in the kitchen instead of joining the others in the family parlor?

"I've no doubt Olivia will convince her parents in the end. And don't worry yourself about Andrew; he's been waiting for Olivia for a long time."

Samantha slowly shook her head in disbelief. "And I never noticed."

"There's something else you have avoided noticing."

Not willing to go in the direction she feared Grannie headed, Samantha announced, "Duncan's married, and a father-to-be."

"So he said."

Refusing to let it hurt her that she hadn't been the first

he told, she added, "That's three out of four of the Morgan men to fall to amour. Not including Edward, who'd only have to glance down the street to find himself a sweetheart, so I'm told."

"Lydia Snow. Sweet child. She'll attract his notice any day now. Leaving only Ben. And you."

With a casual toss of her head, Samantha pretended not to know what Grannie implied. "I'll return to Chicago in a few short weeks. Ben will probably succumb to some pretty widowed mother of one of his students, or an older sister, a maiden aunt."

Wisely, Grannie didn't try to pursue the issue or offer any unwanted advice. Attempting to muddle her way through the troubling topic, Samantha switched tactics.

"Did you love Grandpa when you two first met?"

Grannie chortled. "Love him? No. I believed I hated him. And he was far from fond of me."

"What changed?"

"I finally listened to what my heart had been saying all along, that we belonged together."

"And did Grandpa agree?" She found herself thinking of Ben, and their pretended courtship.

"With time. And . . ."

"And?

"And," Grannie's eyes went dreamy, her face softened, almost young again, "a need he could no longer deny." At her granddaughter's puzzled expression, she elaborated. "Ah, child. How much you do not yet know about women and men. What foolishness that the subject is not discussed until the eve of marriage, and then generally only in the most dour of terms. I was fortunate to have Sam as my teacher, long before our wedding day."

Understanding dawned slowly, turning Samantha redfaced. "You and Grandpa . . . ? Before . . . ?"

Grannie patted Samantha's hands, locked together on the scarred tabletop.

"My intention in telling you my deep dark secret was not to embarrass or appall you, sweet child, but to help you understand the hugeness of the questions you seek the answers to. Someday soon you, too, will know the longings of true love for one who returns that love with equal passion. Do not deny yourself the fulfillment of that love, granddaughter. Follow your heart, Samantha, it will not lead you astray."

Grannie rose to transfer cups from the tray on the table to the cast-iron sink. Her back to Samantha, her gaze far beyond the view out the window over the sink, Grannie said, "One more secret I entrust you with, Samantha—the reason I never speak of my wedding day. Things were simpler then, especially high in the mountains away from civilization.

"Sam and I," she glanced over her shoulder, saw Samantha's rapt attention, and confided, "Sam and I exchanged vows between ourselves. Without benefit of clergy or the proper papers. After all this time, after everything that's come and gone in our lives together, your Grandpa and I, we might not even be legally wed."

TEN

Later, Samantha couldn't recall what words were exchanged after Grannie's confession, except that as she left the kitchen to retire for the evening, Grannie patted her shoulder and told her not to fret about it.

Fret she did, though. Thoughts spinning, Samantha sought the only release she knew she could count on, her writing. A pad of paper and several sharpened pencils in hand, she settled into the rocker Mama had earlier vacated. Tucking her legs up under her, she wrapped the crocheted afghan from the rocker's high back around her, snuggling deep into the familiar hollows of its worn and lumpy cushions. As fast as her fingers could fly, she wrote on and on through the night, long after her hands cramped and her shoulders burned, until, toward dawn, she fell asleep still clutching her pencil, the pad sliding off her lap onto the floor.

In the early light of dawn, Ben saw the light from the Spencer kitchen tracing a path across the hills and hollows of new-fallen snow and loped next door, hoping Grannie—usually the earliest riser—had coffee burbling on the stove and fat cinnamon rolls baking in the oven. He'd sent the boys on ahead to school as soon as they could see their way to begin a week's punishment of starting the fire in the schoolhouse stove. Now he feared the punishment too harsh, feared more that they might just take off again to Farmer Miller's to help the Baxter kids with their chores, and hoped to ask Grannie for her sage advice in the matter before he headed to school himself. Instead, he found Samantha curled up in the rocking chair by the window, sound asleep. On the floor lay a thick pad of paper. Ben bent in retrieval and discovered it entirely covered, to the last sheet, in her handwriting, neat as a pin on the first page, an almost illegible scrawl fading off to a squiggle on the last.

Being an honorable man, he knew he shouldn't read any of it; being the man desperately in love, albeit possibly futilely, with the author, he couldn't resist a quick perusal. A sentence or two of Sam's intimate exploration of the complexities of romantic love was all he managed before guilt overcame him. He set the pad back on the floor where he found it just as Sam stirred in her sleep and awoke.

Sleepily stretching, she focused on him. "Ben? What're you doing here this late?"

"It's six-thirty in the morning, Sam."

She yawned widely, digesting that information. Sudden concern flooded her face, she looked frantically around for her pad of paper.

"On the floor," he helped, thinking how lovely she was on awaking, sleep-tousled hair, eyes vague with last night's dreams, and one rosy cheek imprinted with a row of small crescents where her fingertips had pressed in sleep.

She reached for the pad where Ben had replaced it, her legs unwinding from under her, stocking feet protruding beneath the crocheted coverlet. Ahead of her, Ben picked up the pad for her; without thanks she snatched it out of his hands, protectively hugging it to her chest in over-lapped arms.

"It's private."

"I know. I mean—"

"You read this?"

"Only a line or two. Unintentionally. When I first came in. You were sleeping—"

"And that makes prying excusable?"

"I figured you'd been writing an article for Jasper. Soon as I realized it wasn't, I stopped."

Flush-cheeked, Samantha relented. "All right then."

She raised a hand to the back of her neck to rub at the kinks settled there, wincing at the cramps she discovered in both shoulders.

"I wouldn't recommend sleeping in this chair any length of time to friend or foe."

"Here, let me."

He came around behind her, resting his hands over tight muscles, kneading gently. Her skin warmed his palms through the fabric of her shirtwaist; her long drawn-out "mmmmm" of contentment heated his heart, and his groin. Her chin dropped down on her chest, exposing the soft, slender nape of her neck with its fringe of whiskey curls, and Ben's hands trembled at their task, his fingers sliding up seemingly of their own accord to let those silky curls twine around them. Heaven and hell, all at the same time, though he wouldn't have stopped to save himself from either. He rubbed the heels of his hands against the taut muscles in her neck a couple of times until they unknotted under his touch, then resumed kneading her shoulders to the sound of her happy sighs. Soon, God willing, he might finally enjoy this sensuous pleasure every day for the rest of his life if he wanted to.

Eyes closed, Samantha gave herself over to Ben's touch,

breathing deeply of the clean scent of the soap, detecting, more faintly, the cold freshness of all outdoors, and still faintly, burnt toast. She winked one eye open, asking lazily, "What'd you say you were doing here so early?"

Without pausing at his loving labor, he replied, "Hoping for a hot cup of coffee and a cinnamon roll. Turned out it was you burning the midnight oil instead of Grannie Spencer up early baking." He glanced at the clock on a high shelf. "Looks like I'll have to do without in any case, or teacher's going to be late for school."

Reluctant to relinquish his chore, he rested his hands on her shoulders; as reluctant to give up the creature comfort he offered, Sam let her head fall back and to the side so that her cheek rested on his knuckles.

The swinging door slammed against the kitchen wall with resounding force as Aunt Jane burst into the room, trailed by the mild-mannered, often absent pair, Noble Sr. and Jr. After a stunned second of silence on her part, the plump woman—red-faced and quivering all over with indignation—screamed a tirade against what she thought she saw.

"Samantha Spencer, for shame! Shame on you, too, Benjamin Morgan! At this hour. Under your own father's roof, Samantha! You should be ashamed of yourselves, both of you!"

With every shouted word she shook her pointing finger at the two of them, causing Ben to drop his hands from Samantha's shoulders and step back, putting a discreet distance between them.

"Aunt Jane, we didn't—we weren't—What are you doing here at this hour? Surely not attempting to catch Ben and me engaged in some impropriety, which we weren't."

"I know what I see, missy. Just like you to flaunt everything that is proper. I told Preston no good would come of your going off alone to that wicked big city. And *look* what tragedy has come from it." She waved a slip of paper over her head like a banner. "My poor little girl! Oh, my poor sweet child!" She burst into huge, loud sobs punctuated by bansheelike wails loud enough to wake the dead.

Uncle Noble, at a loss as always in his wife's considerable presence, snatched the piece of paper out of her hand and passed it to Noble, Jr., a man of twenty-five years with no more backbone than his father. They could've passed for brothers, with thinning tan hair, high receding hairlines, long, pale faces, and light eyes of uncertain color; slender and slight, neither measured up to Aunt Jane's considerable bulk, nor her unspoken family domination. Holding the single sheet of paper gingerly between thumb and forefinger, Noble, Jr., stepped farther into the room and fluttered it in Samantha and Ben's direction, clearly peeved at all the unsettled disturbance to comforting, mundane routine. Casting an accusing glance between them, he announced in a weak voice,

"Olivia has eloped. With your brother, Ben."

Stunned speechless, Samantha and Ben exchanged stares of incredulity. Ben recovered first, quizzing Noble Sr. and Jr., since Aunt Jane continued to sob, beyond conversation.

"How long ago'd they take off? Where're they headed? Maybe there's time to catch up, stop them."

"Don't know when; don't know where. Mother and Olivia quarreled heatedly last evening over the unsuitability of her abrupt engagement to Andrew. Olivia was sent to her room, but she wasn't in it this morning, and some of her clothes and her satchel were gone."

One eye on the clock, Ben said, "Then what's done is done. Likely they're wed by now. Look, folks, I'd like to help thrash out this problem, but I've got a schoolroom full of kids without a teacher. Junior, if you've come in your buggy, I'd appreciate a ride."

With a quick, apologetic glance at Samantha, Ben left with Junior, the young man's lean, pale face clearly mirroring his relief. By now family members, haphazardly dressed and still working buttons into their holes, began descending upon them. One of the first was Grannie, and when Aunt Jane saw her, she wailed, "Aunt Maddie, oh, Aunt Maddie, the most terrible catastrophe has befallen our family." She returned to sobbing incoherently.

Grannie looked to Samantha as the only calm in a sea of turmoil.

"After a quarrel with Aunt Jane, Olivia slipped away, supposedly to elope with Andrew. She left a note to that effect."

The babble of voices ceased at once. Mama raised her good hand to press fingers to a mouth shaped like a tall O. Papa and Uncle Noble exchanged bewildered, helpless stares. With an impolite snort, Grandpa began to chuckle low and deep in his throat, then building in volume.

"Uncle Samuel, this is no laughing matter."

"But it is, Janey, don't you see? After living the life you've plotted and planned for her all these years, our Livie's finally stood up for what *she* wants instead of what you do. Andrew's a mighty fine young man—upstanding, conscientious, smart, trustworthy—as Preston here can tell you, can't you, son? And soon to be a junior partner at the bank, I've heard. Livie couldn't've chosen any better to my way of thinking. And all this carrying on, well, it's about the biggest bunch of damn foolishness I ever did hear."

The room fell silent. Silver-haired and upright, weathered of face but still muscular and strong as a team of

oxen, the patriarch of the family had spoken, and like it
or not, he made a lot of sense.

Grannie put on coffee and started taking breakfast orders as if it were any other morning: who wanted flap-
jacks, who wanted eggs, who wanted both. Sausage or
bacon?

"Corrie, could you set out the bread and butter and
jam? Samantha, count noses and lay out plates, please,
while I whip up some of my cinnamon buns. You fellows
make yourself useful and fill the woodbox."

Doing as she was bid, Samantha made a mental note to
save a couple of Grannie's cinnamon buns for Ben, since
that was his excuse for coming over before dawn. Had it
been just that, an excuse? Why else? Certainly not anticipating he'd find her asleep in the kitchen rocking chair,
where Aunt Jane now sat, sniffing and dabbing at her red-
rimmed eyes and dripping nose with a kerchief more lace
than fabric, and trying to collect herself. Her crying had
dwindled away to a few sighs and hiccoughs and she
seemed appreciably calmer, but what fate Olivia would
face upon her return—*if* she returned—Samantha didn't
dare guess.

She spied her notepad under the rocker where it had
somehow ended up, and retrieved it on the pretense of
kneeling to pat her aunt's hand and offer platitudes of
comfort. Rising, relief palpable, she didn't dare imagine
what might have happened had anyone chanced to pick
up the forgotten sheaf of paper and begun reading. Within
lay evidence of her inner confusion, the questions she
asked herself, her theories and queries about the subject
uppermost in her mind—the validity and varieties of love.
Especially after this morning's sweet intimacies between
Ben and herself, the two of them alone as color filled the
sky and dark shadows receded for another day. Ben knead-

ing the tightness from her shoulders as if they were the only two alive in the awakening world. As if this was *their* kitchen, in their home. As if this was how it was meant to be. So sweet. So simple. So right. So utterly frightening, Samantha dropped a fistful of knives and forks onto the table in the dining room with a clatter that solicited exclamations and admonitions from the kitchen through the open door between.

Breakfast occasioned more talk of Olivia. Speculations flew around the room as to where the runaway couple might've gone. Fortunately, Aunt Jane appeared at least temporarily mollified after her third cinnamon bun, though she continued to glare occasionally at Samantha as if she still held her partially, if not entirely, responsible. She, however, kept her suppositions to herself, for the time being. Samantha nibbled on a strip of bacon, examined her conscience, and came to the conclusion there was little she could have said or done last night when Olivia threatened elopement to change her willful cousin's mind. In fact, she found herself fervently wishing Eliza and Charlie would follow that same path. As breakfast concluded, Mama informed Samantha that she was expected to go with Eliza to visit the seamstress for a final fitting this morning, in her stead.

"Mama, I have a column to write for Jasper. It's due on his desk tomorrow morning."

"And I am scheduled to visit the doctor." Cordelia held up her injured arm in its sling to imply Samantha had forgotten. "Time enough when you return for your writing . . . And don't even think of suggesting Eliza go alone."

"I-I-I could, Aunt Cordelia," timid Eliza offered.

"Nonsense. I won't hear of it. It is your family's duty and pleasure to assist you with every phase of your wedding preparations. Besides, Samantha, if you don't go, Eliza will be tempted to skimp on such things as nightwear and unmentionables and day dresses, though I have clearly instructed Miss Tyler as to the quantity desired for this, our wedding gift. Preston and I would find it unthinkable to do less for the niece we raised as a loved and loving daughter. Wouldn't we, Preston?"

Papa offered the proper platitudes, and Samantha realized the subject had been settled and closed. If only the appointment were any other day!

Eliza regarded her as if she could read her mind and very much regretted imposing on her time. Beside her at the table, Samantha reached out to squeeze her cousin's hand.

"Mama's right. The column won't take more than a couple of hours. I'd much rather spend the morning gallivanting with you, anyway. What do you say to luncheon at the Tea Room afterwards?"

Relieved, Eliza admitted, "I'd like that. If you're sure you can spare the time."

Insisting she could, and then some, Samantha rose to begin clearing away dirty dishes.

"Leave those for Janey and me," Grannie spoke up, over Aunt Jane's protests that she no longer did menial tasks better suited to her hired girl. "Do you good to occupy your hands and your head with something besides fretting over Olivia. Go on you two. Pretty yourselves up and have a good time on the town."

Duncan exited the Morgan house as Samantha and Eliza passed by, headed downtown. They paused at his hail, waiting for him to join them.

"Where're you two off to?"

"The dressmaker's shop, then luncheon at the Tea Room. And you?"

"To the livery stable to rent a rig. Business out of town. How about my inviting myself to join you lovely young ladies at the Tea Room when I get back?"

They agreed on a time, then chattered all the way to Main Street, filling Duncan in on community happenings since his departure more than two years ago, until they came to a parting of the ways.

Orders had been left at the dressmaker's to create a bridesmaid dress for Samantha in addition to Eliza's wedding gown and trousseau. Mama's less than subtle way of coaxing her out of her tailored, serviceable suits and dresses for the occasion, Samantha had no doubt, wondering if her mother had had a doctor's appointment at all, or if it had simply been a ploy to get her there. In any case, the two-piece gown was absolutely gorgeous, a vision of peach satin and matching lace. A low square neckline with sheer lace insert and a high band collar of satin. Sleeves form-fitting to the elbow and worn with long, dyed-to-match gloves with pearl buttons. A skirt that fell straight to the floor in front, with fabric draping in back emulating a bustle, but without the bustle's bulk, and a detachable train for formal wear. Mama had even thought of the proper hat, peach-dyed straw, brim rolled upward on both sides, and appropriately shaded trims of flowers, ribbon, and feathers. Quite the most elegant attire Samantha had ever worn. When she had finished putting everything on for her fitting and stepped out for a turn before the standing cheval mirrors, Eliza clasped her hands together above her small breasts, exclaiming,

"Oh, Samantha, you are beautiful."

About to issue an automatic protest, Samantha caught a glimpse of herself in one of the mirrors. Mesmerized by what she saw, she slowly pivoted, viewing herself from the many angles the mirrors provided, heart fluttering a bit by the lovely sight she was met with at every turn.

"I believe the ugly duckling has at last become a swan, at least temporarily," she joked to cover any hint of vanity.

"You were never an ugly duckling, Samantha, but you certainly obtain a swanlike elegance in those clothes. Wait until Ben sees you all dressed up! He won't be able to take his eyes off you."

Samantha made an unladylike sound and a rude comment. Secretly, she was more pleased than she dared admit, even to herself, that Ben might find her half as beautiful as Eliza had. The very thought of his reaction left her trembling with anticipation. Unnerved by the unexpected response, Samantha thrust such thoughts into the darkest recesses of her mind for later examination. With a glance at the clock on the wall, she reminded her cousin that by the time they had set aside their finery and dressed in their street clothes, it would be time to meet Duncan.

They stepped out into a brilliant winter day of a clear, robin's egg blue sky and blinding white snow, soiled only along the curbs where wheels of countless passing vehicles had sprayed. Duncan waited for them at a table, already sipping a steaming cup of coffee.

"Been waiting long?" Samantha asked, sliding into a chair on one side of him while Eliza took one on the other.

"Not long."

"Did you manage to get everything done you'd planned to?"

"Just about."

"You've changed," Samantha countered. "Once you would have talked my ear off over your morning adventures."

Duncan shrugged. "Nothing to tell. I drove over to Isadore to apply for ordination at the Methodist headquarters there. Took a test, the results of which won't be available to me until after I return to Colorado."

"Speaking of Colorado. I've been wondering how you dare come home almost a full month before the wedding, leaving your wife behind to suffer alone the discomforts of being with child!"

Duncan chuckled. "Alice would appreciate your indignation on her behalf, Sam, but the truth of the matter is that she insisted I take advantage of the wedding so near the holidays to mend fences with my family. As to leaving my poor little wife all alone," he teasingly imitated, "half of Luckless is related to her by blood or marriage. I doubt she'll have a lonesome moment without me. Well, maybe one," he added with a wicked glint in his eyes that set both virginal young women to blushing.

Eliza quickly changed the subject. "Did you have a church wedding, Duncan?"

"We were married on a magnificent June afternoon in the cathedral of a cloudless sky on a snowcapped mountain top, witnessed by every last soul of Luckless, Colorado. Alice's father married us with every single one of her six unmarried sisters as bridemaids."

"She is one of seven sisters?" Samantha asked, incredulous.

Duncan raised a hand, placing the other on his heart, and opened his mouth to pledge the truth of his words. Samantha interrupted.

"I believe you. No one could make up such a fantastic coincidence."

"Or whimsy on God's part?" queried the future preacher.

"Will you have a church of your own when you return to Luckless?" Eliza wanted to know, obviously hungry for knowledge of her home-to-be once she and Charlie were wed.

"There is no church building yet, nor school. Matthew and I will be saddlebag preachers for some time to come, I'm afraid. Luckless could as aptly be named Lawless for its eight saloons and three bawdy houses. A general store, a brick bank, and a blacksmith—that's about the extent of the town. Alice and I are just grateful that Colorado became a state in '76. We couldn't have legally wed in a territory."

Samantha immediately thought of Grannie Spencer's confession to her the night before, stricken to realize that there couldn't possibly be any validation to their marriage vows without their having gone beyond Colorado's territorial boundaries. Knowing they had not. To all intents and purposes, Grannie and Grandpa Spencer were not really married, and never had been. What repercussions that could have on her grandparents' large, extended family, she couldn't begin to imagine. Perhaps no one ever need know. For the time being, she decided, she'd bide her time, and offer up a few fervent prayers that her grandmother's secret never be exposed unless Grannie herself so chose.

Duncan walked them to their porch. Propped against the oval-paned front door was a flat package wrapped in paper and ribbon. Duncan picked it up, read the name on the accompanying card, and handed the package to Samantha.

"It's for you. From your secret admirer." He grinned. "Not that it's much of a secret who it might be. Young Edward has talked my ear off since I got home about you, Sam, clearly as smitten as a lad coming into his manhood can be."

Samantha undid the wrappings, opening the box to reveal three expensive, elegant lace hankies.

Eliza breathed a small "Oh, my" of dismay.

Duncan blew out a slow whistle. "The boy has taste, you have to give him that for what he lacks in etiquette. Even *I* know the error in so personal a gift, and I've been far from the social scene in the Wild, Wild West."

Samantha ignored his tongue-in-cheek comment. "This situation has clearly gone too long unattended, and I intend to put a stop to it right now."

Slapping the lid on the box over hankies, paper, and ribbon, she ran down the front steps to cross the worn path to the Morgans' front door, wondering what in the world she'd say to the poor love-struck lad now that she'd decided to confront him, hoping inspiration would strike before she came face to face with the sixteen-year-old .

ELEVEN

He must have been watching from one of the front windows. Before she could open the front door, Edward flung it wide, hope and fear warring on his adolescent face. Samantha's high dudgeon died an abrupt death. Relenting at once, she forced a smile, casting about for the best approach in this touchy situation. Too much candor could devastate the infatuated lad; too little would give the wrong impression, prolonging his agony.

"May I come in?"

Dumbstruck and awkward, he stepped aside to let her pass him into the front hall. Biding her time, Samantha did a slow turn to examine the familiar entry, seeing it afresh after her long absence. Years without a female's touch evident in the lack of adornment, this room, like the rest of the house, looked clean and tidy almost to the point of appearing uninhabited. Absently, Samantha wondered when Ben found the time to see that it was kept that way, along with all his other responsibilities. A man of many unsung talents, obviously.

"No Christmas trimmings?" she asked, evading the obvious, holding the package of hankies behind her back.

"Not yet."

Edward shifted uneasily from one foot to the other, but Samantha could think of nothing to ease his discomfort.

She knew so little of love, puppy or otherwise. Too bad he'd picked her as the object of his affection. He should've chosen someone, anyone, else. Someone who understood the workings of a teenaged boy's mind. Someone of his own age. Someone who . . . who lived right across the street. Of course!

Inspiration dawning, Samantha offered Edward a broad smile.

"Something's been puzzling me since I arrived home," she said. "It occurred to me you might be able to help me figure it out."

"M-M-Me . . . I-I-I mean, I will if I can."

His eagerness to please her almost broke her heart. Of all the brothers, Edward had always been the most sensitive. The one who brought home injured birds and frogs, and an occasional orphaned kitten or puppy—including Zeus—to try to nurse back to health, find a home for. The one who wept as if his heart were broken for those he couldn't save. She could not bring herself to wound this sensitive boy, no matter what. Had her hands not been full, she'd've crossed the fingers on both for luck. Instead she offered up a simple silent prayer for the right words.

"I'm concerned about a neighbor across the street. Lydia Snow? Do you know her?"

Edward's ear tips turned bright red; he nodded without speaking. Samantha took that small encouragement to continue.

"I've seen her . . . more times than I can count . . . standing behind one of the pillars on her front porch, peeking across the way. And I was wondering if you might have some clue to such odd behavior." His confused expression indicated he hadn't. *Men could be so dense sometimes, especially Morgan men. "I* think she finds someone at your house of interest," she prompted, with no growing comprehension from Edward. "Aren't you and she about the same age? Classmates? Has she perhaps been paying more attention to you lately?"

Edward's cheeks flushed scarlet.

"We . . . we've been walking home from school together a lot. Just her and me usually, 'cause Frankie and Georgie take off right after to meet up with some new friends of theirs."

"And . . . ?"

He had no idea.

"Do you talk together?" she prompted.

"Oh! Oh, sure! She's got lots to say, lots of ideas. I mostly just listen."

"Just what every good talker needs," Samantha agreed. "But you must have opinions of your own. You're an intelligent fellow."

Edward flashed a brief grin. "That's what Lydia tells me all the time." He shrugged. "I don't want to make her mad by maybe disagreeing."

"I'll let you in on a little secret, Edward. Young women enjoy a stimulating verbal exchange as much as men. And I'll tell you another, because Lydia herself probably hasn't the courage." Samantha lowered her voice conspiratorially. "She's sweet on you."

The boy went pale except for two mottled blotches in the center of his cheeks, but for the first time, Samantha saw the dawning of comprehension, and hope.

"She . . . she isn't. I mean, she can't be, can—?"

"Oh, but she can and is. And I mention it only so you . . . if you're so inclined . . . won't hesitate to express your interest in return. Youth, and the pleasure thereof, are more fleeting than you can imagine."

It was evident that this shy, sensitive boy had much to ponder, alone. As if in afterthought, she added, "By the by, is Ben at home? No? Too bad. I found this on my doorstep, addressed to me," she pulled the package out from behind her back, "and wondered if he might have sent it, to tease me. You know how he can be. If so, the joke's on him. These three lovely handkerchiefs," she showed him, "are going to provide Eliza, Olivia, and myself with three pretty tokens to carry at the wedding. And Eliza's shall be her required 'something new.' If you see him, tell him so for me, will you please, Edward?"

"Yes, ma'am, I-I-I will. A-A-And thanks, Samantha, f-f-for . . . for . . . well, aw, thanks."

She exited quickly and ran for home, tangibly relieved. Annoyed, too, that fate kept putting her in these awkward amorous situations of late. Hopefully, this was the last of them.

Belatedly, she heard her name called out in a stage whisper, two voices strong. On the Morgans' back stoop stood Ben and Duncan, gesturing wildly for her to join them, grinning like a pair of Cheshire cats.

Duncan caught her hand when she reached them, enclosed it in both of his, pumping vigorously.

"Never saw anyone let down easier, Samantha. If you'd've been as gentle with me, I wouldn't have had to leave town."

"Balderdash! If you had listened to my first five hundred refusals, the five hundred and first wouldn't've come as such a wound to your pride you had to turn tail and run away. Shame on the two of you for eavesdropping."

"Ben was already there when I arrived, listening at the kitchen door."

"So naturally, you had to join him. Duncan, will you please stop yanking on my arm like a pump handle? You're about to free my shoulder from its socket."

Duncan did as bid, puckish grin not in the least diminished at her chiding. Ben stood a couple paces back, his smile more thoughtful, and a little bit sad.

"It was kind of you to let the poor foolish lad down so gently, Sam. I've a feeling he'll never quite figure out how you transferred his infatuation from you to Lydia Snow."

"You give me too much credit. It's not at all what I intended when I stormed over here, but seemed to be what was needed once I got into the middle of things."

"You did just right, Sam. Thanks," said Ben quietly, a twinkle finally sparking in his eyes. "You've made my parental duties a whole lot easier, and those as teacher a heck of a lot harder. Now I'll have two budding lovebirds on my hands, more interested in each other than their school work."

"Which I've no doubt you'll handle with consummate tact and skill," said Samantha, tongue-in-cheek. "As much as I'm enjoying this little tête-à-tête with you boys, I'd best be heading home. My first column for Jasper is due tomorrow, and it won't write itself."

Ben wasn't willing to let her escape so soon. "I'll be heading out Saturday to hunt up a couple of Christmas trees, one for the school and one for here at home. If your folks'd like me to cut one for them, too, I'd be happy to."

"I'm sure they will, since Mama can't participate as usual. Thanks, Ben. Can I come, too? I haven't been along on the hunt for the perfect tree in ages."

Ben had hoped for just such a request, counted on it. An afternoon alone with Sam, far from home, on a carefree mission in the great outdoors, was about as close to heaven as Ben expected to get any time in the near future.

"Great idea. The three of us'll have a grand time," exclaimed Duncan. "I'll even rent the wagon box sleigh from the livery to haul them home in."

Ben thought he saw a flicker of disappointment on

Sam's face to mirror the one in his sinking heart. Without knowing for sure, he didn't dare try to dissuade Duncan. Ben was doing his damnedest to keep things between him and his brother on an even keel. He'd managed to do that so far by staying strictly out of his way, avoiding one-on-one confrontations. Looked like that distancing would end Saturday, hopefully without any major blow-ups between them. Though he'd be danged if he'd let any man, Duncan included, come between him and the progress he'd made so far with Sam. If Duncan'd come back to stake his claim next door, he was going to have one helluva fight on his hands, figuratively and physically if need be.

They all agreed on a time for Saturday's expedition. Samantha hurried home, disappointment keen, not quite certain why, knowing only that it'd begun as soon as Duncan invited himself to join her and Ben on Saturday. Not daring to face the reason for her jumbled emotions, she entered the kitchen where dinner preparations were well under way, Mama reigning supreme over her domain from the rocker.

"It's about time you came home," she chided the moment Samantha stepped into the room. "There's so much to do, and you're never at home, though you left Chicago early for the express purpose of helping me with wedding preparations."

Samantha refused to be baited into a sharp retort.

"What is there to do? Where would you like me to begin, Mama?" She stood contritely in front of her mother's chair, planting a kiss on her mother's still-smooth cheek. "Thank you, Mama, for the new dress. It's exquisite. And such a lovely surprise."

Somewhat mollified, her mother harrumphed. "Consider it your Christmas present, young lady. And you may help me out by writing while I dictate. A menu must be decided upon, a seating arrangement, last-minute invitations for persons inadvertently omitted in the first mailing."

"That might take all evening, Mama," Samantha protested. "I have to write my article for Jasper."

"The morning is soon enough for that, Samantha. It is time you learned priorities. Family, in all instances, comes first."

At the older woman's growing agitation, Samantha relented, patting her mother's good hand gripping the arm of the rocking chair.

"You're right, Mama. Let me get paper and pencil, and we'll get to it at once."

Before and after dinner until bedtime, Samantha wrote to her mother's dictation. Knowing she'd never sleep with her assignment for the *Weekly Review* unwritten, she burned the midnight oil in her room, bundled in quilts and wearing her gloves to ward off the chill. She watched dawn come and go through her bedroom window, refusing to give in to sleep until her task was completed.

Eliza found her at her desk at noon, asleep on crossed arms.

"Didn't you go to bed at all?" she asked when her cousin stirred slightly.

Samantha turned her head on her arms, too tired to raise it. "No, but the article's finished. Read it through for me, will you, before I deliver it to Jasper. I've grown so foggy-minded, I no longer can determine if it has any merit at all."

She passed a thin stack of papers to her cousin, who perched on the bed to read them. She looked up when finished, her plain features pretty with pleasure.

"This is wonderful, Samantha. How I do envy you your talent for making the person reading your words feel so uplifted for having done so. They took me back to when we were children, how magical Christmas seemed then. I could smell the ham baking, taste Grannie's gingerbread men, hear sleigh bells and carols. Feel that delicious anticipation, like no other, while awaiting our gifts Christmas morning. Reading this left me covered in goose bumps of delight."

Though her spirits soared at Eliza's lavish praise, Samantha started to yawn and could not stop.

"Then I'd better freshen up," she said and yawned again. "See what I can do about the bird's nest tangles in my hair." She yawned. "And get this to Jasper." Yawn. "It's twelve-thirty already, and I promised delivery by noon."

She stood, wavering exhausted on her feet. Eliza scrambled off the bed to rush to take her arm.

"You'll do no such thing. You're going straight to bed for a few hours' sleep. I—I'll deliver your article to Mr. Cooper, with your apologies."

She put Samantha to bed, fussing over her briefly. When she left, article in trembling hand, Samantha was already asleep.

Just before dinner, Samantha awoke rested and wandered down to the kitchen, tempted by the aromas of beef stew and baking powder biscuits. Expecting to find the kitchen full of busy womenfolk, she found Grannie cheerfully laboring alone. A prick of fear shivered up her spine.

"Did Eliza get my article to Jasper in time?"

"I imagine so," Grannie responded without turning, "if that's what she set out to do. Haven't seen her. Could be she's running other errands. Or maybe she's in the parlor with Corrie, going over wedding plans. Oh, here she comes."

Eliza entered through the back door on a blustery breeze, red-cheeked, sparkling-eyed, and apologetic.

"I'm so sorry to be late. I hope you weren't worried about me. Jasper and I . . . that is, Mr. Cooper and I, we got to talking about plants. He generously showed me all through his marvelous conservatory, and the next thing I knew, it was late. Here, Grannie, let me at least set the table for you."

Still in her outerwear, she took the stack of plates from Grannie's hands, as flustered and fluttery as a bird learning to fly. Samantha grabbed the dishes from Eliza, suddenly fearful she'd drop them.

"Let me. After all, you did me a tremendous favor. Did Jasper like the article?"

Unwinding her muffler, Eliza nodded. "He sang its praises as sweetly as I did earlier. You'll see it in print Saturday," adding for Grannie's benefit, "with your famous mince pie recipe for all to envy and attempt to emulate."

Grannie made an undignified sound, but her expression proved she was clearly pleased and proud.

"Let that old man of mine find something lacking in my pie recipe once it's all printed up in black and white."

She chortled loudly, and the young women chimed in. Only later did it occur to Samantha to wonder about that special light she'd seen glowing on her cousin's happy face, recalling a time when the mention of Charlie's name put that look upon it. Certainly not Jasper Cooper's! Denying that what she was thinking might hold a grain of truth, Samantha promptly thrust the thought from her mind.

Saturday morning, the *River Valley Weekly Review* passed quickly from hand to hand for a reading of Samantha Sarahannah Spencer's column, Seasons and Seasonings, with nothing but lavish praise for the contents, even from Mama. Never tired of seeing her words set in type, Samantha read the article through and found it surprisingly good, considering her state of exhaustion when she wrote it. She almost regretted inviting herself along on Ben's tree hunting excursion, so many ideas for subsequent articles filled her head.

Once bundled into a lap robe between Ben and Duncan, with hot, flannel-wrapped bricks under her feet, Samantha forgot everything but the pleasures of the afternoon. A brilliant blue sky interspersed with cottony clouds and a sparkling white blanket of snow intensified all the other subtle shades of winter—stark black branches on tree and bush, forest green pines, dried grasses of ivory and russet and gold. Duncan told one tall tale after another of his prospecting attempts in Colorado, claiming as truth that a day as mild as today would be taken for midsummer high in the Rockies. He said nothing of his wife, nor the coming blessed event, nor his commitment to the ministry, in fact seemed to avoid those subjects altogether. Samantha suspected he had not spoken of them to Ben as yet, so she avoided any mention herself, not wanting to spoil the peaceful pleasures of the afternoon.

Also left undiscussed was her article in this morning's paper. No number of veiled hints broke the silence, forcing her to come right out and ask.

"Have either of you read today's *Weekly Review?*"

Unabashed deviltry flashed in Duncan's eyes. "I took a few minutes to skim a write-up by some new contributor. Something about Christmas. Not half-bad."

Knowing full well that to rise to his bait would only lead to more teasing, Samantha satisfied herself by punching his arm, hard, then waited for Ben's remarks about the article, usually astute and often helpful.

"Skimmed the paper, my ass," he muttered under his breath. "Hogged the *Review* right up until time to go is more like it."

"Patience, brother," chortled Duncan. "This evening you can read and digest the paper to your methodical heart's content, with no interruptions and sharing with no one."

"Definitely no sharing and no interruptions, brother," Ben echoed on a threatening note, without rancor, grinning onesidedly.

Good humor restored, Ben slapped the reins lightly, offering a gentle 'giddap,' the subject shelved for the time. Samantha found herself looking forward with anticipation to his analytical review of her work, later, in private.

They rode beyond farmland, deep into open country to a county forest frequented by surrounding towns for an annual harvest of Christmas pines. In the woods, where the winter sun did not often reach, the snow mounded knee deep in spots. Ben and Duncan made a sling of their crossed hands for Samantha to sit upon and carried her with all the pomp of a queen on her throne. In imitation of the reigning Victoria, Samantha directed her knights this way and that, in search of the perfect tree, until they threatened to dump her in the closest snowbank.

"Ah, but we have arrived, knaves. You may set me upon my feet. There stands the perfect tree for Mama's parlor."

It grew alone in a small clearing, seven feet or more in height, symmetrical on all sides. Not far away, Ben claimed two more for his home and the school. Stumps, some with fresh sawdust ringing them, gave evidence of others who had recently come.

In her mind's eye Samantha saw all the parlors in River

Valley adorned with brightly decorated trees and bough-draped mantels, thanks to the seemingly endless bounties of nature. Eager to capture her thoughts for a possible future column, she perched on the tallest of the stumps, pulled off her gloves to locate pencil and paper in her pockets, and scribbled a few notes to that effect.

A snowball landed with a wet plop in the center of her page. With a mewl of dismay, Samantha glared up to see a grinning Duncan prepared to fling another. Brushing frantically at the spreading dampness, she warned, "Don't you dare, you . . . you . . . There's no name bad enough for someone who would attempt to destroy another's creative efforts, Duncan Morgan."

Duncan's grin faded. Before he caught on to her ploy, Samantha slipped her notebook into her pocket, scooped up a ball of snow, and struck him squarely on the chin, and the battle was on with ringing challenges and rising mirth.

Ben stood apart, dwelling on his own snowball fight with Sam, and its unexpected conclusion—their first kiss. Ax over his shoulder, he flexed his hands around its hickory handle when he would've rather been throttling Duncan. Shaken by the intensity of that image, Ben vented jealousy on the first of the selected trees. Iron blade slicing deep into soft northern pine sent vibrations from his locked wrists up his arms to his shoulders and down his spine, releasing physical tension, though in no way easing the turmoil thundering inside his head. One refrain echoing again and again. *Duncan and Sam. Duncan and Sam. Duncan and Sam.* Always it had been Duncan and Sam. Those two against the world, into mischief, sharing secrets, friends from beginning to end. Until Duncan took off. Now Duncan was back, apparently picking up where he left off in pursuit of Sam's affections. And damn him to hell, it looked like he was winning her over. What chance did he himself have against those odds? *None.* The one word rang inside his head along with the shotgun crack of the falling pine, scenting the forest with the pungency of needles and pitch.

The playful gamboling ceased at the sound. Samantha and Duncan joined Ben beside the fallen tree, breathing hard. Duncan reached for the ax.

"Let me tackle the next one, brother."

Ben reluctantly relinquished the tool. Before Duncan could move on, Samantha spoke softly.

"Look. Over there."

Following her pointing finger, they watched a trio of deer, mother and two speckled fawns, step daintily into the clearing at the far edge, cautious but calm. Warily the threesome crossed diagonally on a faint animal trail far older than their own random, crisscrossed human tracks, so lovely a sight Samantha instinctively moved closer to Ben and slipped her hands around his forearm, leaning one wind-reddened cheek against his shoulder.

Crazy, irrational hope burst within him. Dammit, what was he whining for when he ought to be giving his brother a run for the money! He wanted—loved—this woman with every fiber of his being, and all hell could freeze over before he'd cease doing battle—even against his own brother if that's what it took—to win her.

Side by side, he and Sam watched Duncan attack the next pine. Ben had to admit his brother cut a fine, manly figure; a surreptitious glance in Sam's direction to see if she noticed reassured him that he might have nothing to fear after all. Her attention had wandered to something she'd spied off in the trees, a rabbit hopping an erratic trail through new-fallen snow, soon out of sight, leaving behind only characteristic tracks—pairs of exclamation points close together—and a few bunny pellets to mark its passing.

The Sam of old would've followed in hot pursuit, most likely gotten herself lost in the process, as she had a good many times over the years. Often enough so that he and his brothers threatened to tie a rope to her—a good long rope—so she could follow it back home, to save themselves the hours it took to find her. Locate her they always did, usually sitting on a rock—waiting—knowing with indomitable spirit and perfect trust that one or the other of them, or all of them together, always would.

It seemed as if Sam had always been a part of his life and his memories, from the moment she came into the world kicking and protesting when he was three, little more than an infant himself. But he paid little attention to the annoying tag-along next door, until one sweltering August afternoon when he was forced to save her all by himself.

After a week of unrelenting high temperatures and humidity thick enough to swim in, Ben longed for nothing more than the shade of his favorite tree and a good adventure tale to read. He'd no sooner sat down Indian-fashion with book spread open on his knee, when leaves and then twigs began raining down on him as if an early fall had come. He looked up and saw the five-year-old sitting high up in the old red maple, legs dangling, grinning ear to ear, and about ready to toss another load of twigs.

"You cut that out!"

She made a face, eyes crossed, tongue extended.

"What if I don' wanna?"

"And get down from there before you fall."

"No!" she shouted back, stubborn chin out-jutting.

"Come down."

"Can't. I'm stuck."

She pointed at the ground and he saw the rotted limb that had given way under her slight weight, leaving an open expanse on the gnarled trunk she was too small to breach.

Young Ben sighed heavily with an exaggerated lift of his narrow shoulders, and reached for a branch overhead.

"I'm comin' to get you."

Swinging her legs, she offered, "Better not. Better get Andy or Charlie. You don't know nothin' 'bout climbin' trees."

Which unfortunately was true. But Andy had run to the bakery for bread for Ma, and Charlie and Duncan were off building a fort in some secret spot they didn't want him to know about. If he waited for one of them to return, or his pa or hers to come home from work, it might be too late.

"I'm comin' up."

She shrugged, swinging her legs all the more vigorously.

"Well, okay. But hurry up, will ya, I gotta go, real bad."

"I'm comin', I'm comin'."

He reached her faster than he expected to, considering his heart was hammering so hard in his ears he could hardly hear her complaints over his slowness, her urging him on with suggestions where to find foot- and hand-holds. He sweated with more than the heat, a cold kind of overall wetness that left him shivering. He discovered, miserably, that he was afraid of high places, but continued doggedly on, convinced that only he could save Sam. And save her he did, sort of. She jumped with confidence into his awaiting arms from her perch, and he managed to keep his balance. He inched his way groundward branch by branch, leading the way, each time making her come to him before continuing on. He kept from looking down until the very end; and when he did, his stomach rolled over and his eyes behind his glasses went all blurry, and he knew without a shadow of doubt he couldn't take another downward step. Sam led *him* the last ten feet; and had never breathed a word from that day to this of his cowardliness, in fact, sang only his praise whenever the story was retold.

Ben smiled to himself, remembering, recalling how that incident when she was five to his eight defined their odd relationship from that day onward. He saw her that day for what she was: foolhardy, curious, creative, adventuresome, bossy, brave. She was loyal to a fault to those to whom she believed she owed a debt, loyal and protective—and unconditionally loving—to family and friends alike. In her way, she loved him as she did each and every one of the Morgan boys—like a brother. Maybe differently now, Ben amended, maybe, in fact, differently then, too. As much as she made fun of him and his role on the sidelines of life, he'd always been the one to be there when she needed someone—whether she knew it or not—needed *him*.

It was he who found her one day not too long after that time in the tree, squatting beside the riverbank off in the woods (she was thought to be lost again), weeping as though she'd never stop. At her feet, in an open grain sack, a litter of kittens heartlessly drowned by some farmer soon after birth. He was the one into whose arms she flung herself, who comforted her awkwardly, finally convinced her to come home. He suggested a funeral might be in order and helped her plan and carry out the grandest feline funeral known to childhood, with all the kids in the neighborhood in attendance.

Ben himself encouraged her love of books, challenged her to write one when she protested over a sad ending, even bought her her first dictionary for her ninth birth-day—so she wouldn't keep bothering him to correct her atrocious spelling, he claimed. And then ended up missing her when she no longer came to him for help. He had no one to blame but himself for fostering her love for reading and writing, though he never dreamed back then it would become her all-consuming passion.

Or her his. She grew on him, slipped into his life and into his heart until he couldn't tell where she began and he ended. And he never said a word, not even when Duncan first declared himself to her. It almost killed him, but he said nothing, only because, thank the blessed Lord, she didn't reciprocate. He watched his foolish, smitten brother beat his heart against her stubborn single-mindedness until it drove him away. And he knew just how his brother felt when Sam announced she was going off to Chicago to live and work, leaving his own heart shattered like shards of glass within him.

Now all the players in the game were back, and glory be, it looked like he might be making some headway with Sam. At long last. The big question was, how much, and would it be enough to keep her at home for good and all come January?

"T-T-Timberrrrr!"

Ben started like a sleeper suddenly awakened. At his side, Sam jumped up and down as the pine began its ever-swifter descent groundward, taking other small trees and branches and dried autumn leaves with it. The earth shuddered faintly as it landed; a shower of snow rose up and fell.

"Bravo!" Sam shouted, bare hands locked just below her chin, her cheeks ruddy, eyes brilliant. "My turn! I get to cut the third one." Over Duncan's protest, "It's only fair. I picked it out."

Ben knew, and Duncan did, too, if he'd recall, that there was absolutely no future in arguing with Sam once she set her heart on something.

How about picking me, Sam, to pin your heart's-desire on next time around? Crossing the fingers of both hands in his pockets, Ben conjured up a wish and a prayer that it be so.

TWELVE

Singing carols all the way to the schoolhouse, Duncan and Ben complaining that Sam sang more off key than Grannie Spencer and no wonder she'd been banned for life from performing with the church choir, they arrived with the afternoon on the wane. Tinges of pink and orange streaked a cloudless sky, promising a clear, if cold, day tomorrow.

"I'll bet this frigid snap has frozen Johnson's Pond already," prophecized Duncan, struggling beside Ben to stand the Christmas tree on its base of crossed boards in one corner of the classroom.

"Heard it was," Ben agreed, suspecting where Duncan was headed, determined to get the jump on him. "Sam, how about you and me going skating tomorrow after church?"

Feigning regret for his brother's sake, Duncan admitted, "I promised to visit a few old friends with Eliza and Charlie after services. You two'll have to go without me."

Setting a carton of donated decorations on Ben's desk, Samantha caught Duncan's wicked wink. For a preacher-to-be, he had a lot of the old nick in him yet. Clearly he'd arranged things to fall into place just this way.

Looking smug, Duncan excused himself, headed outside through the attached shed to the boys' privy beyond.

Almost immediately he stuck his head back into the classroom.

"Take a look at this. I think you have trespassers. Or very creative mice."

They crowded with him into the small, slant-ceilinged shed. Crammed to the rafters with supplies at the far end, the two lowest shelves had been emptied of their load, the boxes stacked in a half wall for privacy. On these make-do beds, all the emergency blankets were in use as pillows and covers. A scattering of grease-stained, brown paper wrappings littered the floor; a basket had been toppled, and with it, the contents—winter apples, a loaf of bread with a generous corner torn off, a broken jug of milk seeping into the dirt floor.

"Isn't that Mother's favorite blue willow pitcher?" Duncan asked.

Ben moved in for a closer look, kicking at apple cores, stooping to retrieve the half-eaten loaf of cinnamon raisin bread, his personal favorite.

"It is. And this is the fresh baked bread Grannie Spencer sent over only this morning."

"Henry and Molly," Samantha guessed.

Ben privately agreed. Frankie and Georgie had taken to aiding and abetting old man Miller's orphans again. He couldn't fault their tender hearts or their desperation to save brother and sister from the farmer's cruelties, only their methods. Running away could only hurt the children's chances once Jasper came up with some legal means of freeing them from their unwilling bondage. Examining the signs of obviously hasty departure, he wondered where the pair hid now, and where they'd go with their hiding place discovered. Experiencing a gut-twisting need to help, he could only stand helplessly by waiting for word from Jasper.

"So, who're Henry and Molly, and why've they been hiding out in the school?" asked Duncan, returning from his trip of necessity out back on a current of crisp, cold air.

Ben related the incident in the classroom and Jasper Cooper's educated conclusions. None of it surprised Duncan.

"In my travels, I've yet to see indentured orphans treated like members of the family."

Ben eyed him suspiciously. "Doesn't seem to me you'd have all that many opportunities from high up in the mountains in a mining camp," he observed caustically.

Time for Duncan's confessions, Samantha realized, regretting the end of the happy mood of the day. She saw by his expression that he wasn't looking forward to it either.

"I haven't exactly—"

"Hallooo! Hallooo . . . Anybody here? Door's wide op—Oh, there you are, Ben. And, er, well, well . . . Miss Spencer, isn't it, from Chicago?" His voice laced with disapproval, Mayor Chester, as round as he was tall, filled the doorway, fairly quivering with indignation as he observed the scattered food and bedding. "See here, Mr. Morgan,"—no longer "Ben"—"we cannot have this sort of thing going on in the school . . . Between our teacher and a . . . a *newspaper reporter* no less . . ." He began to sputter.

"What sort of thing?" Ben cut in, his tone cold, calm.

Mayor Chester gestured widely to take in the disarray he considered evidence of some misdeed. Duncan stepped from behind the half-opened door between shed and classroom hiding him from the mayor's view.

"Nice to see you again, Mayor."

The mayor's florid face mirrored obvious relief.

"Oh, Preacher Morgan. You're here, too. Well, then. Well, then. That's dif—I'd thought—One hears—Nonsense, apparently. Beg your pardon, Ben. Miss Spencer, Samantha. Can't be too careful of our teacher's reputation. Heh heh. Looking forward to your sermon Sunday, Preacher." Forgetting whatever he'd come for, His Honor made a hasty retreat, footsteps thudding through the classroom and beyond.

The echo of his departure dwindled to a weighty silence. Samantha shifted from foot to foot, throwing apprehensive glances between brothers. Uncertainty marred Duncan's usually cockiness, as he awaited some sign from Ben. Ben studied the packed earth under his feet, bent toward them, hands locked over hips. Turning his head sideways, he leveled Samantha with a questioning stare.

"You don't seem surprised," he told her, deceptively calm, not bothering to elaborate.

Making no excuses, Samantha shook her head, resenting being trapped in the middle between them. Ben straightened on a deep inhale, exhaled, cleared his throat, faced his brother.

"Any other little revelations, Preacher?"

Trapped, Duncan shrugged, offering a halfhearted grin. "Correction, that's preacher-in-training. Sunday's sermon is for practice, though a good one, if I say so myself." A waiting silence. "And, well, I'm married. To the sweetest girl in the world. Alice Fletcher, that is, Morgan. Alice Morgan. You're going to love her. Like a sister. She's . . . we're . . . I'm going to be a daddy six months from now. Congratulate me, Ben."

He thrust out his hand for shaking, the hopeful gesture for more than pre-parental good wishes, to include "is all forgiven?" Ben distanced himself with a backward step.

"Congratulations. Anything *else* I'm the last to know?"

He acknowledged Duncan's headshake of denial, bobbing his own in understanding. He tossed a lingering look around the shed. "Doesn't appear there's anything more to do here. I'd suggest we head on home. That rig you rented has got to be costing a month's wages for a poor preacher in the making."

He latched the back door so it couldn't be opened from without, thought better of it, and unlocked it. Let the runaways have a place out of the winter cold, should they return. Hell, leave the whole danged school wide open for anyone with a mind to winter there. On a surge of sudden anger, he stormed through the building and out, leaving the others to follow.

Duncan caught him by the shoulder before he could climb up onto the wagon seat. Ben spun. Duncan backed off, raising both hands in peace.

"You wouldn't hit a preacher, would you, Ben?"

"Don't count on it," his brother warned, tight-jawed.

"I didn't come home to fight with you, you know," Duncan admitted, "only to set things right between us."

Jaw jumping, saying nothing, Ben waited.

"Grannie Spencer suggested I help out with Eliza's wedding." Nothing. "She also suggested—very strongly—that it was time I came home to mend fences." Not a flicker in Ben's ice blue eyes. "Look, I've made peace with God and my fellow man . . . everyone but my favorite big brother." Skepticism flared through the ice. "It's true. *You're* the one I've always tried to please. Especially after our parents died. Tried and failed and tried again. Right? Can you deny it? Who'd I always come running to in a jam? Andrew? Charlie? That pair of stuffy bankers? Not likely. Who always got me out of trouble? Set me on the straight and narrow, again and again? Had the patience of Job—?"

Ben interrupted with an unkind sound. "This sermon going to be over any time soon, Preacher?"

Duncan fell silent, studied his brother's unrelenting, frozen stare. With a rueful shake of the head, he capitulated.

"I'd say the first sermon in my short ministry has fallen on deaf ears, brother. But we're taught to turn the other cheek. Try, try again. I know you, Ben. You'll go off good and mad, only to come back later having reasoned away your anger with that analytical mind of yours and ready to forgive."

Ben held to silence for several long seconds. "Don't hold your breath, Preacher. And don't count on it."

Blast, Duncan was right. A sleepless night, his mind churning, left Ben foggy-minded, but clear on one point. He was going to dissect and bisect and think yesterday's quarrel to death, and when push came to shove, he was going to resolve the issue by making peace with Duncan one more time. With the dawn, and the acid of an entire pot of thick black coffee eating away at his insides, Ben tried to figure out what he was so crazy mad about anyway. Duncan just being his same old self in a slightly different guise. Keeping secrets. Making a conspirator of Sam. Leaving Ben in the dark until he found out from someone else. So what was different?

Ben slammed his fist on the kitchen table with force enough to set his cup rattling in its saucer. "Nothing. Nothing's different." *And nothing's the same.*

Duncan had run off a boy and come back a man—a married man, father-to-be, and a minister of God. All on his own, without anyone's help, especially not his. And he'd treated him like the same wicked, clever lad who'd tried his patience, caused him towering rages at every turn. The one brother he always felt he had failed. Why else

would he've run off, except to escape Ben, who hadn't
taught his young brother the lessons he ended up learning
the hard way from strangers in a far-off mining camp?

Some great teacher he was! Ben upbraided himself,
tearing at his tangled forelock.

And now on top of everything, it looked like his two
youngest charges had gone astray, too. Frankie and Georgie's beds hadn't been slept in. Not that Ben was worried
where they were. He knew. Taking care of business because the grown-ups hadn't, wouldn't, and waited with
hands tied for the legal system to grind slowly on its ponderous gears.

Damned if he was going to wait, doing nothing, until
Jasper found some precedent in those dusty law books of
his, or received a reply to his written inquiries. Those kids
needed help. His help. Now, not a week or a month from
now.

Galvanized by his decision, he left his warm kitchen
and grabbed mackinaw, cap, and gloves from their pegs
by the back door. As an excuse for his impromptu visit,
he gathered up Frankie's outgrown winter coat, thinking—
he wasn't sure what—and strode off in the direction of
Miller's farm. Buttoning his coat with impatient fingers,
he figured they'd do better service wrapped around old
man Miller, to shake some common sense into the man.

A bitter wind struck him full in the face, a north wind
promising snow tonight at the latest, maybe as early as
noonday. Ben welcomed the frigid blast to cool his temper,
forcing cold clarity where hotheaded delusion had
reigned. The thought of him throttling the burly farmer—a
full head taller than him and a hundred pounds heavier—
into listening to him, was laughable at best. Reason was
his ally, always had been, always would be. If he couldn't

make Miller understand the error of his ways, he wasn't the fair-minded man brother Duncan claimed him to be.

He reached the farmer's back field by cutting diagonally across the schoolyard, finding the worn trail doubtlessly made by his young brothers and the Baxter children during their frequent elicit meetings. He had it all worked out in his head what he intended to say. First, offer the coat. Then ease into conversation about Henry and Molly in general, finally getting specific regarding to their care and education, hopefully using the training of his chosen profession to bring the man around.

His heart sank into his boots when he saw the place. The Miller farm's most obvious crop turned out to be pigs, and they seemed to pretty much have the run of the acreage, including what passed for a yard around Miller's house, nothing more than a crude, drafty shack. Stumps littered the churned-up muck where a dozen big porkers rooted, giving testament that this had likely once been some logging firm's poor, sandy cut-over land. Not far from where Ben stood observing, the farmer himself labored over restocking his woodpile, the sound of his ringing ax covering Ben's approach. All too soon he spied him. Ben thanked his lucky star as Miller set the ax aside, at the same time knowing with all too clear certainty that, by the glowering rage on the farmer's face, coming here had been a big mistake, maybe the biggest in his life.

A short half-hour after his arrival, he skirted the schoolyard clearing, stumbling from tree to tree for secrecy and support, hurting in so many places he didn't dare-stop to take inventory, for fear he'd fall face forward unconscious into the snow. God, he hurt! Everywhere. There wasn't a square inch anywhere on his body, save his leather-clad feet, that'd been spared by hammy fists and well-placed kicks from boat-sized boots.

Not given the opportunity to use outstanding reason on the man, Ben fortified himself dangling inches off the ground, gasping beneath his shirt collar, twisted into a knot against his windpipe. Miller thrust his ugly, unshaven face into Ben's, demanding on fetid breath, "Where's them kids?"

Ben couldn't've answered if he wanted to. Spots danced before his eyes. He figured his last thought was going to be that this was the stupidest trouble he'd ever walked into. His own damned fault, for thinking he could reason with the stinking hairy beast.

"Where's m' kids, teacher? Them's got chores to do, whippin's t' face up t' fer runnin' off like they done. Ya don't tell me where they're at real soon, I'll beat on ya 'til ya wish ya had."

Ben didn't, and Farmer Miller made good his threat. Dragging himself off into the woods after Miller was through with him, Ben's convictions held despite his hurting. Those kids had to be kept out of old man Miller's beefy grasp at all costs, including another one-sided battle in his frozen, rutted farm yard, if need be.

Staying out of sight of the few individuals out and about during Sunday morning services, Ben made it home. Barely. Collapsing in the parlor in his favorite easy chair before a thawing hot stove, he slipped into an oblivion where his hurts couldn't find him.

Ben wasn't in church to hear his brother preach, and though she suspected he was simply being his stubborn self, there was no one around for Samantha to question afterwards. Duncan left with Charlie and Eliza, Edward with Lydia Snow and her family, and the two youngest Morgans she could not recall having seen at all.

She expected Ben to appear at her door soon after Sun-

day supper at one to go skating, but he did not. Helping
with dishes afterwards, she spent more time staring out
the window toward his house than drying, until Grannie
commented on her unusual slowness.

"Not like you to linger over your least favorite task,
Samantha. Dreaming up another column for the paper?"

Grannie had been pleased as punch with the write-up
including her mincemeat pie recipe, and had become
Samantha's staunchest supporter, even against her daughter-in-law. Cordelia wasn't pleased with Samantha's announcement at dinner that she'd be spending the afternoon
skating on Johnson's Pond instead of addressing enve-
lopes.

"Let the poor girl have a few hours' fun, Corrie. She
can help you out once it's too dark for skating. The wedding's weeks off yet."

"Less than four, Maddie, less than four." Desperation
laced her mother's voice. "Oh, very well, Samantha," she
relented, "but please return no later than five. There's still
so much to do."

Dishes finished without Ben putting in an appearance,
Samantha concluded he wasn't coming at all. Probably
because of yesterday. Contrary to Duncan's prediction that
Ben's anger would give way to reason, he was apparently
holding on to his grudge against both Duncan and herself,
she decided. Not that she intended to permit him that luxury. With a blizzard pending, she might not get another
chance to skate, alone with Ben, before she returned to
Chicago. Good temper or bad, he was going to take her
on this outing. Bundled for the weather, catching up her
ice skates, Samantha headed for his house.

Silence hung so heavy at first she thought nobody was
at home. Unable to believe good ol' punctual, dependable
Ben Morgan could've forgotten their assignation, Saman-

tha passed through the tidy, austere kitchen into the short, shallow hall off which fanned all the rooms on the ground floor. The Morgans' house, a reverse floor plan of the Spencers', kitchen and dining room on one side, front and back parlors on the other, so familiar she could've traveled it blindfolded, reminded Samantha of all the good times experienced within these walls before the parents' untimely deaths. Not a stick of furniture had been replaced or removed from the exact spot Hattie Morgan had last set it in. Nothing new had been added, but all Hattie's personal touches—seasonally fresh or waxed flowers in a vase, porcelain figurines, the familiar, honored cut glass fruit bowl on the dining room table—had disappeared from sight. Samantha's palms itched to explore possible hiding places, kitchen cupboards and dining room sideboard, to set Hattie's trinkets out once again. To bring back something of the personality of the woman who had once lived, and loved, and raised her brood in this house. Make it a home again for those left behind. For Ben. Not on a personal level, of course, but because the kind-hearted, hard-workingman deserved so much more than Fate had dealt him.

A small sound nearby in the seemingly empty house sent shivers of apprehension up and down Samantha's spine. Prepared for flight, she listened harder, all senses alert. Tales were told of transients finding no one at home from whom to beg a handout, seeking what they could in an unoccupied house, bludgeoning the unwary who returned too soon. A year in Chicago had made her unnaturally suspicious. The slight sound came again. A pained groan, from the back parlor. Fearful but determined, Samantha caught up from the stand beside the front door an umbrella with a strong curved handle and pointed tip.

Wielding it over her shoulder like a baseball bat, she cautiously advanced on the room.

In the dim light of the glowing potbellied stove, a man slumbered stretched out in Ben's favorite chair, a man with the profile of Ben Morgan himself. With half a mind to give him one good whack with her weapon for neglecting her in favor of an afternoon nap; she advanced on tiptoe, circling to face the culprit as he slept. At the sight of him close up, Samantha dropped the umbrella in horror and fell to her knees at his feet.

His poor, once-handsome face sported two black eyes, a split lip, and swollen jaw. His clothes were torn, filthy, and smelled of barnyard offal, and his knuckles battered as if he'd given as good as he got. He reclined with both arms wrapped around his middle, protecting ribs she suspected might be badly bruised, possibly broken. The slightest movement elicited pained groans from swollen, bloodied lips, and he tossed his head back and forth against the back of his chair in sleep that looked suspiciously more like a state of unconsciousness. Fearing the worse, Samantha gingerly sought an uninjured spot on his upper arm and patted it, calling his name, first softly, then louder, panicked. He responded at last by forcing open one swollen eye, then both in growing comprehension.

"Samantha, what—?" he croaked, and winced.

"Shuush. You're hurt. Someone has beaten you, badly."

"Miller."

She rocked back on her heels, understanding, knowing the size and temperament of the brutish farmer from infrequent sightings in town.

"You confronted that man all alone? Oh, Ben, no wonder you look like death warmed over. Of all the stupid—"

"Don't . . . scold. I . . . hurt."

"I can see for myself why." She kept her tone tart for

fear of breaking into tears. Blinking hard, she scrambled to her feet. "You need a doctor."

"No!"

He struggled to sit up, grunted, fell helplessly back, clutching the shirt covering his ribs.

"All right, all right, then. Lie still. I'll go fetch Grannie. Ben, please, I have to. *I* don't know how to help you." Tearful and frightened, she wailed.

"Just . . . her. No . . . no one—"

"Just Grannie. I promise. Lie still. Don't you dare move 'til I get back."

His eyes closed, his face went slack.

"Ben?"

"Hurry!"

THIRTEEN

"Nothing broken," Grannie declared.

Ben attempted a sigh of relief and cut it off short as pain stabbed through his midsection.

"Hurts like a—"

"And going to for some time. A lot of bruising there. Danged fool thing to do, getting into a fight with Cyrus Miller. Never knew a meaner bully, young man and old. Samantha, lend a hand. Here, hold the end so I can wrap him up good and tight."

While Grannie scolded, she stripped off the tattered remains of Ben's shirt, leaving him bare to the waist. Samantha stifled a gasp of sympathy for the massive bruises covering much of the exposed area, then fell to studying in fascination the characteristic bulges and ripples of the male anatomy she'd never before seen. Purely scientific curiosity, she told herself, well aware that she lied. Something had changed deep inside her on discovering Ben so badly injured; her pain had felt as real as his, her fear for him monumental. She flew home for Grannie thinking, *If anything happens to him . . . ,* unable to finish the thought, suspecting that should she lose Ben, she would lose the most important part of herself as well.

Grannie busied herself with a roll of bandages she'd brought from home. Finding an end, she wrapped the cot-

ton once around Ben's waist, cautioning Samantha to hold
the beginning there, just so, while she wrapped round and
round upward.

Samantha couldn't take her eyes from the process,
Grannie's gnarled yet nimble fingers unrolling and wrapping, Ben's taut stomach disappearing inch by inch. He
arched his arms outward, elbows cocked as Grannie
reached the lean hardness of his upper chest. The defini-
tion of his arms detoured Samantha's attention, muscle
and bone and sinew sculpted into limbs of beauty and
strength, ending in wide, capable hands with long, blunt-
tipped fingers.

". . . Let go now, Samantha. Samantha, I'm all done."
Grannie's jolly tone mirrored her amused grin.

Samantha's cheeks flamed hot, as if it burned, she drew
back her hands from touching Ben's hot flesh. Still grinning, Grannie lifted herself off the straight-backed chair
she'd drawn up next to Ben's easy chair.

"I think we can all use a cup of tea about now. I'll
rummage around in Ben's kitchen for the makings. You
can tidy up here a bit." She thrust the remnant of Ben's
shirt into Samantha's hands.

Clutching the garment to her heart in one fisted hand,
Samantha put Grannie's vacated chair between herself and
Ben, free hand gripping the chair's back. Now that the
worst of it was over, her legs began to quiver until the
unmanageable trembling coursed the length of her body.
Attempting to hide her reaction from Ben, she let her gaze
follow Grannie's departure. As trim and straight-spined as
when young, from the back, the tiny woman's age betrayed
her only by the silver in her hair. Always candid, ever
capable, was Grannie, making it all the harder to believe
that as a girl she'd been pampered and indulged to the
point of spoiling. Her journey westward and subsequent

marriage to a craggy mountain man had taught her many lessons she'd willingly passed down to children, then grandchildren. Samantha had been blessed, or cursed, with Grannie's stubbornness, her independent streak, her conviction that she was always right, that she must correct every wrong. Grannie disappeared from view, and everything Samantha'd felt since discovering Ben injured and barely conscious rushed back in a flood. Hot, angry tears flowing freely, she turned on the cause of them.

"Ben Morgan, how could you scare me like that? You're so hurt, I thought . . . I thought. . . ."

Ben gingerly spread his arms wide. "Come here."

Hitching a sigh, she longed to throw herself at him, instead Samantha cautiously slipped onto his lap and lowered her head to his shoulder.

He wound comforting arms around her, feeling better than he could ever recall in his entire life, hurts and all. Each curve and hollow the length of her long, slender body fit every corresponding one of his to perfection, just as he'd always imagined. He ran both palms up and down her back along her spine, feeling her tremors slowly cease. The warmth of her flesh through all the layers of her clothing heated his skin as no fire made from wood or coal could have. The dampness on his bare shoulder under her cheek told him she shed tears for him. For him. Because she cared. Maybe even loved him a little. At last. At long last. Ben relaxed against the chair's padded back, the most contented man on God's great earth.

Samantha sat suddenly upright, doubled her fist, and slammed it into his forearm, careful to choose a spot with the least bruising.

"Ow! What'd you do that for?"

"What *were* you thinking, taking off all on your own to challenge a brute twice your size to a battle of fists?"

she demanded, knuckles to hips, balancing her round bottom on his hard thighs, precariously high up.

Fighting his mightiest to concentrate on words instead of physical sensations; Ben admitted his folly.

"I was stupid enough to imagine I could reason with the man. Took along Frankie's outgrown coat for Henry as a peace offering. He ground it into the manure of his pig wallow with his heel. The oaf had no interest in reason. He wanted *his* kids back and figured I knew where they were."

"And you wouldn't tell him," Samantha commented, knowing Ben's strong sense of right and wrong would never permit otherwise.

Ben shook his head and winced.

"Head hurt?" Samantha asked, all sympathetic. "I could get you something for the pain."

His strong fingers circled her wrist. "Don't go."

Samantha settled back into his arms.

"Every inch of my body hurts," Ben admitted, "but your being here, like this, is better than any medicine."

He caressed her soft cheek with a cupped palm. She turned her face, feathering his hand with her gentle kisses. He slid his fingers down to her chin and directed her lips to his.

The rough pad of his thumb brushing over the velvet of her skin, Ben thought there was likely to be no more perfect time to tell her he loved her than now.

They parted for breath. With a hitch in his, Ben said, "Samantha, I—"

"Children, refreshments."

The gentle clatter of china against china preceded Grannie down the hall from the kitchen. Samantha quickly slid off Ben's lap onto the straight chair as Grannie appeared in the doorway with a wicked, knowing glint in her eyes, but a serene smile on her lips. Balancing a tray of cups and a plate piled high with buttered bread, she crossed to the library table in the center of the room and slid her burden onto its unadorned, polished surface. She faced the guilty pair, pretending not to notice their obvious discomfort.

"Not a leaf of tea in the house, so I made coffee. I looked for that loaf of bread I gave you yesterday, but couldn't find it, so I used some fit only for toasting."

Before Ben thought up an excuse for the missing bread, Duncan stepped into the hall from outside, slapping snow from his overcoat, and on his heels, Frankie and Georgie, looking more like snow children than human.

"Snow's really coming down. Found these two halfway home and—Glory be, Ben, what happened to you?"

Three brothers with ruddy cheeks, side by side like stair steps, took in Ben's injuries with identical gape-mouthed stares. The whole story came out, including Cyrus Miller's visit to the school that first time, for Grannie Spencer's sake. Near the end of his tale, Ben leveled the two youngest with his sternest look.

"Found evidence in the shed behind the school that those Baxter kids have been hiding there. Trouble with that is ol' man Miller's going to figure out soon enough that it's a likely place for those two runaways to hole up. They'd've been better off sticking it out on the farm 'til Jasper Cooper discovers a legal way out for them."

Coming to sit cross-legged on the floor, as close to his injured brother as possible, Georgie spoke up.

"Ol' man Miller hurt Molly. Made her cry real hard. She's only five. Just a baby. He oughtn't hit her. Henry says he can take the beatings, but no one's going to hurt his sister. It was *his* idea to run away. Frankie and me thought of hiding out at the school. We fed them, too."

"Bread and apples and milk, I know. Where did you plan to hide them come Monday?" Ben's tone was more tired than challenging.

Georgie looked expectantly toward Frankie, who stood at Ben's chair on the opposite side. Frankie shifted from one foot to the other, a sullen expression on his twelve-year-old face.

"Could've thought of some place."

Ben quizzed him with a probing stare.

"Where are they now? Back at the school? When did you plan on coming up with another hiding place? And moving them there?"

With an obstinate jut of his chin, Frankie declined to answer.

"We was . . . were coming to tell you, Ben, so's you could help us figure it out," Georgie admitted.

Ben carefully eased himself forward out of the deep comfort of his chair.

"That's the best idea you two've had since this whole mess began. Under the circumstances, we'll keep them here temporarily."

"No!" Samantha all but shouted her dismay. More calmly, she insisted, "You will do no such thing, Ben Morgan. The first place that brute will look for the children is at the school, the second, the teacher's house. They'll stay with me . . . with us, won't they, Grannie?"

"You're to stay clear of this, Sam," Ben warned.

"I agree," Duncan spoke up. "We can't have that madman knocking at your door."

"Why would he?" Samantha demanded of the brothers, united for the first time against her. "Why would it even occur to him to find them at my house?"

"Samantha's right," said Grannie. "Those youngsters belong with us, where they'll be safe and sound out of harm's way. Time's awasting. Sooner you go get them, the sooner we can protect them."

Ben struggled to his feet.

Samantha caught his arm when he swayed her way. "Where do you think you're going?"

"To the school. Sam, they know me, maybe even trust me enough not to run away."

"They know us," Frankie said.

"We gotta go, too," Georgie chimed in.

"You'll need Preston's sleigh," advised Grannie. "The storm that's been threatening all day kicked up into a real blizzard over an hour ago. Snow's already knee deep, and you can't see your hand in front of your face."

"I'll hitch up and drive," Duncan volunteered.

Everyone but Ben headed for the door.

"Whoa. Three adults and two kids, plus two more, out in this weather? Frankie and I can handle things without putting any of the rest of you in jeopardy."

"I'm going," Samantha insisted over Ben's protests. "The little girl might be less frightened with another female around, and I can handle the sleigh if necessary."

Grim resignation settled onto Ben's battered face. He was hurting too much to put the effort into convincing Sam otherwise. His head felt like it had grown two sizes, and waves of blackness tended to come and go unexpectedly.

"You pass out on the road, brother, who's going to take your place at the reins? No offense, Samantha, but this rig requires a man's strength."

Samantha gave in to his logic, fearing for the Baxter children's safety should they continue to stand around disagreeing. She helped Duncan throw the protective oilskin tarp off Preston Spencer's two-seated sleigh, then hitch up the mare and her mate. Night had fallen dark as coal, and the temperature had dropped dangerously low as the storm built in velocity. A trip of only minutes in good weather took what seemed like hours. Visibility at zero, Duncan kept the team's pace to a slow walk; Ben and Frankie held lanterns aloft overhanging each side, searching for a road now only a memory.

At last, with everyone chilled to the bone and longing for the warmth of home and hearth, a faint glow of light pierced the distance off to the right. The schoolhouse at last, every window blazing with welcoming illumination, a billowing plume from the smokestack promising blessed heat.

They approached cautiously, the team's hooves making only a muted *thump-thump* on the newly fallen blanket of white, sleigh runners whispering a quiet *swish*. Ben pulled up close to the front steps.

"You take the back," he suggested to Duncan.

His brother nodded in understanding.

"You two stay here," Ben ordered Samantha and Frankie.

Samantha promised nothing, Frankie nodded in tenuous compliance. Hoping he could count on them, Ben climbed down out of the sleigh like an old man, taking shallow breaths, protecting his bandaged ribs with an arm held tight across them. Duncan waved a ready sign from a corner at the rear; Ben gingerly returned the gesture.

They burst into the classroom at the same time, capturing the children before they could bolt. Duncan caught Henry sprinting for the back door, lifting him clean off his feet with an arm around the waist. Ben didn't have to lay a finger on the little girl; she darted under a desk and cowered there like a cornered rabbit, scared half to death. With an effort, Ben squatted beside her.

"Come on out, I'm not going to hurt you."

"Don't listen to 'em!" her brother shouted, flailing help-lessly beneath Duncan's grasp. "Run, Molly! Run!"

She obeyed without question, and ran directly into Samantha standing just inside the schoolroom door. Making no further attempt at escape, the child buried herself in Samantha's skirt, clinging to the fabric by fistfuls.

"Don' let 'em git me, don' let 'em git me!" Molly wailed.

Instinctively, Samantha wrapped her arms around the child's bony shoulders to still the poor baby's trembling and shaking from head to toe.

"Shush, now. Ben won't hurt you . . . either of you."

"Heck no!" declared Frankie, pushing past her into the room. "We come to rescue you an' take you home to Sam's house. Golly, gee! What've you been doing?"

The adults now saw what the boy first noticed, causing a rush of quick tears to Samantha's eyes. Henry and Molly, homeless and hopeless, had made Christmas for themselves in the austere classroom. They'd decorated the tree Ben and Duncan had hauled in yesterday, using all the donated ornaments, and many more they'd fashioned themselves from bits of colored paper and paper lace. Their efforts were both pitiful and grand, for now the tree listed precariously to one side, heavily weighed with trims as far as their arms could reach on all sides, but the back pressed into an unreachable corner. A porcelain and fabric angel for the top lay on the floor beside the chair they'd dragged over from behind Ben's desk; Henry had obviously been prepared to mount it before the interruption.

Because her brother remained hostile and silent in Duncan's custody, Molly spoke up from the protection of Samantha's skirts. Turning her sweet young face up to Samantha, ignoring the men, voice quivering, she confessed.

"Henry an' me made Christmas fer ourselfs, 'cause we figure it'll be the only one we're goin' get."

A strange sensation, totally foreign to Samantha, surged outward to encompass the waif with the dirty face and dirtier body. Judging by the smell alone, this little one mucked about in the pig yard, laboring beside her big brother. Barely out of babyhood, with a face far too thin under a tangle of filthy hair indistinguishable of color, and round eyes of changeable hazel, the little bit of an urchin slipped straight into Samantha's heart and lodged there. Prying her gaze away, she found it immediately focused on the boy, seeing similarities to her young friend Willie Klem in the mature acceptance of responsibility far too soon. Those similarities ended in Henry's steel gray eyes, where she recognized anger and defiance and scarcely concealed terror. Staring at Henry, Samantha absently patted Molly's shoulder. Finding her voice, though it came out choked and rough, she praised the childrens' handiwork.

"I've never seen a lovelier Christmas tree."

Taking her cue, Ben cleared his throat, obviously the victim of some of the same emotions as herself.

"Samantha's right, and with your permission, I'll place the angel on top to finish it off."

Taking silence for assent, Ben reached for the back of the chair, and grunted at a sudden stab of pain.

Duncan stepped up. "Allow me." He effortlessly rose on one braced foot in the center of the seat, placing the treetop trim over the crown. Everyone murmured approval, though the angel tipped precariously earthward as if about to take flight. Henry turned his attention to Ben, head tilted inquiringly, his keen gray eyes missing nothing.

"Someone beat the daylights outta ya."

Ben hesitated, unwilling to burden the boy with the truth

on top of everything else he bore on his scrawny shoulders.

"Let's just say I took a fall," he compromised.

Henry studied the battered face a moment longer, shrugged. "Yeh, sure. If that's what ya want everyone ta think." He addressed Frankie, fresh anger hot in his voice. "What'd'ya bring all of 'em here for? Thought we was friends."

Frankie stood firm. "I didn't tell 'em. Saw for themselves you'd been here when they came with the tree. My brothers and Sam're here to help."

Henry snorted disbelief. "Grown-ups idea of helpin' usually means orphanages, or trainloads of kids hauled away from the only home a fella knows an' handed out to anyone that'd take 'em. Molly and me're free've that kind'a help, an' plannin' on keepin' it that way, thanks all the same." He faced Ben, man to man. "If ya'll let us spend the night, we'll be long gone by mornin', an' leave ya a warm room when ya come ta teach besides."

Ben pretended somber consideration of the boy's proposal. "Don't mind saying, a warm classroom has a certain appeal. But Frankie'll tell you, our reason for coming out in this blizzard tonight was to offer more satisfactory shelter for you and your sister at Sam's house." He indicate Samantha with a nod. "A friend of mine is looking into a more permanent arrangement for you out of the grasp of Cyrus Miller, and has been since that man barged into my school to haul you out like a bag of grain. He won't know where you are, and soon won't be able to manhandle you again without finding himself thrown in jail. Ben crossed his fingers behind his back, hoping his words prove true.

Henry's shoulders sagged as if a burden had been lifted,

and his face mirrored abject relief for one brief moment before scrunching up in disbelief.

"How come ya puttin' yerself out fer us? How'm I supposed ta know yer tellin' the truth?"

Without hesitation, Ben replied, "For the same reason I know two runaway kids are welcome in Samantha's home." He rested a hand lightly on Henry's bony shoulders. "I know you and your sister are good folks facing hard times, and you can believe—because it's true that all of us here, and a whole lot of others beside, want nothing more than to help you make better lives for yourselves."

Henry gave Ben's words lengthy consideration, studying the faces of those around him, coming to rest on his sister's hopeful, wide-eyed countenance.

"Kin we stay with the pretty lady, Henry, kin we? Please?"

The last of his resistance crumbled. He shrugged.

"Fer a couple of days, I guess, 'til I figure what ta do next."

"How about at least through Christmas?" Samantha suggested, pulling the little girl more closely to her, little caring that her skirt might be soiled beyond repair. "You'd like to share Christmas treats and presents with us, wouldn't you?" she prompted.

"Oh, presents! Please, Henry, we gotta stay fer Christmas."

Giving in, not too reluctantly, Molly's brother agreed.

"Okay, but right after Christmas, don't plan on us hangin' around if I kin come up with something better."

FOURTEEN

Beckoning lights guided their way to the Spencers' front door; welcoming arms wrapped them in warm, woolen blankets. Appendages tingling to life so painfully as to bring smarting tears to their eyes, the travelers huddled in the back parlor around the pot-bellied stove, thawing, surrounded by family and friends grateful for their safe return. Stories of the hazards of their journey they chose to save for another time, preferably in the light of day. Preferably a hot one in the middle of August, Duncan added. Grandpa Spencer excused himself first, his seamed face slack with relief, claiming it was well past his bed-time and he knew they'd make it home unharmed anyway. Mama and Papa soon followed, leaving Grannie and Eliza to minister to the numb, weary crowd.

Surprisingly, Jasper Cooper was on hand to help, and had been there since mid-afternoon, staying on to confer with Ben and Samantha upon their retrieval of the orphans.

"A matter of some urgency, don't you know, about the, ahem," he nodded toward Henry and Molly sitting Indian fashion on the floor, side by side, as if afraid of being sepa-rated, "but can wait 'til you warm up. Ah, here's Eliza . . . Miss Upton . . . with hot cocoa all around. All around."

Samantha, sitting beside Ben on the sofa, observed with growing dismay Eliza's and Jasper's behavior in each other's presence—awkward and shy and aware only of one another. He followed her with his gaze as she went from person to person with her tray of steaming cups. When she reached him, and his hand brushed hers in the exchange of a cup, she poised motionlessly before him, their gazes locked, until Frankie protested he hadn't received his drink. She moved away with discernible reluctance, and a final glance his way over her shoulder. They reminded her, Samantha realized with a sinking heart, of the love-smitten teens, Edward and Lydia.

You're tired, and your imagination is overworked, she chided herself, blaming the stresses of the last several hours for such a wild flight of fancy. Eliza was betrothed to Charlie Morgan. *She loves him, for heaven's sake!*

When Henry and Molly had drained their cups and slumped together half-asleep, Grannie Spencer suggested it was time for baths and bed.

"Don't need no bath," Henry protested, but without vigor, his eyelids drooping.

Grannie chuckled. "In this house you do, my lad. Unless you'd rather sleep in the barn with Dolly and Dub . . ."

His objections died immediately; Grannie led them off to the kitchen, an arm encircling the narrow shoulders of each, to a brimming tub of steaming water in the pantry, where they'd take turns privately bathing. After feeble protests, Frankie and Georgie raced each other home where Edward awaited news, Frankie practicing his version of the night's events in ever-growing proportions.

"Georgie has been a big help, collecting some outgrown things of his and Frankie's for Henry, and Edward volunteered to solicit some of Lydia Snow's for Molly," Eliza explained at their departure. "Jasper . . . Mr. Cooper . . . and I, we tidied up the spare bedroom for Henry, and I made up a bed on the chaise lounge in my room for Molly."

Jasper spoke up from his chair. "Miss Upton took the matter well in hand, don't you know. Thought of everything, she did. Indeed she did."

Eliza's cheeks turned rosy at his praise, lingering in the doorway to the hall as if not certain where she belonged now that her chores were completed.

"Come, sit by me, Eliza," Duncan offered from his perch on one slipper chair, patting the seat of another close at hand. "Jasper apparently has news regarding his research into the children's plight."

Eliza slipped into the chair he offered. Jasper fumbled from pocket to pocket—jacket, vest, pants—at last coming up with a crumpled, much folded paper.

"Ahhh!" he breathed a sigh of relief, working the wrinkles out over his knees with his palms, and addressed the others. "My typesetter, Gus, came up with what I think might prove to be the solution to our troubles and theirs. I had thought to run an advertisement in next week's *Review*, seeking to learn if an Orphan Train had passed through town, don't you know, and he recalled setting this for the Children's Relocation Society sometime last fall. Took the majority of the weekend to locate it in our files . . . they're a bit, ahem, disorganized." Jasper read the entire flier aloud.

ASYLUM CHILDREN!
A Company of Children, mostly Boys, from the
New York Juvenile Asylum, will arrive in
RIVER VALLEY, at the Harmond Hotel
Saturday Morning, Sept. 8, 1888
and remain until Evening.
They are from 5 to 15 Years of age.

Homes are wanted for these children with farmers where they will receive kind treatment and enjoy fair advantages. They may be taken at first upon trial for four weeks, and afterwards, if all parties are satisfied, under indentures—girls until 18, and boys until 21 years of age. They are desirable children and worthy of good homes.

The indenture provides for four months' schooling each year, until the child has advanced through compound interest, and at the expiration of the term of apprenticeship, two new suits of clothes, and the payment to the girls of fifty, and to the boys of one hundred and fifty dollars.

All expenses for transportation will be assumed by the Asylum, and the children will be placed on trial and indentured free of charge. Those who desire to take children on trial are requested to meet them at the hotel at the time above specified. T. Fairweather, Agent.

He searched for understanding on the expectant faces of his audience. "It is my belief Henry and Molly were part of that company of children."

"I believe they were," Duncan interrupted. "I sat in the back of the sleigh with those two all the way home. We talked some, mostly to forget how cold we were. Henry admitted they have no kin, and that they were in some kind of institution in New York before being shipped here with a trainload of others like themselves . . . A few months ago, he said. Could've been September."

Excitement alive on his bland, scholarly face, Jasper slapped his paper against one thigh. "Then as such they are entitled to the benefits implied by this document," he waved it aloft briefly, "including," he read, " 'kind treatment,' 'fair advantages,' and 'good homes.' Additionally, ahem, 'They may be taken at first upon trial for four weeks.' Four weeks' trial, mind you, without indenture or adoption. And from what I've been able to gather through inquiry, there has been no follow-up on the part of this Children's Relocation Society regarding the children they've placed. Often, I'm told, they legally remain the wards of the communities in which they were born."

"Miller has no right to lay claim to Henry and Molly without some kind of legal document," Duncan discerned.

"Correct. That is correct. And in my research I was unable to find one shred of such proof."

"Which means someone else could still adopt them," Eliza's soft voice contributed on a note of wistfulness.

"That's true, my d—Miss Upton. Someone else willing to give them a home and meet the requirements stated in this flier could take them away from Cyrus Miller for good and all, don't you know."

"If a family could be found to take both of them in," Ben interjected a note of reason. I can't think of one family hereabouts in a position to take on two more mouths to feed."

"What about yourself?" Jasper suggested.

"Me? I'm single."

"You're also a teacher with a sterling reputation, they trust you, and you've helped raise your young siblings all these years. Glowing recommendations, don't you know."

Before Ben could counter Jasper's conclusions, Eliza spoke up.

"Those children need both father *and* mother, especially Molly. Unless I'm very much mistaken, she is very frightened of men."

"I agree," said Samantha, who'd held to silence until now, listening. She related how the child had hid under a desk at Ben and Duncan's approach, then ran to her for protection, shaking with fear. "I'm not surprised, given their treatment in the hands of that awful man."

"So how do we go about finding a family to take them?" asked Duncan. "I'd take them back to Colorado with me if things were different. An unemployed apprentice preacher with an expectant wife is a hard enough beginning for a new marriage without an instant family besides." He shrugged eloquently, turning to Eliza. "What about you and Charlie? The kids already like you, and my brother's not such a bad sort."

Eliza paled, then flushed, then paled again. She twined her fingers through the folds of her skirt, clutching fistfuls. Samantha recalled the intimacies of their talk when her cousin confessed she was barren, and that this bothered Charlie not at all. That he preferred the exclusivity of just the two of them, especially in light of their plans to move to Colorado right after the wedding.

"I-I-I will speak of the matter with Charles when I see him next. Probably tomorrow evening, if he doesn't have to work late."

"Time is of the essence, Miss Upton," Jasper cautioned. "We shall make a much stronger case against Cyrus Miller if we have already found a more satisfactory home for them, don't you know."

"Then I-I-I shall seek him out at the bank tomorrow afternoon," she agreed tremulously, gaze downcast, visibly and acutely uneasy at her own suggestion.

Jasper rose, took a hesitant step forward, then stayed where he was, fingering the already frayed document he held.

"And I will go with you . . . to lend my arguments to yours. I can answer any questions of a legal nature your . . . fiancé might have. Legal questions . . ." His

voice dwindled absently, his gaze upon her more eloquent
than his bumbling words.

"T-T-Thank you, Mr. Cooper." She didn't look up.

"Until tomorrow, then, Miss Upton."

Eliza raised her gaze briefly. "Until tomorrow, Mr. Cooper."

"I'd best make for home," he commented to no one in
particular. "Bound to be slow going, what with the additional snow. Good night all. I'll come for you at one
o'clock tomorrow, Miss Upton. One o'clock." He caught
up overcoat, bowler, and muffler, heading for the front
door.

"Thank you, good night, Mr. Cooper." Eliza rose. "And
I'll say good night to the rest of you. I-I-I'd like to check
on the children." She followed Jasper into the hall; their
quiet conversation could be heard for several long moments more before Jasper finally departed.

"What'd you think that's all about?" Duncan asked in
a stage whisper, nodding his head toward the departing
pair, answering his own question. "Looks to me like
brother Charlie's got some competition for his bride-to-
be's affections." Ignoring Samantha's sound of dissent, he
stood, stretching his arms high and wide toward the ceiling, yawning hugely. "I'm off home to bed. Coming,
Ben?"

Ben raised his head a fraction from the soft sofa back.

"Be along shortly. I'm going to enjoy being warm and
relatively free of pain a little longer before I move a muscle."

"Ahh!" breathed Duncan knowingly, giving the pair on
the sofa a long once-over.

Too weary and too comfortable, both Samantha and Ben
let the innuendo go unchallenged.

Samantha angled toward Ben, cocking one knee onto

the seat, letting an arm drape across the back, fingers almost brushing his tousled hair, ash blond turned silver by firelight.

"Shall I ask Grannie for something for the pain before you leave?"

He turned his tired, bruised face toward her open palm, his breath warm on her hand.

"No, don't bother. She's probably gone up to bed. I'll survive." He attempted a grin, and winced when he couldn't, thanks to a split lower lip scabbed over and a jaw swollen as large as a bad case of the mumps. "Kind of like you worrying about me and fussing over me, though," he admitted.

Unnerved by his nearness, she teased lightly, "Don't get too used to it, I'll be going back—"

He faced away. "To Chicago, I know, I know." He took a deep, stabbing breath and glanced back. "Haven't changed your mind about that, have you, Sam?"

The question shook her, the answer suddenly not so certain. "I . . well, no . . . of course not."

Silence fell, heavy and long. Logs spit and crackled in the stove, setting off explosions of sparks like miniature Fourth of July fireworks behind the glass window in the door.

"You know what your next article for Jasper should be, don't you?" Ben broke the silence to ask.

"I've a few ideas related to the Orphan Trains. The treatment received by the children in their new homes. The lack of legal protection for them," she hesitated, "It's just that I . . ." She chewed on her lower lip.

He waited for her to go on. When she didn't, he studied her face, finding it troubled.

"You what, Sam?"

She dropped her hands into her lap, palms up in defeat.

"If I fail again, Henry and Molly Baxter will be the ones to suffer, as were Willie Klem and his family, thanks to my interference. They could be forced to return to Cyrus Miller. Or given to others who are no better. Possibly separated."

He clasped her upturned hand, lacing his fingers with hers, pulling it gently onto his lap to trace the life lines on her palm with an index finger, his expression thoughtful.

"You don't know that some good hasn't come from your attempts, and those of that other reporter—what was her name?—Nell Nelson. One thing you both accomplished with your efforts, is that those deplorable conditions can no longer be ignored. Maybe you need to allow more time for changes to get under way. You know how slowly the wheels of bureaucracy turn. If you write about the orphans, at the very least, you'll help Henry and Molly and the others left behind in River Valley by alerting those who took them in of the need to protect the children's interests, and their own."

Ben fired Samantha's enthusiasm anew. She pulled her hand free to jump up, restlessly pacing a few steps in each direction before him, stuffing her hands in the side pockets of her practical gray gabardine skirt.

"Maybe Jasper would let me write an article independent of my weekly column. This is far too serious, and too important, to fall under the homespun heading Seasons and Seasonings. I've already written several columns ahead for that anyway. Do you think he'd let me do it? Write another article beyond those he's agreed to?"

"Wouldn't surprise me. You'll have your chance to ask him tomorrow, anyway, when he comes courting sweet Eliza." Ben offered a lopsided grin. She bristled indignantly, as expected.

"Stuff and nonsense! He is not courting her; he knows she's engaged to be married. Eliza loves Charlie."

"Maybe she does," he agreed. "Or maybe she loves him like a brother. I wouldn't count Jasper out until the wedding vows are spoken," he conjectured, then yawned. "Now, if you don't mind giving me a hand up, I'll head on home to bed."

He stretched out one large hand, which she grasped in both of hers. Between them they eased him onto his feet, holding hands, toes touching. A good night kiss seemed the most natural thing in the world, long and lingering and oh so tender, and incredibly hard to bring to an end.

Ben was tempted almost beyond restraint to tell Sam what he'd meant to when Grannie had interrupted earlier—that he loved her, wanted her, needed her. But now was not the time. Something might compel her to respond in kind—something like friendship, or compassion for his injuries, might prompt her to say the words, only to regret them later. It'd kill him to have her retract the words, once spoken. Better to let things stay as they were, for now.

He backed off abruptly. " 'Night, Sam. No need to see me to the door, I know my way out."

"Yes, well, good night, then. Take care."

Fingertips to lips, bewildered and hurt, she watched him hobble into the hall for the coat he'd left on the rack beside the door. Something—probably the return of common sense, knowing Ben—had made him retreat from her. Ever-practical Benjamin Franklin Morgan would know a little friendly or flirtatious kissing could not possibly lead to anything more between them. Soon she'd return to Chicago, as planned, and he'd stay behind. Why did she face that prospect now with more dread than joy? Certainly not because she'd fallen hopelessly, passionately, unreasonably in love with her next-door neighbor and childhood playmate. In love with Ben Morgan? Absolutely not.

Samantha turned out the lights in her progress upstairs protesting the possibility, and continued her protests through a long, sleepless night.

Jasper arrived a full half hour early to pick up Eliza, like an overeager swain. And he brought small gifts for Henry and Molly, dropping on one knee before them in the front hall to pull from the deep pockets of his overcoat a jackknife for the boy and a pretty picture book for the little girl. For a crusty, confirmed bachelor, he had a way with, and unconcealed affection for, the two. Henry's words of thanks were stilted and unsure, Molly's a shy "me too," and they quickly ran off to examine their new treasures in private.

"That was kind of you, Jasper," Samantha told him.

His ear tips turned bright red. "I'm fond of youngsters. Always thought . . . that is I hoped . . . Well, some things are not meant to be." He looked wistfully up the stairs.

"I'll go see if Eliza is ready."

"No rush, no rush. I came early purposely to have a few words with you, don't you know. Shall we?" He gestured toward the family parlor at the end of the hall.

"I have some ideas to go over with you, too."

Jasper tossed his coat onto the seat of the hall tree. They spoke at the same moment.

"I've been thinking I'd like you to take over more responsibility at the newspaper. If you have the time, that is."

"I'd like to write some articles for your paper that aren't suited to my weekly column."

They then repeated themselves, ladies first.

"What kind of articles did you have in mind?" asked Jasper, leading the way down the hall.

"First and foremost about the Orphan Train's rather cavalier attitude toward their charges once they've found a home for them."

In the parlor, Jasper paced, hands locked behind his back, head tilted toward the floor. He spun to face her.

"An excellent idea, excellent. How soon can you have it written?"

"I can meet this week's deadline. Is this what you had in mind about my assuming more responsibility?"

He paused. "Actually, no. You see, well, I've discovered . . . rather *rediscovered,* what a challenge, what a pleasure, it is to dig around in my law books looking for the solution to difficult problems. Didn't realize how much I missed that kind of work, don't you know. And I thought, well, I hoped, that you could sort of, well, manage things . . . oh, just for a few short weeks, so's not to interfere with your return to Chicago, while I prepare a case for the children against Miller. In the event it should go that far."

"I'll do what I can," Samantha promised, tone hesitant, "if you think I'm capable of handling everything."

"There's nothing to it, nothing at all. Gus lays out the format, sets the type, runs the presses. There's a fellow comes in Friday evenings to collect the papers and deliver them. All the editor's required to do is write up the week's national news as comes to us by telegraph, and throw in whatever local news the citizens of River Valley feel necessary to share with the town—weddings and births and such. Any empty space I fill up any which way I can, like with your column. Very popular it is, by the way, if one can believe all those who stopped me on the street or dropped by today. Most wanting to contribute memories, recipes, and the like for future columns." He gave her a moment to digest that tidbit and to savor it. "I figure this Orphan Train story ought to be given front page headlines, don't you?"

"Oh yes!" A thrill went through her from toes to crown. Her first headline! Imagining how it might read, she almost missed his next words.

". . . Spoke to Mayor Chester about the situation. He wasn't very helpful. Not at all. Seems he's afraid of making enemies of those of his constituents who've taken in children from the train, especially ones the size and temperament of Cyrus Miller. Sheriff Tupper wasn't much more help, except to say he'd lock Miller up in jail for a couple of nights if Ben pressed charges for the beating he took from the man."

Indignation flared. "Ben's injuries aside, Cyrus Miller ought to be tossed into jail and the key thrown away for what he did to those two innocent children! And Mayor Chester ought to be ashamed for refusing to take a stand. He should be more concerned about what the townspeople will think of him if he turns his back on Henry and Molly in their time of need. And I shall tell him so at the first opportunity."

Jasper smiled hugely. "I would suggest you tell him that, and anything else which comes to mind, in print, for this Saturday's edition."

"You may depend on it, Jasper. On that you may depend."

FIFTEEN

"Hello! Hello? Samantha? Eliza? Aunt Cordelia? Aunty Maddie? Where is everybody? Oh, pooh! Andrew, there's no one here to appreciate our homecoming."

Olivia rolled out her lip. Her husband smiled indulgently, but his tone was firm.

"Then we'll return this evening. They're probably out Christmas shopping, as you should be, my dear."

Olivia brightened at once.

"Oh, yes, let's do go shopping."

Andrew spoke as to a willful child.

"I have to get to the bank. I've been neglecting my duties these last few days, enjoying the company of my lovely bride. My responsibilities won't wait forever, you know."

Ever volatile, Olivia frowned. "Very well, if you must. But don't stay away a moment longer than necessary."

He bent and kissed her offered cheek. From the top of the stairs, Samantha marveled at Olivia's unwonted docile demeanor and Andrew's newfound air of authority.

The sound of voices had brought her out of her room, where she struggled over the most important words she might ever write, the pile of discarded paper at her feet testimony to how difficult it was proving to be. The newlyweds' arrival offered a much needed respite from her solitary pursuit of those elusive words.

"Welcome home, you two."

She ran lightly down the stairs, enveloping Olivia in a brief hug, kissing Andrew on the cheek. "And welcome to the family," she told him.

"Where is everybody?" Olivia wanted to know.

"Grannie and Grandpa took Mama to the doctor to see how her arm is mending, with lunch at the Tea Room afterwards. They'll be quite late, I'm afraid."

"And Eliza?" asked Olivia, obviously seeking more attention than Samantha had been willing to give to their return.

Suppressing her mirth, she said, "Eliza's taken Henry and Molly Christmas shopping."

She omitted mentioning Jasper Cooper's going along, and the plan to visit Charlie at the bank later on the children's behalf. They'd all agreed Eliza's request would prove more persuasive if her fiancé could actually meet them first.

"Henry and Molly? More relations?" asked Andrew, mildly amused.

"Not yet, well, maybe some day." She briefly explained the situation that had brought the Baxter children into the Spencer household, and Eliza's hope that Charlie would be favorable about adopting them.

Andrew shook his head. "I wouldn't count on it, Sam. Doesn't seem to me Charlie's plans for the future allow for a ready-made family."

He only put voice to what Samantha had already concluded. "What about you two as parents, now the honeymoon's over?"

Chuckling, Andrew patted his bride's hand resting on his forearm. "All in good time, Samantha, don't rush us.

Olivia hasn't a domestic bone in her lovely little body. She can't cook or keep house, but that's what my housekeeper's for. Besides her obvious beauty," he bent to kiss her upturned cheek, "my wife's true talents are in knowing the right things to do and the right things to say at the proper time. Perfect assets for a future assistant bank vice president, wouldn't you say, my dear?"

Olivia blushed prettily, her gaze never leaving her husband's face. "Yes, dear," she agreed mildly.

Samantha's mouth dropped open. This new Olivia was either a consummate actress, or had found a serenity of unbelievable measure in her marriage to Andrew; or perhaps she was merely besotted with the romance of it all. Whatever the cause of her cousin's metamorphosis, Samantha hadn't the time to dwell on it now, nor the inclination.

"So, are you planning on living in your apartment in town?" she asked Andrew, hoping to hurry things along.

"That we are."

"With Charlie?"

Olivia tittered. "No, of course not, silly. Andrew is going to ask him to move back home until he and Eliza are married."

"I see."

Ben would certainly have a full house again, with all the brothers except Andrew reunited under one roof. She doubted he'd mind in the least, family meant just about everything to him. He'd make a tremendous husband and father one day. At the thought, a pain twisted in her heart like a knife, realizing quite suddenly that someone else would someday exchange vows with Ben Morgan, live happily ever after in the house next door while, she attempted to help shape the world with her written words, alone, in Chicago. Before the idea could shatter her, she forced a too brilliant smile and a feigned interest.

"I assumed you'd take an extensive honeymoon, to avoid Aunt Jane's wrath, if nothing else," she told the pair, sarcasm thinly veiled.

"Pooh! We've already been to see Mama. She claims to be very happy for us, and has already made plans to announce our marriage with a wedding supper Sunday evening. And she's promised to talk Great-Aunt Maddie into another sewing bee, this one for the completion of *my* hope chest. Then, of course, there's Sissy's party Saturday night. We wouldn't miss it for the world. Won't Sissy be in a rage to have all attention on me instead of her at her very own party! There's so much to do beforehand. I haven't forgotten my promise to choose a dress among mine to alter for you, Samantha."

Samantha let Olivia prattle on; there was no stopping her. She had half a mind to tell her cousin she had no intention of going to Sissy's silly party, but knew the family outcry that would arise if she didn't. When Mayor Chester sent out invitations, *everyone* was expected to comply, even her visiting grandparents and Mama, cast and all. She guessed she owed the newlyweds the support of her presence, should there be unkind gossip concerning their hasty wedding.

Then there was being escorted by Ben, the very thought of which sent her anticipation soaring, a sensation she decided to enjoy rather than dissect.

As soon as possible, she shooed them out the door, for once her need to spend time at her chosen occupation going unchallenged.

An hour later, the very vocal return of Eliza and the children interrupted Samantha's labors. After dealing with her somber subject for hours on end, their happy voices—

and her desire to know how things went with Charlie—drew her downstairs. Arms overflowing with bundles, showing off new winter boots and coats, the children chattered cheerfully about Christmas shopping and Christmas secrets just barely kept.

One glance at Eliza's stricken face, her eyes swimming with unshed tears, her skin parchment and translucent under wind-chilled red, told another story altogether. When Samantha opened her mouth to ask what had happened, her cousin held up a staying hand. She then turned her palm to herself, showing the absence of the "engaged" ring she'd worn on her right hand these many months, awaiting transfer to the left during the exchange of vows.

Samantha quickly suggested cookies and milk, herded Henry and Molly into the kitchen, and left them to find the treats on their own.

In the back parlor, Eliza had dropped her outerwear on the nearest chair to stand with hands stretched toward the heat in the stove, tears streaming, silent sobs heaving her narrow chest. Samantha folded the slight young woman into her arms. Eliza's dam of resistance immediately collapsed. Samantha led her cousin to the sofa. Eliza clung to her arm, fingers biting deep, but Samantha made no protest, waiting until the weeping dwindled to a trickle. By then, she was furious at the man who'd caused her poor cousin's suffering.

"I cannot believe that Charlie Morgan. How dare he break off your engagement just because of those darling children!"

"H-h-he d-d-didn't. I-I-I d-d-did." Eliza hiccoughed with the aftermath of her tears, dabbing her eyes with her hankie. Resolve took the slump from her shoulders. "H-h-he was most u-u-unreasonable from the first, a-a-and downright hostile to J-J-Jasper, who kindly led the children outside so Charles and I could talk privately. H-h-he would not begin to consider taking the children with us to C-C-Colorado, and, oh, Samantha, h-h-he accused me of such . . . said J-J-Jasper and I-I-I . . . That we . . . Ohhhh!" On a low moan, she wept anew, but briefly. Dabbing her eyes, she admitted, "T-t-the worst of it is that I-I-I'm not so sure Charles is entirely w-w-wrong about . . . about my feelings for Jasper."

"Then breaking your engagement was the best—"

"No, oh, no! I-I-I must marry Charles. I promised. The wedding plans are all made. P-p-people are coming long distances to see me wed. The gifts . . . all those gifts! No, I must make amends to Charles, beg him to take me back. He l-l-loves me. I could not h-h-hurt him—"

"Which would hurt him more, a broken engagement, or a lifetime married to one who's given her heart to another?"

"I still love Charles, truly I do."

"But you have doubts . . . ?" Samantha prompted.

Eliza's lips narrowed, her small chin tipped up with uncommon determination.

"Doubts or not, I will marry Charles. I'm only suffering from those prewedding vagaries all brides fall prey to. Or because he did not want us to take the children. And . . . and, on second thought, I believe he was right about that. We shall have enough to deal with, moving to a new place, setting up our banking business, b-b-building a h-h-home and a l-l-life together." Her voice quavered off, but she pinched her lips together. "D-d-don't try to talk me out of it," she pleaded. "I am going to marry C-C-Charles, as planned."

Samantha said no more, and kept her opinions to herself. Maybe Eliza was right and everything else was merely the growing stresses before the wedding. Maybe

Eliza did love Charles and not Jasper. Only her cousin knew what was in her own heart. As confused as she herself was over her volatile feelings for Ben, who was she to tell Eliza what to do.

Dinner was scarcely over before Charles rang the front doorbell, bearing a bouquet of florist's roses and an enormous box of chocolates, and a contrite expression that must have gone right to Eliza's heart. For when they emerged from the chilly but private front parlor some time later, Eliza again wore his ring upon her right hand. Hours later, when Samantha put down her pencil, satisfied with her first draft, to listen to the silence of the house at midnight, she thought she detected the sounds of muffled sobbing through the thin wall dividing her bedroom and Eliza's. As tempted as she was to rush to her cousin's comfort, she knew in the end this was a quandary Eliza must face and resolve on her own.

She overslept until nearly noon. Mama was not pleased. Not about Samantha lingering in bed, or the mess she'd allowed Henry and Molly to make of her kitchen, or having forgotten—for the third time—to pick up from the dressmaker the samples of tulle from which to choose Eliza's veil. What she was mad about was Ben Morgan coming over at the crack of dawn that morning, demanding to see Sam. Of course, Mama had not allowed Grannie to awaken her at such an early hour, but it was very unseemly. What would people think? What would people say?

Mama's frequent use of those particular bromides never ceased to tempt Samantha to throw a glance over her shoulder to see just where these people were, and wonder why they should care. Biting back what she would really like to say on the subject, Samantha asked, "What was so urgent that it couldn't have kept until after school? He's not suffering any ill effects from his beating, is he?" Her heart beat double time at the thought.

"Not so one would notice, though he looks ghastly. He should've known better. Fisticuffs at his age! He didn't say why he insisted on seeing you so early, and when I refused to wake you, he said he would return right after school. That you should wait here for him. He was adamant that you should wait."

Samantha wasted precious minutes throughout the day trying to guess why Ben needed to see her so badly. She concluded that it would have to do with the children, and not her more fanciful notions that he might think it was time they resume their pretended courtship, or . . . she was afraid to think it . . . make the game reality! But no, that was preposterous. She and Ben were friends, nothing more. And merely friends they must remain, or it would break both their hearts when she left for Chicago in a few short weeks.

Forcing herself to concentrate on more important matters, she revised her story until satisfied it was the best she could manage, then spent the rest of the afternoon with Eliza and the children, wrapping gifts and helping them make their own ornaments for the tree, and recalling the snowy Saturday afternoon when the tree had been harvested. The picturesque clearing, the heady pungency of pine, watching the deer pass by. The rough wool of his mackinaw against her cheek; the familiarity of his steadfast presence. Her life and his linked forever by the shared past and present, but, regrettably not in their separate futures. How greatly she would miss him when she returned to Chicago, she dared not even imagine.

An hour later, she was wondering how she could even tolerate being in the same room with the insufferable, pig-headed man, no matter how like a wounded hero he looked with his bruised face blooming purple and yellow and green.

"Sam, I don't want you to write that article about the kids." He kept her protests at bay by talking over them. "I was wrong to agree to your writing it. Miller's likely not as dumb as he appears. Seeing your by-line in print, even *he* might figure out where they are. Put you and your family in harm's way." Her stubborn chin went high. "Let Jasper pursue the problem by legal means. Come on now, Sam, be reasonable."

"You are the one being unreasonable. My article will help Jasper's case immensely, put public support behind his efforts. And . . ." How could she tell him the most important reason of all?

"And?" Only the gravity on her face kept his temper at bay. "Give me one good reason for putting yourself in danger?"

"Because I failed Willie Klem, and hundreds others like him in Chicago. I absolutely *cannot* fail Henry and Molly, too. I could not live with myself if I didn't do everything in my power to assure them better lives."

No other argument could've swayed Ben but that one, nor could he stand up against her pale-faced determination. Cupping her cheek, he used his thumb to urge her chin upward until their lips met. The kiss was hot and sweet and brief. He backed off to lock his gaze on her amber one, his smile gentle, pleading.

"Will you at least keep the article anonymous?"

"I can't. Who is going to give importance to an issue to which I am unwilling to sign my name? The people of this town have expressed enthusiasm over last week's Seasons and Seasonings, and should be made aware that I can deal with journalism of greater substance as well. My position on this issue must be perfectly clear, no other choice of conscience can be made if my words are to have power and effect change."

Ben conceded, rubbing her chin with the rough pad of his thumb. He heaved a weighty sigh.

"You're right. But promise me you'll be careful. Watch your back. Cyrus Miller won't let this go so easily."

She promised. Ben left soon after, giving her a quick peck on the cheek as Eliza walked into the room. With a wicked wink for Sam's cousin, he headed for home, his mind no more at ease than before. Knowing Sam, sooner or later she'd do something to get herself in hot water. And danged if he wasn't going to have to keep an eagle eye on her to see that she didn't get herself drowned.

Her promise to Ben fresh in her thoughts, brought to mind Willie Klem's innocent, trusting face. Impulsively, she sat down to write her employer on the *Chicago Evening Star* for any possible news of the boy. She hadn't much hope that R. W. Reed would come out from behind his massive desk to honor her request, but she felt compelled to try.

Wednesday morning she delivered her article to Jasper and went over it with him line by line to make certain she had not stepped over any bounds, possibly putting the children in jeopardy. Jasper took her through the steps of putting a paper to bed, a side of the newspaper business she'd not seen before and found thoroughly fascinating. She envied Jasper the complete control of format and content, thrilled at the opportunity to take charge herself, if only temporarily.

Eliza had flatly refused to accompany her, showing an unaccustomed stubbornness by saying she couldn't and wouldn't enter Jasper Cooper's house or place of business ever again. She had better ways to occupy her time in the last few weeks before her wedding. The decision, though, did not make her happy, not in the least.

On the way home, Samantha stopped by the dressmaker's with the gown Olivia had chosen for her to wear to Sissy's party, of bottle green velvet, slender-waisted, with a daringly low neckline and tiny cap sleeves, and a high-collared, elbow-length cape of the same fabric. She stood impatiently for a fitting, arranged to return on Friday afternoon for another final one, escaping at last from the tedious task with Mama's tulle samples wrapped in brown paper.

On Thursday afternoon, Edward came over after school, requesting to see Samantha. With sinking heart, she found him in the family parlor, having declined a piece of Grannie's hot apple pie in favor of privacy. Great was her relief when he told her, shuffling from foot to foot, twisting his knitted cap in his hands, red-faced and stammering, that he had invited Lydia Snow to Sissy's party, and she'd accepted. Duncan promised to teach him how to dance, and said to tell her he'd rented the sleigh so everyone could travel together. Edward puffed up over her congratulations, and left looking more like a man than a boy.

On the afternoon of luckless Friday the 13th—if one believed in superstition—Samantha headed out for her appointment with the dressmaker, Molly holding fast to her hand and Henry on her other side. They had won out over her protests that they must stay close to home. Three days of heavy snow had left them housebound and overenergetic, much to poor Mama's despair. It was agreed that they need not start school until after the excitement of the holidays and the general upheaval of their lives had settled down; they'd have adjustments aplenty without it, Ben, as teacher, decided.

The day proved cold and crisp and sunny. The whole out-of-doors had a fairyland quality to it. Well-traveled roadways and walkways wound paths through unblemished white as far as the eye could see. Ice-laden branches of every tree and shrub sparkled like strands of crystal. A day so brilliant as to be blinding, which, Samantha later suspected caused her not to see him until it was almost too late. Cyrus Miller. Loading his wagon in front of the feed store.

She pulled the children into the nearest shop, Bailey's Books and Stationery, offering the excuse of needing a ream of writing paper, promising a storybook for each if they were good. From the children's happy, hopeful expressions, she knew they'd not seen the horrid man, but had he seen them? Samantha couldn't be certain.

They lingered in the bookstore until Henry began to fidget and Molly to whine. Watching at the window behind a display of Christmas books, Samantha saw the farmer drive off at last, leaving them free to safely complete their chores.

Samantha's borrowed, altered dress fit to perfection. Molly clasped her hands to her chest and declared her "jest bootiful, like a princess," and though Henry pretended indifference, admiration lit his eyes.

Already they both looked so much healthier, entirely different children, their too-skinny bodies filling out with Grannie's good cooking, the haunted shadows and hollows all but gone from their young faces. Scrubbed up and suitably dressed, they proved to be handsome youngsters with identical gray eyes and russet hair, Molly's a shade lighter than Henry's, and delicately curled. They were both being so good and helpful as to be unbelievable, probably fearing rejection, or worse, if they were not. How anyone could meet them and not immediately find them appealing, Samantha couldn't understand; how anyone could abuse them, was beyond comprehension. For the remainder of the day, in town and at home, Samantha fretted guiltily that her shopping expedition with them might've alerted the bullying brute, Cyrus Miller, to their whereabouts. She didn't rest easy until night fell and bedtime arrived without his pounding at their door demanding the return of "his" children.

On Saturday morning, the paper with her Orphan Train article was left at every subscriber's doorstep, but Samantha had no time to relish seeing her words in print on the front page she herself had tried her hand at setting up. Unprepared for the amount of preparation involved in getting ready for Sissy's party, she found it turning into an all-day affair. Olivia arrived early with the accessories for Samantha's outfit and stayed until mid-afternoon supervising the transformation of both her cousins with scented baths, crimped curls, and the tiniest, most tasteful application of cheek and lip color. Painted, powdered, and corseted, Samantha endured the lengthy make-over in silence, to keep the peace. Not, of course, hoping to put a glimmer of admiration in Ben Morgan's blue eyes. In the end, Olivia's handiwork turned both her and Eliza into unexpected visions of loveliness. Eliza's dress of deep mauve warmed her sallow skin and heightened the soft brown of her hair and eyes. Studying herself in the cheval mirror, Samantha could scarcely force her gaze away, seeing herself reflected there like a pretty, poised stranger. Ben wouldn't believe her transformation; she'd have to murder him if he teased her about it. Eliza came to her side; they exchanged lengthy, appreciative perusals, catching each other's eye in the glass.

"Charlie's going to fall in love with you all over again,"

Samantha told her cousin, usually so shy and plain, now blooming and beautiful.

"As Ben will with you."

Samantha tried to laugh off the remark, though it left her shaken and confused.

"Nonsense. Ben doesn't love me."

"But he does. I think he always has."

Refusing to continue along those lines, Samantha dropped the subject, knowing that if she dared believe Ben loved her, everything she thought about herself and all her plans for the future could irrevocably change.

"The others have arrived. Time for our grand entrance," she said, voice a bit unsteady.

They were gathered in the small hall. Eliza hung back shyly, letting Samantha go ahead. Heart beating hard and fast at the base of her throat, Samantha began her descent to a cluster of upturned, admiring faces. Among them, she sought out only one; Ben's gaze never wavered from her every step of the way. She looked for some sign that what Eliza said was true, not at all certain she would know if she saw it. This was Ben, neighbor, playmate, friend, his lean, craggy face as familiar to her as her own. Dressed in suit, overcoat, and bowler, in spite of his bruises, tonight she thought him the handsomest Morgan of all. Dependable, reliable, small town bound and content with it. He would never leave River Valley, and she could not stay. But, oh sweet Lord, if she ever found out he did love her, she wasn't sure she could bring herself to go.

Ben couldn't get enough of the sight of Samantha coming slowly down the stairs to him. To him. This vision in green, flyaway whiskey hair tamed into a regal crown, looking so long and lean and lovely it was unbearable. For a few brief seconds he forgot to guard his expression, saw her understand it, read confusion, panic, in hers.

Good! Let his love shake her up, trouble her, torment her as it had him all these years. Let her think long and hard about it and, good God, let her come to the right conclusion. For tonight he'd pretend she had, that they were—like the others—committed to each other with passion and with love. Leave reality to tomorrow.

Looking scared half to death, Samantha backed away from the coat he held out for her, clearing her throat.

"I promised to show Henry and Molly how I turned out. They're having supper in the kitchen. I won't be but a moment. The rest of you go on, I'll catch up."

His smile on the grim side, Ben insisted, "I'll wait."

Samantha fled to the rear of the house, reappearing almost before the kitchen door stopped swinging. Her face was ashen, her eyes stricken.

"The back door is standing wide open. The children are gone."

SIXTEEN

"He's got them, damn him."

Ben had pushed past her to sprint through the kitchen. She joined him at the gaping back door. Tracks, big heavy work boots, small, scuffling imprints on either side, trailed through the backyard behind the barn to the alley beyond. Ben sprinted for the alley, Samantha racing after him, hampered by velvet skirts dragging through calf-high snow. He stopped abruptly where the tracks changed from footsteps to wagon wheels, slamming a fist into his palm in frustration, uttering another oath.

At his side, Samantha wrapped her arms around herself. "It's my fault. All my fault." Her voice quivered; he glanced her way. "I took them to town. He was there, at the feed store. I didn't think he had seen them. I was almost positive he hadn't."

His jaw jumping, Ben clenched his fists, anger great, but not directed at her. With effort, he regained control.

"You're not to blame, Sam. Those kids can't live their lives in hiding. Sooner or later Miller would've seen them somewhere, or heard some mention of them."

He flexed his hands, open and shut, open and shut, knowing what he had to do. Hating it, the memory of Sunday's beating fresh in his mind, evident just about everywhere on his body.

"I'm going after them."

She gripped his arm, hauling back, feet sunk deep in the snow. "You will do no such thing, Ben Morgan. The last time you did that, you were beaten within an inch of your life. And the children were no better off than before. In this instance, discretion is the better part of valor. Not to mention how foolhardy it'd be to try to follow on foot a man driving a wagon, and with a head start."

Ben looked down into her furious, beautiful face and knew she spoke sense. Saving Henry and Molly from old man Miller required more than misplaced heroics. Still, his idea, foolish as it might've been, proved something, he discovered, suppressing a grin. Sam'd do about anything to keep him from getting hurt again, including knock him down and sit on him if she had to, to keep him out of danger. She'd finally come around to caring about him. Impatiently, he wondered how much longer it was going to take her to realize it herself. His chest swelled with fresh hope. Her fingers digging into his forearm brought him back to the task at hand.

"The sleigh Duncan rented is swifter than a wagon. With any luck, Sheriff Tupper and Jasper will be at the party by now. The three of us ought to be able to persuade Miller to hand over those kids, one way or the other."

His plan seemed sound. Samantha hoped he was right. She let go of his arm, already having decided to go with him and the others to the farm, a fact she thought best to save for later.

Duncan raced the team through streets narrowed to one track by snow, his face alive with the old, wicked pleasure Samantha remembered from more mischievous days, before he decided to become a man of the cloth. But the glint in his eyes was as dead serious as his brothers, from Andrew to Edward, all of whom were prepared to do battle.

Olivia clamped her hat to her head with one hand, and clung to Andrew's arm with the other, demanding, "Duncan, slow down. And do try to avoid the worst of the bumps and holes; you're tossing us around back here like baggage. We'll arrive for the party all in disarray. What kind of entrance will Andrew and I make then? Slow down, I say."

"Sorry, can't do that, Olivia. For once something's more important than how you appear in public." He took the next turn on one runner. "Here we are, safe and sound."

They tumbled from the still-rocking vehicle. Olivia's strident complaints never ceased.

"We *will not* rush the house in an unseemly manner. I won't allow it."

"Olivia's right," Ben agreed "No need to cause an uproar. Duncan, you find the sheriff, while I look up Jasper, then we'll head out."

Inside the door, before the maid could take their outerwear, Samantha linked her arm with Ben's. "I'll help you find Jasper. I'm going with you."

A voice interrupted Ben's immediate protest.

"Looking for me?"

Round-faced and balding, Jasper peered around from behind the closet door in the entryway. At the first words of Ben's explanation, he shrugged back into the closet.

"With Sheriff Tupper's help, I believe I have information enough now to make Cyrus Miller more than willing to hand over those children," he told them. "Ah, and here he is now. Here he is."

It helped that Jasper had been keeping Roger Tupper informed throughout, little more needed to be said before they set out in pursuit. Ben quickly found out nothing he could say to Samantha would keep her from joining the rescue party.

"I was in on the beginning of this, Ben Morgan, and I shall be there for the conclusion, if nothing more than as a reporter. The public deserves to be informed of the outcome."

Ben reluctantly gave in to her logic. As they prepared to depart, Samantha saw Eliza standing beside Charlie at the fringe of the gathering, her face pensive, more involved with the activity near the door than with the party beyond. Samantha knew she loved those children as the ones to which she'd never give birth. Her cousin's gaze slid past her to Jasper. With a last pained look, she slipped her arm through Charlie's and turned away.

A glance at Jasper's woebegone expression as he watched her walk away left no doubt in Samantha's mind that he returned her cousin's obvious affections. What an unlikely pair of star-crossed lovers—the confirmed bachelor of forty, and the shy, betrothed young woman of scarcely twenty. And yet not so unlike in temperament and tastes. Another testimony to the fickleness of the impractical heart.

The swift journey proceeded for the most part in silence. As the isolated farm came into view, Jasper announced, "I should act as spokesman, if no one minds." His voice quavered a bit, but echoed his resolve.

"So long as you make the fellow understand he's got no claim to those kids, it's okay with me," Sheriff Tupper announced. A man of settled middle age, with little demands on his office except to officiate over the starting gun at picnic races and keep order during the annual Fourth of July parade, he'd grown unaccustomed to heavier responsibilities.

Not a light shone from the few windows of the farmer's

house, little more than a shack with lopsided, haphazard lean-to additions here and there. Off to the left, the barn and long pig shelter and the pen, in no better condition than the house, dominated his few acres. These, too, lay in total darkness. Either the man hid in waiting, or he'd gone to bed. Somehow Samantha doubted the man too stupid not to expect them, doubted also that he wouldn't have prepared in some way for their eventual arrival. Forced to use his authority, the sheriff stepped up to the plank front door. His knock received no response. Ben reached past him, pounding with knotted fist.

"Open up, Miller, we know you're hiding out in there."

The door flew inward, Miller's considerable bulk loomed. A head taller and a hundred pounds heavier than every man standing on his porch, he also carried a shotgun draped in the crook of his arm. His face, so like one of his own rooting hogs, contorted with rage, he roared, "Git off m' land."

No one backed down, but no one spoke until Jasper stepped forward.

"We've come for the Baxter children, Henry and Molly. For the children."

Miller's roar changed to one of laughter.

"Like to see any one've ya puny whey-faced townies try. Them kids're mine, give to me free an' clear. Now, git."

He wrapped a hand around the stock of his gun, finger caressing the trigger. Jasper cleared his throat.

"Point of law, Mr. Miller, they are not yours free and clear. Unless you have an official document of adoption or indenture, they are still wards of New York State. Nor have you lived up to the terms you agreed upon when taking them off the Orphan Train last fall, including," he retrieved the flier from his vest pocket and furled it, reading, "ahem, 'kind treatment' and 'fair advantages,' as well as 'four months of schooling each year.' " He looked up, chin stubborn, voice steady. "If you do not relinquish Henry and Molly Baxter into our care at once, Sheriff Tupper has received the authority from the circuit judge to proceed with a warrant for your arrest. You will then be jailed until such time as you either agree to comply with the Children's Relocation Society's requirements, or forfeit the children to a more suitable home. A far more suitable home." Jasper concluded his rather lengthy speech without stammering and without his telltale "don't you know."

"Here, here!" exclaimed Duncan. "And if that's not persuasion enough for you, Miller, I'm prepared to remove my figurative clerical collar and help my brother give you as good as you gave him the other day to change your mind."

"If you turn us away tonight, more of us will come in the morning," Jasper stated. "Our small delegation may not intimidate you, but I assure you a mob of angry townsfolk will prove far more daunting. And, I might add, possibly not as nonviolent. The misuse of small children as slave labor is not kindly looked upon hereabouts. Not to mention your having to then face the far more serious crimes of kidnapping and resisting arrest."

Bravo! thought Samantha, watching the brute of a man backing down bit by bit with every word. Typically the bully, when faced with intimidation of the scope Jasper described, he speedily retracted his stand.

"Take 'em then, an' good riddance. They're 'bout worthless anyhow. Cain't even whup a good day's work out'a 'em."

"One thing more, Mr. Miller," said Jasper. "Should you ever attempt to make contact with Henry and Molly—

even a word spoken on a street corner—you will be carted off to jail. A restraining order has been issued against you and is in effect indefinitely."

Minutes later, Duncan drove the sleigh away from the farm. Molly sat on Samantha's lap, arms wrapped around her waist in a death grip, face pressed hard against her bodice. Henry sat between Duncan and Jasper in front, pretending indifference to the horror he'd just experienced. But his dirty face had been streaked with the tracks of tears and his eyes haunted when he emerged from the farmer's house. It would take time, and a warm and loving family, for the children to recover from their ordeal. She saw Jasper's arm snake across to the boy's bony shoulders, give a squeeze and a pat, then fall away. He had a father's comforting instincts. And Eliza, a loving mother's. Too bad they couldn't somehow . . . Samantha stopped herself from speculating further. Eliza would soon marry and leave for her new life in Colorado. The children would find a good home somewhere else. And that was that!

As soon as they gained the road off Miller's rutted drive, Ben told Jasper, "That was some fancy legal palavering, old friend. You made a big mistake, giving up your law practice."

Jasper bobbed his head in a nod. "So I'm coming to understand."

Duncan drove directly to the Spencers' house, dropping off Samantha, Ben, and the children, taking Jasper, Roger, and himself back to the party to relate their tale of success. Samantha and Ben herded the exhausted children up to their beds, forgoing baths for needed rest. Ben went with Henry to his room and lingered. In Eliza's room, sitting beside Molly on her reclining lounge bed, the child's hand tight around her fingers even in sleep, Samantha could hear the rise and fall of Ben's soothing voice relating outrageous exploits of the wild Morgan brothers' youth, hearing her own name mentioned with frequency. She'd like to have been a fly on the wall for those stories, especially when she heard Ben laugh and Henry chime in, his laugh rusty with disuse.

With a wife at his side, Ben would make the perfect father for a boy like Henry Baxter, Samantha thought, gently slipping her fingers out of Molly's sleep-relaxed grip. His wife would never have to fear for her children in the hands of an overly stern or indifferent father. His wife. Jealousy, and longing, rose high in her throat; she pressed locked hands to its base to press them down, only partially succeeding. Tears smarting behind her lids, she struggled to accept the inevitability of Ben marrying some day, aching with sorrow that it wouldn't be her.

All these weeks, she'd made such an issue of returning to Chicago, he couldn't doubt she'd go back, though she was beginning to have grave doubts herself. Thoughts of Chicago no longer brought to mind dreams of adventure and success, only the harsh realities of its hugeness, indifferent crowds, ceaseless noise, and noxious smells. Of a tiny one-room efficiency on the top floor of a four-storey walk-up, spartanly furnished, and a filthy, leaking, shared bathroom at the end of the hall. Samantha shuddered at the thought of leaving the comforts of home, family, and the work for Jasper she'd only begun and already come to love—and Ben, whom she also had to admit she'd grown to love—for the uncertainties and unpleasantness of the Windy City.

Leaving Ben, that would prove the hardest. What else could she do after all her talk of becoming a renowned stunt reporter like Nellie Bly. Anything else would brand her a coward and a failure, in her eyes as well as those of her loved ones. Her written words were expected to make a difference in the world, help free the downtrodden from the shackles of cruelty and poverty, alert the public to horrific wrongs, crimes, vice, indecencies of the rich and powerful. As did Nellie Bly's and her more successful followers. It was the reason for this God-given talent with which she'd been blessed. Though at the moment it seemed like a curse and a burden.

Samantha stood, brushing away the tears that had rolled unheeded down her cheeks, refusing to give in to her maudlin fancies. She was exhausted, physically and emotionally, the only reason she'd given in to them in the first place. She moved to the bedside table to turn down the light and caught a reflection of herself in Eliza's cheval mirror across the room, aghast at her appearance. Olivia's borrowed dress was completely ruined. The green velvet had not taken well to snow and mud and heaven knew what else she'd splashed through at the Miller pig farm, leaving it soiled beyond repair. She hadn't fared much better. The lovely hair arrangement Olivia labored over had lost half its pins and slid off the crown of her head to her nape, damp curls coiled around her face like Medusa's snakes; and the delicate coloring her cousin so expertly applied now streaked her face like war paint, along with mingled tears and dirt.

She brushed at her skirt with both hands, only making things worse. Grabbing a linen handkerchief off Eliza's dressing table, she scrubbed at her face with no better result. Nothing to do but face Ben as she was. No longer the poised and pretty woman Ben had stared at so admiringly only hours ago; with a feminine pride she didn't know she possessed, Samantha keenly regretted he'd seen her in this state of dishabille. Pulling the last few pins from her hair, she finger-combed as best she could, letting it hang over her back to her waist, suddenly wishing it were any other color than an ordinary shade of brown.

She emerged from Eliza's room, gently closing the door behind her, at the same time Ben exited Henry's diagonally across the hall. Their gazes locked. For the longest time neither moved or spoke. A new shyness, an uncertainty, stretched almost palpably between them. Samantha moved first, only because the stairs were at his end of the hall. He waited for her to come to him through the shadows, his hand still on the doorknob, as if he'd forgotten it was there.

She'd undone her magnificent whiskey hair, leaving it loose and swaying with every step she took toward him. God help him, he was struck dumb at the sight. Dirty and disheveled Sam might be, but she ignored it with a queen's grace. She closed the distance between them, spine straight, head high, unflappable in spite of the harrowing adventure they'd so recently shared. Any other woman would be weeping over her appearance, trembling and faint over what they'd seen and done. Olivia would, Eliza would, but not Sam. Never Sam. She was the bravest, smartest, most beautiful woman he knew, and for this little while, he dared to believe she was his. Watching her approach, he found it easy to imagine her his wife, saying good night to a son and daughter of their own, the evening ahead of them full of promises of loving intimacy.

All this time wasted, Samantha thought. How could she never have realized the inner strength and honor in this person, boy and man, this beautiful, beautiful man, inside and out? Why had she taken so long to recognize that she loved him, when there was so precious little time left to be together? Overwhelmed by emotion, she paused before him, suddenly as awkward and uncertain as a shy schoolgirl. Or a young bride on her wedding night, coming to her husband for companionship and love.

"Ah, mmm, is Henry asleep?"

He nodded, looking as discomforted as she felt.

"Molly, too?"

"Yes."

Silence stretching long. His hand fell away from the knob, he lifted it to rest on the round of her shoulder. The other caught under her chin, tipping her head upward until their eyes met. She tried to look elsewhere and couldn't.

"W-W-We should go down. My family might come home—"

"In a minute. This first."

He kissed her long and deep and slow, and she returned it with matching passion, toe to toe, her hands gripping his elbows for support. He pulled away first, but not too far, resting his forehead against hers, taking a deep, shaky breath.

"I've been wanting to do that for hours," he admitted.

"Me, too." She hitched a sigh.

He lifted his head to gaze deep into the amber depths of her eyes. He wanted to tell her he loved her, he wanted to ask her to marry him. He wanted somehow to find the courage to make her admit she loved him. Calling himself the worst kind of coward because he couldn't. Because he might be dead wrong.

Kiss me again, she silently begged. *Hold me, Ben. I love you. And I'm scared to death. I never dreamed this would happen to me . . . I never expected . . . this. I don't know what to do.*

"Could you please kiss me again?" she begged, voice weak, breathing shallow.

Ben complied with an intensity that thrilled, and terrified her, from her crown to her soles. Sensations she had never even imagined coursed through her to settle in her innermost reaches, shaking her to the core. If she didn't make him stop, at once, who knew where such emotions might lead, alone in her parents' darkened house, with two innocent children sleeping mere feet from where they stood? Afraid to imagine, still she couldn't pull away from the touch of his hands, encircling her, the exploration of his lips. And hers. She was as guilty as Ben. He was an excellent teacher here, too, far beyond the classroom, and herself an apt pupil. Each nuance he initiated, she mimicked; where his hands explored her body, hers followed to the same intimate places on his, discovering by touch alone the strength and beauty of his lean, muscled body. She could so easily lose herself in this wondrous experience, she grew afraid. She went still in his arms.

Ben lifted his head like a dreamer waking, eyes unfocused, breath panting through parted lips. Thank the Lord she'd stopped when she did, he hadn't the strength to, longing for nothing more than to follow his urgent need to fulfillment here and now. He saw the confusion in her eyes, and the fear, her love for him too new, too unexpected, not at all a part of her clear-cut plans for the future. Sam needed time to get used to the idea, that was all. He'd resume his courtship of her, this time in all sincerity. She'd come around. He was almost sure of it. He had to believe that she would. He didn't even want to imagine a life without Samantha Sarahannah Spencer at its center. She shivered, the hall was unheated. Ben rubbed the length of her velvet-clad arms, no softer and smoother than he imagined the flesh of her arms and all the rest of her to be. He forced the thought aside before the stirrings of his desire became all too painfully evident.

"Cold?"

"What? No, I . . . Not really . . . We should go downstairs to wait for the others."

His hands stilled on her arms, near the elbows. "I have to go home, Sam," he insisted gently.

"Yes, well, I guess, if you must. Frankie and Georgie are home all al—"

Ben chuckled. "They're fine. But I'm not."

Concern put a frown of worry on her sweet face.

"Your injuries are bothering you—"

"My injuries are nearly healed. It's . . . well, it's not something a gentleman talks about with a lady."

"What—?"

"Ask Grannie. Good night, Sam."

He gave her a quick, hard kiss and released her. Before she could gather her wits, he sprinted down the stairs and out the front door.

"You forgot your hat and coat," she called after him from halfway down the stairs, but too late.

Samantha retreated to her room, lonely to the point of bereavement, not certain why, puzzled and faintly offended by Ben's abrupt flight.

Hours later she awoke from a restless, dream-filled sleep, and it came to her. She needn't ask Grannie after all. She and her grandmother had already had numerous such discussions, especially just before she left to live alone in a large, wicked city. About men. About women. About men and women. Together in good ways and bad. About waiting. About how hard it was to wait—especially for men.

"You silly, innocent ninny," she chided herself aloud, smug with the knowledge that Ben had barely been able to contain his desire for her, but had been gentleman enough to try. What a dear, sweet, wonderful man. Happy tears stung her eyes, tickled her nose. She snuggled deeper into her covers and fell back to sleep, smiling.

SEVENTEEN

Sunday morning Samantha awoke to the familiar sounds of the banked fire in the kitchen stove being brought to life, the dull *thunk* of the woodbox lid, the creak of the pump handle, and the splash of water into the pot for coffee. Stretching long and slow like a contented cat, cozy and secure beneath mounds of Grannie's quilts, she recalled every minutia of the passionate embrace last night in the hall just beyond her bedroom door. Bay rum aftershave and the freshness of all outdoors, rock hardness of sinew and muscle on a whip-lean frame, the faint taste of peppermint on his exploring tongue. The very essence of Ben Morgan forever imprinted on her senses. Warmth spread from the region of her heart downward to that other place where love resided. *Love,* she thought, grinning, *I am in love with Ben Morgan, and he loves me.* And for a few long minutes, she gloried in the thought, refusing to dwell upon its complications.

The mingled smell of boiling coffee, frying bacon, and baking cinnamon rolls finally brought her out of her comfortable cocoon. She scurried into her clothing and dashed for the warmth of the kitchen, then immediately wished she'd stayed in her lofty retreat.

Dressed for church in a deep purple walking suit. Mama sat in her accustomed chair in the bay window, the rapid rhythm of her rocking demonstrating her displeasure, as did her narrowed lips and disapproving frown. Papa's presence in this strictly feminine domain attested to the seriousness of her aggravation. He stood beside and slightly behind Mama's rocker, staring out across the backyard, hands linked behind his back, the expression of his profile clearly speaking of his desire to be anywhere but here. Grannie cheerfully labored over her breakfast chores, ignoring her son and his wife, staying completely out of the matter. Mama spoke as soon as the swinging door swished closed behind her only daughter.

"It's about time, Samantha. I was afraid we would have to leave for church without speaking with you. I see by your casual manner of dress you are not planning to join us. Again. You'll be missing yet another of Duncan Morgan's fine sermons."

"Sorry, Mama," Samantha apologized on all counts, and when more seemed expected of her, elaborated. "I must write a follow-up story on the Baxter children while it is fresh in my mind. Tomorrow, I'll be working at the *Weekly Review* with Jasper, and I want to be fully prepared." That he might not need her services—what with the matter of the children having been resolved so swiftly and simply—occurred to her much to her keen disappointment.

"It is last night's escapade your father and I wish to discuss with you."

"I wouldn't call the rescue of two innocent children from the clutches of a kidnapper an escapade, Mama."

Mama sighed heavily and rolled her eyes. "What exactly would you call running off into the night with four men on a man's errand, Samantha? Your presence was expected at Mayor Chester's party, and your obvious absence noted by one and all. What could I say when asked, but the truth, that you were off alone heaven only knows where with both Ben and Duncan Morgan."

"Duncan's happily married—"

"Ben is not, and you have been observed too frequently of late alone in his company at all hours of the day and night. Miriam Jones commented on having seen you rolling around on the ground in the snow, embracing and kissing, on Main Street. On Main Street, Samantha! I did not give much credence to her chatter before, one has only to consider the source. But now, what else is one to think but that you and Ben—" She struggled for words. "You and Ben are behaving in the most unseemly manner for all the world to see."

Samantha found herself speechless. What could she say? In a way, Mama was right, yet at the same time so horribly wrong. The sweet playfulness of that kiss after they slipped on the ice was nothing like the town gossip, Miriam Jones's sordid interpretation of it. The warm glow of new love that had been with her since the evening before, dissolved with the implications of Mama's harsh words. Samantha looked past her to her father still studying the view beyond the frosted windowpane. A strong, silent man of few words, and those to the point and unquestionably fair, Samantha appealed to him now.

"Papa?"

He faced his warring family. "Samantha, my dear, you must admit your mother and I have allowed you more freedom than is customary for a single young woman, what with Chicago and all. All we ask is that you and Ben practice a little discretion and good common sense when in public. If the two of you have reached some, ah, understanding, that is your matter. We'd be overjoyed if something more were to come of your friendship. Ben Morgan is an admirable, conscientious young man.

Please, just keep in mind that this a small town, not the big city you've grown accustomed to over the past year, and conduct yourselves accordingly."

"Yes, Papa." She looked from one parent to the other, chafing under inaccurate suppositions and binding restrictions, but determined to be the cause of no more family dissent. "I'm sorry to have distressed you, Mama. I'll try to behave more acceptably in the future. I'll be helping Ben decorate his house for Christmas this afternoon. Rest assured, we will not be alone, Eliza and Charlie will be helping, too, now that Charlie's living at home temporarily, as will Henry and Molly."

Preston glanced at his wife for confirmation. "Very well, then, we see no problem with that."

Greatly relieved the inquisition was over, Samantha hastened to help Grannie set out the food for breakfast. They exchanged wry grins over the dining room table; Grannie chuckled deep in her throat.

"Well done, granddaughter. Hopefully, on reflection, neither of your parents will recall you promised only to *try* to behave."

Glancing through the doorway into the kitchen, Samantha held up both hands with fingers crossed, her grin as wide as her grandmother's.

"I kept my hands behind my back, just so, in case."

Ben caught Samantha in his arms as she passed from hallway to front parlor, where the tree stood awaiting the chain of cranberries she carried in her arms. He planted a smacking kiss squarely on her lips. Samantha made a halfhearted protest before happily succumbing, though he'd already pulled the same stunt in the dining room doorway and between hall and kitchen.

"Did you hang mistletoe balls in every doorway?" she demanded when he released her.

His devilish grin went wide and he pointed a finger upward. Above their heads hung yet another ball of green leaves and red berries festooned with gold ribbon.

"Didn't want any missed opportunities."

"Did you make all these?"

"Talked Eliza into it."

He nodded to where she sat on a slipper chair beside the tree, sorting through a carton of ornaments. She was watching the goings-on in the doorway with unabashed pleasure. Her cousin then threw a hopeful glance Charlie's way across the room. He never looked up from the strands of strung beads he frowned over in his futile attempt to untangle them. Since the party last night he'd barely looked at Eliza. Samantha suspected they'd had words, probably about Jasper Cooper, though she hadn't had the opportunity today for a heart-to-heart with Eliza. Trouble was brewing for all Mama's carefully made wedding plans, Samantha feared.

At Eliza's feet sat Henry, Molly, Georgie, and Frankie, competing to construct the longest paper chain. The old spotted hound, Zeus, that Edward had found as an abandoned pup, slept contentedly among them, oblivious to the noise and the paper chains draped over him, wet, black nose to twitching tail. Molly, covered with snips of colored paper and strips cut from old Christmas cards thanks to great globs of white library paste, took as much pleasure from the process as the boys with their friendly competition.

Edward and Duncan attempted to decorate the fireplace on the far wall with branches trimmed from the tree, arguing amiably about the quality of their workmanship. Duncan called to Ben to referee.

"What do you say, brother, is it heavier on the left than the right, or the other way around?"

Ben threw up his hands, his face alight with amusement. "I'm not getting in the middle of this."

His two younger brothers turned back to the friendly squabbling, finally agreeing to tear it all down and start over. Samantha made note of the new ease between Ben and Duncan, grateful that these two feuding brothers had finally made peace between themselves, offering up a quick prayer that it prove permanent.

The doorbell rang. Ben welcomed Samantha's parents and grandparents into the front hall.

Stomping snow off her boots, Grannie said, "We've come bearing refreshments. There's mulled cider in this old coffeepot, and Sam here talked me out of a tin of my Christmas cookies to go with it."

Ben took the pot by its wire handle, and Samantha the cookie tin from her mother's one-handed grip. Cordelia smiled at her daughter with hopeful love in her eyes.

"It was lonesome at home with everyone gone, especially knowing what fun you all were probably having over here. Do you mind if we join you?"

Samantha hugged Mama's shoulders, giving her a quick peck on the cheek.

"Of course not, the more the merrier."

And merry they were, filling up on cider and cookies, fighting over nonsense. Duncan lit a fire in the hearth once he and Edward came to an agreement over the mantel arrangement of boughs and candles and bows Eliza had fashioned for each end. Charlie relented at last and came to sit on a low stool beside his fiancée. At everyone's prompting, he lifted the lid on the old upright piano and played accompaniment to a round of Christmas carols.

No one heard the doorbell, though its ring became strident and prolonged. Andrew finally used his key to let himself in, trailed by his bride and her mother, both quivering with indignation, Olivia in tears.

From the doorway, she accused, "How could you hold a family party and not invite Andrew and me, especially when he is this family's rightful head as eldest?"

Every face turned her way, every mouth dropped open. Grannie found voice first.

"Stuff and nonsense, Olivia. Don't go stirring up a tempest in a teapot over a very impromptu gathering. Get down off your high horse and come join us. You, too, Jane. Andrew."

Only partly mollified, Olivia let Ben take her coat. Andrew, looking greatly relieved, shrugged out of his and accepted a mug of cider from Eliza. Aunt Jane made a bee-line for the plate of cookies, selecting a large assortment, then found herself a seat in which to enjoy them. The party resumed, having lost none of its former fervor by the interruption.

Toward evening, Samantha gathered empty mugs on a tray, taking them to the kitchen to wash while Grannie and Grandpa Spencer entertained with stories of the good old days. She'd heard them a million times, but never tired of the retelling. She hoped Ben would follow her for a few private moments, so she could tell him about the morning's conversation with her parents, and hopefully for a comforting stolen embrace complete with a shower of kisses.

She heard the door swish open behind her and turned, expecting her wish to have come true. It was only Olivia, carrying an empty cookie plate which she dropped with a clatter on the worktable in the center of the room.

"I should still be furious with you, Samantha. Aunt Cordelia told me of the rumpled, stained mess she found my dress in on your bedroom floor. You can be assured I'll never lend you another." She thrust out her lower lip.

"I'm sorry, Olivia. The damage was unintentional. You needn't pout. You know I will not be impressed. I've apologized, and if it will make you happy, I'll replace the dress with one of my own."

Olivia immediately pounced. "I'll take the lovely blue traveling suit you wore on the train. *And* your promise to attend the sewing bee Great-Aunt Maddie has agreed to arrange for me Friday after supper. *No excuses.*"

"I'll be there." She'd already promised Mama. Giving up her favorite suit, the pride of her wardrobe, proved far harder. But fair was fair. "The suit is yours, too, though it breaks my heart to part with it. I bought it with my very first paycheck. You'd better consider my debt to you paid in full, Olivia," she warned. "I know I shall."

Olivia's satisfied smile went smug, as though she knew all along how Samantha valued that particular garment, and her choice had been because she did. Shortly after Olivia returned to the parlor, without volunteering to help with the dishes, Ben came in. He stood behind Sam at the sink, brushed away stray curls at her neck, and gently kissed her nape while encircling her waist with his arms eliciting the most delightful sensations.

"Don't let Mama see you," she warned when she could catch her breath, then proceeded to relate the morning's conversation, omitting nothing, including the implication that she and Ben were now considered a couple by most of the population of River Valley, thanks to Mrs. Miriam Jones.

He kissed her nape again, sending shivers coursing her spine. Ben lifted his head to stare into her eyes as reflected back at him in the frosted window over the sink.

"Forget the gossip, Sam. Either old lady Jones'll soon

go on to fresher, juicer tidbits, or we'll make gossip impossible by getting hitched, thereby giving her nothing to talk about."

Samantha frowned at his grinning reflection. "Don't you take anything seriously?" She turned away out of his arms. "I have half a mind to—"

"Kiss me?" His lips covered hers for a hard, quick kiss.

She swatted at him with a damp dish towel upon release. "I prove my point."

He laughed, grabbing the towel from her, whipping it at her once in retaliation, holding up his weapon like a white flag.

"Thought you didn't know what one of these things was for! Never saw a female like you before, Sam, without a domestic bone in her body."

"Rest assured, there are many, many more like me. Besides, I really don't mind washing dishes and cooking. I even tolerate a good spring cleaning . . . occasionally." She threw a mocking glance around the room, lightly taunting, "I must admit, though, you are a far better housekeeper than I."

He let the teasing barb pass. "Then between the two of us we ought to come up with some superior decorations for the school for the box social Saturday night. There's only a half day of classes Friday, so we can begin by noon. I'll even supply lunch. All you have to do is come."

"Alone? You know we can't—"

"We'll ask the others to join us, any who are available."

Ben intended to make darn sure no one was.

Samantha looked doubtful. "There's to be a sewing bee Friday night, to work on Olivia's unfinished hope chest, at her request. I've given my word not to miss attending, under any circumstances."

Ben placed a hand over his heart, raised the other in the air. "You'll be home in time for supper."

"Very well, then. It sounds like fun."

Early Monday morning Samantha sat at Jasper's enormous, littered desk at the *River Valley Weekly Review,* shirred cotton protective sleeves covering her shirtwaist from wrist to elbow, a printer's green celluloid visor keeping the hair out of her eyes. She studied back issues of the newspaper with fresh interest. With knowledge gleaned from having worked on the *Evening Star,* she saw several techniques that could be applied to the *Weekly Review* to attract new readers, increase circulation, bring the publication from the constant threat of going into the red into prosperity. She jotted down notes as ideas spilled from her fired imagination to share with Jasper when he came in later in the day, stopping now and then to quiz Old Gus, the typesetter, on one related subject or another.

Old Gus, whose last name proved to be Webber, was a veritable encyclopedia of newspaper information she quickly discovered. A man of uncertain age, obviously very old, he was small and scrawny, but wiry and amazingly agile. Gus claimed to have once been a reporter on a major newspaper in New York, though he neglected to mention which one. He lost any claim to fame, fortune, and family to John Barleycorn, and hit bottom right here in River Valley. Since his recovery, he'd been with the *Weekly Review* through several ownerships. With his vast experience, he could've run the whole operation himself, were it not for his advanced age.

It occurred to her that Gus Webber had an interesting tale to tell, if he would. It further occurred to her that many citizens of their small town had life stories, memo-

ries, histories of equal interest. The mayor's mother, for
instance, was the first settler's child born in the newly
populated valley, her parents the first married, theirs the
first permanent residence, a log cabin. Grannie Spencer's
family had been River Valley pioneers, too. She'd related
accounts only the night before of their arduous journey
and travails while carving an encampment out of the wilderness. Samantha and her cousins knew them as well as
Grannie herself. But what of future generations once
Grannie, and she herself, were gone? Who would preserve
River Valley's history then?

Samantha lifted her head, excitement tingling right
down to her fingertips with the swelling bud of an idea
for biographical sketches of various men and women in-
strumental in making her hometown what it was today.
Material enough to last a lifetime. Grabbing up a sharpened pencil, she pulled a stack of blank paper toward
her and began to write. She didn't pause until the pencil
lead wore down to wood and her paper pile diminished
to a single sheet. She flexed her cramped fingers, looking
longingly at the typewriting machine standing neglected
on one corner of the desk. Wishing she knew how to use
it, she promised herself to learn as soon as possible, realizing suddenly she wouldn't be in town long enough
to do so. By the desk calendar she saw only three short
weeks remained before she was due to leave for Chicago,
the very thought of which filled her with unexpected
dread.

Samantha set her pencil down, linked her fingers, resting elbows on her desk, and bent forehead to knuckles.
She needed to face what she had refused to consider for
days now. Only this morning, a telegraph was delivered
to the newspaper reporting that Nellie Bly had departed
from Ceylon Friday after a day's delay, and for the first

time the information failed to excite her spirit of adventure. All she'd been able to think about was Ben, and his joking suggestion last night that they'd get hitched. What if he'd said that not simply in jest? What if he asked her again in all sincerity, on bended knee? Knowing now she loved him, how would she answer?

I don't want to go back. I want to stay here at home. With Ben. Forever, with Ben.

The realization struck her like a blow, but before she recovered from the shock, Aunt Jane descended upon her on a wave of cold air and instant chatter. Her aunt marched up to the editor's desk, pulling a much folded slip of paper out of her brown seal fur muff to plunk down on top of Samantha's notes.

"This is the announcement of Olivia's marriage to Andrew. Since you haven't taken the time to collect the information, I've taken the liberty of writing it up myself. Please print it as it is, Samantha. Also," she fished another bit of paper out of the muff and laid it over the announcement, "here is my recipe for transparent pie. As you've published Maddie's mince pie and Cordelia's springerle cookies, I knew you'd be asking for my contribution soon, so I'm saving you the trouble. I can also get you Josephine Reed's recipe for speculatius. They're the best little tea cookies you'll ever taste. Melt in your mouth. Not to mention Maggie Moss's potato pudding, and Franny Burton's brandy snaps, sinfully delightful." She paused for breath.

"T-T-Thank you, Aunt Jane. I had not thought of starting a column devoted to recipes, but it sounds as though it might be a good idea. I'll ask Jasper about it when he gets in. My Seasons and Seasonings column for this week is already being set in type. I'll make every effort to include your transparent pie in next week's. Thank you for coming in." Samantha stood, circling the desk to take her aunt's arm, urging her toward the door.

"Yes, well, all right, if I have your assurance it will appear next week. I'll take my leave. I'm to meet Miriam Jones at the Tea Shop at noon. It's nearly that now."

At the last moment, just when Samantha thought her aunt safely out the door, she came up short.

"Do not forget Olivia's sewing bee Friday night, Samantha."

"I haven't. I'll be there."

Aunt Jane pursed her lips. "Very well. I'll hold you to your word in the matter. Remember, my dear, family before . . . friends—single, available males like Ben Morgan included."

Five minutes after Aunt Jane left, Eliza arrived, a basket over her arm.

"I've brought you lunch. There's enough for . . . for e-e-everyone," she explained, her gaze flitting about the single big room housing editor's desk and the press and related equipment, hopeful smile fading fast.

"How thoughtful. It's just Gus and me to enjoy it, since Jasper's driven over to Isadore on business and not expected back 'til mid-afternoon. Thank you for thinking of us. Will you join us?"

"I . . . no . . . I have to pick up a whole list of sewing notions for Grannie Spencer, for Friday evening. I'll leave the basket, just remember to bring it home with you when you come."

Disappointment etched in the droop of her shoulders, Eliza left. Samantha bit back the temptation to ask her to stay for a chat, or a shoulder to cry on if need be, but she couldn't spare the time. As Gus reminded her, quite caustically Samantha thought, they had a newspaper to run. He did admit there was time enough for lunch, once

Samantha laid out the plentiful repast Eliza had provided upon a tablecloth spread over the work on her desk.

She'd taken her first flavorful bite of succulent fried chicken when Charlie Morgan burst in, still pulling on his overcoat.

"Eliza . . . Where is she? I saw her come in." His angry gaze darted over the room, coming to rest on Samantha.

"Shopping. She left lunch." Samantha waved the chicken leg, irritated but amused by his jealous ire. "There's only Gus and me, Charlie. Jasper's out of town for the morning. You can search the storeroom if you'd like."

"No, I, that is, I thought—"

Samantha laughed briefly, without humor. "You're as unstrung with premarital nerves as Eliza. Never fear, in less than three weeks you'll be wed and all this nonsense will mean nothing. Just as it already does, if you'd but think about it. She loves *you*, Charlie. Now, get back to work. You know what a tyrant Papa can be," she teased with the blatant lie.

Reluctantly agreeing, he departed, shaking his head, running fingers through the cowlick at his nape. Samantha went back to her chicken, chewing absently, realizing afresh how difficult, how painful love could be. Did she wish to experience that kind of suffering? The answer? Emphatically yes. Loving Ben. Loving only Ben.

In spite of the many interruptions throughout the morning, Samantha was fully prepared for Jasper when he returned at three-thirty. He thumbed through the pile of ideas and notations she handed him as soon as he hung up his coat, but his attention kept wandering to the lunch basket on the corner of his desk.

"Eliza brought lunch. Want some? There're plenty of leftovers. Eliza's a fabulous cook."

"I would. I would. Missed lunch myself, don't you know. Miss Upton stopped by, did she? How is Miss Upton?" His cheeks turned ruddy. He rummaged through the remains to cover his discomfiture.

Tempted to say "Disappointed at having missed you," Samantha left well enough alone. "Did your business go well in Isadore?"

"Well indeed. Well indeed." He chewed reflectively on a crisp wing. "Mmmm. My compliments to Miss Upton. Excellent. Excellent. Ahem. My business in Isadore, it concerns us both, Samantha."

She looked up from a note she was scribbling to herself, interest immediately piqued.

"It seems I'll have little trouble reinstating my qualifications to practice law. Paperwork's under way. Someone else will have to run the *Weekly Review.* I was thinking you . . . A female editor's not unheard-of in these . . . If you are at all interested . . ."

Samantha resisted the impulse to throw her arms around Jasper in a grateful embrace for a perfect solution to an unspoken prayer.

"I couldn't buy the paper outright from you, Jasper. I haven't a cent to my name."

"Something can be worked out."

She studied his earnest, kind face.

"Are you certain you want to do this, that I can fill your shoes?"

"Not hard. Not at all hard. Wasn't that good an editor. You'll be a far better one. Without a doubt."

"Then, yes. Yes, yes, yes! I'd love to be the *Weekly Review's* new editor."

She thrust her hand across the desk, and he wrapped it in his large paw. A quick shake and the agreement was sealed. When she headed for home two hours later, she all but danced down the path worn in the snow over the sidewalk. Only the ice underfoot and a belated sense of propriety kept her walking sedately homeward. But her heart danced to a happy beat, her dreams soared.

Wait 'til I tell Ben. Wait 'til he discovers there are no more obstacles keeping us apart.

EIGHTEEN

Ben stared down at the unopened envelope addressed to Miss Samantha Spencer from R. W. Reed, editor of the *Chicago Evening Star,* laying dead center on his schoolroom desk, dread and regret a palpable thing.

Dammit, why'd I have to go and do the noble thing? The right thing, he reminded himself, silently cursing his impulse to send Sam's Chicago editor a copy of the Orphan Train article.

Jasper had showed him a rough copy set in type almost two weeks before, prior to its inclusion in last Saturday's issue. It was so incredibly well written and probing, he thought Reed should see it, if only to discover what a huge mistake he'd made in demoting Sam instead of giving her a second chance.

I didn't figure on this!

Beside the envelope addressed to Sam lay spread the two-page letter thanking him for the article, agreeing with its superior quality, also agreeing his hasty decision had been a mistake and admitting he'd gladly hire her back in her former capacity as female stunt reporter for his paper. Having misplaced Samantha's address—"if you could see the mounds of paperwork on my desk, you'd know how this could happen"—he was sending his congratulations and his offer to Miss Spencer care of Ben, obviously a very loyal friend.

Ben barked a bitter laugh. *Some loyal friend I am, sitting here considering not giving Sam the letter. Maybe never. At the very least not until we've had more time together.*

She was just beginning to come around. Maybe beginning to fall in love with him a little. A few weeks, a few days more, and she'd realize it. Knowing Sam, he'd be the first to know. He'd declare his feelings, propose, she'd say yes. *Then* he'd give her the letter, when it no longer mattered.

Ben buried his head in his hands, gaze riveted on R. W.'s bold script, most especially the words "a very loyal friend."

I can't do it! Dammit, I deserve more time with Sam.

That decided, Ben propelled himself out of his seat with a violence that toppled his chair with a crash. Forcing a calm he didn't feel, Ben carefully righted it, then paced to the town-side window to check on Sam's impending arrival.

The snow had stopped mid-morning, but a solid bank of clouds hung dark and heavy close to the ground, promising more, possibly of blizzard proportions from the looks of it.

Maybe Sam wouldn't come. *I should've told her I'd come for her.* Except, if he did that, she'd catch him in a lie. He'd promised her they wouldn't be alone, that maybe Duncan and Edward, and others, would help out with the decorations, told her he'd rent the two-seated sleigh for that very purpose. If he drove up in the one-horse sleigh now stored in the barn out back, Sam'd know him for the liar he was.

Just when he had about decided he'd better go for her anyway, and hang the consequences, she came trudging down the road toward him, bundled up so only the tip of her nose and her eyes slitted against the cold peeped out from behind her muffler. She carried a basket on each arm, her steps labored under the weight, or the struggle through the most recent snowfall.

Not bothering with a coat, Ben dashed down the schoolhouse steps to take the baskets out of her arms.

"I should've picked you up."

Samantha paused to catch her breath. "It wasn't so bad closer to town where more feet have trampled recognizable paths, and I got a ride for all but the last half mile. Milly Adams and her brother Martin were heading home to Isadore and dropped me off at the turn-off. I didn't even know the family had moved out of town until I met them on the road. Am I the last to arrive?"

Because he didn't answer at once, Samantha studied his lean, handsome face and found chagrin in his lopsided grin. He lifted his flannel-clad shoulders in a shrug.

"Looks like it'll be just you and me, Sam. I won't tell if you don't," Ben offered an old, childhood challenge.

Samantha heaved a sigh, doubtful and hopeful in the same breath. Throwing caution to the wind, she smiled widely.

"I won't if you won't," she repeated the familiar response. "Now, I'd suggest we head inside before you freeze to death. Whatever were you thinking, coming outside on a day like this without a coat?"

She continued scolding him like a mother—or a wife—all the way into the building and while she divested herself of her outerwear. Ben gloried in every shrewish word, proof positive that she cared.

At the last minute, Ben remembered the letter for her lying on his desk in plain sight. He left her working on her wet boot laces and slipped from the cloakroom to bury the missive under a pile of uncorrected arithmetic papers.

"Oh no, you don't!" Sam spoke at his elbow.

They spoke together.

"Sam, I—"

"No more schoolwork today—"

Relieved, Ben assured her. "No schoolwork, I promise. Just getting some tacks." He pulled out the slim center drawer and grabbed up the small cardboard box, showing it to her. "We'll need these for pinning snowflakes to the wall. Remember when we used to make these?" From under his desk he retrieved an enormous mound of folded paper snowflakes cut out in a myriad of shapes and sizes. The sheer quantity of them overflowing the carton barely containing them was daunting. "I've had the kids snipping away all week. It was the only craft project I figured all different ages could handle."

Samantha giggled. "If we put all those up, we'll find ourselves with a snowstorm inside the school."

"If we omit a single one, some child's feelings will be hurt."

Samantha lifted her shoulders in a shrug. "I'm game if you are. Let's get started."

More than an hour later, Samantha tacked the last paper snowflake to the north-facing window framing and turned triumphantly away, a comment dying on her lips. Ben stood at the window on the opposite wall, staring toward town, hands locked behind his back, head tipped downward, face pensive.

For a moment, he reminded her for all the world of himself as a boy, usually inside the house looking out the window at her and his brothers at some form of rowdy play or other. Always left out, the outsider, the skinny scholar who couldn't throw a ball or run a race. And she loved him so fiercely at that moment that all she wanted to do was throw her arms around him and kiss the sorrowful look off his face, but not quite daring.

"Is it snowing again?" she asked from her side of the room.

His head jerked up, his hands dropping to his sides, but he didn't so much as glance her way. "What? No, not yet." He sounded as forlorn as he looked.

She went to him then, slipping her arms around his waist, pressing her cheek to his backbone. Feeling the muscles of his back tense at her touch, she backed away, hurt and confused.

"Where's the mistletoe ball when a girl needs it?"

No response.

"What's wrong, Ben? Did I say or do—?"

He spun. "No. *No,* Sam. You haven't done anything wrong. I have. A couple of things. First off, I never invited anyone but you to help decorate the school."

She grinned. "I suspected as much."

He looked even more grim. Pulling out of his rear pants pocket the envelope he'd retrieved from his desk when she wasn't looking, he presented it to her.

"There's this, too."

Puzzled, she glanced at the envelope, then at him. "It's for me. That's R. W. Reed's scrawl. I'd know it anywhere." She took the envelope, turning it over and back in her hand. "It hasn't been mailed. How did you—?"

"It was enclosed with a reply to my letter to him in which I included a copy of your Orphan Train article."

Another puzzled glance.

"I wrote to him on your behalf after Jasper let me read the first rough draft. I thought Reed should see it, too. Told him I believed you deserved another chance to prove yourself capable of being the best female stunt reporter in Chicago. And I wouldn't doubt he'll give you that opportunity, now he's seen for himself what you can do, given the chance. Congratulations on an outstanding piece of reporting, Sam."

Stunned to silence, emotions in turmoil, Samantha opened the envelope with trembling hands, read the contents of the single page within.

"Well?" Ben wanted to hope he was wrong, even knowing he wasn't.

The one word held such eager anticipation, she didn't doubt what he wished the outcome to be; it was the same thing she'd longed for with every fiber of her being, until she realized the depth and breadth of her love for Ben. Believing he loved her with the same intensity. Now it would seem he wanted nothing more than for her to go back to Chicago. A new thought struck her like a blow. Had all the embracing, the kisses, the soulful glances been only for the fulfillment of their joking agreement to pretend to court to spare the matchmaking of friends and relatives, or perhaps only the male urges Grannie warned her about? *Sweet heaven, what if either, or both, were true?*

"Well, Sam, what does R. W. have to say?" She appeared so stricken, Ben's hopes rose as if on wings. "Didn't I get your old job back for you after all?"

He wanted so badly to have accomplished this for her, she hadn't the heart to disappoint him, though it broke in the process. She forced a too-bright smile.

"Yes. I'm speechless. I didn't believe R. W. Reed capable of reversing a decision once made. You must have been most persuasive. How can I thank you?"

A sheen of tears turned her whiskey eyes dark brown. Ben took them to be tears of happiness. False enthusiasm laced his best wishes.

"Your writing convinced him, Sam. You could've sent him a copy of your article in print when it came out Saturday with the same results. I just thought of it first. When . . . when does he want you to return to Chicago?"

"After the wedding, as he earlier promised."

Maybe there's still a chance to get Sam to fall in love with me, stay here where she belongs.

If he cares even a little, maybe there's still time for him to discover we belong together, here in the valley.

I won't stand in her way, no matter what the price, come hell or high water. But I'm begging you, Sam, tell me I'm more important to you than your writing. Say it, Sam, say it.

Tell me you love me enough to keep me home, Ben. Please?

Silence hung thick and heavy between them. Ben rubbed his palms over the wool fabric covering his thighs to keep from clenching his hands into angry fists. Samantha nervously folded her letter and stuffed it into its envelope. Impulsively, she raised up on tiptoe to plant a kiss on his cheek, balancing herself with hands on his shoulders, the letter from R. W. crumpled between them.

"Thanks, Ben."

He heaved an uneven sigh and hauled her hard against him. His lips came down over hers, so urgent he left her breathless. Samantha responded with every fiber of her being, hoping to persuade him to speak by the sheer intensity of her need. They clung together, exploring, demanding, imploring, until they swayed on their feet. Simultaneously, they broke contact, taking deep, shaky breaths. Samantha searched Ben's face, saw clearly his desire in the depths of his eyes the color of dark, fathomless pools, knowing hers reflected the same passion. She pressed her forehead into his shoulder, fighting it. Failing. She lifted her head.

"Love me, Ben. Teach me the way between a man and a woman."

Arousal turned his eyes obsidian, the ardor etched on his face akin to pain. She saw the battle between what he so desperately wanted and what was right.

"Please, Ben. I promise never to regret asking."

"You sure, Sam? You don't know—"

She offered a tremulous smile. "I know more than you imagine. Grannie has been a thorough teacher."

"God bless Grannie." His own grin flickered briefly. He took her hand and led her nearer the pot-bellied stove in the corner. She went willingly. "No regrets, ever?"

She shook her head. "Never."

Uncertain what came next, Samantha waited expectantly, her heart beating so hard against her ribs, she thought it would explode. Ben held up a staying hand.

"Wait."

He disappeared into the storeroom, noting through the small window beside the back door that a storm had kicked up in earnest. The thought flitted through his mind that he should call a halt to this, here and now, head for home. Knowing he couldn't, come what may. He gathered up an armload of blankets off the shelf. Returning swiftly to the classroom he discovered Sam standing exactly as he'd left her, seeing on her face a wanting as great as his own. No turning back. Ben spread out blankets close to the welcome heat of the stove, creating a thick mattress over the hardwood floorboards. He faced Sam, finding her where he left her, clearly scared, as clearly eager.

He stepped close, kissing her lightly, his hands coming up to work free the buttons of her suit jacket at her throat. He found the pulse there fluttering like a hummingbird's wings. He relieved buttons to her cleavage, waited, silently questioning.

Samantha lifted trembling hands to begin on buttons of Ben's plaid flannel shirt, opening his shirt to the waist, discovering with a gasp that he wore no longjohns beneath. Upon his bare chest, golden curls spread thick and lush between taut, dark nipples, forming a *t* that disappeared into his pants at the waist. Her cheeks went hot. Eager to discover more, she worked to loosen his belt. Succeeding, she reached farther down. Ben caught her hands, grip just short of painful.

"Enough for now, Sam. My turn."

He released the last button on her jacket, helped her out of it. Impatient, she undid the waistband buttons of her skirt and it fell in a heap around her feet, followed swiftly by her petticoats. She stood exposed in pantaloons, corset cover, corset and chemise, utterly vulnerable, utterly free.

Ben took her hand and she stepped out of the pile of clothing at her feet, moved with her onto the blankets, and lowered her onto her knees. Casting aside his shirt, he sank down beside her. Knees bumping, they each made a tentative exploration with hands and lips. With impatient fingers, Ben lifted her camisole cover over her head, tossed it aside, unfastened the hooks on Samantha's corset until it fell away, followed by a knee-length chemise. Resisting, at the same time, her efforts to help him off with his pants.

Pressing his lips against hers, stilling her protests, he murmured, "Not yet, Sam. Patience."

He began a patient perusal of the rises and hollows of Samantha's lean, lush body; she imitated his every move, including flicking the very tip of one nipple between thumb and forefinger. He shuddered, she experienced a sense of unexpected power, then succumbed to the same

sensation as the range of Ben's exploring fingers spread
in wider and wider arcs. He spread two hands flat just
below her breasts, kneading them, hands slowly sliding
downward over her ribs, to part at her waist. One pressed
in the small of her back, the other continuing the journey,
down, down, beneath fragile lawn fabric, stopping just
above the tantalizing throbbing between her legs. Her head
fell back and she moaned.

Taking encouragement, Ben dipped lower, his fingers
cupping her there. Pausing. Waiting. And watching.

Her head came up, desperation in her whiskey eyes.
With fumbling fingers, she worked the buttons on his fly,
frantically slipped his pants down over his buttocks, exclaiming "Oh, my!" at what she discovered. More curious
than daunted by his arousal, she wrapped the fingers of
one hand around it. Rock hard and velvet smooth. The tip
she rubbed beneath one thumb. Ben quivered and growled,
capturing her hand, holding it still.

"Not so fast."

He lowered them both onto the blankets, lifted her hips,
tossed away the last of her undergarments, leaving only
stockings, sheer and black over long, shapely, incredibly
tempting legs. He captured her foot and kissed it, then
her arch, her ankle, her calf and knee and thigh. There he
lingered with lips and tongue. The small of her back came
up off the blanket, pressing shoulder blades and hips deep
into its folds. She clutched fistfuls of woven wool, twisting them and hanging on.

"Please. Ben, please . . ."

He lifted his head. "Stop?"

"No. Oh, no. Hurry!"

Ben divested himself of his remaining clothing in an
instant, covertly watching her study his male parts; her
expression alive with interest, without embarrassment. He

stretched out beside her, turning her to him, his backside arched away and a thigh covering his arousal. For Sam's sake, he had to go slow, something that would've proven impossible pressed belly to belly with her.

He led another intimate perusal with hands and lips, Sam imitating his every move precisely. Finally, knowing he couldn't last much longer, nor would she, he slid himself between her thighs, pressing for entrance.

"It'll hurt, but only for a second," he warned into her ear.

"So I've heard."

She grasped his buttocks and thrust hard against him, a sharp intake of breath the only indication of the tearing pain that came and went so fast she scarcely had time to acknowledge it as he began a gentle, rhythmic thrusting within her.

A wildfire of sensation spread inside her upward and outward from where they were joined, swelling and surging until nothing else mattered, nothing else existed. Slowly dissipating, leaving her satiated and weak-limbed. Ben followed after a half-dozen sharp thrusts, throwing back his head and moaning out his pleasure.

Still joined, they lay together, damp and spent and fulfilled. Outside, a howling wind rattled windowpanes, threw hard pellets of snow against the glass. Safe and warm within, they lay languidly in each other's arms, bodies touching from shoulder to thigh, legs entwined.

Tell me you love me, Ben, that what we just did has meaning beyond uncontrolled urgency between man and woman. Ask me to stay. Only ask, and I will gladly comply.

Oh, God, Sam, how can I let you leave me? How am I going to keep from begging?

Her hand reached for him and he stirred to life. Ben

rolled away and onto his feet in a single, fluid motion. She sat up, her expression hurt and puzzled.

"I thought you liked—?"

He held up a hand. "No more, Sam. We can't."

Now she looked crushed.

"Did I do something—?"

"No. *No.*" He grasped at straws. "It's the storm. We can't linger. We'll be stuck here all night if we do."

Like a dreamer awaking, Samantha turned her gaze toward the nearest window, surprised to have been unaware of a blizzard of obvious intensity. She scrambled to her feet, gathering her scattered clothing. Ben found his. They dressed quickly, without speaking. Silently, they folded the blankets. Ben replaced the stack of them on the shelves—on second thought, took all of them with him to the barn—leaving her alone to bank the fire in the stove while he struggled through knee-high drifts to harness horse to sleigh.

He gave her a hand into the vehicle, their clothing whipping about them as if about to be torn away. Wrapping themselves in every last blanket, they burrowed deep within, seeking warmth out of the bone-chilling cold, finding the wool fragrant with their lovemaking. Samantha snuggled closer to Ben, slipping her hands around his arm, leaning her cheek against his shoulder. Making no comment, giving her scarcely a glance, his face grim, jaw jumping, he gathered up the reins in both hands.

It took several slaps of the reins and increasingly loud threats to set the beast in motion. The snow lay deep in the road, no vehicles had passed this way in hours. The mare floundered, sometimes belly deep. Ben hated torturing the poor creature, but had little choice. Visibility went no farther than the tips of her twitching ears and disappeared immediately behind them. After a time, he lost track of how far they'd gone, if they still continued in a homeward direction, uncertain whether they should go on or turn back.

Samantha burrowed deeper, shivering, releasing her hold on Ben's arm to wrap both of hers around his narrow waist, seeking warmth and comfort. Ben stiffened under her touch, and squirmed uncomfortably. Curiosity got the better of her fear. She let her hand trail downward and found him throbbing.

"Dammit, Sam, stop that," Ben barked.

At her touch, he jumped, twisted away, the reins in his hands following his lead. The mare struck a shoulder-high drift and shied, overcorrected, struck the opposite side, ricocheted back the other way, the sleigh swaying and skidding in increasing arcs. Ben hauled back on the reins, which suddenly snapped in his hands, giving the mare her head. The sleigh veered toward a particularly steep bank, and there was nothing Ben could do to stop it. The vehicle began a sideways slide. The mare screamed and broke free as a runner struck some protrusion, tipped sharply sideways, tumbling over and over downhill.

NINETEEN

"Where's Samantha? I thought you three young ladies were going to spend the afternoon together." Preston Spencer invaded the gathering of the females in the family in the cozy back parlor with greatest reluctance.

"I haven't seen her since before noon, Uncle Preston," said Eliza, glancing up from the tea towel upon which she cross-stitched a border.

"You two didn't go with her to help Ben Morgan decorate the school for the Christmas party?" His usually mild tone held a sharp edge.

"This is the first I've heard of it," retorted Olivia tartly. "She was to attend this sewing bee in my honor, and as you can see she's not here as promised."

His wife, perched on a slipper chair, cast him a worried look, alarm in her query. "Is she out and about in this ungodly storm?"

"Now, now, my dear. She's not in her room, but has likely lingered next door with the Morgan boys, having forgotten the time, as usual."

Aunt Jane tut-tutted. "Talk is rampant enough without Samantha encouraging more by her wanton behavior. You should keep a firmer rein on your daughter, Preston."

Preston glared at his cousin. "Like you've done with yours, Janey?"

"Children, children," interrupted Maddie, a twinkle in her eyes. "Squabbling as you did as youngsters won't help locate Samantha."

"You're right, Mama," Preston said. "I'll run next door. That was always the first place to look for her when she was a child. Apparently little has changed, though she's old enough to know better."

"You do that, son," said his mother, "and leave us to our sewing. Rose, pass me the yellow floss, please."

Preston opened his mouth to say he'd be right back with Samantha, or news of her, when Duncan burst into the room, trailed by Jake Carter, owner of the solitary livery in town, rage on his bony, unshaven face. Shaking a fistful of leather tack under Preston's nose, he demanded, "Who's going to pay for the damage, I want to know? Harness and bridle don't come cheap. He," Jake thumbed at Duncan, "says his brother's to blame for my mare comin' back to the stable all lathered an' winded. Took more'n an hour to clean her up an' settle her down fer the night. Had my doubts, rentin' to Ben Morgan in this kind'a weather. Told him he was crazy. Didn't pay me no mind. What I want to know is, who's payin' fer replacements, him or you? An' where the hell's my sleigh?"

"Well, I suppose I—"

"Sir, look at the harness," Duncan interrupted.

Carter whipped the objects in question behind his back, where Duncan captured them and yanked them from his hand. Preston accepted Duncan's offering, conducted a thorough examination, leveling the stable owner with a glare to match his own.

"Neglected. Fraying. Snapped clean apart. No wonder the poor beast came home alone. As to your sleigh, Mr. Carter, my guess is my daughter and Ben Morgan are stranded somewhere in this blizzard without transportation, thanks to your rental equipment."

"Well, now if you put it that way—"

"Did my brother say where he was headed? When he'd return?" Duncan demanded.

Preston's face went grim. "Samantha told me she was going with a group of you, including Ben, to put up Christmas decorations at the school."

"Samantha's missing, too?" asked Duncan.

"Oh, Preston!" Cordelia rose abruptly. "What are we to do?"

"Firstly, my dear, we'll all remain calm, or we'll be of no help to anyone. Carter, you will seek out Sheriff Tupper, have him round up every able-bodied man in town for a search party. And I would strongly suggest you not fail at the task. Your reputation would suffer, should it be learned that what you rent out is faulty at best, possibly downright dangerous. Duncan and I will take my sleigh, head on out for the school, see if we can find them." The air of authority that earned him the respect of his bank employees galvanized the worried gathering.

Eliza stood. "I'll gather up blankets, Uncle. You'll want them for warmth in this horrid weather, and so will Samantha and Ben, when you find them."

Maddie set down the pillowcase she was embroidering in an elaborate floral pattern of Olivia's choosing. "I'd better put on your biggest coffeepot, Preston. I have a feeling we're in for a long night."

"I'll help," Cordelia insisted. "There must be something I can do, even one-armed. I cannot just sit and wait."

"We could continue with our handiwork," Jane suggested hopefully. "I personally find it calming. And you all did promise Olivia—"

"Not now, Jane," Maddie snapped at her niece. "Anything we would work on while waiting would be fit for nothing but the ragbag."

"Pooh!" Olivia pouted.

"Where are Andrew and Charlie tonight?" Preston asked. "We could use their help."

"Charlie's next door. I'll get him," Duncan offered.

"And, of course, Andrew is at home, as well," Olivia offered, voice sullen. "At *our* home, where he belongs."

"Carter," Preston addressed the stable owner, "you'll stop by to inform him on your way to the sheriff, he'll want to help. Here's the address."

"I won't have my husband traipsing around in this weather," said Olivia.

Preston threw her a disgusted glance. "If you kept him from trying to find his brother before it's too late, it would not bode well for your marriage, Olivia. As for how you may help, though you haven't asked, I would suggest you continue as you were with the rest of this sewing party. It *is* in your honor, after all. Ah, Eliza, thank you." He took the pile of blankets she silently offered. "We'll be off, then."

Samantha felt herself falling, striking surprisingly hard, tumbling endlessly over and over. Coming to an abrupt stop on her back, her head hit something all too solid. She blacked out for an instant, barely recovering before struck by a huge and heavy object dropped squarely on top of her, stealing her last breath.

"Sam, Sam, are you all right? Speak to me, Sam."

"Stop . . . hollering . . . in my ear," she gasped when she could. "My head's already throbbing."

Ben uttered a relieved chuckle, too close for comfort. "Alive and well, same old Sam. Thought for a minute landing on you might've done more than momentarily left you speechless."

"I'd be a whole lot better if you'd get off me." She pushed with hands pinned between them, apprehension making her request sharp, shrewish.

"Can't. We're trapped under the sleigh, me unfortunately on top. Sorry, Sam, this is as roomy as it gets."

"Push it off."

"Tried. Can't get into position in such cramped quarters. My feet are trapped somehow. I'm stuck."

"Let me try." She squirmed frantically, only managing to free one arm from between them, nothing more.

Ben stifled a groan. "Never mind, Sam. You can't lift a five-hundred-pound sleigh single-handedly anymore than I can. All that wriggling is killing me."

"You're hurt!" She instantly fell still. "I'm sorry. I didn't know." She felt something long and hard poking her right thigh, and struck Ben's shoulder blade sharply with her doubled fist. "Ben Morgan, you're . . . you're not hurt, you're . . . How can you be thinking of such things at a time like this?"

"Ouch, dammit, Sam, cut that out. It's more your fault than mine, with all that wiggling around. A man can't help these things, given certain stimulation."

"Really?" A thoughtful pause. "I had no idea. How curious. No control whatsoever?"

He couldn't stay mad. She sounded so hopeful. "There are a few exceptions, I imagine. Unfortunately, I'm just a teacher, Sam, not a preacher like Duncan, and sure as heck not a saint. Especially not with my face buried in a tangle of blankets smelling of our lovemaking. We'd've been a lot better off if they'd landed on top of us instead of underneath. Are you staying warm enough?"

"I'll manage 'til we're rescued. What about you? Are you all right? Your feet . . ."

"Okay, as far as I can tell. It's these dang heavy boots, with soles like bricks and laces double-knotted. They probably saved me from serious injury, but I can't work them free and I can't get my feet out of them. The seat's got me wedged down tight. Sorry, Sam."

"This predicament's more my fault than yours. I distracted you."

"And more Jake Carter's for renting us faulty equipment. If the mare hadn't broken free, I could've kept us from capsizing. Somehow."

"Then there's nothing left to do but wait for rescue."

Ben fell silent.

"Ben?" He didn't speak. "What are you keeping from me?"

She felt his chest heave in a silent sigh.

"We will be found, won't we?"

"I don't know. I hope so. But . . ."

"But if it's still snowing as hard as before, we could be buried from view, if we aren't already with the small avalanche we created on our own. There's a very real possibility we will freeze to death trapped under here, and go undetected until spring thaw," Samantha concluded fatalistically.

"That won't happen. We'll get out of this, Sam, I promise. You've got a great new job waiting for you in Chicago. And I've got a lot of people depending on me."

A chill slithered up Samantha's spine, unrelated to the cold snow upon which she lay. Without a doubt, Ben was telling her there would be no shared future for them. In two short weeks, she'd leave for Chicago, and Ben's life would return to normal. She shivered, tears close to the surface.

"If I could, I'd give you my jacket to keep, you warm," Ben offered, ice-cold more from Sam's silence than the wind whipping in beneath the overturned sleigh. So that was that! He had given her every chance to contradict him. More than once, he brought up Chicago, hoping against hope every single time to hear her say "I'm not going back."

"Keep your coat. I'm warm enough pressed between you and the blankets. If you could, though, would you remove your elbow from my ribs? Ah! That's better."

Because there seemed nothing more to say, they fell silent. After a while, Ben noticed a slackness in Sam's body against his. Able to lift his head no more than a couple of inches, he managed a glimpse of closed eyes and parted lips.

"Sam? Samantha! Don't you dare go to sleep, dammit."

"Leave me alone, Ben. All I need is a few minutes' nap. I'm so tired."

"Oh, no, you don't! You know better than that. You go to sleep now, and you'll never wake up. Tell me a story."

Samantha smiled sleepily. "Like when we were children? When I made up all kinds of fairy tales and insisted you boys act them out with me?"

Ben chuckled. "Except that you'd never play the damsel in distress. You always had to be a knight or a rogue, whichever was the hero, and poor Eliza forever requiring rescuing."

Samantha laughed softly. "It got so she'd run and hide in the coat closet to avoid the role. I'm surprised you remember, you so seldom joined in, forever in the house, nose in a book. Or acting so put upon if you were talked into performing with our impromptu troupe, we finally left you alone altogether."

"I was always given the part of slave, or captive, or

faithful manservant. Not very challenging roles," Ben commented without rancor. "Fortunately, once Edward was old enough, they fell to him instead, so I could go back to the books I much preferred."

"I thought you felt left out, that you envied your more . . . mmm . . . outdoorsy brothers."

Ben laughed aloud. Samantha felt it rumbling through his chest pressed so hard against hers.

"Sorry to disappoint you, Sam. I was never the poor, awkward 'four-eyes' you all thought me, at least not in my own mind. In my opinion those brothers of mine were a bunch of danged fools for letting you lead them all around by the noses like that. Ouch! Quit slugging me every time I say something you don't like."

"It helps me stay awake," said Samantha sweetly.

"I can think of something far less painful that we'd both enjoy."

He lightly kissed her neck just below her ear, then her pulse, beating like trapped butterflies at her throat, her round chin, her soft cheek, and at last—when she faced him—her waiting lips. Samantha's fist unfurled, her fingers spreading through the soft, clinging hair at his nape. Before intimacy became something they could not consummate in tight quarters, Ben turned his head away, breathing hard.

"No more, Sam. Shouldn't've done that. Tell me . . . tell me about . . . Chicago."

"What about Chicago?"

Disappointment laced her words; her too-rapid breathing tickled his ear.

"Anything that strikes your fancy. Since I've never been there, everything'll be new to me. What's living in a big city like?"

Because she had no choice but to go back, she wasn't

about to tell him how much she hated everything about cosmopolitan living. Instead she told him about all the museums, the zoos, the parks, the beautiful Lake Michigan shoreline so near at hand. The handsome, towering structures of brick and steel built since the devastating fire eighteen years before had destroyed so much of the city. Lavish with her tributes to its grandeur and conveniences, she waxed eloquent over her small apartment, her job on the paper, the fascinating people she'd encountered. Pride kept her praises glowing and growing, until the place sounded like heaven on earth, rather than her own private hell. No one, especially Ben, must ever know she had come to loathe residing there away from home and loved ones. Finally she simply could think of no more favorable exaggerations.

Ben cleared his throat as if it had become rusty with disuse. "Sounds great, Sam. I'll have to bring Georgie and Frankie to visit you some day."

Samantha spoke, too hastily. "I don't think you should." To see her in that environment would prove every word of praise a lie. "A-a-a female stunt reporter works such odd hours. Long hours, sometimes all day and all night. I'll never know from one moment to the next where I'll be asked to go, under what guise . . ."

Her excuses dwindled with the growing tautness of all Ben's muscles beneath her. If he could've walked away from her, she had no doubt he would've. Instead, he withdrew inside himself, abruptly dropping the subject.

Close quarters grew far closer with nothing left to be said. After an undetermined time, Ben's forehead bobbed down against her shoulder and she heard his soft snores. Knowing she should attempt to rouse him, too tired to care, Samantha turned to him, pressing her lips gently to his temple where his pulse beat with a slow but steady rate. Laying her cheek against his forehead, she closed her eyes.

A loud, incessant hammering directly overhead roused Samantha from her deadly sleep. She found Ben, with his cheek pillowed over her heart, undisturbed by the sound, though she shouted an urgent response to her rescuers. The sleigh began to rock violently, and with a shouted "Heave ho" flipped over onto its runners, releasing its captives at last. Frigid air and needle-sharp snow against his face awoke Ben. He rolled over onto his back, breathing in deep gulps of fresh air. Duncan leaned over him, hands to bent knees.

"So this is where you've been hiding yourself, brother." His voice quavered, and his eyes shone with moisture.

"Not by choice," Ben retorted from where he lay.

Duncan reached down to offer a hand up.

Ben raised his, palm out. "Give me a minute. My feet have gone numb with the weight of the sleigh on them all this time. What time is it, anyway?"

Duncan shrugged. "Near midnight, I imagine. Took us a while to track you down. An hour more, maybe less, we never would've. The sleigh's already buried up to the runners. Your feet, they haven't been injured, have they?"

Ben sat up, experimentally flexing his ankles this way and that, quick, pained tears smarting in his eyes.

"Nope. Sure burn and itch like crazy coming awake though."

Hands fisted on hips, Samantha stood indignantly over the pair. "No one bothered to ask how I am after our ordeal."

Said Charlie from behind her, "The way you jumped out from under like an escaping bunny, Sam, you couldn't be suffering from any serious injury."

Ever proper Andrew, standing shoulder to shoulder with Charlie, betrayed his anxiety, commenting tersely. "Both of you were damn lucky to survive an accident like this. Never took you to be anything but a cautious driver, Ben."

"Mare spooked at something, and the harness fell apart when I tried to rein her in."

"So I saw when Jake Carter came by demanding the whereabouts of his sleigh and the replacement of his gear," said Duncan, indignant anew. "Man ought to be tarred and feathered for renting out defective equipment."

"I'll see to it he doesn't go scot-free. You have my word," said Sheriff Tupper near at hand. "The pair of you could've met an untimely end as a result. Got to be some law against that, somewhere. If there ain't, soon will be."

More shouting from nearby sent Charlie and Andrew scrambling up the steep incline to alert the others that the lost had been found safe and sound. As a crowd gathered, it appeared that every able man and teen-aged lad in town had been marshaled into a rescue party, including its large-girthed mayor, so florid of cheeks and winded, he seemed on the verge of a heart attack. Nevertheless, he managed a disapproving stare for each of them, requesting an audience with Ben and Samantha the moment they had sufficiently recovered from their ordeal.

"Your presence won't be required tonight at the box social, under the circumstances. I'm sure your brother, the preacher, won't mind officiating in your stead." His tone rang with displeasure rather than consideration for their harrowing experience.

Later, huddled together beneath every available covering in the back of Jake Carter's commandeered wagon, Samantha whispered into Ben's ear.

"I'm afraid we've stirred up a great deal of trouble for ourselves, though the mayor can't begin to know the full extent of our impropriety. I hope this won't compromise your reputation, or your job. Mine can't suffer anymore than it did when I decided to live all alone in wicked Chicago, but you could lose everything you've worked so hard for all these years."

Ben gave her hand a reassuring squeeze. "It won't come to that, Sam. I'm the best teacher this school system's ever had. And my family's been here nearly as long as the mayor's mother's. No lasting harm will come of this, never fear."

TWENTY

Mayor Chester, speaking for the School Board committee, wasted no time in presenting their decision. Sunday, after church, he drew Samantha aside while her parents complimented Duncan on this week's sermon. He proved to be an inspired and inspiring orator, which surprised Samantha not at all after the childhood pranks he'd talked her into.

His hand on her arm, the Mayor cast a hasty glance toward Preston and Cordelia, clearing his throat. "We have no desire to distress unnecessarily your highly esteemed parents with your indiscretions, Miss Spencer. Therefore, the committee has decided to request that you join us at the Townline School precisely at four o'clock tomorrow afternoon to hear our decision in this . . . ahem . . . delicate matter."

Samantha held her tongue for Ben's sake, seething within, relieved only that her parents needn't immediately know of this latest mess she'd gotten herself into. Her first coherent thought after Mayor Chester left her standing alone in the dim, shadowed narthex was that she ought to enlist Jasper to act as mediator on behalf of herself and Ben. After his eloquence at the Miller farm, who better to plead their case?

Almost immediately, she realized the folly in the idea.

The more who were involved, the more likely the public would find out, jeopardizing Ben's future. Between the two of them, surely they'd be able to make the committee understand. Understand what? That they were innocent of intimacy? Not possible. Especially when heat and desire burned deep within her whenever she thought of their afternoon of lovemaking before a cozy classroom stove while a blizzard raged without. Better not to borrow trouble in any case but wait to hear the arguments presented by the School Board committee before attempting to come up with a suitable response.

"Before announcing our decision," said the Mayor, standing behind Ben's desk, which he had appropriated upon arrival, "let me read to you from our guideline in all matters, this invaluable volume." He held up a slender red book, clearing his throat. "I quote from *How to Organize, Classify and Teach a Country School* by W. M. Welch, A.M.:

> *"The personal influence of a teacher, in molding the character of his pupils, is the most important element in their educations . . . not the teaching of morality in words by rote, but the living of it, breathing it, exhaling it . . . Reputation may be concealed for a time, but character, like the atmosphere, pervades all with its influence. Let teachers teach by precept and example."*

He closed the book before him with a second clearing of his throat, noticeably relishing what was to come no more than anyone else.

His small audience, Ben and Samantha and four town fathers, sat across the front, deskless row of backless benches intended for the smallest scholars—committee to the left of the center aisle, Ben and Samantha on the right, a discreet distance apart on opposite ends of the long board seat.

"The committee has decided, Mr. Morgan, Miss Spencer, that it would be in everyone's best interest for the two of you to wed with the greatest expediency, or we shall be forced to find a new teacher for the Townline School."

Samantha leapt to her feet. "Mayor Chester, I cannot believe you and your committee have a legal right to come to such a decision."

The Mayor bristled, face florid. "That may very well be, missy, but I sure as hell—pardon me—have a moral one to every child and parent in this school district to uphold the dictates in this guide." He slammed his fist down on the book's cover.

Ben stood, facing the mayor, unable to look at Samantha, his heart hammering in his chest so hard he was sure everyone present would hear. Let the committee slander his reputation, replace him with another teacher. He'd get by, somehow. But the damage to Sam's reputation in her own hometown, he could not allow. In a small town, people talked, gossip spread like oil on water, growing by leaps and bounds with each retelling. If Sam was to hold up her head, he had no other choice, whether or not she ever forgave him for it.

"I'll do it. I'll marry Sam . . . Miss Spencer. By the first of the year, sir, if that's all right with you."

"Fine, fine!" blustered the Mayor.

"It is not fine," said Samantha, fury in her voice and on her face. "And we most certainly will *not* marry, Mr. Morgan. You need make no such sacrifice on my behalf, nor need I on yours." She faced Mayor Chester, no calmer. "I shall be returning to Chicago immediately after my cousin's wedding—sooner if you insist upon it. I hold a valuable position with a well-read and well-respected newspaper with a national readership. Mr. Morgan's credentials were impeccable before I came home, and shall be again soon after I leave, unless some malicious gossip-monger deems otherwise. In which case, most of this town would simply consider the source. Ben Morgan is the finest, most dedicated teacher River Valley has ever had. Only the foolhardy would cast aside the good he has done for the youth of this town, and will continue to again, given the opportunity. All for the few innocent moments we've spent alone, a few platonic kisses between friends—if unwisely in public. What man among this committee has not done the same? And I for one will have no part of your outrageous decision. Good day, *gentlemen.*"

Samantha ran from the room, caught up her coat and muff, and escaped outside into blinding winter sunshine, but not before the first sob escaped her.

"Sam. Wait!" He caught up with her where walk met road, capturing her elbow though she tried to twist away.

Enraged, half-blinded by tears, she squirmed furiously, spewing forth her outrage.

"How . . . dare . . . you . . . humiliate . . . me . . . like . . . that! I-I-I . . . wouldn't m-m-marry you . . . if . . . if . . . if—"

"If I was the last man on earth," Ben finished, anger rising to match her own. "Why not? Is the thought of being married to me so repugnant? Don't answer that. I can see for myself that it is. I was trying to save your reputation—"

"You . . . you *idiot.* You have only helped to . . . to *ruin* it by fueling the committee's assumptions. *H-H-Hang* my reputation, in any case! I *will not* have you make some

monumental sacrifice of your cherished bachelorhood to
save it, nor will I permit your saving your precious job at
my expense. I *loathe and despise* you, Ben Morgan. If
you *ever* so much as speak to me again, I-I-I'll . . ." She
couldn't think of anything cruel enough to make him hurt
as badly as she herself did right this moment. She broke
free and spun away; Ben let her go unchallenged.

Nellie Bly was expected to arrive in Hong Kong sometime Wednesday, Christmas Day. Samantha awoke hours
before dawn, wishing she was there with her, or in Chicago, or anywhere else but here at home on what was
supposed to be the happiest day of the year. Except that
for Samantha, this year, it was the worst Christmas morn
in memory. In the early afternoon, the Morgan men would
arrive for a dinner-time feast and the annual exchange of
gifts. She'd be forced to face Ben for the first time since
the disastrous inquisition with the School Board Monday
afternoon.

And why should she have to face him? If he did not
have the decency to stay at home, she would remain in
her room, pleading illness, until he left. And indeed she'd
not be lying, the pain of a broken heart swelled and spread
until there appeared to be little unaffected—body, heart
and soul. Love equated heartache, as she'd always suspected. She should've known better. Observation of others
in the smitten state, especially during these last few weeks
she'd been home, should have taught her precisely what
the hazards were in the giving away of her own heart.
Fool that she was, she'd gone and done it anyway, taken
a chance that the wonder and glory of loving Ben Morgan,
anticipating his in return, would never suffer the agonies
of disappointment and loss.

Never again! Samantha promised herself. *"Once bitten,*

twice shy," Grannie would say, and the old saw is true.
Love is the cruelest of Fate's little tricks perpetrated on
we poor mortals, and I'll not fall under its spell again.

That decided, Samantha pulled her covers up over her
head, buried deep in her feather pillows, and attempted to
go back to sleep. An endless time later, she peeked out
of her burrow, anticipated full daylight, was surprised to
find dawn had not even begun to streak the clear winter
sky after what she'd judged to be hours of sleepless tossing
and turning.

Time had slowed to a crawl these last few painful days,
without even the comfort of her writing, as lost to her—all
thanks to Ben Morgan—as her sound, untouched heart.
More tragic than the loss itself was that she simply didn't
care that writing might never again fulfill her to the exclusion of all else.

Quick tears filled her eyes, overflowing. Samantha sat
up, brushing them away impatiently with the backs of both
hands.

Enough! I've cried tears enough since Monday to fill
a dozen buckets, and I'll weep over that man no more.

She caught up R. W. Reed's letter from her nightstand,
plumping her pillows to read through the contents once
again. She'd all but memorized the first page with its
words of praise and promise.

"Too late," she whispered. "Sweet Lord, I don't want
to go back to Chicago, but what else can I do?"

No answer came. R. W.'s letter trembled in her hands,
and a second sheet of paper slipped out, fluttering down
onto her colorful log cabin quilt. Samantha had paid little
attention to the editor's missive beyond the promised job,
too much had transpired from that moment onward. She
replaced one page with the other, read, and reclined back

upon her pillow, to read again that last portion of R. W.'s letter.

Odd that you should ask after the Klem family at this particular time. An acquaintance of mine recently returned with his bride after a world tour of some two years, desperate to staff the new home he had built during their absence. Providence brought the Klem family to mind, and I promised to look them up. As you might imagine, Sophia Klem and her daughters, Olga and Clara, were more than delighted to trade what amounted to virtual slavery for positions in his household as cook and maids. Enterprising little Willie has taken to his new occupation as stable boy with the same enthusiasm with which he sold papers for the Evening Star.

Dropping the letter onto her lap, Samantha let her head fall back upon her pillows, wishing she were capable of feeling more joy at the Klem family's good fortune. But her thoughts never strayed far from Ben. She had truly believed he loved her enough to ask her for her hand in marriage. Instead, he made his responsibility the task of making sure she return to Chicago by contacting her employer. Bitter was the pill, knowing the only way he'd marry her was to be forced into it to save his teaching job.

Feeling tears building, Samantha was prepared to let them fall, when her bedroom door cracked open and Grannie slipped inside.

"Knew you'd be awake," she said cheerily, a suspicious grin on her face, like a cat having swallowed the canary. She carried a bulky bundle wrapped in brown paper tied with twine. Dumping the package onto the bed, she hiked up a hip and perched on the edge.

Vigorous and spry, Grannie relentlessly embraced all that life had to offer with the same fire in her sixties as led her to leave home for the West in her twenties. At this moment, her violet eyes sparkled wickedly in a sun-weathered face creased with countless laugh lines. That particular look usually foretold some delightful surprise for herself, blatantly Grannie's favorite grandchild. Samantha sat up.

"I've always meant for you to have this when I felt the time was right. Jane's going to be furious that I've chosen to give it to you; don't let her try to talk you out of it."

Curiosity overcoming grief for a time, Samantha worked at the knots in the string, asking, "A Christmas present, Grannie? What is it?"

Grannie's leathered hand covered hers. "Not a Christmas present, my dear child, a coming of age present. For unless I'm very much mistaken, I do believe you've finally learned you are more than your writing, that you've discovered your heart, how it can love, and how it can hurt to love again."

Samantha sadly shook her head, pressing the flat of her palm over her aching chest. "Never again. I've no desire to experience this kind of pain anytime soon, if ever."

Grannie chortled, patting Samantha's cheek with a callused palm. "Sooner than you know, dear heart. In the meantime . . ." She pushed the package closer.

Samantha freed the last knot, tore away paper with impatient hands, revealing a beautiful double wedding ring quilt, obviously of some age. Samantha passed her hand reverently over the surface, feeling tiny, even stitches in an unfamiliar pattern.

"It's so . . . so lovely. Did you make this as a bride?" she asked with some awe.

Grannie cackled a rough laugh. "Not I. Sam's first wife. This was her bride's quilt." Grannie referred to the thirteenth of the traditional baker's dozen a young woman brought to her groom upon their marriage.

Samantha's gaze snapped to Grannie's face. "Grandpa's first—?"

"She died very young. A tale for another time. Look at the quilt more closely," her grandmother urged impatiently.

Samantha unfurled the quilt with a snap. "Oh, Grannie, what a shame. What happened?" Her fingers followed a row of uneven stitches repairing a tear that went from one side seam to the other two-thirds of the way from the bottom. Apparent now, too, were the numerous stains of uncertain origin spoiling the perfection of fabric and workmanship.

"Someday I'll tell you the entire tale. As Sam's namesake, you'll appreciate the story more than anyone else since you are blessed—or inflicted—with the same adventurous spirit as your mother and me, and your Grandpa Sam. There isn't time for that today. Come, get dressed. Join me for a cup of bracing coffee before the rest come down clamoring for their breakfast and their presents." She hesitated at the door. "You do understand how much that quilt means to me, don't you, Samantha?"

Her granddaughter nodded solemnly, hugging the coverlet to her. "Because I see how you value it, Grannie, I'll cherish this and pass along its legacy. Especially after I learn what that legacy might be," she hinted.

Grannie put a warning finger to her lips. "Later, when you are a young bride yourself. Then you'll understand."

"I won't—"

Grannie shut off her protest with the quiet closing of the door. Samantha hurriedly washed and dressed, hoping against hope she'd be able to convince Grannie to relate the deep, dark mystery of the bride's quilt in the comforting warmth of Mama's kitchen. She dressed for the holiday in a two-piece dress of garnet velvet, rich with ivory lace at collar and cuff. In the chill of her room, she found no need to pinch color into her cheeks, grown pale with pining, but she found no solution for the lack of luster in her sad eyes. She needed a cup of Grannie's fortifying coffee as much for courage to get through this day as its welcome warmth.

She heard the murmur of voices as she laid a palm on the door and swung it inward. Too late she discovered Grannie's early morning companion was Ben, coffee cup in one hand and a gingerbread man, minus his head, in the other. Samantha immediately reversed her steps and retreated into the hall as he called her name. That Grannie had arranged this folly, she had no doubt, probably with Ben Morgan's help. But she had no intention of falling into their trap. She stopped, dead in her tracks. On the other hand, why should she run from any room in her own home simply because *he* chose to frequent it? She spun and reentered, taking the steaming cup Grannie offered in both hands. Ignoring Ben entirely, she strode to Mama's rocker and sat, facing her grandmother.

"Not even going to wish me a Merry Christmas, Sam?"

She pretended not to hear him, or see him. Childish, but it gave her a grim satisfaction.

"No forgiving and forgetting?"

She tossed him a scornful glance. "What *are* you doing here hours before invited?"

"Grannie asked me over. She always gives me my own

box of gingerbread men for Christmas. She knows they're my favorite and . . . I'm hers."

His crooked grin was all too familiar, but did not light his dark blue eyes, which remained questioning and hopeful. This morning he wore his Sunday suit, minus the jacket, which he'd draped over his chair back. Sporting no tie, his white shirt over snug vest gaped free of the top two buttons, revealing the base of his throat. There she had felt his strong pulse against her exploring lips only days before, when lasting love between them had seemed a possibility, when the throes of passion had clouded her vision of the truth, reality. Even now, her rose-colored glasses shattered with her dreams, her body betrayed her with longing and . . . lust.

To cover her discomposure, Samantha made a rude sound of incredulity. "Well, you're not mine, so why don't you take your cookies and go home? Grannie and I had planned an uninterrupted chat before anyone else got up, hadn't we, Grannie? Grannie?"

"She left, Sam. Wise woman, she knew we had to talk this out."

Samantha rose carefully, mindful of the hot liquid in her cup, setting it down on the table, prepared to retreat. He caught her hand and would not let her break free. She went still.

"There's nothing more to say, Ben Morgan. Your proposal of marriage to save your teaching position said it all. Come to think of it, it wasn't even a proposal. You simply stated we would wed without ever consulting me."

"Will you?"

"What?"

"Marry me?"

"To preserve your job and your standing in the community? I think not." She pulled free, heading for the swinging door.

"I quit my job."

She spun. "You did *what?*"

"Told the committee it was an insult to your character and to mine to assume the worst when no wrongdoing was involved. Their apologizes were profuse, but too late. The damage's been done. Years of loving you—all my life, in fact—not to mention weeks of careful plotting on my part and Grannie's, trying to convince you to reciprocate, all for nothing." He shrugged, shoulders slumped. "Told them I planned to follow you to Chicago, take up residence there, become a ditch digger or a push-cart vendor or a street sweeper if need be, until I finally convinced you somehow to fall in love with me, through dogged persistence if nothing else."

More confused than ever, Samantha asked suspiciously, "If you care for me as you claim, why did you send R. W. my Orphan Train article in an attempt to persuade him to take me back as stunt reporter? It seemed to me that you were overeager to get rid of me."

"Becoming a big city reporter was all you ever talked about. All you ever wanted," Ben barked, his fist coming down hard on the table, rattling cup and saucer, sloshing coffee everywhere.

Samantha grabbed up a dishcloth, swabbing angrily at the mess, her every furious phrase accented with a swipe of the cloth.

"A lot you know, Ben Morgan. I haven't wanted to go back to Chicago for weeks. R. W. had fired me altogether. Because I wouldn't return to the society desk. I have no intention of returning to Chicago. I hate Chicago. Jasper asked me to manage the *Weekly Review* in his stead, and

I fully intend to take his offer and stay right here at home until we get married."

He stood, toppling his chair, and caught her by both arms, gently forcing her to face him.

"You *do* love me, then?" he asked gruffly, hope and fear warred on his face.

Her expression went tender, her voice soft. "Yes. More than I thought possible. I love you, Ben Morgan, heart, soul, body, and mind, forever and always."

"And you'll marry me?"

Her heart leapt within her, but she pretended to give the matter serious consideration.

"I am not at all certain an out-of-work suitor would be my best choice in a husband."

Ben grinned widely. "Weak excuse, Sam. Can't get out of it that easily. The town fathers have already asked me to come back. Repeatedly. Begged, actually. At a raise in salary."

"Then, yes. Yes, Benjamin Franklin Morgan. I will marry you—"

Ben let out a triumphant *whoop,* then captured her lips in a quick, hard kiss. Samantha responded with abandon before pushing at his chest with hands trapped between them.

"You didn't let me finish. I'll marry you . . . so long as you don't expect me to stay at home and keep house," she warned. "I love you with all my heart and soul, but writing is my sustenance."

Ben ran a thumb over her full lower lip, longing and love in his eyes. "I know that, sweetheart, I always have. That's why it nearly killed you to give me R. W.'s letter. I almost didn't, you know."

"I saw you staring at it by the schoolroom window,"

she admitted. "You looked for all the world as though you had lost your last friend."

"I believed I would, as soon as I gave you that letter. My best friend, my heart, my soul."

Samantha's throat tightened with sudden, unshed tears. She could scarcely speak. "But for me, because you thought it was what I wanted, you were willing to risk all that."

His smile went tender. With his thumb, he brushed away the single tear that traced a path over the fullness of her cheek.

"If your heart lay elsewhere, how could I keep you here?"

"It doesn't, and you don't have to worry. I'm here to stay. I love you, Ben."

"Took you long enough, Samantha Spencer," commented Ben dryly, and swept her up into another impassioned embrace, oblivious to the silent *swish* of the kitchen door swinging shut, and Grannie Spencer's self-satisfied chuckle.

TWENTY-ONE

For a day begun so unhappily, never was there a more glorious Christmas in Samantha's memory, dawning sunny and crisp, every color intensified against the pristine whiteness of sparkling snow. Duncan's uplifting Christmas sermon gladdened every heart; the combined adult and childrens' choir sang in a single voice to rival the angels. Every church-goer's face wore a joyful smile, from youngest to eldest, every greeting offered glad wishes and blessings for this glorious day and the new year ahead.

Christmas dinner far outdid Thanksgiving's in Samantha's estimation, each dish a feast for eyes and nose and pallet. Good cheer radiated around the dining table—extended to seat the crowd with the kitchen worktable—both covered with one long, linen cloth. Candlelight put a sparkle in every eye, camaraderie ran like an undercurrent, strong and powerful, among this huge gathering of beloved family and friends where no one seemed immune to the almost unbearable anticipation of the opening of gifts as soon as dinner concluded.

Never had she felt so alive to every one of her senses. Her love for Ben continued to swell and bloom within her with an intensity that left her fairly trembling. She stared across the table at him so frequently and so lengthily, she often forgot to eat altogether, noticing, with pleasure, that he seemed afflicted with the same difficulty. How much she ate, she was unaware, nor did it matter, she felt gloriously satiated with Ben's love.

When the last plate was cleaned of the last generous slice of Christmas fruitcake, Grandpa Spencer, with a flourish, slid wide the double doors to the front parlor. There a fire burned in the hearth in honor of the day, and mounds of wrapped gifts surrounded a towering tree, lavishly adorned and topped with a benevolent St. Nick. Uttering a joyous cry one by one the children spilled into the room, restrained by a gentle admonition from the family patriarch, who designated himself Santa, handing out presents as fast as eager hands could reach for them.

From Mama and Papa, Samantha received a ream of writing paper and two dozen pencils; Eliza had embroidered a collection of pretty hankies with Sam's initials—assuring her as she opened them that it'd be no trouble to change the *S* to a *M*. Olivia had purchased for her a ridiculously tiny bit of navy straw covered with feathers and fruit that she insisted was the latest thing in headgear in Chicago, where she and Andrew had honeymooned. Molly shyly presented her with a colorful hand-drawn picture of uncertain subject matter; Henry had laboriously whittled an animal, possibly a horse or a dog, over which she lavished praise, genuine tears of pleasure in her eyes at their efforts in her behalf. She burst into brief, happy tears when she opened Grannie's gift, a framed, embroidered sampler, bearing the motto Home Is Where The Heart Is; and unabashedly exchanged secret, knowing glances with Ben after she unwrapped his, an astronomy book, marked with a slip of paper at a detailed rendering of the constellation Cassiopeia. On the inside cover he'd written "To remember us by, yours always, Ben."

As each one of her senses had heightened, so had each emotion, much to her delight, and dismay. Every last rite of the season, every last person in the whole wide world seemed wonderful, beautiful, perfect. Accepting her euphoria as the fleeting pleasure it was, she enjoyed the rare sensation to the fullest.

Grannie brought out her tins of Christmas cookies to pass, Papa carried the big punchbowl of her equally famous eggnog concoction to the table reserved for it in the center of the room, and again they all feasted like the starving. Should there be bellyaches all around tomorrow, no one gave them a thought today.

If there was anyone in the front parlor happier than herself this Christmas, it could only be the Baxter children. Clothes, toys, candy, oranges—everyone had remembered to bring them gifts, until treasures piled up around the delighted siblings, in an overwhelming array. Eliza sat cross-legged on the floor, skirt decorously tucked around and under her knees, as excited over the unwrapping and discovery as they. When refreshments appeared and the children had consumed their fill, Molly curled up on one side, her head in Eliza's lap, and promptly fell asleep. At her other side, Henry—under Eliza's extensive tutelage—read from a new book. Eventually she slipped an arm across his shoulders and he rested a cheek against her chest, eyes drifting close.

The soft beauty lighting Eliza's face spoke of her deep affection for the children, and of her unfulfilled longings. Samantha saw her glance toward Charlie, who stood with one arm stretched over the fireplace mantel, staring moodily into the fire. Sensing his fiancée's searching gaze, he lifted his head; instead of a smile in return for the timorous one she offered him, he frowned more deeply still. Eliza immediately turned her face away, eyes glittering with unshed tears, but she did not abandon the dozing youngsters, even to please him.

Soon thereafter, during the annual carol sing to Grandpa Spencer's accompaniment on the fiddle, the doorbell rang. Samantha, the nearest to the hall, jumped up to answer. Jasper stood on the stoop, hat in hand, apology and excuses on his lips, saying he had some questions about this week's issue of the *Weekly Review* and had thought their Christmas celebration would be over by now. All the while, his stare never wavered from the front parlor where, beyond the open double doorway, the Spencers and Morgans still reveled, abject yearning on his face. He shifted uneasily from one foot to the other, working his hat around and around by the brim, until Samantha snatched it from his hands and tossed it onto the seat of the nearby hall tree.

"For heaven's sake, Jasper. You're as welcome here as anyone in that room, and you know you want to join us. Come on in."

Insisting on taking his coat, she convinced him to relinquish it to her. When he entered the front parlor, her hands around his upper arm tugging him onward, the happy greetings he received left no doubts in his mind that he was welcome, and his round, pleasant face lit up like a Christmas candle. He perched on the ottoman beside Ben's chair. Samantha curled her legs under her, sitting on the Oriental rug close by the pair. While Jasper refreshed himself with the eggnog and plate of cookies forced upon him, the three of them fell to discussing the future of the Baxter orphans and the possible prospects for a home. When Ben and Jasper drifted off to other subjects of lesser interest to her, having not yet resolved the problem of Henry and Molly's future, Samantha fell to observing how Jasper's attention frequently wavered from the topic at hand to Eliza and the children curled up together on the hearthrug at the far side of the room.

Long before Eliza's gaze found his, he studied her with such hopeless ardor on his face, Samantha, observing, felt like an unwelcome invader of his private suffering. From the moment he caught Eliza's attention, the expression on her face a mirror of his own, neither could've looked away if either had so desired. Samantha turned aside first, certain her observation of the raw emotion in their eyes would not be welcomed if found out. At the hearth, Charlie watched, too, seeing for himself what Eliza could not bring herself to tell him. Samantha saw his expression go from anger, to pain, and finally to resignation. Quick tears smarted behind her lowered lids for the unhappy trio. She offered up a silent, fervent prayer that somehow this impossible situation be resolved without breaking anyone's heart. Knowing she prayed for one of her own on this day of miracles.

On Saturday, December 28, Nellie Bly departed for San Francisco, arriving in Japan the following day. Charlie Morgan had not visited or in any way contacted Eliza since Christmas evening, when he had left the gathering early without a word. Ben admitted, when Samantha asked, that he hadn't seen much of his brother the last couple of days, that Charlie had been keeping to himself in the room he shared with him, or disappearing altogether for hours on end, offering no explanation.

"I guess I haven't paid that much attention, Sam. Had my hands full keeping track of four kids with more after-Christmas energy than they know what to do with." He chuckled, admitting he didn't really mind that Henry and Molly had taken to playing with Frankie and Georgie at his house of less restrictions than hers. "Good practice for Monday morning, when there's a whole classroom full of boys and girls regretting the end of the holidays, instead of just four."

"I'm worried about Eliza. I hate seeing her so confused and unhappy, but I don't know what to do to help her."

Ben wrapped her into his arms; she pressed a cheek against the comforting flannel of his shirt, breathing deeply of the fresh, out-of-doors scent that always lingered about him.

"Anything you might say would only be resented as interference sooner or later. Eliza and Charlie will work out their problems in their own way and their own time, Sam. We did." He kissed the top of her bowed head, smelling the light flowery fragrance of her freshly washed hair and faint scent of her bathing soap.

"I know, I know," Samantha admitted with a sigh. "It's just that I wouldn't wish that kind of suffering on anyone, especially a sweet, gentle, loving soul like Eliza."

Resolution came quickly and unexpectedly Monday night, a scant day and a half before Eliza and Charlie's impending wedding—New Year's Day at noon. Charlie came to invite Eliza for a walk immediately after supper, both of them somber and quiet when they departed, looking for all the world as if they'd rather be anywhere else but in each other's company. No more than a half hour later, the doorbell rang, and Charlie stood on the stoop, alone. Samantha glanced past him expectantly.

"Did you lose Eliza somewhere along the way?" She attempted to lighten his grim mood with humor.

"I left her at Jasper Cooper's house." His tone held more sadness than bitterness. "She insisted I come by to tell you our decision. She thought that if your family heard it from you it might lessen the blow. Can I come in?"

She led him to the heated back parlor, where they stood facing each other unhappily.

"So the wedding's off," Samantha stated rather than asked.

"You're not surprised?" He saw she wasn't. "We found we were not suited to each other after all. Didn't take much to see she'd discovered in Jasper the kind of love she couldn't give me, or me her." He gave a brief, mirthless laugh. "On reflection, I came to realize I didn't so much love Eliza with that kind of passion, as that I wanted to take a bit of home and family with me to Colorado. To bolster my shaky self-confidence, if nothing else. Had you been available, Sam, it might as easily have been you I asked to head West with me. Not that I don't genuinely care for Eliza," Charlie hastened to add. "I do love her. Like a sister. Not a prospective wife with whom to spend the rest of my life. I spoke with Duncan at length before coming over tonight. He helped me finally come to a decision. His assurances that he and Alice would always have a place for me at their table and a spare bed, will get me by until . . ." he offered a fleeting grin, "well, Duncan tells me there are women sufficient in his wife's family alone that I'll have no trouble finding myself a bride when and if I'm ready."

Samantha reached out to take his hand. "I'm so sorry, Charlie. But you and Eliza both can thank the powers that be you didn't make this discovery *after* the vows were spoken."

He squeezed her hand. "Thanks, Sam. You're right, of course. I think I began to understand that watching my brothers fall in love. Especially Ben. Lucky guy."

He looked so downhearted, she gave his hand a little tug. "Colorado. The very name makes me shiver. How I envy the adventures awaiting you there. And just think, once Grannie Spencer returns, between her and Duncan, you'll have no shortage of matchmakers with which to contend."

Samantha brought forth a chuckle from him then, rusty though it'd grown; she giggled with him. He kissed her cheek.

"Thanks for everything, sister-to-be. I don't envy you facing your mother with this news, and I'd help you out if I could, but I've got a ticket for the 6:00 A.M. train, just time to pack and say a few more goodbyes. Don't look so woebegone. I'm not going off to Colorado forever; I'll return for holidays with Grandpa and Grandma Spencer, and Duncan and his family. Take care."

"You, too, Charlie. Godspeed."

She closed the door behind his departing figure, dread seeping into her bones far colder than the outdoor temperature. Mama was bound to take the news very badly. Better get it over with before she lost courage.

Cordelia took the news with all the ire and drama Samantha anticipated, and more. In the kitchen where she and Grannie had been sipping coffee at the worktable and chatting, she raged and wept and claimed she felt faint, though Samantha and Grannie both knew she had too much gumption to carry out that threat.

"Ohhhhhhhh!" Mama moaned, stricken. "This is awful, just awful! The plans. The work. The expense. Merciful heaven, Preston will throw a fit of temper when he learns how much has been spent, all for nothing. Cake. Caterers. Complete new wardrobes for everyone. And the gifts. All those gifts! They've been arriving in droves and now must all be returned. I'll *never* be able to hold up my head again in this town." She wound to a stop, took a deep breath, during which she reached a decision. "Someone else will have to get married in her stead. You, Samantha. You and Ben shall simply have to—"

"Mama—"

"Now, Corrie, you sure you want Samantha getting married only days after becoming engaged? *Someone* might take it to mean they *had* to get married," Grannie reminded her, barely suppressing a grin.

"Mama, I—"

Cordelia glanced briefly at her mother-in-law, then back to her daughter.

"Mama, I—"

"Nonsense, Maddie, everyone will merely assume we've made the most sensible arrangements, what with Eliza and Charlie's rash decision at the last possible moment."

"Mama—"

"What is it, Samantha? Speak up." Her tone said clearly that she would tolerate no arguments.

Samantha bent briefly to hug her mother, kiss her cheek. "I've been trying to tell you, Mama, that if Ben's willing, I'd be more than happy to get married day after tomorrow. On the condition that Grannie exchange vows with Grandpa at the same time."

Cordelia blanched, tossing a frantic glance between grandmother and granddaughter. "Please, oh, please, don't tell me all the wild speculation I've heard about you and Sam not really being married are true, Maddie. I could not bear another blow of that magnitude today."

Samantha realized her error in the paling of Grannie's complexion under the nut brown of her weathered skin.

"Oh, no, Mama. I misspoke. I meant to say, Ben and I shall be happy to if Grannie will *renew* her vows with Grandpa."

Grannie cackled. "I'm willing if your grandpa is,

Samantha. Serves him right, having to marry me all over again, for allowing folks to have their doubts."

Cordelia heaved a heavy, relieved sigh. "Thank the dear Lord the matter has resolved itself so quickly and simply. Bless you both for saving our family from disgrace."

"Happy to, Corrie," retorted Grannie, winking broadly at Samantha behind her daughter-in-law's back. "Happy to."

Samantha echoed Grannie's sentiments, and her gesture.

Eliza came into the kitchen as the trio celebrated over fruitcake and mulled apple cider. She was not alone; she clung to Jasper's arm as if she feared he might try to escape. She was radiant; Jasper appeared both overjoyed and proud, and more than a little bit apprehensive at having to face the formidable matriarch, Cordelia Spencer.

"Mrs. Spencer," he began, "your niece and I, we've come from speaking with your husband, and, well, Miss Upton . . . Eliza . . . and I would like very much to add your blessings to his. I've asked for Miss Upton . . . Eliza's . . . hand in marriage. Ahem, in marriage. Mr. . . . that is, Preston, has given his permission, and I . . . we . . . would appreciate yours as well. I must warn you, with or without, Eliza and I have already given our pledge to one another, don't you know," he concluded, tone milder than his words.

Cordelia studied each face in turn, resignation crossing her own. She threw up her hand.

"Very well. You have it. And why not? What is one more scandal averted most unconventionally!"

The ladies exchanged hugs and kisses all around, and

would have included Jasper except that he looked as if he would bolt from the room if they tried.

"We'll have a triple wedding," Samantha exclaimed when the excitement dimmed a bit. "You and me, Eliza, and Grannie and Grandpa renewing their vows!"

Eliza shook her head, leaning against her love's ample side. "I'm sorry, Samantha, but we can't. Jasper and I . . . we've already decided a spring wedding would be lovely."

Jasper interjected, patting her hand on his arm, his expression adoring. "Early spring, my dear. Very early."

"Early spring. We . . . we hope to adopt Henry and Molly if they'll have us, knowing we . . . all . . . need more time to grow accustomed to one another."

Hugs and kisses flew around the room once more, and even Jasper's best efforts didn't keep him from being included.

"Everything worked out absolutely perfectly for everyone concerned," said Samantha with a happy sigh, snuggling more deeply into Ben's embrace as they sat on his sofa before a fire in the hearth.

He'd listened to her tale and her request, objecting to no detail, already wishing the elaborate wedding—far more than he personally cared for—was over with, so Sam and he could set up housekeeping as soon as possible here in the Morgan homestead, for the rest of their lives.

"Eliza offered us all the wedding gifts she's already received, but I declined, what with my overstuffed hope chest and your house needing nothing anyway. I can't wait to settle in here, so I can discover where you've hidden your mother's lovely things. My memories of her—so many happy years running in and out of this house as if it were my own—are tied to them. My hands itch to rediscover all those treasures, so I can put them back exactly where I remember them residing."

Ben held her a little tighter, pressed a kiss to her whiskey crown, heart so full he was near exploding.

"You're my most cherished treasure, Sam. You're the only adornment around here that I need, now and forever."

She lifted her face to plant a kiss on his faintly whiskered cheek. "And you, dear husband-to-be, are the very unexpected, most valued discovery of my heart. Who would have ever dreamed my coming home a failure only a few short weeks ago could result in the greatest good fortune of my life, sufficient to last the rest of my life! I love you, Ben Morgan."

He grinned at her crookedly, spreading a hand over his heart. "I think you'd better remind me of that a dozen times a day for the next hundred years, Sam, after what I've suffered waiting for you to figure that out."

"You do believe me, don't you?"

"I do! I do! But telling me frequently sure beats pinching myself so I won't think I'm dreaming. I . . . Ouch! What was that for?" He rubbed his arm where she'd grabbed his flesh between two fingertips and twisted.

"I thought I'd simply save you the trouble," she said sweetly. "Actually, I had in mind a dozen hugs and kisses and . . . whatever . . . per day. But if you'd rather—"

He interrupted her with a dozen tantalizing kisses, some brief, some lingering, some feather-light, some open-mouthed and passionate.

"That takes care of today. Only four hundred thousand, more or less, to go."

Samantha ran the tip of her tongue around her lips, tilting her head thoughtfully.

"Mmmm! I rather liked that. Could we please begin on tomorrow?"

Samantha wrapped her arms around his neck, pulling him to her. Letting her lead the way, Ben obligingly complied.

EPILOGUE

Wednesday, December 24, 1890

The howdy bell jangled, the *Weekly Review's* glass-paned front door opened to a blast of bitter cold and Jasper Cooper. He stepped just inside, stomping snow off his galoshes onto the door mat, blowing on red, chapped hands. *So much for Eliza's endless reminders to her husband to remember his gloves,* Samantha thought with a smile. She did notice, however, that eight months of marriage and a ready-made family had in other ways given him a new lease on life. He looked ten years younger, leaner of face and form, his color healthy instead of office-pale, and so much happier now that he'd found everlasting love and an occupation to which to wholeheartedly dedicate his life. As advocate for the organization he and Eliza had founded—the Society for Fair Practices Regarding Orphan Train Innocents—he was making great strides in locating and documenting records to verify the whereabouts and status of children so arbitrarily distributed throughout the Midwest. Samantha greatly admired her cousin-in-law, and prayed the articles she'd written on the subject throughout this past year somehow assisted him in his ongoing efforts.

"Train's in, don't you know," said Jasper, unaware of

the pedestal upon which Samantha had placed him. "Going to pick up the family now."

Flexing her fingers, she glanced at the clock behind her desk, surprised to discover it was already five to five.

"Thanks for alerting me, Jasper. I'll be along soon's I can."

Jasper turned up his collar, opened the door to another icy gust, facing back to her, hand on knob.

"Nearly forgot. Ben says to wait here. He'll come for you directly. Says not to try to walk home—too slippery, don't you know and you in the, ahem, and you with, mmmm . . ." He blundered to an uncomfortable stop, stammering and blushing furiously.

"I'll wait," Samantha promised, resting both palms on her hugely swollen belly.

"Yes, well, won't be long," he said. "Won't be long." He hesitated, brow furrowed as if pondering whether or not he'd forgotten anything else.

"See you and Eliza later on at Mama and Papa's?" she suggested.

"You surely will. You surely will. We'll be there, us and the kids. Six o'clock sharp." He raised a hand in parting and left, this time his departure final.

Intending only to finish her edit of next week's front page, she went on to page two without a thought, making notes for Old Gus on changes, deletions, corrections, so immersed in her work she didn't hear the howdy bell the second time.

"Samantha Sarahannah Morgan. Shame on you, wife. Can't you quit early even on Christmas Eve?" Ben asked at her elbow, causing her to jump.

"That's Samantha Sarahannah Spencer Morgan," she corrected automatically, wrapping her arms protectively around her unborn infant, who kicked a vigorous response to daddy startling mama. "And shame on you for waking Junior; now I'll have no peace 'til he falls asleep again. And, no, I can't quit early. It may be Christmas Eve, but it's also Wednesday, with Thursday a loss altogether, and all copy must be ready for Gus by dawn Friday morning if we're to stay on schedule. I'll have you know, Ben Morgan, I haven't missed a deadline yet, nor will I today." Immediately contrite for her snappish tone, Samantha rubbed the frown between her furrowed brows. "Sorry, Ben, I didn't mean to be so sharp with you. Again." She sighed heavily. "I can't seem to find a middle ground these days. I am either very, very happy, or very, very sad, or very, very quick to fly off the handle, without having a single say as to when or why."

Ben bent to kiss his wife's frowning brow.

"Oh, really," he teased, "I hadn't noticed."

Before she came up with some argumentive retort, he stepped behind her to knead her taut shoulders. She dropped a cheek to his hand, sighing now in contentment.

"You're too good to me."

"I agree. Ready to go home?"

Samantha wrote a quick note of reminder to Gus, dropping her pencil on top of her work with a sense of satisfaction that she was proceeding on schedule once again.

"All ready. I can't wait to see everyone together again, all in one place at the same time, at last."

Ben held her coat out for her to slip into.

"Let's be on our way, then, m'lady. Your chariot awaits."

"After you, sir knight," responded Samantha with the same playful tone.

"No, together, sweet lady, now and forevermore."

He kissed her hard and long, squarely on her smiling lips until she swayed on her feet, before releasing her only to capture her elbow.

"Merry Christmas, a little early."

Grinning, Samantha retorted, "And not a kissing ball in sight."

"Here she is," cried Duncan in his most carrying Sunday sermon voice. "And about time."

He swept Samantha into his arms for a hearty bear hug; Samantha's baby kicked out in vigorous protest. Duncan immediately held her at arm's length, laughing.

"That one's got the kick of a good ol' mountain mule, Sam. Plannin' on making his entrance anytime soon?"

Samantha rested crossed hands on the shelf her belly had become, sighing.

"Hopefully before the end of the year. Ben and I were expecting a Thanksgiving baby."

"Christmas child's got to be at least twice as good," said Duncan with an ecclesiastical nod.

He still reminded her of Puck, escaped from *A Midsummer's Night Dream,* but different somehow, more peaceful—a man blessed with a purpose and a passion. Nevertheless, Samantha couldn't resist laughing in his face.

"My, my, how sanctimonious someone's become, now that *he* is perfect."

Duncan's grin went wide and rueful across tanned cheeks almost as sun-weathered as Grandpa Sam's. "Sorry. 'Fraid I'm not ready for sainthood yet, as my loving wife so frequently reminds me."

Her gaze immediately swept the front parlor, beyond the vestibule where she stood alone with Duncan. Ben had relieved her of her royal blue, fur-trimmed coat, which no longer buttoned in front, and joined the others, leaving her for a few private moments with her lifelong friend and confederate.

"Where is Alice? I'm dying to meet her, and little Adam." Her lips curled into a teasing smile, her eyes crinkled with mischief. "By the way, tell me . . . you aren't by any chance considering starting your own alphabetical dynasty by naming your firstborn Adam, are you?"

"Possibly, Sam, possibly." Duncan chuckled, confessing, "We've already begun on a Betsy or Benjamin, due sometime in June. Come, meet my wife and Charlie's, and the brood he inherited by up and marrying Alice's widowed sister, Charity."

His hand on her elbow, he wove for them a path through her parents' parlor crowded almost beyond capacity with every available relation, be it through blood or marriage, unerringly headed for the pretty young redheaded woman sitting in a slipper chair near the Christmas tree, baby in arms. At her side, stood another fiery-haired young woman, her hands resting on the two raven-headed toddlers pressed against her legs in the folds of her hunter green suit skirt. Copper-crowned and self-contained, she regarded the large gathering with more curious amusement than intimidation, leaving Samantha certain she was going to like Charity Fletcher Morgan, Charlie's beautiful bride.

Passage was slow, hugs and kisses and heartfelt greetings enfolding the newly arrived at every turn. Alice rose as Samantha and Duncan reached the two women, thrusting the sleeping infant into her husband's arm. When Samantha would have offered her hand, Alice swept her into her arms for a hearty hug before passing her on to her sister for another.

"And these are my children, Chenoa and Elan," said Charity by way of introduction. Faint defiance tinged her words, challenge lit her steady gaze.

The attractive young pair of approximately four and

seven bore little resemblance to their mother, with the nut brown skin, black hair and eyes, and high cheekbones of mingled cultures, Indian and white. Intrigued, Samantha bit back the overly inquisitive questions crowding her mind, and stretched out a welcoming hand in greeting, smiling encouragingly.

"Happy to meet you, Chenoa. Elan." She accepted each small brown hand in turn. "Did you enjoy the train ride to come visit us?" she asked Elan, the oldest, with bold, candid eyes and a rather adult demeanor, but his bright-eyed sister spoke up first.

"It was toooo long."

"I find most train rides seem to be," Samantha agreed, eliciting Chenoa's vigorous nod.

"Pah!" said Elan. "Only girls notice such things. Boys do not." He gave Samantha a steady, challenging stare, informing her, *"I* am the son of a Lakota chief, and I shall be one, too, someday."

"I can see that you have the potential for the task, Elan," Samantha responded with serious sincerity, fighting with difficulty the temptation to ask Charity for an interview for her paper, not quite certain how such a request would be met. She could see there was likely more than one fascinating tale to be told regarding Charlie's new wife, including how he met and married her. Determined to find the right time for a long, long chat with Charity Morgan née Fletcher, Samantha offered her a warm smile. "Charlie's a fortunate man to have you all in his life." She glanced toward his advancing figure, close enough to hear her every word. "He left so certain he'd end his days a crusty old bachelor. Looks like you and yours helped him overcome that dire prediction, and so quickly! I'm happy for him and pleased to welcome you into this ever-growing family. I hope you haven't been too overwhelmed?"

"Everyone's been very kind, very friendly," Charity replied softly, a smile on her lips that reached her amber eyes, sheened with tears.

"Samantha! I see you're making friends with my blushing bride."

Charlie spun her around into his arms for a hug and a noisy kiss, as robust and seasoned as his next younger brother, and seemingly as happy. *Must be something in the air out there in Colorado, or the women,* Samantha mused.

"I hope we'll be good friends, as long as she understands your overly exuberant embrace represents nothing more than two old friends exchanging greetings." Samantha threw Charity a conspiratorial wink, which she reciprocated. To Duncan, at her side, she held out her arms, asking of Alice, beside him, "May I hold Adam? I promise not to drop him. I've been practicing with Andrew and Olivia's little Andy ever since I discovered I'd soon have need of the skill. He's only three months old, but I think I have the hang of it."

With Alice's urging, Duncan relinquished his sleeping son. As soon as the blanketed bundle that was their sleeping six-month-old settled into her arms, Samantha's abdomen contracted, hard and strong and with surprising sharpness, until she feared she would drop the child, or be forced to thrust him at his closest parent. Before she could make a complete fool of herself, the wave of pain thankfully passed. To be on the safe side, she kissed the infant's warm, fragrant pate and transferred him to his proud mother.

"I wish the deed were done and I could be holding my own sweet child," she admitted. "Is . . . is the experience . . . giving birth . . . very . . . painful?" This last false contraction had quickly heightened her concerns.

Agreeing with her sister that it was, Charity—more experienced, being the mother of two—immediately amended, "But once over, the pain is forgotten the moment your child is placed in your arms."

Somewhat comforted, Samantha scanned the crowded room, frowning.

"Where are Grannie and Grandpa Spencer?" she asked Duncan.

Charlie answered for his brother. "In California. Seems your Uncle James's wife was put out because they visited your family two years in a row, instead of alternating as usual."

"Mama had a broken arm," Samantha protested. "And there was the wedding. I wanted Grannie here when my time came." She hated the sulky whine she heard in her own voice, though her disappointment was keen.

Charlie shrugged. "To keep the peace, they felt they had to go."

Duncan nudged Samantha's shoulder, saying, "I have a special present for you from Grannie. For after the baby's born."

"Oh, what is it? Can't I have it now? Please?" Samantha eagerly begged, hands locked above her stomach in pleading.

The two men solemnly shook their heads; at the same time, the baby kicked and Samantha's belly squeezed taut as if in a vise. In spite of herself, Samantha gasped.

"Doesn't look like you'll have that long to wait," advised Charity, adding, "Grannie suggested I might assist you, should your time come while we're here. I learned a few ways of helping things go more smoothly from my first husband's people. May I?" She placed her hands over the roundness of Samantha's taut abdomen, sagely bobbing her head as she made a gentle exploration. "Grannie

is one wise old woman. She must have had a premonition.
I believe you shall very soon have your wish, Samantha."

"Oh, no! Not tonight?"

More afraid than she'd anticipated, her exclamation
came out a wail that attracted the attention of those nearby,
including Ben, who hastened to her side. Regaining her
poise with difficulty, because Ben looked so unsettled
himself, she masked her fear with a reassuring smile that
went no farther than her lips.

"You all right?" Ben asked in a low tone.

Her small outburst had been quickly relegated to one
of the vagaries of a mother-to-be by the others, especially
the men. Conversation resumed, discussing recent news
world-wide and local as mostly gleaned from the *River
Valley Weekly Review*—the global influenza epidemic as
yet not diminished (a terrible disease from which no one
seemed safe), speculations regarding the viability and
practical application of the genuine motion picture films
being shown in New York City, the admittance earlier in
the year of Idaho and Wyoming as the forty-third and
forty-fourth states in the union (how many more, for gosh
sakes!), and just where it was Buckner's heifer with a bad
case of wanderlust had ended up this time.

Samantha slipped her hand into Ben's, squeezing hard.

"I'm going to be a mother," she whispered urgently.

He grinned, whispering back, "I know that, Sam. I was
there at conception, remember?"

"Charity, who is in a position to know, says it might be
tonight."

"Tonight?" Ben squawked in her ear, gaining the attention of the entire gathering once again.

"I say, brother, what're you all up to over there?" called
Andrew from across the room. Perched on the loveseat
beside his wife, proudly holding his namesake, he man-

aged a tone of authority appropriate to that of the brand-new vice president of Preston Spencer's bank.

Ben thrust out his chest. "I'm about to become the newest Morgan papa, brother. Tonight, it seems."

"More likely sometime tomorrow morning," Charity commented softly. "These things take their own good time."

"Tonight or tomorrow," Ben amended.

The females in the family surged forward as one, the gentlemen staying put, expressions more than a little uncomfortable. Their talk resumed, but in low, hushed tones, as if not to unsettle the mother-to-be into anything untoward before their very eyes.

Eliza and Olivia, simultaneously embracing their cousin, Eliza offering her blessings, Olivia characteristically offering dire predictions of the bloody, messy, unbearable agony soon to be faced.

"*I* shall *never* allow myself to suffer in that manner again, as Andrew well knows," she insisted tartly, throwing a challenging glance at her husband lingering reluctantly at her side, thanks to an overfirm grip on his upper arm.

Andrew juggled the infant into one arm to pat his wife's shoulder. "Indeed, my dear, I would not dream of asking you to. Andrew, Jr., is quite blessing enough." Aside, he advised Ben with eyes rolled skyward. "Wait until you hear the curdling screams coming from the birthing room. I thought poor Olivia was in the throes of death."

"I *wished* I was!" retorted his wife.

Her emphatic declaration led to other, similar sentiments, first from Aunt Rose, then young Cathleen Murray while attempting to hang on to her toddler Betsy, and finally, most vocal and graphic of all, Aunt Jane—mother of two—who declared the misery of childbirth only increased pregnancy by pregnancy. By this time, Charlie, Duncan, and Andrew had managed to escape, leaving only Ben, who stood his ground, though looking rather green about the gills. Concluding, Aunt Jane nodded in Cordelia's direction.

"I'm sure your mother can concur, Samantha, having miscarried so many times. How many was it, Cordelia?"

"More than I care to recall, or to discuss at this time, and in the company of the gentlemen and children, Jane," Cordelia retorted tartly. Her face softened as her gaze sought out her daughter. She took Samantha's cheeks between her work-roughened hands, kissing her lightly on the forehead, advising her, "Just remember, my child, that no matter how badly it hurts, you must keep telling yourself the pain cannot go on forever. You will, indeed, give birth, one way or the other."

Samantha felt herself growing light-headed, apprehension soaring into panic. With a faint *ohhh,* she leaned against Ben; he brought his arm around her wide girth to support her.

"See here, you women don't have to try to scare Sam half to death."

Charity spoke up, poised and only slightly hesitant. "Please, take no offense. I don't know any of you well, and only long enough to believe you are all kind, compassionate women who would not intentionally frighten a mother in her time of travail. But could we please all go back to what we were doing before this came up? It will be hours before Samantha need seek confinement. Let's all go on with our party, maybe open a tin of Grannie's gingerbread men, as planned, remembering there can be no greater blessing for us all than the bringing of a new life into the world at this most precious Christmas season."

"Spoken like a true pastor's daughter. I agree," said Ben, too loudly and heartily. "Gingerbread men for everyone. And more eggnog all around, too."

With contrite apologies and more hugging and kissing, friends and relatives dispersed. Samantha found a place on the loveseat along with Eliza, Ben hovering close at hand; Jasper pushed up a footstool to perch on beside his wife.

"Jasper and I have had an unexpected happy blessing this Christmas, too. Our adoption of Henry and Molly was made final yesterday," Eliza confided abruptly, her happiness obviously too great to contain.

Samantha and Ben offered their congratulations to the overjoyed couple.

"Tell them our other news. Tell the rest, my dear," Jasper encouraged with pride and pleasure.

Eliza's pale complexion glowed rosier still, her soft brown eyes alive with inner joy.

"We're taking in Addie's children, too, hoping to adopt them as well."

"Addie Stone's?" The farmer's widow had lost her land, then her life to a wasting disease late in the fall. "Those twin boys of hers are a real handful, and they're, what, five now? And Clara's little more than a baby," she cautioned.

"A challenge we feel ready to meet, with Henry and Molly's help, of course," Eliza gently amended. "Jasper and I, we're so enjoying our new charges, we're thinking . . . well, we're hoping," she glanced at her husband for confirmation before continuing at his encouraging nod, "we're hoping to take in as many who need us as our big old house will hold."

"You're opening an orphanage? Or is it to be a school?" Samantha's fingers itched for pencil and paper, ever the reporter, in spite of her baby's impending birth. Her contractions were growing increasingly difficult to ignore. A wave of crushing pain clamped down on her belly as Jasper offered an answer to her questions, and she missed most of what he said before it receded.

". . . Adoption. As many as are free to will carry the name of Cooper, don't you know. Those who are otherwise legally encumbered, we'll take on as our wards until relatives can be located, or declared out of the picture altogether, as it were."

Ben patted Samantha's arm.

"Samantha, maybe we'd better be heading on home," he suggested worriedly.

Panic leapt high in Samantha's throat. "Oh, please, not yet."

Charity appeared at her side to place a gentling hand on her shoulder, as if somehow sensing the fear swelling and growing as the contractions came harder and faster.

"You will know when the time for confinement arrives, Samantha," she reassured. "Should you bring your babe into the world here among your family, in your old room, I'm sure neither your mother nor your husband would have any objections."

Ben appeared noticeably relieved. "Excellent idea, Charity. And Charlie can herd all the men and children over to my house if . . . things . . . get too noisy."

Samantha held on to her husband's hand like a lifeline, ashamed of her cowardice; she turned an apologetic look Charity's way as she recalled Olivia's description of Andy's delivery.

"I don't want to make a fool of myself, or frighten my poor baby . . . or anyone else . . . by screaming like a madwoman over a little pain."

Charity squeezed her shoulder. "Then I shall tell you

the simple secret a Lakota medicine woman told to me as I was about to give birth to Elan. Cry out if you must. Only make it a joyful noise of thanks unto Your Maker, and your babe's, for this precious life that has been given into your care."

Samantha felt tears splash off her chin without knowing she was crying. She rubbed the backs of her hands quickly over hot, flushed cheeks. Charity patted her shoulder reassuringly, but Eliza appeared both awed and distressed at her cousin's uncharacteristic behavior. Samantha offered a shaky laugh.

"Don't mind me. This happens when least expected lately, and I don't seem to have any control over where or when."

"I can attest to that," Ben admitted. "You heed Charity's suggestion, Sam, if you can when the time comes." He cleared his throat, obviously uncomfortable. "All this female talk isn't doing much for my male sensibilities, or Jasper's, here. Would you mind . . . Is it all right if we . . . ?"

"Go," Charity urged. "You have performed well your husbandly duties, the results are best left to women's hands, and eyes. When your wife again has need of you, we will bring you to her."

With a peck on his wife's cheek, and a weak, relieved grin, Ben took his leave with Jasper.

Lifting her gaze to Charity's calm, lovely face. "Thank you for your advice . . . and . . . everything. I hope I can remember what you said when the time comes."

"I will do what I can to see that you do. In the meantime, here is some sweetened papoose root tea which will calm and relax you, perhaps ease your travail. Very soon your family, which has made me feel so welcome here tonight, will celebrate yet another infant's birth this blessed Christmas season."

She drifted away to join her husband on the far side of the room, where he oversaw the board game being played by a quartet of youngsters. He welcomed his bride with love-light in his eyes such as had never been there for Eliza. How wonderfully it had turned out for both Charlie and her cousin after all, far better than if they had wed last New Year's Day as intended.

Samantha sipped her tea, finding it unusual in flavor and slightly sweet. Whether by its warmth or content, she found herself relaxing enough to listen to Eliza and Jasper's plans, and to observe the family party under way, every last soul from youngest to oldest alive with the celebration of the season, the company, and the delectable refreshments—in which Samantha had been cautioned not to indulge until after her baby's birth.

For the most part, the men and women would eventually segregate, as usual, into separate clusters. The men would take their ongoing discussion of the condition of the world at large and River Valley in particular out onto the back porch, ostensibly for fresh air, in reality to smoke cigars Uncle Noble had accumulated on his sales trips and Aunt Jane refused to allow in her house. The women would adjourn to the kitchen to lay out even more food and drink, to gossip, to tell stories of courtship and marriage, horror stories of childbirth and death, recipes for the latest variation of sponge cake, or tried and true remedies for gout. The children, left in the parlor, would play games, tell ghost stories, and attempt to guess what gift lay beneath the wrappings of a box bearing their name with a shake or a squeeze.

For a little while yet, everyone lingered in the front parlor, maybe because of her. Samantha observed friends and family she encountered day in and day out, and faces she only faintly recalled, or not at all. Only Grannie and Grandpa absent, it seemed. Still, there *was* Grannie's mysterious present to look forward to, and her baby's birth, Samantha reminded herself, for no other reason than to bolster her sagging spirits, and her waning courage.

She saw Edward, now seventeen and maturing rapidly, take Lydia Snow's hand and lead her to the doorway to the hall for a quick kiss under the mistletoe hanging there. Samantha glanced Ben's way—he'd tease poor Edward mercilessly if he saw the kiss—but he had eyes only for her, though he chatted with his married brothers and Jasper. There was talk of an engagement between the young pair being announced as soon as they graduated come June. Freddie, at thirteen, and Georgie, now eleven, immersed in a game of Parcheesi, were growing like a pair of weeds. She could scarcely keep them outfitted in clothes that were long enough in sleeve and cuff. Fourteen-year-old cousin Sally, sharing the game with the boys and her sixteen-year-old sister, Prudence, flirted shamelessly with both of the two youngest Morgan boys. Samantha reflected that before she and Ben realized it, the pair'd be off and on their own, leaving them to fill the house once again with children of their own—maybe seven boys or girls, maybe a mixture. Or more. Or less, if each experience of childbirth were as painful as this one.

Contractions were coming faster now, almost on top of one another; Charity's soothing tea no longer worked its wonders. As a new surge struck, Samantha clutched Eliza's arm, whispering urgently, "Will you please go fetch Charity for me? I think I'd better go upstairs now."

Though shy and retiring, Eliza bore a dependable resilience, unwavering when called upon under duress. She rose without question or comment, quickly returning with

Charlie's wife. Together, they helped Samantha rise, then navigate among the clusters of revelers without attracting undue attention. Until Aunt Jane saw them exit to the hall and alerted all the other mothers within her range. An entourage of women, chattering away with unsolicited warnings and advice, followed Samantha's slow and painful progress up the stairs.

"Has anyone thought to check for any items that might be knotted?" twittered Aunt Rose. "A forgotten apron string? A bit of rope? Even a knot in a ball of knitting yarn leaves the baby at risk of coming into the world with a knot in the cord, you know."

"Has the gender of the child been determined yet with her wedding ring on a bit of string? You have only to hold it over her belly . . ." Someone in the back began.

"Too late for that now," Aunt Jane snapped. "We'll see for ourselves if it's a boy or a girl soon enough. Did anyone think to fetch Cordelia's sharpest knife from the kitchen?" Momentary silence. "Olivia, run down and get it. The very sharpest, now, to cut Samantha's pain from beneath the birthing bed."

Samantha's mother pushed her way to the head of the group. "Such tomfoolery is not necessary, Olivia. Better for you to go ask one of the men to fetch Doc Brown, just in case. And the rest of you might as well head back down to the party. Charity and I—"

"Oh, please, let Eliza stay, too, if she will," Samantha pleaded between clenched teeth.

"And Eliza will do what must be done upstairs."

"Very well," Aunt Jane huffed, then shook a fat finger in Charity's direction, "but mind you, I won't have you performing any heathenish rituals on my niece or I'll—"

"Jane," cried Cordelia, aghast. "Go . . . go boil some water. Gallons of it."

"Well, I never. I merely meant . . . I'll have you know—"

"Jane, go."

Red-faced, Jane said no more, lifting her skirts to stomp downstairs, all the rest following like a flock of agitated broody hens.

The three women remaining escorted the mother-to-be into the room of her childhood. Charity and Eliza helped Samantha slip out of her clothing into her nightgown with minimal embarrassment to them all, though her water broke during the process—fortunately as she stood on a throw rug. Cordelia eliminated the mess, then stripped the bed, padding the mattress well first with layers of newspaper, then several worn blankets, and finally a soft, flannel sheet. Charity suggested that if it brought her comfort, Samantha could sit in her rocking chair until the need to push became undeniable.

"I'd like that," Samantha agreed thankfully. "But please, come sit nearby, all of you. Talk to me. Tell me, Charity, how you met up with Charlie," she watched a wary expression settle over the young woman's face, "or, if you'd rather, tell me about growing up in Colorado, tell me all about your sisters." The light in Charity's eyes returned, "What are their names? Their ages? Whether married or single. I'd love to know everything, since we're all related now. Imagine two of the seven Morgan boys marrying into a family of seven sisters! What an amazing coincidence."

Charity chuckled. "The Lakota, and my seventh sister, Violet—who has 'the sight,' would tell you fate had more to do with it than luck, Samantha." She crossed her ankles and sat down on the floor, Indian-fashion, her skirts billowing, then settling around her. She rubbed two fingers against her chin, reflectively. "Where to begin? I am the oldest at twenty-three, then, like stair steps, a year apart, come Dorcas, then Esther, then Alice—who is twenty, and the only other wife and mother—then Patience, and Theodosia, and finally Violet, the seventh, at seventeen. Mama died giving birth to her, or there might have been countless more of us until Papa got his boy and namesake."

"He didn't remarry?" asked Eliza.

"No!"

"He raised the seven of you all by himself?" Cordelia wanted to know.

"Actually . . . no. Papa . . . he was on the road most of every year, traveling from church to church on his circuit. I took care of my sisters by myself mostly, with a little help in the beginning from various women with aspirations of being Preacher Fletcher's second wife. It is a position of much prestige in a small mountain town struggling out of rowdy and wild lawlessness into respectability. But Papa had no heart for any other women after Mama, so eventually . . ." She shrugged. "Well, it was my job as eldest to take on the responsibility."

"And a marvelous job you've done, if Alice is any indication," Cordelia praised.

Charity laughed ruefully. "I'm afraid not. Some of my sisters have proven easier to raise than others. More of their life stories, or mine, however, will have to wait. I believe it's time we helped Samantha to her bed."

"Please," Samantha begged through clenched teeth. The urge to bring her child into the world had grown so powerful, so imminent, she had become unable to concentrate on anything else, even Charity's fascinating tale of herself and her sisters. Finally Samantha had discovered something more compelling than her writing, and a reserve of strength she had never realized she possessed.

Charity rose up in one fluid movement, giving Samantha's hand a gentle, comforting squeeze; the three attending women helped her to her bed. When Cordelia advised her daughter to stretch out prone and keep her ankles modestly crossed until she could no longer avoid spreading her legs, Charity tactfully contradicted her.

"I'm sure your doctors, who had never expelled a newborn from their own bodies, believed they were giving you the best advice they were able. Living among the Lakota, where many of the healers are women who have been mothers themselves, I discovered my own deliveries were quicker and less painful in a more upright position."

"Sitting up?" cried Cordelia, aghast.

"Well, actually, squatting on the ground."

Cordelia's shocked face first went pale, then livid.

"No grandchild of mine shall be brought into the world to fall out upon a dirty floor."

"Excuse me," spoke a pained voice from the bed, "if I have any say in this matter at all, I should like to try sitting up. If gravity helps things go any faster, I'm willing to try it. Oh, Mama, I had no idea how you suffered giving birth to me until this moment. What if I am not as brave as you are? What if I cannot bear the pain?"

Samantha's impassioned plea galvanized Cordelia as nothing else could have.

"You will, my dear child," she replied. "You are the strongest person I've ever known; I was a coward at this time compared to you. You'll do just fine, I know."

Panic that had threatened to overwhelm Samantha receded in an outgoing wave to a more manageable level.

Eliza, who had stood back from the confrontation between experienced mothers, rushed to aid her cousin, propping every available pillow behind her back.

"Better?"

Samantha nodded, unable to speak, in the throes of crushing pain.

"Need to push?" asked Charity beside her.

"Yes." The single word came out a hiss.

"Give it all you have, Samantha, until the urge passes."

The real work began. Time stood still, her labor became Samantha's world. The only thought in her head was that she *would not* scream. Her child must not be born to the sound of her mother's suffering. Charity offered comforting encouragement between contractions, toward the end she massaged Samantha's belly to help ease her discomfort and hurry things along. Cordelia offered no further objection, watching first with lips pursed in disapproval, then agonized concern and wonder mingled, tears rolling unheeded down her cheeks. Eliza stood stalwartly at her cousin's far side, offering verbal comfort and encouragement, pale but composed. When Samantha grew certain she could not live through another session of pain and pushing, her baby slid out into the world with a hearty wail.

"It's a girl," Charity declared triumphantly. "A beautiful, healthy, perfect daughter, Samantha," she added when at last, wrapped snugly, the newborn was placed in her new mother's waiting arms.

Wonderment in her rapt expression, Samantha studied her daughter's tiny face, still puckered with indignant protest, outthrust lower lip quivering. She caught the baby's flailing fists and counted fingers; untangled her kicking feet from the receiving blanket, counting toes. Satisfied her examination revealed no irregularities, she glanced up.

"What time is it? What day is this?"

Her mother lifted her lapel clock from her bodice to check.

"Why, it's twelve-fifteen. Christmas morning, Samantha. Blessed Christmas Day."

No less emotional than before she gave birth, Samantha burst into tears, happy, relieved tears.

"Where is Ben? Please, someone find Ben for me. I need Ben."

Cordelia spoke up. "When you're cleaned up and rested—"

Charity said, at the same moment, "Eliza's gone to fetch him for you."

She tossed a sheet, then a light blanket over Samantha's bare legs and damp, soiled nightgown, brushed her hair, washed her face and the child's, preparing for the new father to meet his family. Cordelia pressed her lips together and said no more, nor did she protest when Ben burst into the room and threw himself down on the bed beside his wife, though the temptation to remind them all how things were done in her day was clearly written on her face. Charity took the older woman gently by the arm, urging her toward the door.

"Shall we give them a few private moments?"

The door closed behind them, leaving the three alone. Ben completed his examination of the babe, as satisfied with the results as had been Samantha. He studied her face, a worried frown between his brows.

"Are you all right? Did it hurt unbearably?"

Samantha patted his lean cheek, caressed his handsome, dear, dear face, rubbed away worry lines at the corners of his eyes and lips with a gentle fingertip.

"I'm fine. Wonderful, perfect in fact, now it's all over. And the pain . . ." she marveled. "Why, I scarcely recall it. Oh, Ben, I have never felt such peace, such fulfillment. All thanks to you and our love."

Ben kissed her lips lightly and sweetly.

"And thank you, Sam, for the best Christmas gift a fellow could hope for." He leaned back to study both their faces. "By the way, when are you planning on telling me if we've produced a boy or a girl? Is the newest Morgan to be Christopher or Christianna?"

"Christianna."

Ben reached out with a single finger, tracing his daughter's pouty lips. In her sleep, she opened her mouth and drew it within, to suckle. Startled, Ben looked up.

"Well, look at that."

"Wait 'til my milk comes in."

Ben licked his lips. "I can hardly wait."

Samantha giggled. "I meant to watch your baby really feed."

"Oh!"

Together they observed their precious child sleeping peacefully.

Finally, Ben asked, "Are you sure you're all right? Can I get you anything? Something to eat or drink?"

"I'm fine, Ben, really. Eliza brought me water and a plate of Grannie's cookies. I'm more sleepy than anything. There is one favor . . . Could you bring me the special gift Grannie sent with Duncan? Remind him it *is* Christmas morning."

Ben rose. "Will do."

He stood stock-still, studying the picture they made nestled together in the covers. His wife. His daughter. He leaned over to kiss his baby's soft forehead, then his wife's. Her cheeks, her nose, her chin.

"I love you, Sam."

"I love you, too, Ben. There is nothing or no one more precious to me than you, and little Christianna, no gift greater than that I share my life with the two of you and all the other little Morgans with whom we'll someday be blessed."

Ben smiled crookedly. "Not even some juicy exposé, one to make you rich and famous beyond your wildest dreams?"

Samantha matched his smile, as beautiful as the Madonna herself.

"*This,* only this was beyond my wildest dreams."

"Mine, too, Sam, mine, too. I . . . ahem . . . I'll go locate that present from Grannie for you."

An unknown time later, Samantha awoke to some faint sound from her daughter, now asleep nearby in her crib. Within a hand's reach lay Grannie's present to her. With impatient finger's she tore the brown paper and string to discover a bound notebook, its pages filled with Grannie's small, perfect script. A letter in a sealed envelope lay between the inside cover and first page, admonishing *READ THIS FIRST.* Samantha slit open the letter with impatient fingers.

> *My dearest Granddaughter,*
>   *If you are reading this, your firstborn has arrived. You have now experienced all that is necessary to know of love and marriage and family so that I may entrust in you—to your discretion—my story, and that of the bride's quilt I gave you last Christmas. May you read it and interpret its value to you with all the love and understanding that went into its writing.*
>   *Your loving grandmother,*
>   *Madeline Preston Spencer*

With hands that trembled, Samantha turned to the first page in Grannie's journal and began to read. She read straight through to the end, thanks to Christianna's sound sleep. When she had finished, she closed the book, happy tears in her eyes. Now she knew the full story of Madeline Preston's journey across country to the Colorado territory in 1845, long before cross-country travel was common, especially for women, most especially women alone. She now knew how Maddie and Sam had met, how their love flourished and blossomed in a most primitive country under the harshest of conditions. She learned of their every failure and their ultimate joy—a joy to match what she and Ben shared—and their mountaintop marriage. All because of another woman's treasure, now passed into her own hands, along with its legacy.

Lying back among her pillows, Samantha vowed to continue the tradition one day with her own firstborn. And to someday—when the time was right—tell Grannie's story, and that of the bride's quilt, for all who loved adventure, and for those who simply loved.

Author's Notes

After Nellie Bly became known world-wide for exposing New York's poverty, child labor, and mental institutions' conditions, many newspapers throughout the country hired their own female stunt reporters in competition, hence the purely fictional Samantha Sarahannah Spencer. Nellie's trip around the world in 80 days that Samantha followed so avidly concluded successfully, and ahead of schedule, in Jersey City, Saturday, January 25, 1890, for a total of 72 days, 6 hours, 11 minutes, and 14 seconds.

Nell Nelson of the *Chicago Times* was real. To my knowledge, no *Chicago Evening Star* newspaper ever existed; the *River Valley Weekly Review* is also a product of the author's imagination, as is River Valley and its citizens.

The Orphan Trains probably did a lot of good for many, but the problem Samantha challenges is a fact of record.

To learn the secret of the quilt Grannie Spencer gave to Samantha, look for *The Bride Quilt,* a June, 1999, release from Zebra.

I love to hear from my readers:
Pamela Quint Chambers
890 76th Street SE
Byron Center, Michigan 49315

Here's an exciting sneak preview of
Pamela Quint Chambers's
newest Zebra historical romance
The Bride Quilt
to be published in
June, 1999

The bride's quilt, the final and thirteenth in her dowry, executed and completed by the bride alone or at a bee with only her closest female relatives and friends upon the announcement of her engagement, represented a lasting testimony to the excellence of her sewing skills and her social status in her community.

ONE

Monday, February 17, 1845
River Valley in the Midwest

"Madeline?"

"Madeline, you haven't heard a word I've said."

"Madeline Genevieve Preston, wake up over there and come join us. Thelma's just been telling us the most delicious bit of gossip. It's about your intended," Thelma's sister Janet taunted.

Madeline stared out, unseeing, through the lace curtains of the parlor's front window, oblivious to the dreary rainlike snow turning the clay road to impassable mire and the teatime chatter going on around her. Lost in troubled thoughts, she awoke with a start, like a sleeper from the throes of a nightmare, when Janet rose to join her, pinching her upper arm, hard.

"I should think you'd be avidly interested in what Thelma has learned about Elmer Chester, since it concerns you as well."

"What concerns me?"

Madeline automatically lifted her right hand to the chignon at her nape to assure herself every last hair had stayed put, neatly coiled inside its hand-woven net.

"You're not wearing an engagement ring," exclaimed Janet, aghast.

Madeline tilted her nose high. "Most likely because I am not engaged to marry anyone."

"Thelma heard that you were," asserted plump and pregnant Susanna White, taking another rich *petit four* from the china serving plate Madeline herself had hand-painted. "She says Elmer Chester proposed on Valentine's Day, this Friday past—how wildly romantic—and that you accepted."

Madeline offered a brief, mirthless laugh. "Papa's partner offered a merger between us last Friday, yes, but hardly romantic since Mr. Chester is older than Papa, weighs not an ounce under three hundred pounds, and has already buried one young wife no more than seven months ago. In addition," Madeline hastened to add, lest there be any doubt as to the man's unsuitability, "Mr. Chester has absolutely no imagination, no sense of adventure. To him, I'd guess, an evening's excitement would consist of two biscuits with his supper stew instead of one, or mutton on Tuesday rather than roast chicken."

"Oh, but she didn't die," corrected Thelma smugly.

"Who?"

"Elmer Chester's first wife. *That's* what I've been trying to tell you. The honorable Mr. Bank President Chester is no widower. He's a *grass* widower. His wife ran off with the butler—"

"To escape her dreadfully dull old husband, I'd wager, if nothing else. Well, I for one have no intention of becoming the second Mrs. Chester, no matter how Papa insists. I have other—"

Madeline bit her lower lip, mindful of her near slip. No one must know the desperate lengths to which she intended to go to avoid Papa's unsuitable arrangement for keeping his lifelong friend and senior partner happy.

"Other what?" asked Maureen Talbot, newly engaged to Gabe Sidwell, her eyes aglow equally with happiness and conspicuous curiosity.

"Other goals. Other expectations. Other hopes for my future, and my life. You and Thelma were allowed to freely pick the men whom you've promised to wed, and Susanna and Janet are already married to men of their choosing; why cannot Papa understand I must be permitted the same freedom?"

"Probably because you have turned down so many suitors, your father fears you will be destined for the life of a spinster unless he takes matters into his own hands," Susanna retorted tartly.

"I'm not yet twenty."

"I was sixteen when Bill and I married," said Janet.

"You believed yourself so in love you couldn't wait any longer," Madeline reminded her, without adding that the childhood sweethearts now had two screaming, crying toddlers to chase after and possibly another on the way, as Janet had today confided. "I myself have never found a person with whom to share the porch swing for two consecutive evenings, let alone the rest of my life."

"You are too particular," said Maureen. "Look at me and Gabe. I know his ears stick out so that they glow red and translucent if the sun strikes them just so, and that our poor offspring, when we begin having them, will probably all have a mouth full of horse-sized teeth like his, but he is kind, and affectionate, and a good provider. And he will love me with an unswerving devotion to last forever."

Had Madeline been an individual given to hugging, now would have been the time to cross the room to where the three others sat around the tea table, and offer one to Maureen in support of her pronouncement; as she was not, she managed the barest of smiles.

"I am happy for you, Maureen, for all of you." She glanced from one to the other of the faces turned her way, as familiar as her own. "By your examples, I am all the more certain I must not marry old Mr. Chester. It would be just my bad luck to meet the fellow capable of sweeping me off my feet the moment the vows were exchanged. Then where would I be? My decision not to marry Papa's partner stands, and if he continues to insist, I will . . . I will . . ." Again she almost betrayed herself to her dearest friends, dismayed at how easily it might happen should this vein of conversation continue.

"You'll what?" they chorused, expectant of some secret to be shared, as they had always shared them since earliest childhood.

She forced what sounded to her like genuine laughter, gay and carefree. "I shall lock myself in my bedroom and hide the only key until Elmer Chester passes on to his reward . . . which shouldn't take any time at all given his ponderous capacity for overindulgence. Have you heard that Annabelle Maxwell and Raymond Butler also recently became engaged?" Miss Maxwell was the town flirt with a less than sterling reputation, always good for a half hour's gossip.

"I've heard," Thelma whispered conspiratorially, "that they *have* to get married, and that Annabelle's not even positive Ray's the father—"

"Well *I* heard," chimed in Susanna, and so the conversation whisked away elsewhere, as Madeline intended.

She followed the flow of talk more closely this time,

not only to keep it from coming around to her again, but to attempt to keep from dwelling on the monumental predicament into which she'd gotten herself. With characteristic impetuousness, she had rashly committed herself to the only recourse she'd been able to come up with to avoid marrying Papa's persistent partner. Not at all certain she hadn't jumped out of the frying pan into the fire, as it were, she grew more convinced by the hour that she had made a terrible, irreversible mistake she would very soon be forced to follow through with, along a path taking her far and forever away from everything she knew and everyone she loved.

Late that evening, alone in her room, she paced, a copy of the document she had signed on impulse Saturday afternoon crushed in her hand. Though reread countless times, Madeline could find no flaw that might free her from her written promise to become a mail-order bride destined for far-off California.

How innocently she had attended the lecture with her parents, given by Major Eben Vance, lauding the beauties and the virtues of the fertile land of lush, exotic vegetation and vistas of mountain and ocean unmatched anywhere else on earth. Here rugged men of sturdy pioneer stock had laid claim to thousands of acres from which to carve their fortunes and their dynasties. All this lacking only bold, adventuresome women to bring home and family and gentility to the burgeoning communities springing up all over that great and wondrous land. Major Vance's mission, and that of the stoic, silent Indian guide at his side, was to bring those women, those brides, across the thousands of miles to their glorious destinies.

To that end, he was offering every unattached woman of River Valley the opportunity to join his expedition, to be among the first of those to write their names in history as pioneers in their own right. Sign-ups were limited to the first ten ladies on this premiere journey, all others would be forced to wait for subsequent trips. And, warned the Major, once this maiden trip had been successfully completed, one might have to wait months, years to find vacancies upon the list again.

Papa and Mama were disgusted, having anticipated an edifying lecture, only to receive a charlatan's pitch for women for sale. But Madeline thought this surprising new practice both a practical and a clever way to solve the problem of an enormous scarcity in the wild and wonderful new West. And an excellent opportunity for the half-dozen young women she watched flock around Major Vance at the conclusion of his lecture, all day laborers and household help by their dress and demeanor, each one eager to be among those allowed to sign. She found herself struggling with an almost irresistible urge to be one of them. Only her father's taking her firmly by the elbow and ushering her and her mother briskly toward the door at the back of the auditorium kept her from it.

A crisp winter chill should have awakened her senses to the foolish decision she'd almost allowed herself to make. Instead, she responded in the opposite manner, awakening to an even greater desire to go. A surge of panic at being left behind so overwhelmed her, she made the excuse of having left her favorite gloves on her seat in the auditorium, and turned back. She pushed her way through the crush of people. Most everyone cleared her a path—seeing her for a person of social position by the couturier garments she wore—allowing her to reach the front row uncontested. The same attention was paid by the Major himself, whose steely gray eyes, identical in color to his dramatic mane of silver hair, glittered the instant he spied her. Without preamble, he thrust papers into her hands. Without another thought, or the foresight to read them through, she signed his copy and hers.

"I simply won't show up tonight, let Papa deal with the legalities should there be any."

She spoke aloud her decision, and hearing her own words, realized she was behaving like a cowering coward, speaking so bravely to her friends of avoiding marrying Elmer Chester in one breath, refusing to follow through with the only viable solution—by leaving town—in the next. Where were her courage, her pride, her self-respect, when she most needed them?

"I shall go."

Decision made, sudden, unexpected excitement burst full-blown within her. Having care to be quiet about her preparations, she lifted her satchel off the high shelf inside her armoire. She stuffed her possessions inside willy-nilly. Time was of the essence. Major Vance had warned that he would depart on the morning train at dawn, with or without all those who had signed on. He'd have little trouble finding other willing souls between here and Independence, Missouri, their stepping-off place into the vast wilderness beyond.

Finding her satchel insufficient for her needs, she dumped the contents out of her copious sewing bag, and loaded that, too. From her handkerchief drawer, she drew every cent remaining from Papa's generous monthly allowance, thanking fortune that she had not spent it as quickly as received this month—the weather having been on the whole too inclement for shopping expeditions. She stuffed the roll of bills into her plum-colored velvet reticule beneath a half-dozen of her loveliest lace-trimmed, embroidered handkerchiefs. From her jewelry box she chose an assortment of her most modest necklaces, bracelets, brooches, earbobs. Her smallest vial of smelling salts, comb and brush, and a handful of hairpins followed, lastly her small pocket Bible. The bead-trimmed bag was now so full she was barely able to pull the drawstrings tight, but there wasn't one item she felt she dared eliminate. One never knew what one might require in a given situation.

Madeline rifled through her wardrobe until she located an outfit she considered most suitable for extended travel, a violet merino coat dress, high in the neck, with a moderately sized cape, and the fashionable new Hungary sleeves over puffed undersleeves, tight at the wrists Because the cape was removable, the dress would do for both cool and warm weather. For coldest weather, she choose a street-length cloak in the latest French style, of serviceable wool. Its color was a slightly darker shade of violet, all of her wardrobe consisting of various shades of purple from deepest indigo to lightest lilac, to complement her violet eyes, raven hair, and porcelain-pale complexion. She spent little time fussing over her ablutions after exchanging wrapper and nightgown for the chosen garments. The grandfather clock downstairs struck three times as she tied her prettiest heliotrope bonnet with matching dyed feathers in place.

With everything in readiness, including herself, she approached the most difficult task of all, penning a letter to her parents to leave propped against her pillow for them to find in the morning. With time fast running out, she kept it simple and to the point, telling them succinctly that she loved them, not to worry as she was safely in Major Eben Vance's competent care, that her decision was based more on an overwhelming need to experience life beyond River Valley than to escape the loveless marriage they'd urged her to undertake. And finally, that she would write at the first opportunity.

The clock chimed four times as she let herself out the front door, so heavily laden with satchel in one hand and sewing bag in the other that her shoulders bowed under the weight. But her resolve remained strong and excited anticipation lightened her steps. She had set her feet irrevocably upon a path leading to the greatest adventure of her life, for a purpose so noble, so patriotic, as to be the stuff of legends in the making. Destiny called her to the far distant promised land of sunshine and bounty, and she had answered. Madeline Genevieve Preston was indeed, in her own eyes, a true heroine in the history of her country for seizing the opportunity when presented, for having the courage to answer its call. She could scarcely contain her soaring expectations for the adventure upon which she was about to embark.

"Where the bloody hell's that female what fancies herself a lady? I want t' have me the gal I bought an' paid fer an', by gum, I mean t' have 'er, now! Flat on 'er back, sittin' an' standin' an' every other way I kin come up with. Fetch 'er fer me, Vance, 'fore I skin yer scalp off'n yer head an' sell it t' the first redskin what heads m' way."

Heart hammering so hard in her chest it hurt, Madeline ducked behind a stack of bulging flour sacks, scrunching down, praying for invisibility from the massive mountain man's detection. Unbelievably, it was herself the reeking beast with a patch over one eye—hiding who knew what horror—a tobacco-stained beard striped black and white like a skunk, and a fleshy lipped leer displaying a half-dozen rotting teeth, searched for, fully expecting to make her Mrs. Cougar Callaway within the hour. As she had so lightly predicted safely back in her parents' front parlor, she had indeed thrust herself out of the frying pan directly into a fire, in a place one would flatter by calling a hell on earth. She made herself as small as possible, screwed her eyes tightly shut, and prayed as if her life depended upon it.

Oh, dear, sweet, merciful Lord, save me from this fate worse than death to which my impetuous folly has brought me.

Only yesterday, fittingly All Fool's Day, April 1, Major Vance's small, bedraggled party arrived, not in warm and sunny California, but at a cluster of log shacks high in the Rocky Mountains—a stockade, or a trading post at best, certainly nothing more—aptly named Luckless, as were the eight new arrivals themselves. *Luckless, Co. Ter.: Poplacion* X X X *All Male n Proud v It* read the sign nailed to a towering pine below another stating *HoTEl, Gen. Stor Hor Hous n Saloon.* In the shadow of the surrounding pines stood the largest of the half-dozen log structures in the tight clearing, the forest crowding close at every turn. To this their small group turned for shelter from the relentless, endless downpour of countless days duration which made pushing onward an impossibility. One more insurmountable difficulty in a series of disastrous mishaps that had plagued Major Eban Vance and his mail-order brides from the very beginning of this ill-conceived, poorly prepared-for journey. The Major himself had neither the knowledge nor the practical skills for the undertaking. His guide proved to be woefully ignorant as well. And the women, including herself, had no aptitude and no training whatsoever.

Immediately upon their party's arrival in Independence, wiser men than himself—other wagon masters, experienced guides—issued dire predictions of the folly in beginning a cross-country journey in mid-February. No one, but no one with a brain in his head left before the first of May, when the last of the snow in the mountain passes melted and the spring rainstorms ceased, turning the land to miring muck. Eban Vance paid the warnings no heed, nor did he give ear to the future brides' collective pleadings, dismissing them as the vagaries of easily frightened females. He was convinced the first to start, arriving ahead of the others, would be the most richly rewarded. Positive that the warnings came from those who planned to try to beat him to the Pacific shore, the Major set his scout to procuring needed supplies and the wagons and oxen to carry them. When he unexpectedly ran low on funds, he turned to his passengers for assistance, discovering only Madeline carried more than a few pennies in pocket change.

The journey, ill begun, went from bad to worse thereafter, horrendous beyond the wildest reaches of one's most terrifying nightmares. Weather which in the first days was balmy, springlike—bolstering the ladies' faith in their chosen leader over the sages' advice in Independence—turned foul before they'd traveled more than ten days. Too late, however, to turn back, the Major insisted, without losing every cent of his investment, making a future, delayed departure impossible. Downpour turned to blizzard, roads became mud holes, knee deep. Known trails ceased to appear, some buried beneath snow, some existing only on the crude map the Major carried and nowhere else. Supplies ran dangerously low, having been vastly underestimated. The two wagons broke down irreparably and were abandoned. Horses grew weak with lack of food and overwork, dropping dead in their tracks. Somewhere in the Rockies, the seven women and two men became hopelessly lost; one young woman, the frailest to begin with, took ill and died and was left buried beneath a mound of rocks as the others moved on.

Eight weeks into their fearful journey, near dusk on the

first of April, Major Eban Vance's ill-fated assemblage arrived in this outpost high in the mountains with little more than the rags that remained of their clothing on their backs and their worn-out, soleless boots on their feet. Their stomachs were as empty of nourishment as their pockets of cash. However, their arrival was greeted with an exuberant, boisterous welcome by the completely male populace of Luckless, a motley collection of mountain men, trappers, and traders. Within the blessed heat of the single, all-inclusive business establishment, the Vance party was wrapped in warm wool blankets and animal hides, fed stew and hard biscuits until stuffed, offered ale all but Madeline indulged in to the point of inebriation. Or beyond, as in the case of the Major and his guide, along with every citizen of this God-forsaken settlement, to the last man. The young ladies—with the exception of herself, of course—grew giggly and silly and alarmingly compliant to the lewd advances of a roomful of women-starved drunks. Madeline, cheeks flaming, slapped away more than one exploring meaty paw, finally leaping off the rough plank seat altogether when she felt a hand sliding over her thigh, simultaneously pushing her skirt waistward and reaching boldly for her most intimate, private femininity.

"Major Vance!" she implored of their self-designated leader. He lifted his drunken head from the impromptu pillow he'd made at the juncture of Coralee's generous breasts, not at all pleased with the interruption. "Major Vance," she cried, aghast. "I must insist that we women be allowed to retire to whatever accommodations you have arranged for us, before something untoward occurs."

Further angered by her strident tone, the Major barked, "Your accommodations are up to you, Miss Preston. You need look no farther than the fellow seated to your right or your left, as have the other young ladies, to find a warm bed and a hot body to share for the night. Now leave me be so I can enjoy mine."

Knowing how useless it was to reason with this man with whom she'd disagreed hourly since the very first moment of their disaster-fraught journey, Madeline watched the debauchery rampant around her, appalled. The supper she'd so recently consumed with such desperate relish lay like a leaden weight in her stomach, apprehension strangling all but the shallowest of breaths. Hands crossed protectively at the base of her throat, she backed out of the lamplight of the single lantern swinging over the one long plank table around which everyone had gathered, into the shadows beyond. Headed surreptitiously toward the door, away from the bold scrutiny of those luckless enough to be without female companionship, Madeline pondered her fate and her future, trapped as she was, penniless, possessionless, in an unrelenting, savage land with only her body with which to bargain for so much as a place to sleep. And not a single male present who wasn't drunk and crude and filthy to the point of probable insect infestation.

If only Papa had not insisted she marry old Elmer Chester, none of this . . . Ah, but that was water under the bridge and too often brought to mind these last miserable weeks! She was where she was because of her own actions, and no one else's, and it would be only action on her part that would see her through her present difficulties. Suddenly, too weary, too sore of body and mind to think beyond where to bed down, Madeline hoped and prayed the fellow who'd welcomed them into this establishment, offering respite and refreshments without questioning their ability to pay, could also provide rooming somewhere, anywhere away from this rowdy crowd. Before she could act upon her decision, the door beside which she stood, burst open so violently she scarcely had time to jump out of the way before it slammed against the wall, missing her by a mere fraction. Cold and rain blew in. Shouts from one and all protested the invasion. The door slammed shut, revealing a terrifying pair—an upright-standing bear, and a wolf crouched at its side, teeth bared.

"Need a room for the night," growled the bear, only a man in a bear robe after all.

"One's all I got to spare," declared the brute behind the plank and upended barrels comprising the counter at the far side of the room, himself distinguishable from the all the others only by the filthy off-white apron he wore tied around his considerable girth.

Madeline comprehended nothing beyond the discovery that a single, private room existed, and that *she* must have it, no one else. With inspiration born of desperation, she recalled the one last object of value remaining, the birth-stone ring she'd worn without removing since Papa gave it to her on her sixteenth birthday. Without a second thought, she slipped it off a starvation-thin finger as she hastened across the room, coming up short just behind the bearlike newcomer when his companion, the wolf—or wolflike dog—lifted his lips in an ugly smile, emitting a snarl warning her to advance no farther. Nothing, however, not even a wild beast threatening life and limb, could keep Madeline Preston from claiming the blessed solitude of a room for herself, not after the indignities she'd suffered sharing the most personal intimacies with others these last several weeks.

"I would like that room, if you please, sir. I have this ring with which to pay for a single night's board, if you'd be so kind as to accept it in payment." She extended the bit of jewelry on an open palm for him to see. Her courage did not extend to stepping any closer to the growling beast, be it dog or wolf.

The aproned fellow squinted at her offering, his stubbled jaws ruminating around a juicy plug of tobacco that dribbled out of the corners of his mouth and down his chin in twin tracks.

"Mebe I will, an' mebe I won't, li'le lady. How many 'sides yerself lookin' to share the room an' willin' to pay fer th' privilege?"

Madeline straightened her spine, hoping to intimidate by stance and demeanor.

"Only myself."

"An' you?" the proprietor asked, turning away his head, but not his squinting, small-eyed stare, to expectorate a stream of brown fluid somewhere in the vicinity of his feet, hopefully, but not likely, into some form of containment. "You plannin' on sleepin' alone, mister? Gotta charge by the head, man er beast."

"Planned on paying for both Wolf and myself, and the five others in my party waiting outside."

The proprietor slammed a meaty fist down on his counter so hard the board bounced on its barrel supports.

"Sold t' th' highest bidder. Mister, ya got yerself a room fer the night."

Disappointment a keen, bitter taste in her mouth, Madeline convulsively squeezed her fingers closed around her meager offering, fighting back tears. Not quite ready to admit defeat, she lifted her chin a notch higher.

"Sir, how dare you let your last room to this . . . this person instead of a lady in need, no matter what he is willing to pay?"

"Did 'n' done, lady," the barkeep glared at her with pure dislike. He bobbed his head sharply, once, at the fur-robed stranger. "Mebe this here fella'll let ya share with him 'n' his friends fer the price of that pretty little ring of yers," he suggested.

Her rival for the room turned his head slightly in her direction over a shoulder. Beneath his fur hood, only his piercing blue eyes—as cold and as deep as a bottomless pool—and a portion of his wind-reddened nose, appeared clear of salt-and-pepper hair, from bushy beard to untrimmed mustache and thick winged brows. Unkempt strands hung too long over a high, broad brow. One could not tell where the animal pelt he wore ended and his own began. Madeline shuddered involuntarily.

"Share with this man? Not in a million years. Not if his were the last accommodations on earth, freely and willingly offered."

Madeline spun on her heel and marched away, not hearing the mountain man's response except for a deep rumble which caused the proprietor to roar with laughter. At her expense, she had no doubt. She sought a far corner where lantern light failed to reach, a place where the owner of this sorry establishment stocked his supplies for sale. She breathed deeply of new leather, oiled steel, malty flour, and lye soap, finding the mingled odors delightful compared to the reek of unwashed humanity, bad cigars, spilt spirits.

No one objected, or even noticed, when she arranged a place for herself behind a wall of crates upon a bed of colorful, patterned wool blankets, with one rolled for a pillow and another to cover her aching, weary body. Snuggling deep, she felt as if she'd discovered heaven. Though she could not shut out the noise, long hours later she dozed.

In spite of exhaustion, Madeline slept fitfully and woke long before dawn, as determined by unrelieved darkness and blessed silence broken only by a chorus of muted snores from behind log partitions. She sat up, prepared to rise and slip out for some very necessary ablutions before anyone else ventured up and about. The creak of leather hinges alerted her to someone entering through the front door. She held her breath and waited, she knew not for what.

"I told you no one was here at this hour."

Madeline recognized the low, conciliatory tone Major Vance used to silence what he considered ungrounded apprehensions. Whoever was with him made not the slightest effort to be quiet.

"Then, where the bloody hell *is* that female what fancies herself a lady? I want t' have me the gal I bought an' paid fer an', by gum, I mean t' have 'er, now! Flat on 'er back, sittin' an' standin' an' every other way I kin come up with. Find 'er fer me, Vance, 'fore I skin yer scalp off'n yer head an' sell it t' the first redskin what heads m' way."

Panic urged Madeline to flee. Common sense told her to make herself invisible. She curled into a tight ball on her sleeping pallet, threw her cover over her head, lifting one edge only high enough to hear. The Major's next words chilled her even more than the trapper's.

"Never fear, sir. You can be certain Miss Preston is somewhere in camp. She is far too intelligent to run off into the wilderness all alone, without provisions."

"Smart er stupid as a post, means nothin' t' me. All's I want is a wife t' see t' my needs, all of 'em, 'n' that's what I paid ya good cash money fer. If 'n we cain't find this a one, give me another'n. Makes no never mind."

"All the other girls are spoken for, and glad to be done with their travels for good and all. I intended to take them all the way to California as brides in a woman-starved land. But you men pay well. And the women won't budge." A pause. Madeline could almost hear his shrug. "In a couple of days, with fresh supplies, my guide and myself will head back East for another batch. Hopefully, we'll have less bad luck and far better weather on the next westward attempt."

The trapper chuckled coarsely. "An' if 'n ya don't, yer always more'n welcome t' stop off here agin. Let's you 'n' me go check that smokehouse out back. Ain't in use right now. Mebe m' gal's hol' up out there. Gotta warn ya, Vance, we don' find her, an' soon, I mean what I says about liftin' yer scalp. That, er get m' good cash money back from ya . . . mebe both."

"Spare me my scalp, sir, and I'll refund twice . . . thrice . . what you paid, and still have plenty left over for profit."

"Done 'n' done."

The men guffawed together with some warped male camaraderie, exiting as they'd come without disturbing anyone but herself.

Madeline extracted herself from her smothering cocoon, taking deep, steadying breaths. The chilling conversation she'd overheard galvanized her to action like nothing else could have. She had thought the disastrous overland journey to inadvertently reach this God-forsaken place had been horrendous beyond compare, but this latest catastrophe, well, it was simply unconscionable. She would die before she'd submit to that uncouth monster Major Vance had sold her to.

The only solution, of course, was to do precisely what those two, discussing her, declared she dare not attempt. She *must* run away into the woods. A fearful choice, but not nearly as frightening as staying. She had absolutely no money to buy her freedom from her prospective husband; there was nothing she could say or do to remain unwed . . . except as in some lesser capacity than married.

She survived eight weeks on the trail, enduring in spite of Major Eben Vance's incompetent bungling. Some small good fortune had placed her alone, in the dark solitude of predawn, within a well-stocked trading post. She would leave far better prepared than at her departure from Independence all those weeks ago. And, thank that same good fortune, she still had her birthstone ring, the gem surrounded by diamond chips, with which to pay for her purchases.

She worked quickly and quietly, picking and choosing from the proprietor's limited stock. She found no knapsack, so used a discarded flour sack; nor serviceable boots in any size she could wear, so she took a pair of knee-high, fur-lined moccasins. Her heavy, woolen cape would serve to keep her warm, both to wear and to sleep under—springlike weather should commence any day now, as soon as the rains passed. The rest of her ring's estimated worth, she spent on easily carried foodstuffs requiring little preparation before consumption out of hand. Water from fresh mountain streams would, as needed, provide her only beverage.

With everything in readiness, Madeline pulled her ring off her finger one last time to set it on the rough plank counter. She eased the front door open, eliciting only one faint squeak from leather hinges, and slipped outside. No one seemed to be about in the predawn dark, not even the pair who searched for her.

The rain had stopped; the air taking on a soft freshness promising a fair, balmy day. Encouraged by that promise, Madeline set off, scurrying to the scant cover from one pine trunk to another, ever alert for any sign of humanity.

Certain that when she was finally determined to be missing, the hue and cry resulting would take whoever sought her back along the way they'd come, she went in exactly the opposite direction, straight uphill, into the thickest of the surrounding forest. She would travel thusly for a day, maybe more. When she was thoroughly convinced her passage had gone undetected, then and only then would she circle back downward, far beyond Luckless, and head straight for home.

ROMANCE FROM JO BEVERLY

DANGEROUS JOY   (0-8217-5129-8, $5.99)

FORBIDDEN   (0-8217-4488-7, $4.99)

THE SHATTERED ROSE (0-8217-5310-X, $5.99)

TEMPTING FORTUNE   (0-8217-4858-0, $4.99)

ROMANCE FROM JANELLE TAYLOR

ANYTHING FOR LOVE   (0-8217-4992-7, $5.99)

DESTINY MINE   (0-8217-5185-9, $5.99)

CHASE THE WIND   (0-8217-4740-1, $5.99)

MIDNIGHT SECRETS   (0-8217-5280-4, $5.99)

MOONBEAMS AND MAGIC   (0-8217-0184-4, $5.99)

SWEET SAVAGE HEART   (0-8217-5276-6, $5.99)